The Way of the Walker

The Stormfall Cycle Book One

By Marius H. Visser

DRAKE
PRESS

Published 2023 by Drake Press

ISBN:
9780645301656 (ePub)
9780645301663 (Paperback)
9780645301670 (Hardback)

These books may contain the use of strong language, graphic realistic
depictions of battlefield violence and fighting.

A catalogue record for this
work is available from the
National Library of Australia

The Stormfall Cycle

The Way of the Walker

Echoes of the Darsfiëre

Dragon Wars Saga

Daughter of the Ageian

King's Plight

Warlock's Path

Tales From Kraydenia

Mercury Dagger

Short Stories

Cracked sky

The Call of Jonas Creed

Acknowledgement

To my wife, I apologise for all the nagging questions about characters, scenes, the various atrocities, and unfortunate events that befall the few in my books. Your grace in answering me with your placated eye-rolls gives me reason to continue.

A big thank you to my Beta Readers! Without you, this would have been a very different book.

To my brilliant cover designer, Andrei Bat, I thank you for indulging all my requests and creating these amazing covers.
https://99designs.com/profiles/bandrei

To my fantastic editor Lindsay Galloway, thank you for all the work done. This book is a better version, thanks to you.

To the Wandering Giant.

You can't eat rocks without breaking a few teeth.

Foreword

Thank you for picking up The Way of the Walker. I really hope you enjoy this novel. If you have a moment, please leave a review on your preferred store as this will allow me the opportunity to write more books such as this. I will really appreciate it. Reviews are especially critical in today's world. Help other fantasy readers and tell them why you enjoyed this book. Thank you!

* Leave a Review: Here

Or scan this:

Want to stay updated with news about my books?

* Join my mailing list at:

https://www.mariushvisser.com/contact

* Like me on Facebook:

https://www.facebook.com/mariushvisserbooks

* Follow me on Twitter:

https://twitter.com/MariusHVisser

Free Novella!

The Call of Jonas Creed **is a short novella set as a prequel to The Way of the Walker. If you haven't already, it is available for purchase right now on Amazon in print edition OR get a FREE ebook when you join my mailing list and get all the updated information of my future novels by scanning the QR code.**

Heroes may be forged in fire...

Legends speak of a shadow realm that echoes our own, called the Void, where gods and demons roam the very paths we mortals tread, hidden from our sight and touch, judging us at our worst moments, laughing at our woes.

The Void is inaccessible to all still living save those blessed, or perhaps cursed, with the means to cross between realms. The lands of the gods are not to be trespassed lightly, but the rewards...

Deep in the heart of Yahrska, past the beautiful Brokar Valley, lies Barren Hollows: a small and peaceful village where all Jonas Creed wanted was to leave his past behind and become the loving husband and father he swore he always would be.

But fate leaves none unscathed. Someone is looking for the Voidwalker, and will stop at nothing to get what they want.

...but Legends are born in blood.

MAYANORE
NORTHLANDS
The Death of Nine
Rochberte
Khort-kamma
Khort-ilise
Velorine
Khort-darvo
Dangrion
Dhumbrook
Forgeholde
Vurmskeep
Falconleigh
Khort-amali
The Silent Seas
Baldurren
EDELBORE
Yelavantia
YAHRSKA
Flaghskeep
Khorvellen
Sistrean Sea
Bashful Expanse
(The Sea of Ice and Shadows)
Port Vellen
The Black Mountains of Khortunand
The Undying Swells
Skala
Ironhorn
TOLOMENE
Kapria
Chariscrag
Baldor
Pikeridge
Barren Hollows
Elderforest
Sterlingshire
Swellergrove
Yuronia
Bottomless Basin
Kerne
Dragons Rest
SOUTHLANDS
Dragon Swells
Copper Crossing
Winterbourne
The Forgotten Strait
Sistrean Sea
KELTORISON
Harkenfell
N
W E
S

Prologue

Jonas dug his fingers into the cool, moist dirt, snapping the thin roots of young plants, and an earthy smell graced his nose. Long breath in, eyes closed, he sucked in the smell, feeling his heart beat deep in his chest. How was it he could be so lucky? He cupped a mound of dirt in his hands and watched a worm curse at him, wriggling around, annoyed at being removed from the earth. He grinned at the worm's anger and placed the soil back in the hole he'd dug. 'There you go, little fella,' came his gruff voice. 'No need to haunt my dreams tonight.'

He rose with a smile on his face, lightened by the fresh scents around him, taking it all in. Pink flowers with a spicy, clove-like scent, red lilies with a sharp, sweet smell, and so many more filled the air. The soft drizzle of morning dew dropped from leaves up high, wetting his hair, and he sneezed again, like he had done so many times this morning. It might have smelled great, but like his father used to say, *'Everything has a price, my boy.'* The various scents irritated his nose greatly, yet he still kept a smile on his face. There were worse things in the world.

The crisp early-morning air left a trail of mist covering the mountains and valley, the forest looking serene and untouched. Moisture in the air wet the rims of his nostrils, forming droplets at the tip, causing him to sniff incessantly. How many times had he walked these mountains, sat on logs and rocks, thinking about his past? Thinking about what he'd done. Wondering if he really deserved to be here in this blessed place called Barren Hollows. He had left the North with nothing but the clothes on his back and a tarnished reputation, and the people here took him in, no questions asked.

He was a man broken by the greed and ambition of others who preyed on his skill and abilities. Young and stupid, he had loved the attention it got him at first, the women he had, the men following his every order, but what they'd done . . . All to empower the name of his employer, the adavey, leader of the eastern Northlands.

The people of Barren Hollows had given him a purpose to live again, given him hope when he met Ayla, and just like that, the rest was history. They had fallen madly in love, and from that love came Jorin, a reminder for him to be a better man.

'Papa!' called a squeaky voice behind him. Jonas turned around, instantly having to stick out his arms and catch the small body sailing through the air towards him, crashing into him and driving him back.

'Jorin, you crazy little monkey! What are you doing all the way out here?' he asked, finding his footing. An owl hooted from a tree on their right, and Jorin imitated it, hooting loudly in Jonas's ears. 'It seems we be eating owl tonight!' Jonas said and hefted the boy, cradling him in his arms and digging his face into his little stomach, growling as he blew onto the soft skin with his lips. The loud farting flaps reverberated through the forest, stirring a commotion in the trees, branches cracking, leaves rustling. 'It seems the owl had enough,' Jonas said as he stared at the big-winged bird flapping to get away from them. He set the boy down and took up his axe.

'I'm not alone, Papa. Mama is here too.'

'And dead tired from the slog up here,' she said, the hem of her dress in hand while she climbed over fallen logs and rocks, ferns and small bushes brushing against her legs. 'Why did you have to walk so far for a tree? There are plenty closer to home.'

'But then I wouldn't have had this view,' Jonas said, gesturing behind him to the lake at the bottom of the valley, shrouded by the mist, a dark blue patch in a sea of green. She drew him in close and kissed him, her soft red lips wet and cool.

'Papa! Let's go swimming!' Jorin's wild brown hair bounced and flopped as he dashed over the rocks through the forest, running down the side of the mountain.

'Jorin! No, wait. You could get hurt!' But the boy didn't listen and giggled instead as he scrammed away from them. Jonas turned and ran after Jorin, with Ayla following behind. Steep cliffs and drop-offs rode the side of the mountain, with enormous, sharp boulders waiting for a fool to tumble down, breaking legs and worse. He lost sight of the boy for a moment and scanned the declivous forest, glimpsing a red-and-black jerkin through the stands of thick trees. 'Jorin!' He heard the boy's laughter bounce between the trees.

'You can't catch me,' sang the squeaky voice, disappearing from his sight again.

'Jorin, stop this!' Ayla shouted behind him.

Heart racing, alarms going off in his head, Jonas sprinted down the side of the mountain and stepped on a loose rock, twisting his ankle. He went down in a hail of dust and leaves, crashing through brush and dirt, dropping his axe somewhere along the way. Dirt and gravel shot into his right eye, the coarse matter grinding harshly, forcing him to close it. 'Argh!' he groaned and jumped back up, searching for the boy with his left eye. The woods were a dangerous place for a lone boy to run around in. Bears, snakes, apes, and jaguars prowled these woods, and a small, easy meal was something they wouldn't readily let go.

Twigs cracked to their right, and an urgent scream followed, setting his heart on fire. 'Jorin? Papa's coming!' His loss of depth perception made him unbalanced, causing some things to appear further away than they were and others closer than they were, messing with his head. He stumbled along, feet getting hooked on stumps he'd seen as far away, nearly going down again. 'Jorin, where are you?'

'Here, Papa!' screamed the terrified voice near to them, and he stopped to scan the area. The ground dropped away from them on their left, and then he saw his boy. Jorin hung by the tips of his fingers clutched to a mass of twisted roots crawling across the side of a tremendous boulder, legs kicking air and eyes wide as saucers. 'Hurry!' he cried, 'Papa! Help me!'

Jonas ran across the top of the boulder and went to his knees, skinning them on the rough surface, breath caught in his throat. The quicker he breathed, the less air made it to his lungs, dark spots enveloping his vision. He reached down to his boy, leaning over the boulder as far as he dared, seeing the menacing rocks far below, just waiting to claim this little body for their own, and he shouted, 'Grab my hand!' It wasn't long before Ayla arrived at his side, screaming and crying at the possible fate they had found themselves in. Seeing the fear in her eyes, he called again, 'You can do it, boy! Grab my hand!'

Jonas started slipping over the side and felt Ayla grab his legs to pin him down, giving him a little more length to worm down. He was so close now, but he could see Jorin growing tired, his tiny hands trembling from exhaustion and fear. 'You're all right, lad. Just take my hand,' he said calmly. Tears welled in his eye. 'Don't let go now, you hear me?' They locked eyes for an instant, and the tiny hands slipped away from him. 'No! No! Jorin! No!' His heart stopped beating for a moment while he screamed and cried, watching his boy fall.

This never happened! He never ran from us. I know this memory. This is a dream!

Jonas woke to a blaze of heat surrounding him, his body bruised and in pain. Blood seeped from wounds on his side and arm, black marks staining him all over. His head pounded, and his sight blurred, the unmistakable feeling of old iron bars pressing against his back a hard thing to forget. Fires raged all over in the cavernous dungeon, and in the distance sat a beast on its throne, eyeing him with contempt.

Just a dream then, he thought and closed his eyes again.

PART ONE

"Our Lord of life inspires those that strive for success. Failure is the devil's work."

Lord Latimus Greyarm
Honourable Dean of the House

1. Bad Decisions

Dust swirled over the hard, trodden roads, pushed every which way by the wind howling through the streets of Skalg, the capital of Tolomene. The harsh sun cast its rays from afar, and in the dying light of day, sweat still dripped from Orana's tan back, wetting her fluttering cloak, thinned and worn from years of abuse. She pulled the hood back, enjoying the wind that cooled her face, and worked her fingers through the clumped, dark hair on the right of her head, the left braided close to her scalp, where a cornucopia of gold and silver rings shone on her ear, all varying in size and ornately designed.

Orana leaned back in the wooden chair, feeling it shift beneath her. Stomach muscles tense with the sudden fragility of the chair, she sat forward again, not wanting to make a spectacle by falling to the ground in any dismal fashion. *It is always best to avoid unnecessary attention,* she thought.

For nearly the last thirty years she'd been on her own, fending for herself. It had been hard during the early days as a young girl, learning how to fight when all she knew was safety. Now, the way of the streets had been embedded deep into her. Caution was always good advice.

Around her, men discussed business with other men, while the women feigned interest in their talks, and children ran around, swinging sticks, playing with one another. She glimpsed her deep green eyes reflected in the dirty pane of glass leaning against the building to her right, locking gazes with herself, before turning to the girl walking towards her. Magnificent polished-steel-and-wood tankards spilled golden ale over their rims, forming a raging sea of alcohol to cover the base of the tray she carried.

'For your troubles,' Orana said as the servant girl handed her a tankard, and she slid a few coins over the weathered table. Marred by deep grooves and gouges where the wood had rotted and crumbled away, a splinter nipped her finger. Orana sucked at her teeth and removed the grass stalk from her mouth, watching the servant girl saunter to the next table.

Cool and refreshing, the ale sloshed down Orana's throat, spilling some from her mouth to run down her chin, and she wiped it with the back of her hand. Down the dusty road, past the tavern walls and the chapel next to it, men were still working, laying cobblestones to neaten the area. To make a show that Skalg was not the dregs everyone made it out to be. They had been laying cobbles and revamping older buildings for two years now. Sure, it made the city look neater, but Orana knew the heart of the city would never change. The people would never change.

As if conjured by her dark thoughts of the city, a brouhaha of shouting men exploded, and she snapped her head to the right just in time to see a man slap the apologising servant girl off her feet, the tray of ale flying to the ground, splashing on the floor, wasting the precious liquid. He towered over the girl as she retreated on her backside, pushing away with her hands and feet to put some distance between her and the shouting man.

'You stupid cow! Watch where you're going! Imbecile!' It was just another day in Skalg. Besides, nobody ever batted an eye over a servant girl getting a slap or two, right?

Orana lowered her head and took another sip of her ale, feeling the last rays of the day warm her neck. The white, flapping coverings above them did little to keep the heat out, but they at least kept the sun at bay. *A man left with nothing,* she thought. *A man running scared and uncertain, his life's work undone, gone, vanished. Stolen . . . Taken away from him in the dark of night while he lay asleep in the very next room, woefully ignorant of the theft happening so nearby. His most precious artefacts, disappearing into the hands of corrupt merchants who will not scoff at the opportunity to buy stolen goods.*

'Something funny to you?' Orana heard the raging man growl. She didn't realise she'd been laughing out loud. Orana cursed within and drew her hood over her head. It was never good to attract attention to yourself in her line of work. Lips pursed, she looked at him and chewed on her ale, swirling it around in her mouth before swallowing, then said, 'Takes a big man to scare girls, eh? Bet ya feelin' pretty darn good right now, eh, making her drop all her drinks. Why? Because she spilled some on yer shiny tunic?'

'Shut your mouth, you filthy shrew! Do you know who I am?' he shouted, voice rough and coarse. He marched towards her, fists bunched and ready to swing them.

Orana slid a dagger from a sheath hanging on her side, spinning it in her hands before stabbing it into the table, hearing the wood groan with the impact, a dull and plaintive sound. The man jumped back at the flash of the steel, eyes wide and angry.

'Do you know who *I* am?' she asked, finishing her ale and obscuring her face with the mug. From the corner of her eye, she saw two men approach, one from the right, one from the left. *Damn! A mark should never see your face, and you, my friend, have just become one. To think I was gonna take the night off.* She pulled the dagger from the table, sheathed it, and rose from the chair. Hands raised, she backed away one step at a time. 'Don't need any trouble. I was just enjoying a drink, is all. Might've had one too many. I don't want to be a bother. How about we forget all this ugly business, and I will see myself out, eh?'

From all around, hard faces stared at them, as if watching a play at the grand new theatre that just opened, waiting for the climax of the show to come to fruition. She glanced around, retreating to where she knew she could turn and run, disappear in the crowds milling about. But it was unnecessary.

The fancily dressed man with his black-and-gold tunic and tight white pants made the smallest gesture with his hand and the two approaching men stopped, waiting for her to take her leave from the tavern. 'Leave now! And don't show your face here again,' the man said and swung around, marching past the servant girl with her wide eyes, clutching her arms nervously, the empty tray grasped under one arm.

Orana kept her eyes on the two she assumed were his guards while she backed towards the street. Once-white masks – now a dust-covered brown – wrapped around their heads, concealing mouths and noses, and blended in with the white-turbans and loose-fitting clothes, so light and breezy. Thick-bladed cutlasses dangled on their hips. Tall, broad-shouldered, their eyes looked sharp and ready, their hands never drifting far from their swords. They would not be easy marks. One more step back and Orana turned on her heel, quickly blending in with the buzzing crowd to make good her escape from the situation.

* * *

The wooden wall was cold and damp against the small of her back, as was the alley she stood in, dark and miserable, tainted with beggars and thieves. Her playground. Small dark figures scurried and scraped in the corners, rats and cats looking for a meal. Concealed in the alley's gloom, Orana watched the fancily dressed man and his two flanking goons make their way down the street, the occasional lantern post casting an orange glow over them. She slipped out from her cover and trailed them at a distance, avoiding the light at all costs. 'Where are you going?' she whispered to herself, seeing him turn down a new street, narrow and busy, crowded with whores fighting for dominion, and drunkards hoping to get a cheap lay.

Men and women wearing scant little fell over each other, shaking their breasts and jingling their bits, studded jewellery and chained piercings glimmering around their nipples as they sold themselves to any willing to open their purse strings. Orana waded through the true heart of the city.

'You want some of this, love?' one shouted, rubbing her naked breasts near Orana's face, close enough to make her step away, only to be cornered by another with both hands on her crotch, pushing her pelvis out, as if trolling for a new victim.

'Nah! She got some class, ya old 'n saggy whore! She's cravin' a lickin'.'

Orana cringed and stepped left to avoid them, hearing them continue their shouting match as both lost the customer. Deeper she went, past the faint glows emanating from the doors to the brothels filled to the brim, overflowing with men and women rutting near the doorways. Some, not even having the benefit of a doorway, lay in the dark corners, while others were pushed against the walls, moaning and groaning, coarse shouts of pleasure keening through the air. More and more hounded her, pushing and rubbing against her.

The cobblestones beneath her feet still looked new, but that would not last long. *The people will never change. Dress it up as much as you like,* she thought. Weaving her way through the harem of hookers, twisting her face up at the sharp smell of urine in the air, she had to lunge out of view as the fancily dressed man turned to survey his surroundings. Through the sliver of a cracked wall, she spied the man in the distance, while she leaned up against . . . something.

Orana adjusted her hand, feeling greasy hairs on a heaving chest, then a rubbing pressure on her right leg, and she twisted to glare at a fat, naked man straddling her, riding his prick up and down her leg with bouldering breaths of pure alcohol. 'Ew! Ew! Ew! Get off me, ya bastard!' She pushed him away, and the drunkard toppled back, tripping over the sill of the doorway and spilling over a rutting pair in the hallway before the steps leading up.

'Hey! 'S'no need fu dat—' the corpulent man began, but he quickly found himself entangled with the pair on the floor and joined their rigorous adventures, sucking and licking any part he could lay his hands on.

Disgusted, Orana turned back to her mark and saw the door swing closed where he had stood only moments ago. *Damn!* She pushed through the throng of bodies and ran for the posts holding up the balcony above and started climbing. The creak of a door sounded, and voices filtered through. Orana scrammed up to the roof and lay flat on her stomach, cautiously leaning over the edge of the roof. His two goons inspected the room, then the man walked in behind them, fervently kissing a blonde foreigner, her milky-white skin a stark contrast to the dark skin of her mark. He fumbled with her clothes until she took over, and the man waved the two guards out of the room. 'Out! Now!'

Orana watched them go at it for a while, then slipped away and turned on her back, gazing at the stars high above, a brilliant conglomeration of sparkling beauties standing out from the dark night sky as the two shagged in the room below her.

She used the sharp edges of the pentagonal necklace to press in under her nail, scraping out the muck from underneath. Subconsciously, she moved on to the next nail, and the next, cleaning them all while she thought of Calimöre: a rider from the east and a hunter of great and terrible beasts. Or so he had said . . .

It felt like a lifetime ago now since they separated on that morning. He had turned to head back east while she carried on to Skalg, leaving Dragons Rest behind her for good. Too many failed ventures, too many missed opportunities, as they would say. Dragons Rest was a more tolerable city to foreigners than Skalg. They had to be, being a port city and all, with many travellers making a stop for a break from the vast, dangerous waters beyond its shores, spending their coin on marketable goods, foods, and women. She and Calimöre had spent a few wonderful nights in each other's arms, bathed in the light of the glowing flames crackling in the hearth. Tender words were spoken but no promises made, for both knew what this was and where it was heading.

A loud, animalistic crow pulled her from her thoughts, and she quickly leaned over the edge of the roof. With every shunt, her mark grunted like a bull in heat, sweating profusely and trembling with delight, curling his toes and shuddering, unable to keep his stomach muscles tense, letting his fat belly hang slack over the milky-skinned foreigner. With a final grunt, he fell next to her on the bed, unable to continue. Orana wanted to laugh again. *How perfectly pathetic.*

She waited for them to finish. He dropped a few coins on the nightstand next to them, the metal glowing with a sheen of orange in the lantern's light. Wheezing, the man cleaned himself up and grabbed his clothes, donning them quickly before leaving, their footfalls fading as they descended the stairs. It wasn't long before the front door swung open and the three men strolled down the street, away from the nest of sex mongers.

* * *

'Oh my, you must be special indeed, havin' a place like this.' Orana sat in a large tree, high in the branches, overlooking a massive fenced compound, with a maze of footpaths crossing ponds and a marvellous fountain spewing water from three dancing dolphins breaching the spectral seas before the looming house. Orana thought it looked more like a palace, but she was sure he would play it off as a humble little home. She was instantly angry. *The arrogant bastard! Somewhere in there, you will have things of value. And soon, they will be mine.* The neighbourhood was quiet. Not a soul stirred so late in the night; not even the animals made a sound, either that, or none dared to go near this place.

Orana slipped from branch to branch, quickly making her way to the ground, and pulled her hood over her head and her scarf over her mouth and nose, concealing her face. *Time to go to work.* She knew of at least two guards that should be nearby. How many more was a wild guess. Dark shadows rustled and shook in the moon's light, a faint breeze blowing through the trees.

The spiked palisade fence had been an easy first challenge. Nimble as a cat, she had jumped up and grabbed the tops near the spikes, flinging herself over with ease to land and roll on the paved path, silently making entrance to the courtyard. She skulked low through the bushes and flower arrangements, a sweet scent drifting from the purple-tongue flowers growing on either side.

A stifled cough sounded on her right, and she dropped to the ground, staying there for some time, not moving a muscle. Leaves crackled under the guard's feet, drawing closer and closer. Her breath caught in her throat, and her heart beat savagely under the thin veil of rustling leaves. The thrill of it all peaked her enjoyment, the danger always present. A voice called from further away, and the guard turned around, headed away from her.

Breathing easy, she sneaked through to the house and climbed through an open window, pulling the shutters closed behind.

Darkness sucked every ounce of light from the house. Orana could barely see what was in front of her, and for the first few steps, she felt around with her hands and feet, making sure she didn't stumble down a step or two until her eyes adjusted.

Hangings decorated the walls with large portraits and tapestries, ornate bowls stood on stands and in corners, with succulents arrayed as little gardens, each one different. Cushions for sitting on the floor, red with gold trim, were placed around a wooden table, with a thick, glass turntable in the centre of the piece, a gargoyle statuette placed in the middle. 'Creepy,' she whispered and fingered the glass, making it spin slowly, the gargoyle turning round and round. 'You can keep that.'

Casually, she made her way down the corridor. The snores began as a whisper, getting louder and louder the deeper she went, until she reached the door from where they were born. Steadily, she pushed the door open and glided into the room as a drifting breeze, soundless.

Moonlight seeped through the wooden slats of the shutters, revealing the pig of a man where he lay naked in his enormous bed, white satin sheets kicked to the side. She reached for her dagger and pulled a pouch loose from next to the sheath instead, retrieving a small glass vial from within containing a clear liquid, looking innocently like water, but she knew not to be fooled by its appearance. A very skilled alchemist had done her the favour of making these.

The man did not look so fancy without his clothes. No, he looked helpless, pathetic, small, and inconsequential. She watched his moustache quiver with every snore where he lay on his stomach, head turned towards her for air, then brought the little vial close to his nose. She broke the wax seal and lifted the small cork, wafting it over his nose. His face scrunched up from the potent smell, his eyes flickered open briefly, and he groaned with a drawl of slurred words. It was a short-lived attempt at waking. His eyes rolled back in his head, and he fell silent once more.

Orana smiled and put away the vial. *You are gonna have a mighty headache tomorrow. Sweet dreams. Now, if I were rich or had something of value, I would have it close-by. Where would you keep it?* She rummaged through the chest at the foot of the bed, finding naught but old clothes and boots. Then she dug through the chest of drawers, but no luck.

Above the bed hung an ugly portrait of the vile bastard, his name inscribed at the bottom. *Yelefant Du Pantè, Royal Bastion of the Lord's Table.* Orana sneered at his smug face, hair combed back and slick, his body swathed in an officer's uniform of blue with red trim, sitting on a chair before a large hearth, burning bright. She pulled a face and removed the painting, grinning as she saw the hollow at the back in the wall, a small wooden chest waiting inside. She removed a pin from her hair and picked the lock, swung the lid open, and nearly giggled out loud. *Oh, you beautiful thing.* Orana emptied the contents into her pockets and replaced the box and painting. She glanced back once to the sleeping man and made for the exit. *Thank you very much.*

2. Friends or Foes

Kunia, Academy of the Arcane, school for the gifted, had been the subject of many controversial discussions in the North over the years. The women had it easier when it came to the subject of magic, for they were doing more than was expected of them, serving the country by becoming mages, druids, wizards, healers, and herbalists. But the North expected men to be warriors, hunters, providers, protectors. They were supposed to be strong and brave in the face of danger, willing to give their lives for others to live, not become figures of obscurity.

After eighteen long years in Forgeholde, Bellard had been ready, and excited, to leave for Kunia. It had been nearly a year now since he joined the academy, and their graduation to continue to the second year was close at hand. For all the patient waiting they had forced him to endure, studying day and night, he couldn't wait to hold his very own isolation crystal in his hands, his very own Pillar.

He wondered what his Pillar would look like, what colour it would be. Cracked and dull? Bright and clear? Would he wear it as a necklace or a ring? A bracelet, perhaps, as he had seen other students on the grounds of the academy wear theirs, while some wore it as earrings, all dependent on many factors. Some he had seen glittered brightly in the sun, while others were dull green, or ruby red, even dark as night. Only time would tell what his would be.

Until now, the masters of the academy had trained all the first-years on the theoretical way to use their gifts without actually being able to harm anyone by mistake, banning any use of magic without the guidance of an isolation crystal. Soon, though, they would venture to the Sacred Hall of the Usha, where their Pillars awaited them. With the isolation crystal, they would create real magic, form a power within themselves, isolated by the crystal to guide it outwards.

The year before, Bellard's power had come to him in the form of a crow knocking its long, sharp beak against his window during a bout of icy rain pattering on the roof. It had cawed and squawked, turning and twisting its head. Its beady black eyes followed Bellard as he rose from his bed and made his way over to the ice-streaked window. Time froze as they stared at each other, feeling a deep connection form between them. One that some would say had always been there, unrecognisable until the day of their awakening, when it blossomed, ever growing until they claimed their Pillar, blooming into existence. It was then that they would realise their power.

He had never been like the other kids in Forgeholde. He had a fascination with the workings of the world, a keen sense of morality and a deep understanding of his own mortality, always erring on the side of caution. Other boys did not seem to accept his way of thinking, though, calling him a coward and a mule. Every day they would mock him, throw stones at him, chase him with sticks and beat his back bloody. Shout vulgarities and make fun of him. And for all the love he had for Gallus, his best friend for as long as he could remember, he grew tired of him always stepping in to protect him.

Little did Bellard know he would soon welcome his transformation, his acceptance of the power of the world and the mystical arts that now coursed through his veins. He had opened that window, and the black bird swooped into the room, settling to the floor before morphing into an ephemeral vision of the bearer, a plague of persistence seeping into his very pores, enshrouding him with the promise of power at his fingertips. He could feel his own potential so close to the surface yet was just unable to breach that final layer. From that day on, the dreams of the Usha hounded him, and they hounded him still, waiting for the Pillar to ground them in place.

But until he claimed his Pillar, gifted by the mystical Usha, he would need to complete the year of studies after an already long and challenging semester, before going on a much-deserved break.

* * *

'Hey, Bellard!' someone called from behind, the voice high-pitched and clangorous. 'Are you going to join us tonight after the lessons? Me, Valdor, and Brethnar are going to sneak into Grandàre Agoras's chambers. We all know he hides his liquor in there.'

Bellard turned for a quick glance and raised his brow, a potent scent of vanilla leaving the beans she chewed on. 'Are you crazy, Mila? Grandàre Agoras will find out. I'm not doing anything that will jeopardise my claim. You shouldn't either.' Bookbag swinging under his arm, the leather strap digging into his shoulder, Bellard picked up his pace to a brisk march across the green grass of the compound, rushing to the building on the far side of the park. He was already late, and Mila wasn't doing him any favours.

'Come on, Bellard. This could be the last time we might actually have some fun.'

'You say that every time. How is this going to be any different?'

Mila's brows scrunched up, her white hair bouncing crazily as she tried to keep up with Bellard's long strides. 'For one, I might get a little drunk . . . Besides, are you going to leave me alone with those two animals?' A year younger than him, yet she had enough confidence for the both of them.

Bellard paused and sighed. She knew how to get under his skin, even if he had no interest in her. There was only one girl he longed to visit, and she was far away in Forgeholde, though he doubted that she even knew he existed. Cora, a fair girl with long brown hair and eyes the colour of steel. She had always been ashamed of the freckles crossing her nose and cheeks, but Bellard thought she was the most beautiful thing he had ever seen. He had watched her so many times where she worked at the inn, scrounging up the courage to speak with her yet never following through. She walked proudly and always had a smile on her face, never taking part in teasing him like the others always did. And even though he didn't really know her, he missed her dearly. His forehead creased with deep lines while he thought of her, then said,

'Fine, Mila. I will join you. But only for a short while, then I'm off to study.'

She squealed with delight, shaking her bunched fists. 'Okay, okay. Just a short while then. You won't regret it,' she said and dashed to the other side of the park, vanishing behind a group of passing students. One would think there were hundreds of wizards in training by the number of students constantly on the grounds, but only a very select few were actually there for their abilities. Others came to study botany, alchemy, the human body, healing, and so much more, all wanting to further their knowledge in the arcane.

Head shaking, Bellard regretted it already, yet he could not deny that those three had been better friends over the past year than he'd had his entire life. He would not let them down so easily. Bellard gripped the bottom of his pack and pulled it up, relieving his shoulder from some of the weight. 'Damn! I'm late!' he shouted and dashed for the building.

A dark wooden ceiling blocked the rising sun, a grey slate floor becoming slippery underfoot, and beige walls flashed by at speed, replacing the blue sky and green grass around him as he ran through the corridor. Classrooms flitted by, the voices inside fading as fast as they started up, a bewildering array of old faces swinging towards him until he reached the next room, and the next. The solid, heavy door of Grandàre Shevira's class came into view at the far left of the hall. It was already closed . . .

Papers went flying with a brief scream as he burst through the door, and the room suddenly twisted and turned, a force pushing him through the air, clear over the other students' heads. Smiles, smirks, grins, and worried faces were all he glimpsed. In a blink of an eye, he was at the back of the room, where a tremendous hit to his right arm and ribs knocked the wind from him. He collapsed on the floor, moments before the rocking bookcase – filled with old, heavy books – toppled towards him. Even with his hands and arms covering his chest and face, he knew the weight would crush him utterly.

He closed his eyes, not wanting to face his coming death, when a force pulled at him, the tables, chairs, students, and marbled floor tiles sliding by him at speed while he screamed. The cabinet crashed on the tiles beneath, shaking the very foundation and billowing dust from the old books, pages drifting from the ceiling, torn away by the impact.

Grandàre Shevira hovered over him, his ears ringing and her voice muffled. 'What?' he shouted and pointed to his ears. 'Grandàre? I can't hear you.' The students were laughing, clutching their stomachs and palming the tables, the sounds coming back to his bewildered mind. He couldn't focus, and the jumble of noises didn't make it any easier. He spun his head from the students to the grandàre and back.

'Quiet!' shouted the grandàre, and the students fell silent. Her spectacles slipped lower on her wrinkled face, and she spun to him. 'Bellard Braxious! What on earth made you think it's a good idea to startle an old mage like me?' She helped him up to lean against the wall. 'Are you hurt? Can you stand?'

His ribs ached, and his nose dripped blood. 'Apologies, Grandàre. It was foolish of me to rush in like that.'

'Is everything all right, Shevira?' asked a stocky man who came running into the classroom, wearing baggy breeches and a chequered scarf draped over his cream tunic, his flabby cheeks and full neck shaking with the twists of his head. Behind him, more students pressed through the doorway.

'Mmm . . . Yes, it seems we are quite all right, Professor. I would gather Mister Bellard here just learnt a valuable lesson in punctuality.'

'Indeed, ma'am. Apologies, again,' muttered Bellard, hiding his face in shame at the scene he had caused. Nineteen years old and resigned to embarrassment. He could not bear to look at the students giggling, speaking in hushed tones with one another while glancing at him. Their stares felt like hot iron burning through his flesh, scoring him with new lines of emotional damage.

'Come on, show's over. Mister Bellard, take your seat. The rest of you, get back to your classrooms,' said Grandàre Shevira, shooing the curious lot out and closing the door. She stomped over to her desk, which was laden with stacks of papers, baubles, ornaments, and a blue feathered quill pen resting in its copper stand, an inkwell standing to its left, and pulled a handkerchief from the top drawer. 'Here you go, Mister Bellard. Wipe your nose and take your seat. We've lost precious time already. Let's not waste any more, shall we?'

'Of course, Grandàre.' He gripped the top edge of the wooden table tightly, drawing it near to press against his chest, something solid for him to hold on to. Something tangible that would not hurt him with sneering remarks.

'We were talking about your Pillars and what you can expect from them,' started Grandàre Shevira, lifting her necklace from her black robe, revealing a bright blue crystal suspended in the centre of a golden talisman. 'This . . . is your power. Never forget that. The Usha have granted your abilities. And they can take it away as fast as they bestow these gifts. Remember this. You will not get a second claiming.'

He had heard the stories before of mages losing or shattering their Pillars, never to do magic again. And for all the power the Pillars brought, they wrought even more danger. For there were those that had stolen Pillars from mages, hoping that it would grant them the wielder's power, but that brought only disappointment and even more resentment to both parties. The Usha would not reward their banality.

'When the time comes for your claiming, be bold, be brave, assertive. Be who you are meant to become.'

Be who you want to become? How do I do that if I don't know who I'm supposed to become? Or what . . . Bellard rubbed at his temples, his face hanging slack in the cup of his hand, eyes closed. *I wonder what Gallus is up to. Probably having the time of his life, getting drunk and lying with all the women in Forgeholde. Why can't I be more like him? Why can't I be brave?*

The classroom had vanished and so did the grandàre's voice. Flashes of the cocksure Gallus with his puffed-out chest raced through Bellard's mind. The son of Brilliard, the adavey, leader of the East. His dark brown hair hanging loose, curling slightly over his ears, his infectious laughter and charm driving the girls mad. They never could resist his friend. Bellard just wished he would leave Cora alone, not tempt her with his wild, seductive personality. Bellard's face was turning hot thinking about it, and a mighty crack on his table made him jump, nearly poking his finger in his eye.

He glanced up at the grandàre looming over him. Twice in one day he had angered her, and the look on her face said little about forgiveness. Her brows were bunched up with her stern stare, and her lips pressed tightly together while she flicked the pointing stick slowly against her palm. Many a student had felt the burn of the pointing stick. It seemed she had no preference for target, given the selection at hand, be it a palm, a back, legs, or even the head, anywhere would do just fine, as long as it inflicted some manner of punishment on the disobedient. All were equal in her eyes.

His heart beat crazily when he saw her mouth move. 'Do you find my lectures boring, Mister Bellard?'

'No, ma'am! Not at all! I just have a terrible headache this morning. Please continue.' For some time, Grandàre Shevira didn't move. She just stood there, glaring at him from over her spectacles, then she swung around and headed back to her desk at the front of the room, laying down the pointer.

'Where was I?' she asked the class.

A girl in the back raised her hand and said, 'You were talking about the claiming, Grandàre.'

'Oh, yes. Of course I was. As I was saying, whatever you do when you go into the Sacred Hall, do not take a Pillar that does not belong to you. Only take your gift. You will be very sorry if you do not heed this advice, headache or not . . .'

* * *

The day had been long and exhausting. Bellard lay on his small bed in his small room, his feet dangling over the end, rubbing against the painted mortar and the cold stone wall. The rough edges scraped over the balls of his feet, pressed gently into his toes. He glanced around his mostly empty room, getting depressed by the few pieces of clothing lying on his bed and draped over the rails in the dark wooden wardrobe. Most other students had such a variety to wear and show off to the world. *One day, I'll make enough to have clothes to choose from. Maybe even own a home . . .*

Since the crash into the bookcase, his arm had itched feverishly, and with all the constant hard scratching, it had turned red and angry, sensitive to the touch. He crossed his feet and breathed a long, unending breath while he stared out the window at the stars sparkling in the sky. He was not in the mood to entertain or be entertained. All he wanted to do was close his eyes and get over this day. That was not fate's plan, though. He reached up over his head and extinguished the lantern light, wanting to curl into a ball and hide from the world, as he had done so many times in his life.

His door swung open with a mighty crack against the wall, and two men barged in. 'No!' Bellard shouted, slapping at the first man, swinging his fists feebly and kicking air as a hood was drawn over his head. 'I said no! Help!'

The bigger of the men grabbed his kicking feet and held them tight as he shouted to the other, 'Grab his arms! Quickly! Tie him up.'

Thick ropes pulled tight around his wrists and ankles, chafing him terribly. 'Help!' Bellard shrieked again and heard the one man's voice excruciatingly close to his ear.

'Call out once more . . . and it will be the last sound you ever make.' The voice sounded eery and deep, forced somehow. Not one he knew. Fear rode him, and he complied, huffing, struggling for air as they carried him out of the room and away.

The air turned chilly. Cold, wet grass tickled his feet, and he knew they had left the dorms. 'What do you want with me? You must have the wrong person! I am nobody.' No answer came.

'Through them bushes, over there!'

He wriggled and squirmed in their grasp as they ran, breaking free from their grip and hitting the ground hard, tumbling and rolling a few times. He couldn't move his arms or legs in any productive manner, barely getting to his feet and looking like a worm, jumping from place to place.

'Help!' he shouted, and air exploded from his mouth, a shoulder driven hard into his side, lifting him into the air. It seemed the world kept spinning around him today, and this was no different. Although he could not see with the hood covering his face, he could sense he was in all wrong positions.

A thorny bush broke their fall, and they rolled further, cursing and flopping on the hard ground, snapping the bonds around his ankles, freeing his legs. They pinned him on the ground before he could run again, and this time, a hand reached under the hood, shoving a dirty rag into his mouth. Hauled back up with little mercy, rough hands steered him left and right.

How can this be happening to me? Do I have a sign on me that reads, 'Please abuse for your entertainment.'? Think, Bellard! Think! How are you going to get out of this? What would Gallus do? He would never be in this position! That's what he would've done. Made sure this never happened!

The creak of a door sounded, and the air turned warm, comfortable. Their footsteps echoed through the chamber, sounding hollow and vast. Another door, and soon after, he was flung down into a chair, nearly collapsing it. Muffled whispers sounded to the right of the room, and he searched for them, turning his head to hear better. Something scraped on the floor, and he jerked his head towards it, hearing something clatter on what must be a tabletop. He swallowed hard, a lump getting stuck in his throat as the thought of pliers pulling out his fingernails and knives cutting into him ravaged his mind.

He worked the rag with his tongue, pushing it and pushing it, getting it hooked on his teeth. His tongue felt numb from all the effort, yet he did not stop until he finally spat it out and coughed. 'I'll give you anything you want. Just let me go! Please!' he begged and nearly wept. 'I won't say anything to anyone. Just let me go!' The door creaked open again.

'Oh, what have you two done?' came a high-pitched voice, the smell of vanilla drifting through the air. 'Get that hood off and untie him this instant!'

Oh, no! Mila, run! He knew where he was, at least. Grandàre Agoras's chambers. He hoped that Valdor and Brethnar were with her. 'Run, Mila!' Vague shapes appeared through the hood, and he ran at the closest, hoping to tackle the man off his feet and give Mila a chance at escaping.

If it was a man, it was the hardest man Bellard had ever run into. He toppled backwards after a tremendous thud and fell in a heap on the floor. Their voices faded, shouts of anger replaced by dreams of Cora smiling at him, holding his hand while they strolled the markets of the busy avenues in Forgeholde. Sweet darkness took him.

3. Order and Chaos

The great doors to the Order of Eternal Sacrament remained closed, as it had for the last four days, a steady stream of white smoke drifting up from the great chimney up high. With the choosing of the new Exarch, the Order of Eternal Sacrament's top officials could not leave the building until that choice had been made. A row of the Shadow Guard, knights of the Eternal Sacrament, stood before the building, shiny breastplates glistening in the sun, white capes fluttering in the wind, ensuring no one gained entry to the Temple of Aztar. Their silver winged helms had a plume of red-dyed horsehair sticking out the tops and hanging down the back of their heads to their necks. Sharp angles skirted their noses, eyes, and mouths, protective leather and metal braces fastened round their arms and shoulders, hips and thighs, shins and feet.

'Oi! What're you doing back here?'

Gawking at the Shadow Guard with mouth agape, Calmantis nearly dropped his mug, splashing ale over his tunic and scrambling back behind the column, startled by the sudden voice. 'Nothing!' he shouted, angry at spilling his ale. The barkeep leaned out from the tavern's doorway and swung his fists, pointing at him.

'Get back in here with my mug! I'm tired of you lot stealing my wares!'

'I'm not stealing your mug, you fool!' Calmantis glared at it and thought, *It is a nice mug . . . No! What am I thinking?* 'I'm a Shadow Guard, sir! A knight of the highest order! I have no need to steal your things!'

The barkeep burst out laughing, slapping his palms on his thighs and mocked, 'Sure you are! And I'm their new Exarch! Haha, ha. The next ale is on the house, if you come back inside.'

'I am so!' Calmantis shouted, but the barkeep was already closing the door. 'Well, I will be soon enough . . .' he whispered to himself at the shut of the door. 'You just wait and see.'

It had been four days since he could lodge his plea to join the knights again, four days where he was not allowed to see the Order's officials to show his worth, to show that he was meant for greater things. There was no doubt they were getting tired of his non-stop requests, with many of his letters never being answered. He would not be deterred, though. Once Calmantis Broviere set his mind to something, there was very little that would keep him from his goal. *Mother always said, 'What is wrong with you, Cal? Did you fall on your head? You are such a stubborn child!' Well, I won't let you down, Mother.*

He turned to look once more upon the noble, illustrious knights before gulping down the last of his ale and setting off down the street, running with his gangly legs, knees nearly reaching his chin. *It is a nice mug.*

* * *

Baldor was a vast city, the capital of Yahrska, where crown and king ruled the lands. Yet, none were more powerful than the Order of Eternal Sacrament. Even the king's forces made way for the Shadow Guard, and the king himself took great council from the Exarch. They were an independent group governed by the book of Aztar, god of life. And they quickly disposed of all who went against their ways or wishes.

Clouds had gathered during the day, grey and unhappy, and the possibility of rain loomed over them. Nervous, arms held firmly against his body, Calmantis looked down and climbed the steps to the temple, seeing the amazing swirling patterns in the sandstone. With military precision, four of the knights stepped forward from the row safeguarding the temple, their boots drumming on the sandstone paving. 'Step back! No one is allowed near the temple during the time of commemoration and Exarchal Conclave.'

Head tilted to the left, Calmantis raised his hands slightly. He mumbled, 'I'm a clerk,' and he coughed, 'of the Order. I have duties to fulfil.' He started back when three of the four stepped back to the line, stamping the butts of their spears on the sandstone.

'For a moment there, I thought you said you were a clairvoy. But you look a little . . . well, you know,' said the remaining man, his voice deep and calm.

'No, no. Ha. Uhm . . . Er . . . I'm a clerk. Not a clairvoy, good sir. Can you imagine me? A clairvoy? Getting the favour of a god. Now that would be something, wouldn't it? Dear me,' laughed Calmantis, placing his long arm over the knight's shoulders. 'Imagine that, having a Shadow Guard bow down to me . . .' The guard did not find it as funny.

'Get off me,' growled the man.

Calmantis abruptly stopped laughing and coughed nervously, lifting his arm with a smirk. 'Of course. Apologies, Knight-Marshal Rechker.' *Yes, I know your name.*

The man stepped back and took out a scroll from beneath his breastplate, unfurled it, and asked, 'Name?'

'Name what?'

'Your name!'

He jumped back a step. 'Calmantis Broviere. Clerk of the Order.'

'You're not on the list. Get out of here. Come back when the new Exarch has been chosen.' *Why can't they see I'm just like them?*

'You know, I've always wanted to become a Shadow Guard. Serve the Order by swinging my sword and upholding the laws of Aztar. You think you can put in a good word for me?'

'I said get out of here! Before we strap you to the gates and strip you naked.'

Calmantis stumbled back, gripping the railing not to fall down the steps, scowling at the knight-marshal. Just as he was about to leave, a loud gong sounded, followed by a steady stream of red smoke drifting from the temple. He laughed and pointed to the sky, overjoyed that the long wait was finally at an end.

The old Exarch had died in his sleep, peacefully and gracefully. Or that was what everyone was told. Rumours of the house's unhappiness with the old Exarch had circulated the city, and rumours spread faster than a disease from a brothel. The day of his burial was a spectacular affair. Supporters of the old Exarch had filled the main street of Baldor, waving banners and throwing flowers while the Shadow Guard carried his wood coffin on their shoulders all the way to the centre of the city, where a gigantic raised pyre awaited. Great, enormous flags of the Order waved in the wind over the pyre, white with a golden broadsword pointed down in the centre, an outline of a golden sun behind it. Calmantis had stood on the roof of his building, staring down at the spectacle below.

A rushing horde of people drew his attention back to his surroundings as they knocked into him, pushing and shoving and dragging him along to get to the gates of the temple. From all over, people surrounded them, wanting to gain access to see the new Exarch, with Calmantis at the front, being squished between a pressing horde and the powerful Shadow Guard and their great shields. A roaring crowd screamed in his ears and pushed at his back while he tried his best not to get trampled, leaving a space between himself and the guard's shield. Arms growing tired, he felt them tremble, and a hit to his lower back caused his left hand to slip from the sturdy shield. His face met with it, a solid wall of iron, dull ringing in his ears from the hit, chipping a tooth and bloodying his nose.

Yet, this was a better angle.

He could now see the doors of the temple swing open over a long rolled-out red carpet, where top-ranking members of the Order formed a line outside. He adjusted his stance to get a better vantage point, catching glimpses in between the members, when pain burst through his side.

'Oof!' Air exploded from his mouth as a woman next to him swung her elbow to get some room, connecting with his ribs. Thinking what would a Shadow Guard do, he elbowed her in the back, getting to his position again. The new Exarch walked between his top-ranking members. *More like the top-reeking members after the four days they've spent together. Ha!*

'Long live Exarch Alicus!' shouted someone to his left, annoying him that they had a better view. *Alicus? Really? That snivelling bum-scratcher . . . I've never been his favourite.*

The man stood and waved, speaking to the crowds, but Calmantis could not hear a thing over the screams of those surrounding him. The back of a spear swung over his head, striking multiple people, him included, forcing them all back from the Shadow Guard. He fervently rubbed his head, where tomorrow there would for sure be a great lump the size of an egg waiting when he woke up.

Calmantis slithered to the ground. Not his finest moment, but it needed doing. He crawled through legs, being kicked and spat on, feeling like he was being punished for some outrageous crime he would never commit – or get caught committing, anyway. One of the two needed to be true.

It felt like ages must have passed by the time he made it out on the other side of the throng, where he got to his feet and stumbled away to a nearby bench, but the sun had just set, the light still a beautiful blue mixed with pink on the far side of the city. He fell with his arse into the seat, panting and cursing, but only in his head. A man of the Order surely wouldn't curse out loud.

A stinging pain confronted him in his mouth, and he pressed his tongue into a gap between his teeth, jerking his head back. 'Hairy tits on a spike!' He jumped up from the shocking use of language, glancing around at passers-by as if one of them had said it and he was looking for the culprit, shaking his head disappointingly. He quickly left the location. A man of the Order couldn't be heard swearing like that. *Time for a drink, I gather.*

4. Judge and Jury

A few days had passed since she broke into Yelefant Du Pantè's home. The riches of that night had put a big smile on her face ever since. Orana had gone to see her fence that very night, emptying her pockets filled with the most beautifully cut gems, rubies, and diamonds of all colours and sizes, selling most of the items. But of all the items she had placed on the table before him, he seemed most interested in the piece of rock she had with her. Bigger than the other gems, a touch of blue sparkled when light caught the black and silver veins coursing through it. The man's round, puffy face had drooped as he lay eyes upon it, becoming flustered and dumb, stumbling over his words as he hastily grabbed the rock from her fingers.

'Oh, this is quite magnificent,' he had said. 'I'll give you five hundred for it.'

Five hundred? That's half of all of them together. The amount had shocked Orana utterly, but she was a professional. She did not show her excitement. 'Five hundred?' she asked with a sneer. 'Is that all you can dream up, Yohtan?'

Bewildered, the fence licked his lips, eyeing the rock in his hands with glee. 'Okay! A thousand . . .'

She snatched the rock from his hands and said, 'I'll take my business elsewhere. It seems you are not ready to talk to me.' Orana spun around and didn't get more than a few feet before his voice bounced off the walls of the small, gloomy room, the lantern behind the fence flickering and dancing to the beat of drafts flowing through from vents near the ceiling.

'Two thousand five hundred for everything! You're bleeding me dry! I know these are not procured goods, they are hot items . . . You cannot get rid of them easily.' Spittle flew from his full, round lips.

Orana had turned back to him, glaring at him for some time,

drilling arrowheads through his face with her stare. 'You want to say that a little louder, eh? I don't quite think all the guards heard you.' She tilted her head and dragged her dagger from the sheath. 'Maybe I should change occupations and become an assassin instead. Cut off your fruits and put them on display for all to see . . .'

'A little testy, aren't we? Take it or leave it!' Yohtan rummaged through a chest behind him and lifted a heavy bag, dropping it on the table to reveal a hoard of silver and gold coins.

He's right, I can't hold on to these. They need to be moved, fast. It was the most coins she had ever seen. *I can live out my days with this. I never have to steal again . . . And to think I was going to take a night off.* The room felt so small suddenly. Her palms were wet with sweat, and it felt like the entire world's eyes were on her, watching her every move. She slipped the dagger back into the sheath and picked up the bag.

'I will see you around, Yohtan.'

'Don't bet on it. If I were you, I would leave town.' Orana would not be scared so easily.

Now, here in the press of people flowing to the Temple of Khylles, Orana had that nagging feeling that someone was following her, watching her from a distance. Bodies pressed up hard against her, hands of men and women grabbing and pushing, all eager to get to the temple to pray for rain. The last few days had been excruciatingly hot and dry. Not wanting to seem out of place, Orana had stuck to where the crowds went, drifting with them towards markets and temples, looking for work or ways to make some coin. Sweat dripped down her face, her hair wet and clumpy, her clothes sweat-stained and smelling foul. She had not bathed since the theft, thinking that a suddenly rich individual wouldn't look like this, would they?

The path to the great doors was a gigantic wyrm, slithering forward, a riled beast ever in motion, the low sun hanging in the distance over large palm trees, planted as decorations for the temple to give it a calming effect. She caught a glimpse of eyes lingering for a fluttering heartbeat too long on her, the dark brows and sharp eyes quickly vanishing into the throng of people. *Damn! How'd they find me?*

A big fat foot stepped on her toes, and she wanted to scream, but she was already the object of attention. More was not needed. She held in her anger, bit her lip, and pushed forward, fighting through the mob of men and women. 'Hey! Watch it!' a man shouted as she accidentally shoved him to the ground, pulling others along and falling like rushing water, opening a wide clearing with tumbling bodies, leaving her exposed. She glimpsed two more men making their way to her.

A sour smell hung in the air, stinging her nose, and she sniffed under her arm, pulling her face at the reek. She wished now she had taken a bath. That was a problem for a later time. Now she needed to get away from these pesky trackers.

People shouted and cursed at her, angry at being pushed by the fleeing woman. Orana turned about and saw the men hunting her were closing in, throwing people out of their way and gaining ground quickly. There was no use hiding anymore. She needed to run. So many people crowded the narrow pathway, shuffling forward and staying away from the thirty-foot drops on either side, blocking her escape. Forwards or backwards were her only choices. 'Move!' she shouted. 'Get out of my way!'

'Got you now, you cow! Ain't no more running,' said one hunter a few feet behind her, and he pulled his cutlass from its sheath, the blade ringing steel as it scraped out.

There was virtually no time between her thinking him an absolute moron and when those surrounding him started screaming and pushing all at once, fearing for their lives and trying to get away from the madman with his sword. The stampede happened fast. No hesitation. No consideration to others, especially not their safety. *That's how it always is, though. Self-preservation trumps all.* Fear drove most people to become survivalists, and blood always flowed at those times, as the man hunting her soon found out.

Men and women fled in all directions, screaming and shoving, while those near the edge of the path pushed back with everything they had. It would not be enough to hold back the terrified crowds, and soon the last row of people slipped down in a hail of cries, grabbing hold of others' clothes, pulling more down with them to fall, screaming. Some of those screams came to a sudden, bone-chilling end on the ground below.

A hard elbow hit Orana in the back, and she stumbled forward. Disorientated, she spun around in time for a rushing man to crash into her, flinging her a few feet away. Her head bounced off the cobblestones, and her eyes swam for an instant. To her left lay a woman clutching her baby, huddled over the blanket, protecting it as dozens trampled them beneath their rushing feet. Even when the man with the sword got knocked down and kicked senseless, the people did not stop. Once the stampede started, there was no stopping it. Fear was a strange motivator. You need only give rise to it, give voice to the possibility of something dangerous, and people would run for their lives.

Orana heard the screams of those being trampled and falling down the side, and decided the fall must be the better option. She crawled away to the side, when a hard shin and foot cracked into her ribs, knocking the breath from her. She groaned where she lay on the ground, and more air exploded from her mouth, her chest heaving and bending under the weight of the boot using her as a stepping stone. Coughing, she sucked in air, heaving her painful chest and scrambled on her hands and knees, fearful groans escaping her mouth. A knee cracked into the side of her head, and she collapsed again. Blood dripped from her ringing ear and mouth, but she was close to the edge now. *This is not how Orana Rille dies! One last bit of pain. I can do this.* She stared down at the ground beneath. *Land on your feet, Orana, tuck and roll. You're a thief, you can take the hit.* She pushed herself over the edge, and a gust of wind enveloped her as she fell, the ground rushing closer fast.

Her body was tired and sore, unwilling to listen to her commands, slow to react. The impact took her by surprise, snapping her legs up, her knees feeling like they were about to pop through the skin, her head whipping back and forth before she rolled forward. Hard stones dug into her shoulder, and she flopped to the ground spread-eagled, panting and coughing. Groaning, her arms moved slowly to her head and came away bloody. Nothing felt broken, but she knew she would be in a world of pain tomorrow. If she could stay alive until then.

She pulled herself up from the ground and turned back to the chaos above, seeing a man glare at her, his face hidden behind a white scarf and turban. She gave him the finger and stumbled away, hobbling along to get out of sight.

*　*　*

Down the gloomy hallway she limped, clutching her bleeding, bruised right arm, hurting all over. A door screeched open just behind her, letting in a streak of light from a lantern swinging in the old woman's hand, who poked her face out the door and said, 'Oh dear, girl. You hear about the trampling on Khylles Walk? Such a world we live in today, eh?' The old woman's foul breath drifted outward.

It had taken her a while to get back home, having walked circles to ensure she wasn't being followed. Still, she couldn't believe the news had spread so fast. Orana didn't turn to her, knowing that if she gave any indication that she knew anything, the old woman would not let her go. But she couldn't say that she had heard nothing as well, for then the old woman would want to inform her, guide the inept young woman to be more vigilant and curious. Knowledge was power, after all.

'Yes, Miss Downere, I heard the news. Must have been terrible to witness.' Orana tried not to stand on her left foot, keeping it suspended above the floor ever so slightly. 'Goodnight, Miss Downere. I've had a long day.' She walked further.

'Goodnight, dear. Oh, and please tell your friends to be quiet. We old people like to take naps, and it's hard to do with them being so loud.'

Orana stopped in her tracks, a cold sweat running down her spine. 'Friends?'

'Why yes, dear. Aren't they? That one man is very fetching. He reminds me of my late husband, Mister Angovic Downere.' She smiled in fond remembrance, licking her dry lips and sighing loudly. 'He was such a catch, that man. Have I ever told you how we met?'

A hundred times, old woman . . . But I wouldn't mind hearing it today. 'No, you haven't. Mind if I come in? We can sit and talk. I wouldn't mind a cup of tea, to be honest.' Tea, spiced water . . . She couldn't stomach the stuff. *I would rather drink warm water or piss. Mind you, I'm sure it tastes pretty much the same. But I will not stick around long enough to drink it, so best get on with it.*

The old woman's face lit up, her saggy skin pulling up around her eyes and bunching all wrinkled around her cheeks. 'Oh, I would be delighted to tell you! Come in, come in.' The door closed, and Orana heard the latches fall away before it swung open fully. The hunched old woman appeared in an old nightgown, the material so worn Orana could see right through. She wanted to scratch her eyes out. Not because the old woman disgusted her, rather it was what her own future held, if she was lucky enough to make it to a ripe old age.

Orana inched through the door, glancing back down the grey hall, searching for movement. All seemed quiet, a faint glow coming from downstairs somewhere. The little home smelled musty, of old wine and pipe weed. She felt the chips and cracks in the old ceramic tiles beneath her fingers as she glided them over the wall. *The younger Mister Angovic, I assume, made you feel pretty special, having made a beautiful home for you both. Now you have no one to fix up the place anymore.*

The old woman scurried ahead of her, leaning on a cane, tapping away on the floor as she dragged her feet, old saggy breasts swinging left and right under the see-through gown. She rounded the corner to where the kitchen was and called out, 'I will put on the water, won't be but a moment. Have a seat, deary.'

'Take your time.' Orana hurried over to the window and opened the shutters, breathing deep the fresh air, peering down to the street below where a few people still walked under the guiding lights of the lantern posts. She climbed through to the tiled roof, stepping lightly on the uneven, sloped surface, balancing herself with her arms spread wide and leaning backwards, touching the tiles with her left hand. Injuries be damned, she had to endure it for the time being, push through the lancing pain shooting up her leg, ribs, and arm. A tile beneath her foot slipped from its position, sending her to the roof on her arms and back, shattering into shards of clay on the road below. Passers-by turned and pointed at her, talking to others and drawing a crowd. She needed to get down and away quickly.

Steadily, she got back on her feet, only to cry out in pain as someone tackled her, a broad shoulder driving the wind from her lungs. She hit the roof again, hard. The world tumbled and spun wildly. There was nothing she could do. Roof, stars, roof, people, a flashing moon, and rushing cobblestones. Darkness.

* * *

The Dragon Swell rode high this morning, breaking far above its usual perimeter, sucking thick white foam back to the sea, reclaiming its own only moments before another monstrous wave beat down on the strand. The wind was gusty, whipping her curls all over, the sky grey and unwelcoming. Orana felt the sand suck her down where she stood away from the breaking waves, letting the water wash over her legs, each time reaching higher and higher. A deep laughter burst out on her right, and she raised Besmitz up by the arms, hoisting him out of the water. Far in the distance on the rocks where great waves thundered against the earth to spray high, her father cast out his net over and over, retracting and casting, hoping to get a good catch for the day. The water crashed over him, leaving only glimpses of him through their unabated slapping. Another wave hit the strand with exceptional force, racing towards them fast and furious—

'Mmm,' she moaned, her chin touching her chest. Water dripped from a height, splashing over itself on the floor somewhere, the incessant *plink, plink, plink* bringing her back to reality. Her head was pounding, throbbing with every move, yet there was an urgency pushing her to wake up.

Her eyes fluttered open. The room was dark and dreary, vacant of anything interesting except for a few buckets of filthy water and a table with some tools lying on top. In the room's corner, on a stand, stood a candle, flickering the smallest flame, barely giving any light, yet it was enough to see the dreaded equipment. A wooden mallet, rusty pliers, a chisel, and a few items she was unsure of, having long silver points, looking terrifyingly sharp.

Tight ropes burned her wrists and ankles. She was bound to a chair, her rump numb and her tailbone painful. *How long have I been sitting here?* Orana yanked on the ropes and kicked to break her bonds or the chair. A futile attempt. Footsteps drummed on the floorboards outside, drawing closer, until a shadow fell over the light streaming through under the door. Keys scraped against iron, and loud clangs sounded, a lock springing open. She knew the sound well.

The sharp-eyed man from earlier on Khylles Walk stepped through the opening door, ducking into the room before straightening. Another man followed him, struggling to gain entry with his pot belly straining toward the ground. Yelefant Du Pantè straightened and breathed a lungful of air, screwing his face from the smell. *This isn't good.*

'What do you want?' Orana shrieked. 'Is this payback for the comments I made a few nights back? Takes a man with a tiny prick to be this insecure. You have a tiny prick, eh?' A yelp of pain left her when a hard fist came from the goon on her left and cracked into the side of her face, spraying blood on the floor, dripping down her chin. She spat red phlegm on the wall and worked her jaw, closing her eyes as unwelcome tears flowed over her cheeks. 'Can we call it even now and just let me go?'

'Where are my gems?' Yelefant asked, rolling up the sleeves of his white tunic without so much as a glance at her.

'Do I look like your maid? How should I know what you do with your things?' Another crack of the fist rocked her head to the side. It hurt like a bastard. Orana huffed like a tired dog, the beatings sapping her energy. She turned to the sharp-eyed thug and glared at him through her swelling left eye. There was a big, purple bruise under his eye, covered up by the scarf wrapped round his face. 'Your mother must be so proud of you killing and injuring so many on their march to pray for rain.'

The thug lunged at her and grabbed her face with his hard, calloused fingers, rough, sharp nails digging into her skin. 'I didn't murder any of them!'

'No, you just scared them all into a stampede, unsheathing your sword like an idiot!' He slapped her across the face and suddenly shrieked in pain as she closed her teeth around his finger. The crunching of bones sounded, and Yelefant had to step in, smashing her hand with the wooden mallet. Orana screamed, squirming and shaking in the chair, blood running down her mouth as she tore the man's finger off with her teeth and spat it on the floor. Stamping his foot on the ground in anger and pain, the thug clutched his shaking hand and tore a sleeve from his tunic, wrapping it around his hand to slow the pulsing blood flow.

'Grab her head!' Yelefant shouted and picked up a bucket, sloshing water over the rim. The thug grabbed her by the hair and yanked her head back, placing a dirty cloth bag over her head, and pulled it tight around her mouth and nose.

Deep breaths, Orana. Deep breaths. Wait for them to ask questions. She sucked in air, thinking the water would come, but they waited her out. Blinded by the cloth, she could only guess when they would pour and when to breathe.

'You want rain, eh? Where are my gems!' *Breathe!* Cold water rushed over her, pouring down her nose, forcing her to cough and open her mouth. More flooded down her mouth, filling her throat and lungs fast, drowning her, and it kept coming. She thrashed in the chair, jerking her arms and legs, wriggling to get out from under the bucket, gurgling water, spitting, and coughing continuously. Her lungs felt like they were about to explode, her chest on fire. It was like being pummelled by the ocean.

Finally, the water stopped falling, the bucket empty. Her head came up and Orana vomited water, coughing it from her lungs in ragged, painful breaths. 'Okay, okay! What do you want? I will help where I can.' They pulled the bag from her head.

'You still expect me to believe you didn't steal my gems?' Yelefant turned the metal bucket over and sat down in front of her, arms resting on his knees, hands hanging to the ground.

'If I had these valuable gems, don't you think I would have paid for a bath at least?'

'So you're a clever thief. You know it will attract attention. My men tossed your room. They found nothing. Give me my gems back and I might let you live.'

Living sounds good. I want to keep living . . . 'If they were stolen, they are not in the city anymore. I guarantee this. If I can find them,' she drawled, 'will you let me go? Forget our business?'

Yelefant leaned back and spread his hands. 'I'm a generous man. If you give me two-thirds of the profit you made, I will give you a month to get my gems back to me. There was one in particular I fancied. Big, black. Silver veins. Yes, you know the one I'm talking about. And don't give me less than I asked for. I will know.'

I should have taken off that night after all. Teeth clenched, she cursed and said, 'Fine. I will get you your gems and coin.'

Yelefant stared at the tools on the table, picking up the rusted pliers, clicking them open and closed in front of her face. 'I was really looking forward to using these. I'm a little disappointed you broke so easily. My coin, tomorrow. No later. I will come to your room when the sun sets.' He sighed, setting the pliers down, and gestured to his thug with a flick of his finger as he stepped out from the room. 'Lofka, you know what to do.'

The smelly bag went over her head again, and Lofka cut her bonds, hauling her up and shoving her out the door. Orana remembered seeing them duck and so did she. She was not about to hit her head for no good reason. One less bump would do her good after the day she'd had. Being a thief had its advantages, and having a good sense of your surroundings was one of them, but that helped nothing if you were unable to see anything.

'Do not remove the bag,' said Lofka from behind, prodding her along. She heard him wince.

'How's the finger?'

'Shut up! I was looking forward to slitting your throat. Guess I'll have to wait a month. Don't you worry, I will get you eventually.' *Don't bet your life on it.*

Orana had to rely on her hearing and touch, feeling the rough walls, cracked and chipped, paint peeling where her fingers glided over the surface. She bumped into something, and soon after, glass shattered on the floor, spraying water over her bare feet. Stripped of her boots, she winced at the thought of stepping on a piece of glass, feeling sharp edges scrape the side of her left foot. She lightly stepped forward, seeing shards of glass everywhere in her mind, and Lofka shoved her from behind. Her foot came down hard, stubbing and scraping the skin off her toes against a rough-textured wall. *Bastard!*

Strong fingers gripped her by the arm, pulling her back. 'Stairs. Climb.' A creak sounded, and he shoved her forward, a hard and worn edge of wood grazing her leg, tearing the skin, then a breeze drifted over her. It was late night, quiet, no one moving around. The door closed behind them, and she stumbled down the road. For some time, they walked, turning left and right. He spun her around and turned and turned, walking down various paths. She had to take a chance on something. 'Lofka, your house is falling apart, while Yelefant sleeps in his mansion.' Silence. *Was that a wrong assumption?*

'What of it?'

'You know, we both can profit if you are willing to . . . deal with Yelefant. You seem the type. Fifty-fifty. I give you half of the profits and we go our separate ways. What d'ya say?' Lofka flung the bag off her head and glared at her.

'Go.' He said nothing else. He simply waited for her to walk away. Nervous ticks pulled at her back, worried that Lofka might slip his cutlass through her from behind. Orana moved away slowly at first, then with more distance between them, she sprinted, running away from the area as fast as she could.

5. Nowhere to Hide

A soft, warm touch tickled his hand, a tender finger following the lines on his palm and down his wrist, giving him goosebumps all over. Bellard lay in bed, and she lay beside him, laughing at something he'd said. Cora picked up a pillow and swiped it at him playfully. It felt like it was early morning, as cold air drifted through the room, the windows all frosted over and the early morning pink-orange hue casting its rays on the bed.

He reached out to hold her hand, and it slipped from his fingers. He tried again, but they seemed to pull further away. Panicked, he jumped from the bed, the room ever lengthening, pulling Cora away from him . . .

'Wake up! Bellard!'

'Er,' he groaned and opened his eyes, and a stinging pain in his head accosted him, making it throb. A girl drifted over him, coming into focus, and he blinked his eyes, seeing the white hair, smelling the vanilla. The memories exploded in his mind, and he sat up, fearing for their lives again. 'Mila! You're okay? What happened?' Brethnar and Valdor stood a good distance away, talking to each other. He realised now that it was her warm hand in his. She pulled him up from the floor and helped him to the chair, scowling at the other two, then spoke to them.

'Don't you two have something to say to Bellard? Now would be a fine time for it.'

The two inched closer, leaving a few feet between them and Mila, fidgeting with their hands. Valdor, the oldest of the four of them by a couple years, shoved Brethnar ahead, gesturing him to continue. For a young man of seventeen, Brethnar sure had a lot of hair and a sturdy build. His brows were bushy and wild, his short, red-brown hair standing in all directions. *Hasn't he ever heard of a comb before?*

Bellard thought, eyeing the nearing man.

'We . . . Er . . . We apologise, Bellard. We took it too far.'

'What?' Bellard shook his head. 'What do you mean?'

Valdor stepped forward and said, 'We heard you were joining us tonight, but then when you didn't show, Mila got upset. So we fetched you. We thought you were playing along, but I fear we got carried away. Sorry, Bellard.'

Only now did he see the scrapes and grass and pieces of thorny bush still hanging on their robes. 'Wait. It was you two who did this to me? I feared for my life. I thought we were going to die! Bloody pricks!'

Valdor turned his face and said, 'If it makes you feel any better, you have a nasty left hook. Caught me on the jaw when we tumbled through the bush and knocked out a tooth. See?' He grinned and turned his head, showing the gap in the back of his mouth. 'And I think you got young Brethnar even better.' He gestured to the younger man, who turned his head as well, showing a faint outline of a black patch circling his right eye.

Everyone was silently staring at Bellard, waiting for his reply. The tension in the room was palpable, and Mila looked ready to deck them with her fists or anything she could get her hands on. Bellard shook his head, then chuckled. 'You bastards deserve more than that. But I'll settle for what I got.' Working his fingers gingerly over his pate, he jerked away from his hand, feeling a thick lump on his head, and asked, 'What did I run into, though?'

'Oh yeah. I nearly forgot,' chuckled Brethnar, and pointed to the door. A large crack spread from the centre through the ornate carvings and out the side. 'I think that got the worst of it. Haha.'

'Come on, Bellard. We're already here. We might as well have a few drinks,' Mila said with a grin on her face. There was a twinkle in her eye that made Bellard think she had already delved into the bottle, but he said nothing.

'Fine, only a few, then I'm off to bed.'

* * *

A breath of heat cooked his nose, a light, sharp and annoying, flickering on his eyelids. Bellard awakened slowly, snorting loudly and lifting his head, regretting it instantly. His ribs, hips, shoulders, and face were in agony. Not to mention his head. With every move he made, he groaned, trying his best to evade the pain. Bellard glanced around, seeing wooden flooring under him. *Where is my bed? Where am I?* Rows of tables and chairs surrounded him, and to the left lay Brethnar, curled into a ball on the grandàre's desk. Silver-white hair tickled his nose, and he adjusted his eyes, focusing on the object lying on his left arm, snoring softly. 'Mila,' he said, his voice sounding groggy and ill. 'What happened?' He shook his head, taking it in, his mind slow to react to the information it had gathered.

'Mila!' he shouted, flinging her head up in shock. 'We have to go!' Mila's head hit the floor with a thud, and she jumped at the pain, waking confused and irritated at his rudeness.

'Ow! Bellard, you boob! Was that really necessary?' she growled at him, clutching the side of her head, muttering obscenities to herself.

He turned to regard her and anxiously croaked, 'Yes! It's morning, and the . . .' he ran to the window to look outside, seeing a few early-rising students and teachers talking on the lawns, then dropped to the floor, hoping nobody saw him, '. . . students and teachers are on their way here.'

Mila's eyes stretched wide, and she jumped up from the floor. She ran over to Valdor and started shaking him. Bellard did the same with Brethnar, but the young man would have none of this incessant shaking and screaming in his ears, so Bellard did the next best thing: he pushed Brethnar off the desk. There wasn't even a shout. The young man dropped on the floor like a brick, in between books and papers scattered about.

'What was that for?' Brethnar groaned, rising to his feet, his plastered hair glowing even redder in the morning sun shining through the windows.

'The grandàre is coming!' Bellard shouted, and both Valdor and

Brethnar snapped out of their drunken haze. The room was in disarray. Tables and chairs were overturned, papers and books lay scattered, and two empty bottles lay on the floor, glinting sunlight back into his eyes. Bellard ran to pick them up, while Mila, Brethnar, and Valdor righted the tables and chairs. Hearts beating wildly, they picked up the papers and books, getting the room back to relative order, before running for the door. They looked a mess and stank like the depths of the abyss.

Ahead, down the hallway, the main doors swung open, and they slowed to a walk, casually looking at everything around them, anything but the woman walking towards them. It seemed the floor had never seemed so interesting before for his accomplices, nor the walls or the ceiling . . . Bellard, though, couldn't help himself from looking. There was a thin black string around her neck, with the most beautiful opalescent Pillar swinging side to side. He wondered how much power she must have, how much confidence that potential brought, knowing she was no vulnerable fool.

She must be a second- or third-year. She's too young to be a grandàre. Her long black hair waved and curled over her shoulder, down her blue robe. Bellard had fallen behind while he stopped to stare at her, then sprinted to catch up with his friends. Like nothing had ever happened, they casually strolled out the front door and over the lawn, back to their rooms.

All Bellard wanted was to drown himself in as much water as he could find. Parched inside out, he felt like a desert had settled in him. Mage or not, it seems liquor did the same thing to everyone. His class would start soon. It was the first one of the day, and Grandàre Agoras was not as kind as Grandàre Shevira. *He* was more likely to let the bookcase fall on him. *A quick change of clothes then, before I head back.* The friends separated without a word to each other, heading in their own directions, heads hanging low.

* * *

Bellard ran across the field of grass, robe fluttering in the wind, a heavy bag of books swinging at his side, bumping into his bruised hip. The hard floor hadn't done him any favours, and neither did the liquor; his mind felt foggy and slow, his eyes scratchy and burning.

A group of students stood on the forecourt chattering away, their whispered buzz droning through the air. Some spoke in hushed tones, furtively glancing back and forth to the closed main doors of the building, raising the hairs on Bellard's arms. To his right, Brethnar sat against the building at the back of a flowerbed between the plants, avoiding the crowd, eyes closed to the rising sun. 'What's going on?' Bellard asked, and Brethnar opened his left eye, closing it soon after.

'Grandàre Agoras is spewing. Seems someone got into his chambers and finished his liquor. He won't let anyone in. Said he's going to find out who.'

'What? How?' Bellard asked, his stomach churning, breaths racing from his mouth.

'He's a grandàre. I'm sure he has his ways.'

'Why aren't you worried? How can you be this calm?' Bellard stormed, shouting his whispers louder than he wanted to, his voice kicking up a few octaves. But Brethnar just flicked open an eyelid.

'What can we do? It's not like we can stop him. As my mother used to say, "Know when to surrender, my boy."' Brethnar jumped up, dusting his bottom, and continued, 'Hey, you want to see how he does it?'

'Do wrexcers have horns? Of course I want to see! But how?'

'I know a way in. Well, sort of. Follow me.'

Bellard glanced around at the students still chattering, working his sweaty palms with his fingers, thinking hard about his decisions. It had been so many months that they had been studying their art, yet could not use it or see it in action. Now, there was a chance of seeing it performed by the grandàre himself, even if it was their futures on the line.

He slipped away, following the crouching Brethnar, staying behind the trees lined next to the building. Bellard broke off a plump nectarine in passing, its yellow skin turning red and soft, tearing at the slightest touch. He took a big bite, and juice burst into his mouth and down his chin, sweet and full of flavour. The blessed fruit restored some of his lost energy, making life a little more bearable.

They sneaked around the corner of the building and reached a thick pipe running up to the roof, and Brethnar grabbed hold of it, pressing his feet against the wall while he climbed first. Bellard's heart fluttered in his chest, skipping beats, as he followed Brethnar up the pipe. He was utterly afraid. Of falling or being caught. Afraid of not completing his claiming. Afraid of failing. Slow and steady, he dragged himself a little higher, his sweaty palms slipping on the glistening pipe, constantly having to readjust his grip.

Now two thirds of the way up to the high roof, his head reeled at the dangers he had found himself in, the possibility of falling, of being caught . . . and he couldn't move. He gripped the pipe tight, not wanting to let go and not wanting to climb any further. In his mind, he saw himself slip and fall, robe and hair fluttering, looking up to the sun and roof stretching further and further away, fearing the rushing ground he hurtled towards. He was stuck, mentally and physically. 'I can't!'

Brethnar popped his head over the edge of the roof and said, 'Come on, Bellard! Give me your hand. You need only climb a little further.'

'I can't!' *What am I doing? I'm not this! I'm not brave!* Eyes closed, he dropped his head against the sun-warmed pipe, arms trembling, growing tired of holding on.

'Don't look down, just focus on me. Look at me, Bellard. You can do this!' He reached down, waiting for Bellard to move up and grab hold.

Okay. Okay. Either up or down, get moving! He inched up with slight movements, keeping Brethnar in his sight, feeling exposed. A gust of wind tore at him, and he gripped the pipe close to his chest, feeling the solid nature of the iron, the heat flowing from it, baked in the direct sun. *This is stupid!*

Something tapped him on the head, and he heard Brethnar's voice close-by. 'Er . . . You're here. Just grab my hand, and I'll pull you over.'

Bellard peeped up and grabbed his friend's hand, straining his muscles to pull himself up. Rolling onto the roof and knocking Brethnar over, he felt like crying, his hands shaking and his body trembling. Yet, he had done it. There was no taking it away from him. 'I did it!' he shouted and jumped up, unceremoniously hugging Brethnar, who seemed a little surprised by the jubilation of his friend. 'Let's never do that again,' he breathed, chest heaving.

'Yes, you did. Now come, we are almost there.' Brethnar stood waiting, waving at Bellard to follow. They scrambled up the side of the roof to a dormer and peered through, cupping their hands over their eyes and leaning against the window to see.

Grandàre Agoras had removed his old, grey mage's hat and was brooding in his chair, spinning an empty bottle between his hands, looking straight through it. 'You left the bottles?' asked Brethnar, scowling at Bellard. 'Why did you leave the bottles?'

'Uhm. I don't know! Why would I have run out with the bottles in my arms, showing everyone, "Hey look, we drank these!" We weren't really in the best state this morning to think clearly, were we now? And whose fault is it we were there in the first place?'

'Oh sure, blame us for having a good time, ya prissy bastard!' Brethnar shoved him away.

'Oi!' said a voice behind them, and both spun around to see Mila and Valdor approach them. She shook her head and pushed by them to peer through the window, then stated, 'You two are the worst spies in the world. We saw you climbing the pipe a mile away and followed. I'm amazed the entire school is not on the roof. Look, he's about to do something.'

A grin appeared on Agoras's face. He rose from his chair and walked to the centre of the room, leaning on a staff with his old hands, magnificent silver and gold rings glinting on his fingers. His Pillar drew Bellard in, a big red gem set in the staff's top, casting bloody shadows on the wall. Twice he stamped his staff on the floor, the sound somehow more prominent, amplified, reverberating through the windows, the walls, and the very stones of the building. A sense of wonder floated around him, a power rippling through the room.

Bellard couldn't pull his eyes from the mage, stuck in awe of what power looked like. Clouds, dark and dense, formed around Agoras, a brilliant display of the night's stars settling through them, glittering purple, yellow, red, blue, orange, and so many more colours, joining the conjunction of lights. Through those glittering stars, the world came into view, a brilliant ball of blue, green, and brown, growing larger still. The land flashed by at ridiculous speeds until Khorvellen came into view. Valdor vomited next to them, yet Bellard didn't glance away like the rest. He kept staring. They raced over Khorvellen's walls, and through the narrow streets of Lowtown, over rooftops of red, grey, and white, some faded with neglect, and smoke rising from chimneys. The houses grew bigger, fancier, the streets wider, cleaner, and at one stage, they were so close to the ground he felt he could reach out and grab hold of the men and women walking there. Over the walls of Kunia, the large grass fields, the orchard, the white-walled monasterium, and on to the classrooms of the chosen, until they saw themselves on the roof, growing closer and closer and closer . . . The roof suddenly vanished beneath them, and they screamed and shrieked.

The clouds drifted away, and still they screamed, staring at Grandàre Agoras, the angry scowl on his grey-bearded face not comforting them. 'Stop shouting this instant!' he roared, and whether they wanted to or not, no sound was forthcoming from their mouths, being restricted by magic.

Bellard stared up at the ceiling, seeing it fully intact, wondering how they had appeared here without damaging it in the slightest, and turned to Mila. He pointed at his mouth, the veins on his neck bulging with the effort to scream, yet not a sound came out.

'Look at me!' Their necks twisted to the grandàre, and they could not look away. 'You four drank the very last of my Ohlerary. Do you know how hard it is to get this? No! You don't. It is near impossible to get! Impossible! A precious wine, that for mages like me, grants a glimpse of a moment in time, any moment! A powerful thing to have at your disposal . . . Now it's gone, forever. For you bumbling idiots, it gave headaches and foul breath. What should I do with you, eh? Well, come on! Tell me!' He whipped his arm out, snapping his fingers, and their voices returned with coughing fits, their throats burning and scratchy. They all started talking at the same time, words bumbling over one another incoherently. 'Stop!' shouted Agoras, and pointed his staff at Bellard. 'You begin!'

'It was a terrible mistake, Grandàre. It will never happen again. We promise.'

'That is not what I asked!' He turned and pointed at Mila. 'You! What should we do with you? I fear casting you out of Kunia is not enough punishment, not even banishing you from every city in the North is!' Agoras leaned in close to them, his coarse voice rumbling like a lion's. 'It better be good, you hear? It better be fitting . . .'

'What is going on here?' crowed an old voice from the door, and all of them turned to see Grandàre Shevira walk into the room.

'Stay out of this, Shevira! These kids need to be punished, and I will see to it,' stated Agoras, turning back to them. 'Out with it. What will it be?' His voice was cold, angry, calm, and dead serious.

Mila looked up at Bellard, then Valdor, and Brethnar, searching for answers, but they couldn't give them. She was their voice now. And they would face her decision. *What could be worse than being banished from all cities?* wondered Bellard. His bowels felt like emptying right here in class, his stomach churning, tying devilish knots with every breath he took. He couldn't let her make this decision. Valdor and Brethnar would hate her. He raced through ideas of punishment. *Lashings maybe? Or to become monks?*

'Send me for my claiming at the stroke of midnight . . .' whispered Mila, her head bowed to her chest, white hair hiding her eyes. 'It was not their plan. It was mine.'

Bellard went deathly cold, the colour draining from his face. 'No, it was my idea!' he heard himself say out loud. *Did I just say that?*

'No. It was mine!' Valdor chimed in.

'Not true. I came up with it!' Brethnar blabbered.

'What? No! Absolutely not! I won't allow this nonsense!' stormed Grandàre Shevira, marching closer, hips swinging, finger pointing at

Agoras. 'You can't—'

'I will not be silenced in my classroom! I am head grandàre here! And I say what we can and cannot allow!' Bellard, Mila, Valdor, and Brethnar had all jumped back at his outburst, eyes wide and fearful. Even Grandàre Shevira had been silenced, her round spectacles dancing on her nose with her start. Agoras turned back to them and tapped his staff on the floor, and for the *tap, tap, tap* it should have been, harsh drums beat in Bellard's ears. 'A suitable punishment . . . Set it up, Shevira. Tonight, we celebrate a night-time claiming.'

Shocked, Shevira stood with her hands covering her mouth, and turned, marching from the room. Bellard stepped forward and burst out, 'Tonight? Please, Grandàre, may we have time to prepare?'

A cold and empty face glared at them. 'You have the day. I will await you when the sun is lowest. Either you complete the claiming tonight, or you leave Kunia forever. Now get out. I have a class to teach.'

Bellard's knees had been cut out from under him. He turned and walked from the room, wobbling on unsteady legs. A cold, bony hand gripped his arm, turning him around in the vacant hallway. Grandàre Shevira waited with mouth agape, her blue eyes pulled wide and tear-filled.

'You four come with me. I will guide you and prepare you for tonight.'

6. Making Strides

The apple crunched in his mouth, spraying sweet juice down his throat, and choked him. Calmantis coughed and spat, hitting his chest while he walked down the street towards the temple and tripped over a rock. Arms flailing, he careened forward, and the red dirt rushed towards his face. *No no no, I cannot go there with a scraped-up face.*

He swung his left leg out at an angle, hoping to catch himself, but did a split instead, tearing his pants from front to back, pulling several groin muscles. He released a high-pitched wail where he sat on the ground, right leg at his back, knee bent awkwardly, left leg straight ahead, unwilling to come back to him. People stared and laughed and walked around him, giving him room while he collapsed on the ground and straightened his legs, rubbing his groin to ease the pain.

A woman and her child walked by right after he got out of his uncomfortable position and must not have seen it happen, because when she saw him rub his nether region, she jerked her child to her and ran from the area, glaring back and shaking her finger at him.

'No, wait!' he shouted, wanting to explain what happened, but she had already turned down a new road. And to make matters worse, his apple was now mushed into his palm. A swell way to start the day . . .

The night before, he had received a letter from the Order demanding his presence, stating his work had fallen behind. They had addressed it to "Disciple 314" and stated:

As a recognition of title, we, as the Order of Eternal Sacrament, wholeheartedly congratulate Exarch Alicus Vitremere on his new appointment and wish him a long reign as leader.

Now, to the crux of the matter, we as the Order are assuredly concerned and disappointed that your work has fallen behind agreed limits. Therefore, we demand you come in immediately and resolve the problems at hand, first and foremost being the cesspits that have overflowed and now run a foot deep. We expect this to be resolved right away.

Our new lord cannot be made to wade through the filth. It is an affront to him and the Order and, most of all, our Lord Aztar, God of Life. We are also deeply concerned regarding allegations of theft brought against you, Calmantis Broviere. In keeping with the respect we have for all workers of the Order and their resolve, we endeavour to hear your rebuttal before any executionary judgement is passed. We simply cannot allow thieves into the Order. There will be a hearing at noon tomorrow. Do not be late.

You have been a valued member, but are ultimately replaceable.
Lord Latimus Greyarm. Dean of the House.

As the good disciple he was, Calmantis had left directly after receiving the letter, donning his filthy apron and taking his trusty shovel, calling forth the might of the gongfermours and their steeds to dispose of the excrement before the night was done. Few had the stomach for the work, and even fewer had the capacity to carry on with it after the first job. Calmantis had other motivation that inspired him. He would become a Shadow Guard, and a little excrement would not stand in his way.

Calmantis shrugged off the pain and pinned his pants together with his fist, walking like he was about to fill a cesspit of his own. He made his way down the road, clutching his pants front and back, his knock knees closing the gap between his legs. There was no way he could turn back now to get another pair. He would simply need to accept his misfortune and move on. He shuffled past the cordwainer's shop, seeing fanciful shoes and boots, some pointy, some flat, some with outlandish colours, and some as dull as daylight in the desert. Shoes would do him no good. He needed pants. And the tailor's shop was just around the corner. If he could only make it through the crowd of bustling workers and marketeers coming and going.

Great, square blocks of grey construction rose into the sky at the centre of Baldor, for those who had chosen not to commute, seeking to be near everything: the jobs, the markets, the shops, and the mania of it all. Where drunkards crawled through alleys and gutters, and murders occurred all too often. Where men and women laboured day and night to make enough to feed their young and where the rich waddled through the streets, bejewelled by gold and silver rings, necklaces, earrings, and bracelets, with expensive clothing cut and sewn by the most famous of tailors, equally rich and fettered. Fettered not by iron chains, but by their own morbid fascination with trivial sophistication, hoping others would see them as more than they were worth.

Calmantis, though, could never quite understand where he settled within the ranks of society. He floated up and down, making up his own titles as he saw fit, usually eking out ahead of whoever he spoke to. He looked up at the rising sun hovering over the plethora of grey towers, and thought, *It's still early enough.* The doorbell clanged loudly as he entered the shop, and he nearly dropped his pants, jerking around at the sound. There were luckily few people in the store. An old man ambled up to him, some yarn slung over his shoulder that he used for measurement.

'What can I do for you today, sir?' asked the old tailor as he approached, and scrunched up his nose, smelling something terribly foul. 'Goodness! What is that reek?' It was hard getting the smell out of you after a night like he had. And they weren't paid in lumps of gold for their work either, so a hot bath was not always possible.

'Terribly sorry about the smell, old chap. 'Tis neither here nor there,' he said, laughing foolishly. 'You see, I was riding my gallant steed across the plains of amber and gold.' He gestured his hand over the imaginary fields, placing his other arm on the old man's shoulder. 'When out of nowhere this, this . . .' He couldn't think of a word and glanced around the room. Pink garments, white garments, stands with fashionable items filled the room. And he smiled. 'Bear!' He lurched forward, growling and bending his fingers to look like claws. 'Jumped out in front of my horse.' Calmantis shook his head sadly.

The old man stood flabbergasted, shaking his head, and mumbled, 'Then what, sir?'

'Well, as brave as poor Nightshade was, that monstrous bear frightened him terribly, and he bolted, me on top, hanging on for dear life, but alas, I am not the greatest of riders, you see. Father used to say, "He's a man of the mind, not of muscle." And I am sorry to say he was correct. We crossed a small creek where plenty of deer had been grazing, and, well . . .' he gestured again, '. . . you know, doing their nasty deeds. It was awful. Excrement everywhere. It was like they knew what was to happen and laid a trap for poor me! And just guess where I landed when Nightshade threw me.'

The old man's face stretched wide, brows raised and eyes bulging, mouth agape when he muttered, 'Oh, no . . .'

'Oh no, indeed. I rolled over heaps of dung. Stones, ground, dung, stones, ground, dung. Couldn't have come at a worse time. I am due to appear before the Order of Eternal Sacrament at noon. And here I stand, a humble man stinking of deer faeces, wanting at least just a fix of his pants after I lost all my coin during the bear's chase. At most, I would accept a new pair of pants, but nothing more I tell you.'

The old tailor looked him up and down and must have thought that no one would willingly roll in faeces, and said, 'Sure, I think I have an old pair back there that might fit you.'

'You are too kind, good sir. I will repay this kind act and make good with you in due time. It will not go unnoticed, I promise you.' Calmantis took the offered pair and tried them on. 'Slightly on the tight side, but you know us nobles . . . always finding something wrong with everything, eh? What a terrible bunch we are. What is the name of this establishment? I would like to spread your generosity through the ranks of the nobles so they may return the favour.'

'Oh, wait, sir. Can't be having a tight pair now, if you are to stand before the Order. Here,' said the tailor, shifting a pair of glasses over his long, pointy nose and grabbing a new pair from the shelf next to him. 'These are a size bigger. What do you think?'

'Oh, lovely! Just splendid, I tell you.' He quickly donned the new pair, twisting and turning, grinning happily. 'They will do quite well! Thank you!'

'The Elegant Thread.'

'What's that, good sir?'

'My shop's name, sir.'

'Is what?'

'The Elegant Thread!'

'Why yes, of course it is! And it couldn't be any truer! Very elegant, indeed. Thank you, old chap! I will see you soon, I would think.' Calmantis bowed extravagantly, retreating from the shop with a flourish, taking to the streets again. The sun had risen higher than he thought and disappeared behind a few puffs of white and purple clouds. A few blocks down this road stood the temple to which he had been summoned. Naturally, he was a little nervous.

* * *

The procession had started, and Calmantis couldn't believe what he was seeing. He walked into the grand temple, filled with dozens of people. They stood with sombre looks on their faces between the great granite pillars that ran all the way to the ceiling where gigantic golden chandeliers hung, spaced equally to the back. Sun streamed through the top windows, while lower vents allowed in fresh air. Behind a row of ornate thick wooden benches, the backrests curved and polished to a glistening sheen, stood the corpulent barkeep, with arms crossed and an angry scowl on his face. *It was careless to steal that damn mug. The fat bastard knew I was outside with it. But it's only a mug! Hardly necessary for this kerfuffle!* Calmantis stood before a panel of the Order's top officials, with Lord Latimus Greyarm at the centre of the row of judges, his exceedingly large grey-black moustache draped over his mouth, sweeping his lips like a broom every time he spoke.

'Calmantis Broviere, Disciple 314. You have been accused of stealing tableware and impersonating a Shadow Guard by . . .' Lord

Latimus swept up a document from the long desk in front of them and glanced over a section before he continued, '. . . Ranickus Beltor, innkeeper of the Black Feather. As you know, we here in the Order take these allegations very seriously, and we will not have thieves work in our Temple. More than that, we will be forced to take your hands from you if this is to be proven true. Do you understand the severity of these claims?'

Despite the crowded chamber of onlookers and their angry faces, the scowls of top officials, and the possibility of having his hands chopped off, Calmantis didn't feel the need to worry all that much. He pressed his tongue into the hole between his teeth, reminding himself that pain was not something he particularly enjoyed. 'May I just say, Lord Latimus and all others here today, how sorry I am for having disturbed your morning so with these ghastly allegations. I understand the severity very well, sir. I just hope that our esteemed Ranickus Beltor also understands this.'

Those in the crowd all turned to one another, looking questioningly at the innkeeper, who had dropped his arms to his sides, nervously moving around in his spot.

'Why do you say this?' asked Lord Latimus, brows no longer in a scowl, but raised curiously.

'Well, sir. We all know the penalty for giving false allegations, don't we? A whipping, is it not? I mean, I do not want to be the reason another citizen of Baldor gets a lashing, but I cannot let a simple thing like this drag the good name of Broviere through the mud, and definitely not that of the Order.'

'A whipping for bearing false witness is still in effect, yes. Please elaborate,' said Lord Latimus with a gesture of his hand. *Ah, the fish strikes the baited hook.*

'To the allegation of stealing. I paid for my drink, sir. In full, with a tip, I might add. The servant girl handed me the mug and not once was I told that I only paid for the contents. How was . . .' A hubbub from the crowd drowned out Calmantis's words, with Ranickus pointing and shouting at him.

'This is ridiculous! It's a sham!' came the shouts of the crowd.

'Silence!' roared Lord Latimus.

The crowd's cries grew less fierce, and Calmantis said, 'How was I to know this detail, sir? It was the first time I've been to the Black Feather. I am more than happy to return the mug if this is desired, but in the future, this needs to be stated clearly. Would I really put my hands on the line over such a stupid thing as a mug? I think not. I have been a loyal worker of the Order for three years now. Why would I jeopardise that? Maybe Ranickus has some vendetta against me, or the Order, I do not know, good sirs. That is something he needs to answer.'

'What about the other allegation? Impersonating a Shadow Guard.'

'Ha! That, sirs, I believe, was nothing more than a miscommunication. You see, Mister Ranickus asked what I was doing out back where I was admiring the Shadow Guard, waiting for the red smoke to appear like everyone else. I simply stated that I would love to become a Shadow Guard. He must've misheard me—'

'Preposterous!' shouted Ranickus over Calmantis's words.

'Where he then claimed he was the new Exarch!' stated Calmantis exuberantly. The temple exploded into a roar so loud, nobody heard the drumming gavel being pounded on the sound block by Lord Latimus, while the other officials palmed the table, shouting for order through the chaotic din.

'No! No! That's not true!' shouted Ranickus.

'Order!' shouted Lord Latimus again, breaking his gavel with the next hit, and glared at the broken handle in his hands. The room was out of control. 'Stop this madness!' Calmantis glimpsed the fuming Ranickus and grinned. He pretentiously waved at the crowd to quiet down, forcing a sincere look upon his face, drawing his brows and his eyes, pleading with them. For some time, the chaos in the temple reigned, slowly growing quiet, with Ranickus Beltor now being the object of everyone's hatred.

'Please! Everyone, listen to the Honourable Lord Latimus. Let not your hatred overshadow the temple in which you sit this very day!' Calmantis pleaded with an extravagant flourish, waving his arms about.

'I have to say!' With the crowd buzzing softly, he continued, 'To continue my previous statement. We were a respectable distance from each other, so it stands to reason that I could have misheard him as well . . .' He did not blink or stray from the locked gaze of Ranickus, rather grinning and waiting for the innkeeper's answer.

The entire temple was silent now. They could hear only the buzzing of the officials speaking amongst themselves, until Lord Latimus turned from them and said, 'Ranickus Beltor. Do you have any more to add before we conclude and deliberate?'

Time fluttered by, and Calmantis could feel the burning, piercing glares from the innkeeper, watching the man decide his own fate. Calmantis would never be allowed back in the Black Feather, but who cared about that? There were plenty more places to have a drink in the city.

Chest heaving, Ranickus did not stop glaring at him. His words came like daggers hidden in sheaths. 'I wish to retract my statements, milords. We were a good distance from each other, so it is possible I misheard. And I guess I could have made it clearer that the mug was not part of the sale. I will not make the same mistake again. Forgive my errors here today. I apologise for wasting everyone's time.'

'Very well. Calmantis Broviere, you are free to go. Ranickus Beltor, you owe this temple compensation for its time wasted, in the amount of three hundred silver sovereigns, by the end of the seventh day after the hearing.' Lord Latimus and the rest of the top officials rose from behind their large desk, retreating from the room, while Ranickus yelled and pleaded for their mercy. *That was a very expensive mug indeed*, thought Calmantis. *Think I will stay in the temple for a few nights until Ranickus forgets about me.*

* * *

Since the finalisation of the hearing, Calmantis had waited to have a word with Lord Latimus, but the top officials were taking their time in the presbytery today. He waited outside the confines of the temple, avoiding the storming Ranickus who had left a little after him. The man had searched the grounds, swinging his fists, while Calmantis watched him through the air vents of the bell tower until the Shadow Guard escorted the man from the premises.

Finally, the door to the presbytery swung open, and the old geese shuffled out under the grapevine-covered awning, carrying thick leather-bound books and scrolls under their arms. The hems of their white robes dragged on the floor, flitting over the stones and dust as they walked from room to room, connected by long corridors. Calmantis waited for them to separate, drifting off to their offices, then ran to catch up with the dean. Ruby-red walls spanned the long distances of the hall, with murals of golden flowers over vast landscapes and the bright sun above, black sconces with short candles burning to their deaths. Some were already burned out, waiting to be replaced, their strings of white wax reaching for the floor.

'Lord Latimus! Apologies, Lord Latimus!' called Calmantis, stopping the dean in his tracks. All the other top officials had slipped away to their duties, leaving Latimus alone.

'Guards!'

'No, please, just listen. I fear for my life after the punishment Ranickus received, sir. All I want is sanctuary here in a cell of the temple. I will be safe here and do my duties quickly and efficiently. Just a couple weeks, sir. Then I will leave. Just until he calms down,' pleaded Calmantis. His dirty hair flopped over his eyes when a Shadow Guard grabbed him by the shoulders, thrusting him against the wall and knocking out his breath. A sword slid out of its scabbard with a rasp, the red flames of the candles burning happily in their sconces reflected on the perfectly polished blade, and he closed his eyes. Had he misjudged this attempt? Possibly.

'Hold on,' came Lord Latimus's voice, and Calmantis opened his eyes. The dean walked closer, clutching green-and-silver prayer beads between his fingers, its frayed strands hanging out from one side, the dull rubbed bronze medallion of the tail-eating-snake on the other end.

'What is wrong with you, man? Are you looking for a quick death? The stunt you pulled in the temple is exactly why you are in trouble. Don't think for a heartbeat that I didn't see through your schemes. If you hadn't got Ranickus to back down, your hands would be mine right now.'

'I know, sir, and I apologise profusely. But I meant no harm. All I want is to be here at the temple, to learn from its people and study and train to become a Shadow Guard. That was never a lie. And I will do anything to one day be worthy of the title.' The Shadow Guard chortled and stood back, dropping Calmantis to the floor. 'You may laugh,' he said, straightening his clothes, 'but is it so bad to be respected and admired by people like me who dream of one day becoming more than they are? Of becoming what *you* are or what *you* stand for?' The guard did not answer.

'No, I dare say it is not bad at all. Step back, Ackelides, give him room to breathe.' Lord Latimus stepped closer, rolling the beads in his hands, and said, 'I will expect any additional services we require to be done by you, without complaint or additional compensation, understand?'

'Yes! Yes, of course, Lord Latimus. You won't regret it. Thank you so much.' Calmantis grabbed the dean's hand and dropped to the ground, kissing the sparkling ring on the man's pale hands. It was not long before Latimus snatched his hand back and wiped it on his immaculate robe.

'One more thing.'

'Just name it, sir. Anything.'

'You will join the others in their daily prayers, and you will study with them the ways of Aztar. If you truly desire to become a Shadow Guard, you will first need to learn the laws.' Calmantis couldn't believe what he was hearing.

'I would be honoured, sir.'

'Good. Ackelides, escort our guest to the cell next to Yeron's. He can show him around. And take a bath. You smell like something crawled up into you and died days ago. I've lost my bloody appetite thanks to you . . .'

7. Bad Debts

Her clothes lay scattered in the room and under the overturned dresser, which used to stand against the wall in the room's corner. Yelefant's men had turned the place upside down looking for the bounty she had received. Orana peeped through the slits of her eyes, feeling heavy and sore, the soft bed beneath her a friendly companion in this time of crisis. She pushed herself up with some effort, moaning at the pain in her side and the sting in her mouth, tasting iron. A big dark patch had spread over the top of her hand where the hammer had struck. She looked at it and slowly closed and opened her fist, turning her wrist round and round. *Don't think it's broken. Maybe fractured, though . . .* Her bedcovers were bloodstained and smeared with dirt, just like she was.

The slow walk back home had given her ample time to reflect, not only on the betrayal of her trust, but that of the honour among thieves. *Yohtan must have given an anonymous tip. He didn't want me coming after him to steal the items back. You could've been free of me, Yohtan . . . Now I have no choice but to hunt you down.* She had made it up the stairs with little noise, dragging her right leg behind her, bare toes scraping on the floorboards. This time, Miss Downere did not confront her. She sneaked into the room and closed the door behind her before crawling into bed, watching the rays of the sun light up the far horizon through the window. *I should've taken the night off . . .*

There was no way she could rest now, with all that needed doing and only a month to do it in. *Or chop, head rolls into the bucket, crowds cheering.* She dragged herself from the bed over to the bath, dropping her filthy clothes as she walked, and placed a few new logs and tinder under the raised tub. The dried twigs and grass needed little convincing before it burned, while the water trickled in. *A good long bath will set me straight for the day.* The smell of smoke soon drifted through the room and out the windows, heating the bricks underneath the bath, warming the water slightly while she settled in.

Eyes closed, she leaned back, resting her palms over the sides of the tub, dripping water to the floor. *First things first, I have to get Yelefant his share, then find some bearing on Yohtan and pack for the trip. He will not have stayed in Tolomene. No, he will be far away, searching for buyers to pay him ridiculous sums of money, indulging in feasts and delicacies.*

* * *

Cicadas screamed in the sun where they baked in the heat, only quieting for the brief moments when the monkeys drew near in search of them, grabbing them from trees and stuffing them into their mouths, crunching on the chewy critters. From tree to tree, the long-tailed basimets swung with their long arms, legs, and tails, hunting for the critters, dropping bark and small twigs on civilians below. Orana watched a troop of floppy-eared primates moving from tree to tree down the street, leaves rustling and civilians cursing and shaking their fists up angrily.

On the far side of the street, a whirlwind of dust raced closer, causing havoc to the markets and stores displaying their wares under stands with shade-cloth coverings. Whipped about, items flew from trays, tables, shelves, and weak hands with the flurry of dust, leaving them strewn on the street, while stall owners ran about to reclaim their merchandise. She watched as expensive la-enole biscuits rolled in the dust, the little limbs of the enoles roving about like hair in the wind. Unique knitted shawls fluttered and waved in the turbulent air, whisked away to be claimed by faraway recipients.

The spinning wind rushed at her, and she smiled. Besmitz had loved to run into those dust devils, and always dragged Orana in with him. They would chase the dancing winds, guessing where it would go to get into its path. To stand brave and courageous before it and await punishment.

She followed the whirlwind and walked into its path, bracing for the convergence. It was a small but fierce dust devil, whipping her clothes and rocking her hair, and as if it understood the challenge, it hovered on the spot over Orana, trying its best to move her, flicking her left and right until she laughed and lost her footing, having to step back for a second. It died soon after, victorious; the wind settled with a showering of dust.

'One of these days, a big one is going to carry you away from here.'

Still smiling, Orana spun to her left and said, 'I would welcome that more than ever today, Malick. I seem to have overplayed my hand.'

The smile on Malick's face disappeared, replaced by dark, furrowed brows. 'What happened?' he asked, dragging her out of the street by the arm, away from passers-by. 'And where are your boots?'

'I did a job, quick and easy, but trusted the wrong people, I think. Now I owe two thirds of what I made, plus the goods returned, or my life's forfeit. But that's not your problem.'

'Huh . . . Who was your mark?'

'Some pompous arse by the name of Yelefant Du Pantè.'

'What? Are you mad? He nearly has the Crown's power! And basically all its backing. If he wants you dead, you are in deep trouble!'

'How should I have known that?' she growled, glancing at the people walking by, making sure they were out of earshot. 'It's not like I'm asking you to get your hands dirty or to kill him. I just need you to find out where Yohtan travelled to. D'you think you can do that for me?'

Malick shook his head. 'You know it goes against the code to steal back what someone fairly compensated you for.' He looked away for a moment, then continued, 'Of course. But where will we reach you? You can't stay here.'

'You can send word to Baldor. It is the biggest city with the most opportunities. I'd wager, if he doesn't get the items sold anywhere else, he might head there. So will I. Address the letter to Besmitz, just in case.'

'Yelefant has men everywhere. If you don't deliver, they will come after you.' He turned her face with a wince, staring at her cheeks. 'And by the looks of it, you've already seen their methods.'

'Up close and personal, yes.'

'Come, I'll buy you a pair of boots. You won't get far like that.' He took her under his wing and walked with her between the stalls, his reassuring arm draped round her neck, while merchants called out their wares.

'You are too kind, Malick. I don't know how I can ever repay you for all you have done.'

'Don't get killed. That's how.'

* * *

Orana walked and walked, taking long, circuitous routes through the scummy area of Skalg, which many would argue was not really worse than any other area, all to make sure she was not being followed. *People will never change.* She was certain that if someone was following her, they would've been properly annoyed by now and either left her in peace or confronted her.

Her new boots needed to be walked in, and nothing but some mileage would do the trick. Great spires of brown and white stood tall in the distance, but here where she walked, the houses were low to the ground, not at all fancy and fairly similar in layout; mostly a square rock hut with a door and a few windows, surrounded by a small garden. For a time, she thought how different life would've been if she lived here, in these quiet areas, and not in one of those spires far in the distance. *Who knows, maybe I would have given up being a thief. Maybe taken a good man, maybe a carpenter with powerful hands. He could work and fix the house while I cook and clean, look after our . . . Haha. What a joke! Who am I kidding? I would drive him stir-crazy. And if I had to hear one more tale of him fixing another broken table, I would drown him in the lake. Hold him under until the bubbles disappeared. Normal life . . . These people are crazier than I could ever be.*

She glanced around and made her way into an old abandoned

home, its walls crumbling and roof falling apart, with enormous holes already visible in its angled slate tiles. The door lay on the ground next to the building, rotting and swelling, its once-lacquered brown faded by the sun. Orana edged into the building, stepping over fallen tiles and stones broken free from the mortar on one wall. She used the wall to steady herself and searched the empty rooms for signs of squatters. *Normal life. I haven't had a normal life since I ran away. How could I? Nobody wanted a young girl for anything other than sex. And I couldn't stomach the idea.*

Devoid of any furniture and smelling of urine and excrement, it was not a place where she wanted to linger too long. She unsheathed her dagger and walked to the furthest wall with the most roof still covering it and placed the tip of her blade in the mortar groove between the stones, scraping out bits of fresher clay. Round and round she worked the dagger, scraping the stone free until she saw it jiggle easily. She worked it a bit more and pulled it free, revealing the bag of coins in a hollow behind.

The bag felt heavy in her hands, the weight considerably more than she remembered it to be a few nights back, but the excitement of that night could have played a part. That feeling of fear, adrenaline, and excitement had never left her, even after years of doing this. If anything, it was only stronger now. Orana stood with the bag in her hands. *It breaks my heart, giving away so much of this wealth. You can't get attached to things. You must always be willing to part ways with anything.* That had been her adage from the start of her career, and it had held true so far. But she was getting a little sentimental of late, wishing to hold on to things for longer. That was how you got to live rent-free with the bugs in the ground, though.

She cleared a section of the dilapidated floor of dirt, vines, and weeds growing through the rotted planks and sat down, plonking the bag in front of her, and started counting.

* * *

It was deathly quiet in her head; she forced herself not to think about the problems she faced, ignoring the screaming cries inside her mind, willing them away. The sun had set already. *He will be here soon. Or he will send one of his goons. Probably that ignoramus Lofka. They look pretty attached to each other.* A single knock interrupted her thoughts, and she kept glaring at the door, willing it to explode, but nothing happened. She swung her legs off the table and rose from the chair, her new boots drumming on the floor. Orana unlocked the door and stepped back, hand on her dagger, and said, 'It's open.'

She snickered, shaking her head at the obedient Lofka who pushed through first and said, 'Put down your dagger, kick it to the room's corner.' After she complied, Yelefant entered the room at the nod from his guard.

'You're late. I have a deadline to meet. Can't be wasting my days like this if you want your goods back in a timely fashion.'

Yelefant glared at her and glanced at the table where the bag of coins lay open. 'Do you think I care about your time? It will serve you well to learn who the master is here, uncouth bitch!' He raised his hand, wanting to slap her – she could see it in his face, how he clenched his jaw and sneered at her, stepping forward as if no one would stop him. Orana would not give him the satisfaction. She let him come in close, following his movements, sidestepping just at the right time for his hand to wave air in her face, and grabbed him at the back of his shoulder, yanking him down hard to the table. The crack reverberated as he jolted upright, eyes drifting, his face a few shades redder on his right cheek. Lofka jumped forward with his cutlass, but she had stepped back with her hands raised.

'That's for what you did to me!' she shouted. 'Remember. Without me, you won't get back your gems.'

Head shaking and eyes tearing up, blood dripped from his nose down his chin, staining his expensive shirt. 'Leave her!' Yelefant roared, and swung back to her, gestured for Lofka to back away, then whispered, 'One month . . . If the sun sets on the last day, your time is up. Listen carefully. I will find you wherever you are, and I will take my time with you. Days, weeks, months, I will make you pay until there is nothing left of you but your bones.' He picked up the coin purse and bounced it in his hands, feeling its weight. 'Seems light . . . You wouldn't be holding out on me, would you? I wouldn't recommend it.' He had been in a bout with a bottle for a while, she could smell the wine on his breath.

'No, that is what you asked for. Everyone has to make something, I guess.'

Yelefant looked around the room in disgust, and for a moment, she thought he would spit on her floor. 'Come, let's go, Lofka. Before we get fleas from this filth.'

The door banged closed, and Orana dropped into her chair, breathing deep and fast, calming herself.

8. Consequences

Now that they had thrust the day of his claiming upon him, Bellard was not sure he wanted it anymore. And judging by the looks on their faces, neither were the rest of his friends. He could see the shock and fear in their eyes, the way they drifted from this world to live in their heads for a while, to think of their loved ones and missed opportunities.

A night-time claiming . . . It hadn't been done in years, and for good reason. Rumours of the last night-time claiming circled the grounds of Kunia every so often, telling of desperation and horror. As the story went, two students had sneaked into the Sacred Hall of the Usha one night, thinking they were ready to claim their Pillars. It was said the tormented screams and cries of the two young men echoed through Kunia, waking the other students and the grandàres from their slumber. All on the compound had run to the entrance of the hall, but none could enter, not even the grandàres, who shouted from the outside for them, hoping to guide them out. But the screams grew faint, fading away to nothing, and the students were never seen again.

There was nothing else to do now but prepare as best he could for the coming claiming. One disturbing thought made Bellard slightly more at ease; he knew he would either die or come out stronger. There was no in between, no middle ground so to speak. Yet, he was sure he was not the worst off. While Grandàre Shevira droned on, Mila sat to his right, sniffing and shaking, knowing she might have doomed them all. He saw how heavy it weighed on her shoulders. And until they all walked out of the hall with their lives and limbs intact, there was nothing anyone could do for her. She had made the call, and they would need to endure it.

He reached out to her and placed his hand on her shoulder, wanting to be there for her. She jerked away and jumped up from her chair, skidding the table forward and running for the door, face covered by her striking white hair.

'Mila, wait!' Bellard shouted, and glanced at Valdor and Brethnar, then at the grandàre all standing in shocked silence, before running after her. 'Mila! Stop!'

The long halls were empty and echoey, their running footsteps bouncing between the dilapidated walls, his calls coming back to him in waves. Shevira had led them to an old area of the school not in use anymore, where no one would bother them for the day. Mila's sobs came from every corner of the mazelike corridors, while the stale old stench of closed-off rooms drifted throughout.

'Mila!' he shouted again and skidded round the corner. There she was, pounding her fist against the wall, before she sagged to the ground, unable to look at Bellard. He reached her side, slowing to a stop, and awkwardly slid down next to her, hearing her sob in between her pleas for forgiveness.

'I've doomed us all,' she whispered, resting her head in her hands.

'Don't count us out yet, Mila.' *We are all probably dead, so what harm is there in making her feel better?* 'If we work together, I'm sure we can get through this. We need you there with us.'

'You really think so?' she sniffed, lifting her head to look him in the eye.

Bellard took her hands and squeezed them. 'Yes!' *No, really, I don't.* 'There are four of us. We will watch out for each other.' *And die horribly, with mutilated corpses.* 'The first one to receive their Pillar will protect the rest of us. The more we get, the stronger we are, and the better our chances. But we have to stick together.'

'Are you not angry with me? Valdor and Brethnar barely look at me.'

'Well, you could have said we should shovel the stinking poop in the moat down to the river, but I think Valdor would definitely make that sound even worse.' He chuckled, and she playfully slapped him on the arm with a giggling sob. 'No, I'm not angry with you, and neither are they. They just need to get over the initial shock of the matter.' She sniffed again and wiped her nose on the back of her arm. 'Come, they are probably waiting for us to continue.' Bellard pushed against the wall and got to his feet, pulling her along with him.

'Why are you so nice to me?' she asked, her green eyes staring up at him. He didn't know how to answer that. His mouth had opened, but nothing had come out. *Why am I so nice to you? What's going on here?* 'Oh, forget I asked,' she said and pulled her hand from his. She stomped away, ashamed she had asked, her teeth clenched. 'We need to get back to the preparations,' he heard her say and followed her, shaking his head at his own stupidity. What could he have said? There was no way out of that question that would not have ended badly for him.

They walked back into the classroom and sat down, ignoring the stares from the other three, and Grandàre Shevira continued talking.

'I will admit that we know little of the night-time claiming. We know it was done years ago, long before my time as grandàre, but there should be some comfort knowing it is not impossible.'

Valdor raised his hand and asked, 'Are there any written accounts of what they witnessed? Something that might help us?'

She shied away from them, and Bellard prodded further, 'Please, Grandàre. We need to know.'

'Yes, there is one. But I do not have access to it.' Their faces drooped, and Bellard fell back in his chair, crossing his arms. 'I do, however, know what they wrote in the account.'

'What?' asked Brethnar, his brooding face lighting up for the first time since this morning. 'What did it say?' *It is amazing what a bit of hope can do for someone.*

'Kanegrin Borna wrote of a place that is cold and grim, not like the hall that I know at all and entered myself a long time ago. He did not go into great detail, but he said there were tricksters messing with his head, whispering a certain foulness. He never mentioned what they wanted or what happened to him physically, but he was said to be dehydrated and starving, and covered in a slew of cuts, although he had only been in the hall for a short while. Something hounded him, steered him to the brink of his sanity. So my advice to you is to ignore anything that is not a voice you know and trust, one that guides you to your Pillar and not your damnation.'

'What are the Usha? Why did they choose us?'

'We are the Usha . . .'

'What?' the four asked in unison

'You are the Usha. Or more accurately, will become the Usha after your claiming.'

'That makes no sense!' Mila burst out, throwing her hands into the air.

'Oh, it will. You know the rumours of the two that snuck into the hall at night, never to be seen again, right?'

The four glanced at each other and nodded, mumbling, 'Yes. We know,' Bellard muttered.

'Well, the rumour has it that no grandàre *could* enter, but there is another side to this story. You see, none of the grandàres were *willing* to enter, and with good reason. Once you receive your Pillar, you are not allowed back into the hall for any reason other than gifting your Pillar back to the ground and laying down your life for the next mages to come. That is the oath you take. When you are nearing your death – natural, of course – you must journey back to the hall and call out to the one you have chosen to take your mantle.'

'So, it is only a burden we carry? To be its temporary bearer until we die and gift it to the next,' Brethnar grumbled.

'Why would you call it a burden? It is a gift, given to precious few.' Shevira started forward.

'I've heard how it haunts those who do not answer the call! It invades the mind and your dreams, forces you to comply. I do not call that a gift. I call that a curse! It is the only reason why I'm here. I wanted to be a warrior, like my father. Ever since my calling, I have been treated differently. They will never accept me now.' Brethnar turned to his friends, shaking his head. 'Unlike all of you, I never wanted to be here.'

'Yet you are . . . And you can still become a great warrior, one with extraordinary skill. And do you really want to live in your father's shadow forever? You can be so much more. As for being a warrior, I think you might have your chance to prove your worth tonight.' She bent down behind the desk. Rasping steel rang out, and Shevira stood before them, an old rusty sword in her hands.

'Whoa!' The four leaped back from their chairs, and Bellard shook his head. *If we are this jumpy around someone we know, what are we going to do tonight?*

'Apologies. I took these from the school's inventory.' She turned the weapon and handed it to Brethnar, who eagerly grasped it. 'It's not much, but it might help. I stowed more under that old sheet against the wall. Take what you need.'

Bellard whipped the covering off, erupting a cloud of dust to the air, making him sneeze mightily, eyes closed, head rocking back and forth. His loud stream of sternutation filled the room, slapping back to his ears with their return from the walls. With the onslaught finally finished, he looked to the four with their grins plastered on their faces. 'Oh, dear. Some mages we are.'

Under the covering lay daggers and sharpened sickles with long curved edges, worn and a little rusty. *Ornaments more than weapons,* thought Bellard, picking up a pair of long-tipped daggers. Mila approached and took the pair of sickles, working her thumb over the blade to feel the edge. Valdor frowned at the remaining dagger. A big, nasty-looking thing with a cracked wooden hilt and a double-sided blade with small curved teeth at the back half, a gleaming edge at the front, tapered to the point.

'That's all I could find at short notice and without being seen,' Shevira said, worryingly rubbing her hands together. 'Agoras will not be happy about this, but I am not sending you in there unarmed at night. Besides, he can't prove it was me who gave it to you, as long as you don't say anything.'

The four of them turned to her. She was risking her position as grandàre for them. They knew it. 'Thank you for helping us, Grandàre. We might just make it out alive because of you,' said Mila, sheathing the sickles and concealing them between the loose fabric of her robe.

'Yes, thank you, Grandàre,' said Bellard, followed by Valdor and

Brethnar.

Shevira smiled her old smile at them and said, 'As much as I like my robes, they are not meant for running and jumping. Then again, neither am I. Anymore, that is. I would wear something more versatile were I you, just in case.'

The last of the sun vanished behind the glorious mountains of Khorvellen on the horizon, and Shevira snapped her fingers, lighting the lanterns on the wall. 'I fear our time is nearly up. The last piece of advice I have is for you to think of the work you've put in throughout this year. You know how to cast spells. You know the workings of your Pillar. When your time comes, be ready and help the others. I will wait for you at the entrance.'

A mighty gust of wind crashed the window shutters against the frame loudly, banging them open and closed with a sudden, fierce push and pull. 'What is that?' asked Shevira and walked over to a window, holding on to the shutter. Through the dark grey of the early night, she could see dark clouds gathering, lightning arcing in the distance. 'Oh, dear. Get to the shelters, now! Your claiming is not happening tonight.'

'Why? What's happening?'

She turned to them, her face pale. 'The World Storm is approaching . . . Go! I will sound the alarm.'

Valdor was the first out the door, with Brethnar hot on his heels, Mila following, and Bellard close behind her, running down the vacant corridor to get to safety. Terrible winds pulled at them as they exited the building. Mila's long white hair whipped in all directions, her slight frame nearly being torn from the ground by the powerful winds. Bellard grabbed her hand and ran next to her. Here in Kunia, they were relatively safe. With the grandàres' protection, they would not feel the full wrath of the storm, but the grandàres could not stop all of it. Some lightning and severe gusts slipped through, lifting and destroying anything in its path.

Bellard glimpsed the Sacred Hall of the Usha a few hundred feet off to their left. Carved from the stone it was built on, great columns rose at its entrance, lit by the violent flashes from above. A layered construction tapering to the top, standing at an impressive five hundred feet high and nearly double in its width, it was rather hard to miss. Soon, they would need to enter the looming beast. He kept running.

A loud howling horn sounded, blowing continuously, picked up by more throughout the city as a warning for all to head for shelter. The terrifying cracks of the constantly flashing lightning roared out in the distance, shaking the earth. Students from all over streamed from their dorms and classrooms, converging with the four friends on their way to the shelters: Deep underground bunkers built all over the city for this very reason. The storms struck suddenly and with little warning; usually strong winds were the only precursor. It was a drunkard's worst nightmare, being caught by the sudden storm while they lay passed out in the gutters.

It always amazed Bellard how people changed in the face of danger. Some became violent, some ran for their lives, and some reacted in a way he knew very well. They froze, like him. They became paralysed, unable to do anything. One thing he had learned about himself over the years was the threat needed to be imminent, unassailable, for him to freeze up, like when he climbed the pipe to the roof.

Two professors ran alongside them, trying their best to keep some kind of order, shouting and pointing to the bunker's entrance, hoping to avoid any injuries or worse. Others were already at the shelters, heaving the doors open and waving for the running students to go down. Pushing and shoving other students, Bellard tried to hold on to Mila's hand, but it slipped from his fingers. 'I'm right behind you, Mila! Keep going!'

Like sheep herded to their pens, they made their way down the stairs, entering an underground system of tunnels and sitting areas, some beds, chairs, and blankets waiting for those that needed them. Cries sounded from somewhere. A young girl perhaps? Then a mighty crack of thunder shook the chamber underground, and the cries of more students joined in. 'Mila! Valdor! Brethnar!' Bellard called, cupping his hands over his mouth.

'Bellard!' he heard over the frenzy of activity surrounding him, and he stretched his neck, rising to the tips of his toes, and saw a hand wave him over near the entrance of the shelter.

'Excuse me. Pardon me.' Bellard pushed through the throng and joined his friends. 'Are all of you okay?' he asked as he arrived, seeing Brethnar and Valdor nod.

'Yes. We are fine, but I nearly stabbed someone by accident with these sickle blades during the chaos,' Mila answered. 'You?'

'I'm good,' Bellard said and lowered himself to the stone floor. 'Might as well relax while we can. It's going to be a long night.'

* * *

The earth trembled with an awful roar of thunder, and cries of fear rode through the corridors, waking Bellard where he sat against the wall, arms crossed on his knees, resting his head on them. Dust drifted from the ceiling with the constant shakes. All around, students sat in little groups, hushed or praying, whispering to one another, all wishing this would come to an end. Since the storm hit, the entrance door had rattled and shook in place, wearing out the lock and hinges. Four professors had been taking turns to hang on to the door, grabbing hold of the iron handles and pulling down hard. Terrible arcs of lightning flashed through the slits in the door as water streamed down in a deluge, funnelled away in troughs leading deeper into the shelter.

A sudden and irrevocable force jerked the door open, flinging the last professor that held on through the air and outside into the storm, where he fell onto the grass, scrambling back to the safety of the shelter. Water gushed through the open entrance, the door flapping and crashing against the frame. Bellard jumped up and made his way to the entrance as Professor Heron tried to close the door again while he shouted, 'Someone is coming! Run, Guthrod! Who is that?' Professor Guthrod dashed back in, shaking the water from his soaked clothes, looking a little worse for wear.

Through the darkness and the bright flashes walked two figures towards them, one unhurried and not concerned, the gait slow and steady, a staff swinging in his hands, as if going for a stroll next to the beach, watching the waves lap the strand. The other – a woman, by the looks of her figure – was talking with her hands, swinging her arms about angrily.

'Grandàre Agoras?' whispered Bellard, growing cold gazing at the figure, and stepped back to give them some room. Hand resting on the dark staff, tapping the rock beneath, Agoras casually strolled into the shelter, dry as month-old bread, and sneered at the unblessed – those who were not chosen by the Usha to carry their Pillars forth – trying to close the door behind Grandàre Shevira. Agoras waved his hand, and the door swung shut, unmovable in its hinges.

Everyone was silently staring at them while Grandàre Shevira shouted at him, 'You cannot do this!' His icy stare silenced her, and she moved out of his way, leaving an open path between Bellard and Agoras.

'Ah, the ones I've been looking for,' came the old voice. Bellard felt so small and insignificant standing before the mage, like an ant about to be stepped on. *And I would thank him for it.* 'Shevira has her reservations about sending you into this storm to claim what is yours. Do you feel the same?'

Go out there? Of course I do! Are you insane? But somehow, the grandàre's words were not a question so much as it was a statement and a warning to say, *"Sure, by all means, cower here, in the safety of others, and never see Kunia again. Or step into the darkness, fight for what you want, or die trying."*

'No.' *Did I just say that?* Gasps and shocked faces stared at him, some taking a step back, his fists bunched and jaw muscles working back and forth. 'I don't speak for anyone here, but I will go.'

Grandàre Agoras tilted his head slightly, as if surprised by the answer. *Wasn't he expecting that? Was he bluffing? Messing with me to see what I would do?*

'Looks like someone found a backbone. We will wait for your return.' Bellard turned back to his friends, seeing the fear in their eyes, feeling the same fear in his gut. He wasn't sure how his legs were moving on their own, but somehow, he drifted by Agoras and felt a hand settle on his shoulder. He heard the old grandàre say, 'Good luck. We will wait for you.'

'I'm going too!' shouted Mila from behind, and she ran to join Bellard at the door.

'Yeah, me too . . .' said Valdor. 'Though I have to say, this is stupid.'

They turned to Brethnar, and Mila whispered, 'It's your choice, Brethnar. You will always be our friend, no matter what you choose.' Agoras waved his hand, and the door swung open.

If anything, the storm seemed ever more frightening, and in the darkness towards the city, they saw buildings on fire in the pouring rain. Bellard dashed over the grass for the building on their right, powerful gusts and rain whipping him around. And like a blow from a runaway cart, the wind threw him off his feet. Flashes above, wet grass beneath, he rolled and rolled, and groaned as Mila collided with him on the ground. A blinding flash arced to the ground a few feet away, sparks flying with a thunderous clap. They climbed to their feet and set off again, catching up with Valdor, who leaned against the wind, his hair whipping back while he covered his face from the stinging rain.

'Wait for me!' Brethnar's shouts were a whisper in the chaos of the World Storm, but they could not wait out in the open. It would be suicide.

'Run, Brethnar!' Bellard and Mila made their way together, arms locked as one, pushing forward. Her cheeks and lips rippled and puffed at the force of the wind, her light frame struggling to move. There was a sudden void with no wind, a pocket where nothing stopped them from moving, and they ended up on their faces, tearing out strips of grass.

Before they could get up, they felt another thunderous clap behind them, and saw Brethnar flung through the dark sky. 'Brethnar!' shouted Valdor as he ran past them, the winds helping him along swiftly, nearly lifting him to the air with the gusts at his back. Bellard saw Agoras standing just outside the shelter, waving his hands around, doing his best to keep the storm at bay. *So you do have a conscience . . .*

'Bring him! Let's get out of this!' Bellard shouted and picked Mila up, dragging her to the Sacred Hall of the Usha. A nervousness enveloped Bellard the closer he got to the building, the monstrous construction looming high above them with a sense of foreboding. They ran for their lives, watching the skies for breaches of the deadly lightning, dodging left and diving right, working their way forward. If only Gallus could see him now, taking on the World Storm. A mighty crack sounded up high where a burning cart, torn in half, hurtled into the Sacred Hall, erupting further and raining debris on them. Pieces of deadly wood swooshed by them, pinning into the ground with sharp points, a heavy wheel digging trenches into the grass behind them.

They crashed into the door, using their arms to stop themselves, and Bellard pulled and hammered on the thick door, not moving it in the slightest. Chaos reigned at their backs, making them stupid. 'It's not moving!' Bellard shouted and grabbed his dagger, plunging it into the wood over and over, his mind readying to flee the area. Valdor and Brethnar joined him, banging, and pushing, and kicking, hacking at it with their blades. But nothing.

'No, wait! Stand back!' shouted Mila, shoving them aside, rain seeping down her wet face. She had never looked more beautiful to Bellard than she did now. He shook the thought from his head and let her pass. She lay her hand upon the door and spoke to it. 'We seek to claim our Pillars! We will bear our Pillars until the day of our deaths, when we will gift it forward to a chosen.'

The building shuddered, and the door rumbled a breath, being freed from its bonds for them to enter. It swung open to an unnatural darkness, and Bellard wished he could rather spend the night with the World Storm as company. Mila glanced back and strode across the threshold, vanishing before Bellard could grab her. *Damn!*

He followed her through, with the other two coming behind him, and the darkness instantly swallowed them. The sound of the door slamming shut was a deafening gong, echoing from all corners, seeming far away, even though they just entered through it. He could not see his hand in front of his face. Not the stones he walked on, nor his friends beside him. 'Mila, you there?' he whispered, afraid to make too much noise and wake something they did not want for company. Even the rumbling storm outside had vanished. There was nothing.

'Yes, follow my voice.' The voice came from up ahead, but it was not Mila's. It sounded hollow somehow, forced. Made to sound like her.

'Who was that? Brethnar, was that you?' Bellard asked, unsheathing his daggers. He inched forward, feeling for a wall or a step, not wanting to stumble and impale himself with his own knife. *I don't like this.* 'Valdor! Stop messing around and answer me!' His heart thundered in his chest. No answer came. He felt alone, vulnerable, like the floor could be ripped out from under him at any moment. He twisted around, swinging his arms to feel for anyone. *Valdor and Brethnar should be behind me, shouldn't they?* Nothing. He swiped cold air. 'What's going on here? Anyone!' His voice cracked, taking on a higher pitch, and he crept forward, hands out, feeling, searching.

'Bellard, ya big baby! Listen to yer father and come over here! Don't make me come and get you.' *'Follow the voice you know and trust,' Shevira said, and you, old man, I do not trust.*

'Don't you want to come out into the light?' the voice changed. *Nor you, Mother.* An icy chill flowed over him. Something sharp brushed his hand, and he jerked away with a start. It tore into his skin, a warm wetness flowing over his hand, burning, blood dripping to the ground. *Tap, tap, tap.*

'Ow!' Bellard grabbed his hand, gently gliding his fingers across his palm to understand what the cut must be like, seeing it in his mind, cursing as he felt the deep wound. He reached out again, but there was nothing now. Just more air. His nerves were a mess; his eyes twitched incessantly while he clenched his jaw, the sharp pain settling into a more bearable numbness. Since they entered the Sacred Hall, he had been subconsciously grinding his teeth. The ache now resonated from his jaw muscles into his locked teeth, yet he was unwilling to relax. He couldn't.

'Over here . . .' whispered Cora, her soothing, calm voice a pleasant treat in an otherwise unpleasant situation. He edged forward, knife shaking in his hand, feeling with the other around him, sweeping left to right. The perpetual darkness was all-consuming, a thing that didn't want you to see. He followed the soothing voice. 'Yes, that's it. Just a little more.' A rumbling growl in the darkness slithered forth steadily, and he snatched his hand back. A sinister shriek screamed in his ears, and as he turned to run, his back burned from a long cut.

'Argh!' he cried in pain, falling to the floor and stumbling away. *Stupid! How can I trust someone that probably doesn't even know who I am?* Back and forth he twisted, swinging the blade ahead of him, and it bit into something that jerked away from him. With every move, his back pained him.

'Valdor! Mila!' No one answered. 'Brethnar!' Now he understood why they never saw those two students again. He himself did not know where the door was anymore. They could be stuck in here forever, dwelling in the darkness, searching for a way out, with no food or water. *Trust?* The word sounded nearly foreign to him. *All my life, people have betrayed and hurt me. How am I supposed to trust any voice?*

'Come on, Bellard. Stop being afraid and follow my voice. You can do this.'

'Gallus?' He edged forward.

9. Duty First

'So you want to become a Shadow Guard, eh?'

Calmantis's head came up from the book he studied, and he turned in the chair, resting his arms on the back. A man in dark brown robes with a thick cream belt around his waist stood in the doorway, hands behind his back. The man had no hair and a day-or-two-old stubble on his face. 'I do, yes. You must be Yeron?'

'I am.'

'Just so I know, should I prepare to be laughed at by all of you or simply those with very little between their ears?'

Yeron tilted his head, furrowing his brows, and entered the little room. 'Do our opinions bother you?'

Instantly annoyed, Calmantis shook his head and stumbled over his words. 'Er . . . No.'

'Then why do you feel the need to prepare? If it doesn't matter, then it doesn't matter. And surely then you do not need to prepare for this.'

'Just because it doesn't matter doesn't mean that it hurts any less to be made a fool of.'

'Ah. So it does matter then,' Yeron said with a wide grin.

'Of course it matters! What soulless creature do you take me for?'

'Merely trying to figure out who I will be working with.' Yeron retreated a step and raised his hands. 'One doesn't simply become a Shadow Guard, you know. It is hard work, dedication, studying, a way of life. Are you sure you are ready for this?'

'Yes—' The left side of his face burned and itched. Calmantis never saw the slap coming. He hadn't even seen the man move. 'Ow! What was that?' Angry, he rubbed his burning face and squirmed in the chair, trying his best to get his long legs out from under the desk, but the chair wouldn't move. Yeron was pushing it forward with his leg, holding it in place. 'Hey! What are you doing?' Arms swinging, Calmantis grabbed at

Yeron's loose robe and cried out in pain when his hand got caught in the folds as the man somersaulted to the small bed, and kicked the chair out. Calmantis crashed into the cool wall and got caught between it and the bed, groaning and staring at the hovering face of Yeron above him.

'If you think you are ready for this, you are very mistaken. A Shadow Guard is much more than just the armour he wears. We train them to ward off evil, to fight without armour, and survive against overwhelming odds. You are too old to become a Shadow Guard. And you're clumsy,' he said while walking around the groaning Calmantis, before heading for the door. 'Your arms and legs are too long. There's little muscle on those bones. And you have no coordination. Does your mind even know what your arms are doing half the time?'

'And here I was thinking you wouldn't give it to me straight. Well, at least I don't smell like faeces anymore,' Calmantis mumbled.

Yeron poked his head back through the door and stated, 'Yes, you do. Take another bath and meet me outside. We'll see how far you are willing to go to prove you have what it takes. And you will address me as Clairvoy Yeron, or Clairvoy, or simply sir.'

'Clairvoy?' Entangled with the chair and the bed and the wall, Calmantis struggled to get up and finally rolled backwards over his head, falling out of his room like a drunken leech, crashing against the far wall of the corridor. Yeron was already gone. The passageway was empty, devoid of people and any decorations. *Clairvoy?* It took him a while to untangle himself and get to his feet.

'Good, I was just about to come get you.' Calmantis whirled around, startled and unbalanced, losing his footing and hitting the wall again. Ackelides stood with his hands behind his back, shaking his head, and continued, 'We need supplies. Go meet Norai in the kitchen. She will give you the list of items needed and the coin to buy them. Get to it, the men are hungry.' Ackelides swung around, his cape flitting in the wind.

'Clairvoy? You never said Yeron is a clairvoy.'

'I didn't? Must have slipped my mind. He's a tough old fellow to please.' This was the first time he'd seen Ackelides's face completely uncovered from the silver-winged helm. It was broader than he'd thought it at first, his golden hair bouncing with every step.

'But Clairvoy Yeron wants me to meet him immediately for training.'

'Then you'd better get those supplies fast. The sun is going down, and he does not like to be kept waiting.' *Damn. No one said this would be easy.*

* * *

Down the shifty alley he walked, hood drawn low over his face, keeping to the walls and watching out for Ranickus Beltor. Three blocks to travel before he could reach the butcher and costermonger. Three blocks where he was a fairly easy target. Ranickus would not let three hundred silver sovereigns slide so easily. *He will want me to pay for his punishment.* The alley had a stench to it, but stenches didn't bother Calmantis. It did, however, remind him that the next cesspit was due for cleaning come tomorrow night.

Puddles of stale standing water reflected the buildings where large birds with long beaks perched on the roof, cawing the most annoying sounds, dragging the low-pitched wail out like a drowning cow; three, four times in a row, and it was driving people mad. A man pitched forward a few feet ahead of him as he tried to throw a rock up at the damn things. But the projectile flew wide, cracking into a window shutter and bouncing back to the street below, nearly hitting an old woman shuffling along. 'Oi!' she shouted at the man, waving her fist at him. 'You nearly hit me! You saw that, you did!' she called to Calmantis. But he held his head low and kept moving.

A large, open intersection of roads joined at the exit of the alley. The sun was getting very low, and dark clouds flashed in the distance ominously. People buzzed around, laughing and talking to one another, paying him little attention. Kids ran after big black ravens in the park across the street, where enormous green trees waved and rustled in the growing winds, their three-fingered leaves sweeping across the street.

A long retaining wall of stone and mortar ran next to the park, where he trotted over the open grounds, nervously glancing around him. Horses neighed and snorted loudly with wagons passing down the wide road. The buildings were getting taller the further he walked, but it was an area he at least knew well. His home was just around the corner, and the butcher and costermonger were opposite his old street. Could it stand to reason he would be safer here? Or would this be the very spot where Ranickus was waiting for him?

The fresh smell of petrichor graced his nose. A delightful scent that was more often than not the harbinger of rain. On the other side of the road he joined stood the stall of the costermonger, already packing up for the day. *No, no, no.* 'Wait, please. Marklin!' he shouted and flagged down the stampeding horses and their wagon and ran across, dodging and lunging out of the way from many others trotting past. Calmantis had not even reached the stall when he saw three men searching the street in the distance, confronting people for information. Big, butch, wearing paddy caps that hid their eyes. *Ranickus . . .*

'Please, Marklin, I just need a couple o' things, real quick.'

'Ah, Cal. Good to see you, lad. It's been a day, hasn't it?'

'It certainly has. Just a cabbage, some ginger, peas, potatoes, and onions. Please.'

'Sure thing, lad. Always like hearing your stories. You have any new fanciful tales of recent adventures?' Ranickus was getting ever closer.

He jumped in behind the stall to hide from their view, knowing how odd it must look to Marklin, and said, 'No, sorry, my friend. No new tales today.'

'Er . . . huh. You in some trouble, son?'

'Let's just say that someone isn't very happy with me of late. Seems I told the wrong tale.' He could hear the costermonger packing the vegetables in a basket for him. 'How much do I owe you?'

'That be four silvers.'

Four? He wanted to shout. It was daylight robbery. But he knew he was buying more than vegetables. He was buying Marklin's silence. *Nothing's for nothing these days.* He held out the coins and dropped them in the man's hand. Ranickus and his two goons were now only a few feet away and shared a striking resemblance. Younger, but the evidence was plain for all to see. Their black hair curled out from under their caps, and they shared the same stubby nose and thick cheekbones that gave them the appearance that they were always dozing off. *His sons, perhaps?*

'Get in the barrel, Cal!' whispered Marklin, pointing round the corner of the stall. Without a second thought, he lifted the lid and climbed in, pulling it closed over him. Many days had gone by where Calmantis envied those with muscular bodies, looking strong and something to be feared. Today was not one of those days. If it weren't for his skinny nature, he would never have fitted in the barrel. His long legs didn't make it easy, though. They were drawn up past his head, and he had no idea what to do with his long arms. It seemed everywhere he turned, his bony elbows banged against the sides of the barrel or his knees.

'Oi! Have you seen a younger lad, maybe thirty or so, skinny and tall? Got big ears, long nose, and stinks like a pile o' shit. Goes by Calmantis,' he heard one son ask. *Oh please, Marklin. Please don't sell me out.* He breathed deep, hoping to calm his raging heart.

'Plenty people come and go, sirs, and most o' them smell like shite. But the name sounds familiar.' The barrel rocked slightly as someone leaned up against it, and Calmantis knocked his head. Nausea crept up his throat while his stomach churned, making him want to puke. 'What's it worth to ya?' The drum rocked again, and through a crack he saw the red pants of one son. He was leaning against the barrel, adjusting his stance, clutching onto his paddy cap in the growing winds. Ranickus stood in front of Marklin, pondering the question, then stuck his hand into his pocket and pulled out two silver sovereigns. Begrudgingly, with a sneer, he handed them over to the costermonger.

'Where is he?' Ranickus asked, his voice cold and edgy. *No, please, Marklin.* The monger weighed the coins in his hands, bouncing them up and down while looking around.

'Seen the lad here a few times. He usually comes from up the road, that building over there. By the carriage with the black horse. That's all I can tell ya.' *Leave, you ape.* Some awkward silence lingered until another customer intruded on their discussion, asking for something Calmantis couldn't hear clearly. 'I'll be right with you, sir. Just a moment to finish up here.'

'Much obliged,' Ranickus said, and grinned at his sons. 'We will have him soon, boys.' Feet crunching over gravel, the three ran across the road, disappearing from his view. To be safe, he stayed in the barrel until the other patron left, and heard Marklin whistle for him before removing the lid.

'They're gone. You can come out now.'

Legs cramping from being bunched up in the barrel, Calmantis struggled up, worming towards the exit with his shoulders and the back of his arms. A rogue splinter pierced his palm, snapping off in his hand. 'Ow!' He winced and sucked at his dirty palm, nibbling at the piece of wood lodged dark under his fair skin. He climbed out, keeping his eyes on the door to the building where his pursuers had run to.

'Here ya go. Take the basket and go before they come back. I hope you have somewhere else to stay for a while. I had to give them something.'

'Not to worry, old friend. I have a place. Thank you.' *Now to pick up half a sheep and get out of here.* 'You take care, Marklin. And send my greetings to the missus.'

'Aye, will do, lad. Now off with you.'

For three years Calmantis had shovelled excrement and not got any closer to becoming a Shadow Guard, working through the nights and smelling of the foul waste daily. He was sure the disgusting faecal matter had seeped into his skin, forever changing his scent. And now, a stolen mug had finally done what he couldn't. He was living so close to his dreams, but these pesky chores were getting in his way. *Clairvoy Yeron must be waiting for me already, growing impatient and thinking of ways to punish me.*

* * *

Wrapped in old, worn rags, the back leg and neck of the lamb stuck out from the basket's side, a swarm of flies buzzing around them. On his way back to the temple, something gnawed at him. Although it was the very first time he'd met Norai earlier in the kitchen, he couldn't help thinking that she was very upset with him. Short and stubby, with a white bandana holding back her bushy black hair, she angrily chopped at the carrots on the wooden chopping block, not averting her gaze from her job. She had given him the instruction without so much as a cursory glance. Calmantis wasn't sure if that actually counted as meeting someone then.

And then there was the old butcher. When he stepped through the doorframe, Pelloch had seemed amicable and had greeted him warmly, clasping his shoulders and shaking him as if he were a branch in a snowstorm. But the moment Calmantis declared he had come for the half lamb for Norai, the man's countenance abruptly shifted to one of ire and displeasure. The sale was done in a jiffy, and he was out the door, with Pelloch pushing him along, mumbling under his breath angrily. *It seems Pelloch was rather looking forward to seeing Norai . . .*

People hastened across the street, hurrying to their homes while gazing northeast where the tempest brewed, the gusts of winds intensifying with every pulse of Calmantis's heart. Their worried faces and the screams caught in their throats echoed a terrible warning to all who listened.

The World Storm was coming . . .

His hood would not stay on his head any longer. It flapped behind his neck, while his hair whipped in the powerful gusts like the knotted ropes of the cat-o'-nine-tails splitting open the skin of a man's back. A cat hissed from behind the large red spokes of a wagon wheel, its eyes wild and alarming. There were rumours that animals could feel tension in the air or sense danger coming. Either way, it was correct. Not that it would make any difference, especially for the poor cat. It was very unlikely anyone would shelter the unfortunate animal. More than likely, it would end up as food on a table for some hungry family.

It was getting harder to walk against the howling winds, but the temple compound was only a few hundred feet ahead of him now. Darkness had taken over, with the heavy, purple clouds gathering above, thunder growling in the distance, making itself known. Dust and leaves whacked him in the face, and a shout behind drew his attention.

'Oi! Ya mangy, filthy, good-for-nothing, son of a whore!'

Feet planted wide against the stones of the road for grip, Calmantis glanced over his shoulder. Ranickus and his sons had found him and were gaining on him. With every morsel of strength he had in his stringy legs, he pushed off hard to run, but it felt like his head was being left behind. He leaned over the basket, making himself as small as he could, hearing the wind rush over his ears, and a brilliant flash lit up the sky, roaring its anger with a mighty clap, spraying bricks and mortar from the high-standing tower ahead, raining debris down on those running in the streets. Some of the Shadow Guard were still at their post, guarding the temple perimeter as always, but most of them had dispersed. *Probably to make sure the top officials are safely tucked away in the reinforced Chamber of Sanctity. What is wrong with this Ranickus? Is he crazy?* 'Get to shelter! We can discuss this later!'

'Oh no you don't! You will just run and hide elsewhere!' *Am I that predictable?*

Their shouts were barely audible, then the rain descended upon them, a downpour beating them mercilessly. 'This is madness! Go home, Ranickus! If not for your own safety, then for your sons.'

All four of them now struggled to move against the power of the wind, yet the wiry Calmantis eked away, cutting through the air. It was unfortunate that he had to carry the basket, holding him back with its bulky frame.

He looked up at the Shadow Guard standing at the gates and yelled, 'Help! It's me, Calmantis!' They did not budge, and one actually seemed to grin at him. *Some type of hazing, I suppose . . . Make the new guy suffer, and all.* The winds tore at him, nearly wrenching the basket from his hands, rags flapping crazily. Had it not been for the half lamb bracing the produce, the food would've been sent sky-high at this moment. 'I brought the food for tonight!'

'What did you get us?' shouted a guard with a grin.

Really? Now is not the time for jokes. 'Lamb and some produce!' Ranickus was getting closer, and his sons were only a foot or so behind their father. *Those knuckles look awfully big from here. And very hard.* 'Tender lamb!' he croaked, and one guard stepped out from the perimeter, sliding forward with the wind's aid, his boots scraping the sandstone floor, cape dancing over his shoulders. Calmantis edged forward, seeing Ranickus reach out to him.

'Turn around and head home now!' boomed the Shadow Guard's voice. And for a moment, Calmantis wasn't sure if it was him being spoken to. Hand on his sword, the guard reached his side and gripped his arm, still glaring at Ranickus and his sons. 'I will not speak again!'

'He owes me three hundred silver sovereigns!' shouted Ranickus, eyes bulging from his head, wet hair plastered to his face. 'The Black Feather is done for if he doesn't pay.'

'Sir! I said step away this instant! You wasted the temple's time with accusations you could not prove. Learn from your mistakes!'

Calmantis had kept walking, putting distance between them. He was not ready for a fight. *Just wait until I train with Clairvoy Yeron. Then I won't hide from you.* A scream sounded behind him, and he turned enough not to be whisked away by the winds. Ranickus jumped at the Shadow Guard, but it all seemed so slow. The veins in his neck and face throbbed with rage, his eyes bulged, and he bellowed, his garments flapping wildly. The guard swung his gloved hand, smacking the innkeeper on the nose with the bottom of his hand. Calmantis didn't hear a thud, but Ranickus toppled backwards, sliding on the ground and being swept away by the winds before his sons grabbed hold of his limp body. *Oh, boy! Oh, boy! Now he is going to make me to pay for that as well . . .*

10. The Storm

She was in trouble. There was never any doubt about that. Once fences ran, it was very difficult to track them down again. That was why they ran in the first place, wasn't it? Not to get cornered by old acquaintances. You should never burn your allies, but someone had burned her. *Could Yohtan really have sold me out like that? Would he have? Surely he must know it makes him a target as well.*

Cool brick pressed against Orana's bare back below her short-cropped top, where she squatted against her room's wall, arms resting on her knees, the dagger's tip drilling slowly into the hardwood floor. She had all her gear packed and ready to go. It was time to leave Skalg behind her to search for Yohtan and get back the stones, yet now she was caged, trapped in Skalg with the World Storm approaching. The men stationed in the towers along Skalg's colossal wall had sounded the alarm just as she had mounted the horse she had acquired for her trek; the bells reverberated throughout the city now, cautioning people to find refuge. Even if she wanted to leave the city, there was no way to get past the gates at the wall. And it would be stupid to go out knowing the storm was approaching. She had no choice but to wait it out. *What is so special about those bloody stones anyway? Sure, they might be valuable, but it's still just a damn stone.*

Her time was running out, and sitting here wouldn't solve any of her problems. It only made her more anxious. Fingers working over the nicked grip, she spun the dagger faster and faster, hearing it bite into the wood beneath, gouging bigger and bigger chunks the harder she pressed. The more her mind raced, thinking about how she was having to sit on her arse and wait for the World Storm to pass over Skalg, the slower time progressed.

Orana couldn't take it anymore. She needed to do something, go somewhere, possibly hit something or someone. She needed to steal something. No one would foresee a thief being audacious enough to break in during a time like this. Nevertheless, this was the most propitious moment, as the fewest number of people were in the street and only a few guards were still on patrol. Homes would be mostly unguarded, and businesses even less so.

She jumped up and grabbed her cloak, wrapping it around her shoulders swiftly as she made for the door. Her face was still swollen from the beating Lofka gave her, the side of her eye burning around the scraped skin. It would take days to fully heal, although the image of Lofka's fist rushing at her would sit tucked away in the distant corners of her mind, ready to be brought up again at the worst possible moments. Down the stairs she went, taking them two at a time, eager to get out of the building.

Dark clouds swirled around above, their ominous droning and rumbling every time they collided with one another created horizontal flashes over the purple ceiling. A soft spray of rain drifted over the city from the approaching deluge, wetting the hairs on her arms, a layer of small dewy drops glistening over her skin. Trees swayed back and forth in the strengthening gusts, the long-tailed basimets quietly clinging to the branches, the terror in their eyes clear for all to see.

Orana hugged the walls of the buildings, where the wind was subdued, venturing out during a respite in the burgeoning storm. She wasn't sure where she was headed, but she was sure an opportunity would present itself soon. Here and there, stragglers made their way to safety, fathers herding their families along like cattle, scouring for cover, while smaller children clung to them.

A few blocks away stood the raised Khylles road, and the grand temple in the distance, glimmering with rain, trees shaking fiercely. She could still not believe what had happened that evening. Four people had died that day on their march to pray, and forty-three were injured, some left with broken legs and arms, heads bleeding and bodies scraped up. *Lofka, I hope your hand festers and rots . . .* To her right, she ogled the long alleyway, littered with empty bottles rolling from the unconscious hands of those unfortunate enough not to have a roof over their heads, clanging over the newly laid cobblestones. *Beggars and drunkards, those that've had hard times fall on them. They will have it the worst of everyone out here in the open. Poor souls.*

Merchants Grove disappeared round the corner between a profusion of houses and buildings, the long, straight, and wide road lined with tall palm trees to the sides. Emptied stalls stood pinned down with ropes and iron spikes beat into the earth, the soil turning dark and soft. Soon those spikes would come flying out and covers would sail off into the night. She would have no luck here. Everything would've been packed up by now.

Orana could hear the cries of a child resonating from one of the nearby buildings, its wails growing with every clap of thunder. *Motherhood . . . why would you bring a child into a world like this? Why would you make another air-stealer? Sure, they're cuddly now, but wait until they walk, talk, and shit everywhere. Then we will see who enjoys them. And don't get me started on when they start thinking for themselves.*

A forceful gust shoved her left, and she fell against a palm tree, its rough trunk scratching her arm, drawing blood. She was not about to leave for home just yet. Two guards struggled towards the bend in the road, fighting the wind and constantly glancing up, their spears lowered as close to the ground as they could. The sweet smell of approaching rain blanketed the entire city, a smell that usually brought peace and relaxation, were it not the harbinger of the World Storm. Especially here in Skalg, where the droughts were long and water scarce. A loud, explosive clap on the right deafened her, a blinding flash splitting the trunk of a tree, instantly burning and trailing smoke, and Orana jumped away from it.

Mid-air, while her dive was taking her to a mud-hole, another brief flash appeared in the corner of her eye, one that didn't make any noise. Brows furrowed, she saw three figures standing now where the flash occurred, one carrying a cane, leaning on it while he scanned the surroundings, the other half dragging, half carrying the last, struggling with the weight. They seemed surprised, confounded about where they were and what was happening, surveying the area as if trying to figure out all these details quickly.

Orana hit the ground, and the mud sucked her up, burying her face in the softened soil, and she tasted the iron in the ground. The basimets shrieked their laughter at her, throwing faeces and snarling with jagged teeth, their screams both intimidating and threatening, while their adorable tails curled over their heads. She climbed to her feet, slipping and sliding, and finally got into her stance. Annoyed, she grabbed handfuls of mud and hurled it at the pesky basimets, then searched for the three strangers that were there only moments ago. Orana set off after them, running through the ever-growing storm to find them again.

The wind was really becoming a nuisance, shoving her left and right, impairing her vision with her lashing hair. It was like walking through a gauntlet of imperiously rude teenagers, or being terribly drunk.

'What are you doing in the streets?' shouted a guard on her right, huddling under the balcony of a building while the decking boards rattled and lifted from its base. 'Get to cover! Can't you see what's coming?'

'I'm looking for some . . . friends of mine. Three of them. Have you seen them?' she shouted back at him, cupping her hands over her mouth and trying to keep her hair out of her face.

The guard shook his head and shrugged his shoulders. 'Thought I saw someone enter that alley over there, but I was not about to risk my life for a better view. You're on your own.' He pulled on the door, making it look heavy and unwilling as the wind buffeted it, before he entered. It shut with a loud clap.

A horse neighed in fear and ran down a connecting street, its handler following behind with arms to the sky, shouting and cursing at the animal. The softer rain turned angry, beating down with thick drops, soaking her through. Feet getting dragged by the winds, it was a struggle to maintain her normal stealthiness. She was closing in on the alley, hearing faint whispers of shouted words come and go. Next to a large square building, a long rail ran to the alley's entrance, its vertical slats giving Orana good grip, keeping her grounded. Behind a shaking bush of green and purple, she leaned out to see them arguing a few feet away, the old one's arms waving angrily.

'We have to . . . of this—'

'But . . . even know wh . . . are!' They were pale skinned, and the younger one carrying the injured one seemed afraid and unsure. *Foreigners in a foreign place. The older one has some fancy clothes. And I wouldn't mind owning that cane.* Stone so white it seemed like milk flowed from the ground to the handle, where a silver hollow-eyed skull screamed from one end, a babe in the throes of birth on the other, elaborate etchings carved into the stone from top to bottom. Orana walked out from her cover, startling them.

'Follow me! You can take shelter in my home until the storm clears!' she said in the common tongue. They seemed hesitant, furtively glancing at one another, saying nothing. 'Come on! This storm is dangerous, and so are the people of this city!'

'How can we trust you?' asked the old man.

Orana shrugged, spreading her hands, and said, 'You can't, but this storm does not take sides. And cover your faces. There are eyes everywhere.'

* * *

'Move it! Quickly!' Orana stood by her door, urging the two men on to carry their friend up the stairs and into the room, closing it behind them. Their groans faded and grew with their heaving effort. It was a big man they were carrying, a slew of old scars keeping company with new cuts covering his arms and chest, most of which were still bleeding. And his face didn't look any better. Blood pooled from his mouth to the floor, staining the wood. If Orana wasn't about to leave this place, this would have upset her terribly. 'Get him on the bed!' *I'm so glad I already packed my beautiful sheets away.*

'Do you have any bandages?' the younger one asked, a note of urgency in his voice. She was saving the bandages for her travels, not to readily give them away to a boy with barely a shadow of stubble growing on his chin. You never knew what might happen out there in the wild or on the road. Predators could attack at any time, man or animal alike. Something in the young man's eyes broke her barriers down, the way he kept staring back at the injured man, the way he fidgeted with his hands and his hair, working out the stress that assaulted him so.

'In that pack against the wall,' she sighed, watching him dash over to it and grab it up, ripping it open and rummaging through it. 'Hey! Do you mind? Stop throwing my stuff all over the floor.'

'Sorry . . .' he mumbled and ran back to the bed to hand it to the old man.

'If you're going to bleed all over my floor and bed, I should at least get your names.' They had not the inclination to answer her. Instead, they carried on working on the injured man. She approached them slowly, arms crossed curiously, gazing over the shoulder of the old man.

Her entire room was wet, and the rumbling storm shook the building to its core, sending tremor after tremor with great white flashes from the sky. Clap after clap, it rumbled and poured its torrent down on the dry city so close to the desert, following the trail over the Rusty Mountains where great iron deposits ran deep in the earth. Many had made their fortune mining those mountains and the desert near Ironhorn, but those metals in the earth also attracted the World Storm's wrath. Once it reached the mountains, they could see a terrifying display of flashing lightning from the walls of Skalg. Truly something magnificent and utterly frightening to behold.

'Vernak,' muttered the old man, nodding his head while he strapped gauze around what looked to be a nasty tear on the man's arm. It was too jagged for a cut, the skin and flesh torn deep into his biceps up to his shoulder. He peeled back the man's eyelids, inspecting them. There was very little life left there that she could see. 'That's Jorin,' he said as he rose and gazed down at the bleeding man. 'And this is Jonas, the lad's father. Do you perhaps have a needle and thread? This wound is too big to just close up on its own.'

His father, yes, I see it now. The broad face, the square jaw, the green eyes. He doesn't have his father's hawk nose, though. 'Yes, of course.' From one of the side pockets in her pack, she retrieved the items, rolled up neatly in a leather case.

'Is he going to be okay?' Jorin asked her from where he paced at the foot of the bed. The man was barely breathing, the air coming out in rasps and his chest stuttering in jerky movements.

'Oh, I'm no healer, kid,' Orana stated, backing away some. 'Ask him. Though I'm not sure I'd want you working on me. I reckon you can see, but them eyes don't look so good. You sure the kid shouldn't be doing . . .' she waved a finger, '. . . that.'

'I'm just old,' Vernak sneered and turned back to Jonas. She noticed that they too carried some scars, wounds recently received. The boy had received similar beating marks as her, she realised.

'What happened to you lot?' asked Orana, cringing with a nearby lightning strike that shook the building, its booming roar quick to follow.

'He's dying, isn't he? Damn! Stupid! No-good bastard! He's dying because I couldn't fight!' yelled Jorin, eyes big and wet.

'Calm down, Jorin!' demanded Vernak. 'It is not the child's purpose to protect the parent! There was nothing you could have done. There was nothing anyone could have done.' He turned to Orana, looking older than a few moments ago. 'We were ambushed. And they took something from him.'

Orana held the wound closed and waited for Vernak to stitch it. 'What?'

'His spirit.'

A long sigh escaped her, and she whispered, 'That's a shame, then. Once we lose our fighting spirit, it's hard to get over wounds such as these. He still has his son. He must have some fight left in him.'

Vernak said nothing further on the matter, and only glanced at Jorin, who was now chewing on his nails. He continued to work the thick needle through the man's flesh, drawing it around for the next stitch until the wound was closed, then bit the thread off.

'Where are you three headed?'

'Don't take it personally, but I do not feel comfortable giving you all this information.' Orana cleared her throat and rose from the bed, crossing her arms and making to speak, when Vernak interrupted her. 'Please. We are very grateful for the help you have given. It's just that we know nothing about you. And I'm sure you mean well, but we can't risk involving people that might get mixed up in this mess. It's better if you don't know.' Now she just wanted to know even more.

'Who gives you the right to say what I should or shouldn't get involved in? Besides, you two won't last a day in Skalg without me. Tell me where you're headed, and I will decide the rest. You're heading to Baldor, aren't you? Got that look on you. That holier-than-thou look.'

'Skalg?' he whispered. 'Maybe, yes. Might have to take a detour first, though.'

Erua is smiling on me today! I will be less conspicuous with the Westerners. Then maybe Yelefant might not even find me again. And mind you, the company wouldn't be a bad thing. Another terrible clap sounded, and Jorin nearly leapt out of his skin. With her finger over her mouth in thought, she tilted her head and said, 'I will be your guide. For a fee, of course.'

'I can't hear a damn thing you're saying through this storm! Speak up, girl.'

'I said I would be your guide. For a small fee.'

'Can you two stop yammering like old friends and fix my father?' shrieked Jorin from the side, glaring at them both, his fists bunched.

Vernak turned back from the interruption and gripped her by the arms. 'Look, where we go might be a little dangerous. I cannot have it on my conscience, were you to get injured. I will have to decline, my dear. We will be fine.' He glanced at Jorin, cupping his hands together, and said, 'Grab a rag and start cleaning up the blood from the floor. Once the storm has passed, we will leave her home.'

Where I'm going, there's definitely danger, and a lot of it, huge fistfuls of them. And they hurt like nobody's business. Orana walked over to the window and peered through the slits where the black night sky flashed violent arcs of white, blue, and purple. The drumming rain on the roof and the shutters softened slightly, pattering away, careless of the damage it had caused. Streams of water flooded the city, carrying pieces of wagons, tools, furniture that must have been ripped from someone's home, a few dead basimets, and an already bloated horse. 'If that is what you want.' *Don't think you will dismiss me so easily, old man.*

Jonas groaned out loud in his haze of unconsciousness, gripping the bed tight, and clenched his jaw while Vernak leaned over him. Jorin dashed to his father's side, wanting to hold his hand, but the man would not release his grip.

'Sleep wherever you can. This storm is here to stay for the night,' Orana said and dropped onto the couch, shifting her pack to use as a pillow.

Vernak reached across the shaking man and lay his hand on Jorin's arm. 'We have done all we can for now, my boy. We require the help of an alchemist for the rest. They will have the needed ingredients to get your father back on his feet.'

Orana turned away from them and muttered, 'There's one on the other side of the city. A woman named Erechol. She is . . . discreet.'

'How do we find her?'

'Head past the Temple of Khylles and over the basalt bridge to the west. She has an enormous villa on Kurtak Lane, with many palm trees. You can't miss it.'

11. Finding a Way

A loud clap sounded, jolting Vernak up from the hard floor, heart pounding and searching for his cane.

'It's just me,' Orana said, sneaking in from the door. 'You three were just about dead. Seemed like you haven't slept in days.'

Vernak twisted around, seeing Jorin roll over on his side, soft snores drifting from him. Old and weary, he got up, rubbed his sore hips, and cursed the clothes he slept on, having done very little to soften the floor. He could feel the deep folds they'd imprinted into his skin. 'How long has the sun been up?' he muttered, seeing the rays light up the room. 'I didn't hear the storm die down.'

'It cleared ahead of dawn. Cleanup crews are already working their way through the city.'

'Where did you go?' he asked, clearing his throat and stroking his silver beard. 'It must've been a mess with all the damage the floods caused.'

'Yes, but I know the city better than most. I went to see an old friend to make sure he was okay. What's it to you, anyway?'

'It's nothing, sorry. My circle of trust just got smaller recently.' He strode over to the bed, tapping Jorin awake with his foot, and lowered his head to listen to Jonas's breathing. It was shallow but steady, if a bit wheezy. Jorin groaned from the floor, forcing his eyes open. 'Wake up, boy!'

'I've told you before. I'm not a boy anymore! And soon, I'll be a father. Can you still call me boy if I have one of my own?' complained Jorin as he rose unsteadily from the floor, careening to his left and gripping the wall for balance.

'Just because you used your prick on some unfortunate girl doesn't make you a man! Now get ready! We have to leave.'

Jorin fell back at the old man's anger. There were times to show your grit, to stand up against being spoken to like a child. Today was not one of those days. He quickly gathered their items, then slung Jonas's weathered pack over his shoulders.

Vernak breathed a calming breath and spoke to Orana. 'Will they have opened the city gates?'

'They might've. How did you get into the city in the first place?' she asked, tilting her head to the side and removing her mud-spattered cloak.

'We, er . . . We snuck in just before the storm hit.' He glimpsed a flicker of triumph in her eyes, the corners of her mouth curling slightly into a grin, quickly vanishing again.

With a great heave, he lifted Jonas from the bed by his arm, helped by Jorin on the other side, grumbling at the weight of the man. Mumbling and drooling spit and blood, Jonas's eyes flitted open, swimming, drifting, and closed again, his legs barely working, folding in under him as the two men dragged him from the bed. 'Come on, Jonas! Left leg forward. That's it.' Between the two of them, they got him up and made their way to the door before Vernak turned and said over his shoulder, 'Thank you, Orana, for what you did for us. We won't forget it. Take care.'

Step by step, they dragged Jonas along over the floorboards of the hall, where an old woman poked her head out of a door, a look of disgust on her old face, a snake's hiss forced out between her teeth. She quickly retreated when they locked gazes, slamming the door closed, and down the stairs they went, floorboards creaking underfoot. Wet patches on the floor stood collecting swarms of mosquitoes, bursting away in a cloud of black buzzing as they drew near. Run-off from the ceiling stained the white walls brown, a constant drip pouring down every crack. Out the door they went, taking to the streets and drawing their hoods over their heads where more people were already walking about, sifting through the rubble pushed along by the floods, walking ankle-deep in water and muck.

Although the floods had caused a lot of damage, the veritable cornucopia of water would lessen the hold that the drought had on

Skalg. They would have drinkable water for weeks. Clever drainage beds ran along the roadsides, funnelling streams of the life-sustaining liquid to great tanks stored all over the city, harvesting the precious commodity for a time when they would see no rain for months.

A thick layer of sediment covered the newly cobbled streets, muddying their city again, but the cleanup would be swift, with a few hundred men and women sweeping for weeks. They could not let the *jewel* of Tolomene be looking like a heap of rubbish.

There was no joyous laughter today. Too many would have perished through the night to call for celebration. First, there would be mourning and giving thanks they survived. Then there would be celebration, laughter, stealing, and murder. Back to the norm. For now, though, everyone moped about to see how their lives had been uprooted.

'Chy'ii!' shouted a guard to a bunch of men pushing to lift an overturned wagon while a man lay trapped underneath, his legs getting crushed as he screamed for them to stop.

'Shouldn't we help them?' asked Jorin as he adjusted his grip on his father.

'Keep moving,' grumbled Vernak. He kept his head low, drawing his hood down to hide his face. 'They will not take kindly to us being here. You heard what Orana said.' All around them, men and women swept water and mud from their homes, knowing in a few months, they would need to do it again. The last World Storm had hit less than a year ago now. It was growing more frequent each year.

'You must know why these terrible storms occur. Why are we being punished like this?' Jorin asked, straining to keep his father upright, arm draped over his shoulders.

'I really wish I knew, Jorin. But some things are a mystery even to us.' Vernak saw the boy's face, felt the need for more answers radiate from him with the stare he received, but he had none to share and turned his gaze away. Thick clumps of mud clung to their clothing, their boots having vanished in the ochre sediment.

The sky was a beautiful blue, with not the slightest hint of the storm that befell them only last night, the sun shining over the steeples and walls of the city. In times like these, it paid to live on higher ground. And they could see that truth made clear as they descended into the lower parts of the city. Cold water covered their feet, reaching for their knees the further they went. It sloshed from their shoes with handfuls of sand, each step getting more difficult. Ahead, some homes were completely underwater, only the tops of their pitched roofs visible, where some men, women, and children sat on the very ends, waiting for the water to recede. *It must have been a frightful affair, having sat there through the storm, clinging to the tiles, just waiting for a lightning bolt to cook you from the inside.* 'We can't go this way.'

'We should've asked her to come with us!' growled Jorin. 'She would've known how to get around this.'

Vernak was tiring of the child's complaints. It was all he'd been doing since they set out together.

A row of flooded and submerged buildings lined the disappearing road where the bright reflection of a harsh sun shimmered in the water, blinding them. 'There! You see? The basalt bridge. That's where we need to get to.'

The cupola bridge stood in the distance, a gigantic, dark, prancing horse statue rearing on the roof, held up by enormous black columns rising from the watery grave, where the liquid gathered into what looked like an old moat. Debris rushed down the old waterway constantly, powerful currents ripping away at the banks and houses, spilling over the columns, gathering the water from the flooded city. *If we can get over the bridge, we should be fine.* 'They must have expanded the city. That must be its original border.'

'So very interesting. But I fail to see how this history lesson will help us. Why don't you snap your fingers and take us to the other side?'

Vernak clenched his teeth, wishing he could smack the boy across the face. It might not be helpful, but it sure would make him feel better. 'We can't go back to the Void! Not now, anyway. Unless you want to have another go at the darcöle? I will indulge your request to witness the outcome of such a meeting, however brief it might be.' He glared at Jorin, watching the man pale, making the bloody blue-purple rings around his eyes stand out even more. 'I didn't think so. So shut it and be helpful.'

Lucky for them, the people of Skalg were busy with their own problems, leaving them to roam freely for the moment. Were it not for this, their saddened state and injuries would've stood out like a sore thumb. *Had we the time, we could wait for the water to recede and make our way across, if the bridge still stands.* He turned to regard the man in their arms and sighed. They could not wait for days to cross. Jonas would not last that long, and there was no guarantee the bridge would still stand after the pummelling from the water it was receiving.

Vernak let out another long breath as he searched for an answer, but only one came to mind. 'It seems we have no choice but to go through it.'

'What? There could be anything beneath the surface. A fallen tree could sweep us away and trap us under the water, drowning us. Or, for all I know, there could be those gigantic lizard things I've heard rumours about, lurking just beneath the surface, waiting to grab its next snack . . . Or what about—'

'Or what about shutting up? There are no crocodiles here,' shouted Vernak, drawing the attention of passers-by. He quickly drew his hood lower. 'I swear, if you weren't Jonas's boy, I would leave you behind in this city to fend for yourself. Come. This way.'

The water was icy compared to the growing heat outside. It was a refreshing change from the building humidity. In tandem, they marched into the mysterious depths, the liquid gradually reaching their calves, thighs, abdomens, and chests, all while bearing Jonas, not letting his head dip beneath the surface. Ahead, they could see the bridge clearly now, the gigantic blocks of basalt being bashed and swallowed by the brown deluge, the angry roar growing louder. The row of houses next to them all sank lower, their frames, timbers, and stone walls getting damaged from being soaked in the water. Their feet left the ground, and the currents pushed them away from their mark.

'Tsuilghawny jyë ghop? Tsaldu ëk,' shouted a worried man from the top of his roof, waving his arms at them. 'Yoi tsefmagh! Eegh!'

'What is he saying?' asked Jorin, jerking his head back and forth between the man and the bridge. 'He is warning us to get out of the water, isn't he?' Jorin floundered to his right, falling behind and dragged both men down with him into the murky water, a sudden gurgle for air disappearing beneath the surface. It was slippery and tumultuous, pushing them around fiercely. Vernak's feet scraped the ground, and he luckily found his footing. He burst forth from the water with a loud gasp, sucking in air, and pulled Jonas out with him, Jorin clinging to his father's tunic.

He ignored the pleas of the man trapped on the roof and pushed ahead. 'Jorin! Kick with your feet! Swim with your arm, boy! You are going to kill us all!'

Something grabbed hold of Vernak's foot and yanked him under. He had no choice but to let go of them, hoping they would make it through. Water rushed over him, and dark shapes assaulted him, cracking into his face and ribs, spinning him over. Eyes open to see in the murky water, he had little warning of approaching items, seeing their dark shapes only moments before crashing into them. Objects rushed by him while he tried to swim, but he was getting nowhere fast. Vernak reached down, moving his hands down his leg until he felt a long, rough vine or a tangled rope around his right ankle, and he tugged on it as hard as he could, fingers working furiously to free himself.

His breath was failing him by now, and his lungs burned like fire, a feeling he had never experienced before. With his cane in his left hand, he reached up and dragged a hidden blade from it. *No time to waste.* He began cutting at his attacker, nicking his skin every so often, releasing big bursts of bubbles to the surface. It was taking too long. His head felt like it was about to burst. He wanted to take a breath so badly, just suck in that wonderful air, but all he'd get would be a lungful of dirt and water. Desperately hacking at his captor now, he felt his mind wandering, drifting away from him to blissful rest. *Is this what it feels like to die? It's not as bad as I thought. Peaceful, actually. I don't know what everyone complains about.* His hands worked back and forth, cutting, hacking, slashing, his ankle burning from multiple cuts and stabs.

The vine snapped, and the world suddenly stalled around him.

But he had not the energy to swim for the surface. He didn't even know which way was up, to be honest. The current was pulling him still, knocking him into debris, but it didn't matter anymore.

Something hard thunked against his head, and his sight was gone. *I shouldn't have done that to Jonas . . .*

* * *

'Vernak!' Jorin shouted, and his head plunged under water briefly, causing him to suck up copious amounts of the liquid while he held on to his hapless father, being pummelled by the raging current. They had slipped into the moat when the water snatched Vernak from them and were now headed at speed towards the cupola bridge. Jorin swam with his free arm, kicking water and sucking up more, keeping Jonas on his back with his head above the surface.

Through the muffled sounds of the water rushing into his ears, and the fogging of his vision, one thing he could see unmistakably was the bridge's thick columns hurtling towards them. Jorin readied himself and spread his right arm out. There was no use in swimming against the tumultuous water. It was difficult to gauge just how fast he was moving, though the sections of houses, carts, timber walls, dressers, and so much more flitting by on the side were definitely at a canter, maybe even nearing a gallop. *This is going to hurt!* he thought, completely at the mercy of the water.

It hit like a kick from Uncle Yurgassun's horse, crashing into his chest with its natural jagged edges and spinning their bodies into each other. They bounced off the column, and Jorin grabbed at it, scraping his fingers raw against the rough stone and tearing off his nails before slipping away. He crashed into the next row with his back, and his grip on his father slipped away with the hit. It felt like he would cough up a lung at any moment. Only his middle finger still gripped his father's tunic, and he wrestled it closer, screaming from the pain of the pressure on his back, arm, and hand.

'Wake up, Father! Please! Wake up! I can't hold on anymore! Father!' He gurgled the mucky water and coughed, spitting it out as more rushed over them. The columns stood roughly six feet apart, and there was not much to hold on to, given their big circumference and the slimy layer of algae covering the wet basalt pillars. Jonas's limp body slipped from the column and nearly broke Jorin's arm as he bent backwards, holding on as his father rode the flow. He could not hold out for much longer. 'Vernak!' he shouted again, but no answer came.

'Please, someone, help me . . .' he whispered, wanting to cry. *Get it together, Jorin. Maybe I can push off against the pillar to the next . . .* A cart came into view, swiftly making its way towards the bridge, colliding with it and shattering to pieces, rocking the bridge with the hit. *No, it would sweep me away like that cart.* Perched against the column with arms and feet, he slipped down into the depths.

Water rushed over his head, forcing him down and scraping his chest against the column, but he held on to his father. Panic set in. He could not get back to the surface, the water was not allowing him, and he could not pull Jonas under. The man would drown. *Tunisia, if I don't make it back to you, please take care of our little one.*

Something scraped against his boots. He ran his foot over it, feeling the straight edges of a railing and strengthening posts arrayed down the length to the next column.

Think, Jorin! This would not be new to this city. In Baldor, a long time back, when his father took them to see the city, he remembered seeing rope lines spanning the length of the bridges for people to grab onto and make their way across. He felt around the column, working his way down, and there it was, thick ropes, pulled taut with the current. He grabbed hold of the rope and wrapped his foot around the railing, curling his toes inside his boot to secure his hold, and inched away from the column. Jorin secured his right foot in the railing and unhooked his left, hooking it in further down the railing while pulling himself closer to the next column on the rope. It was going torturously slow, though he was gaining ground. Soon, he felt the rough basalt column with his boot.

He desperately needed to breathe.

Jorin reached up and searched for a handhold, feeling the nicks and bumps in the stone – the centuries of degradation it had been subjected to – then felt a narrow slit, a crack in the column, and squeezed his fingers into it. With a gradual, aching ascension, he made his way to the surface and sucked in the precious air, breathing deep with his eyes wide. *I made it. I'm alive.* He looked to his left, losing more hope. *Ah shit . . . So many more to go.* He had no idea how many times his father had dipped under water, how much liquid he had sucked up into his lungs, and there was nothing Jorin could do about it now except keep the man's head above water with his one arm, hoping he still breathed when he came to the other side.

* * *

Muffled sounds rang in his ears, and a wet kiss slathered his lips. Air rushed into his lungs, and his face burned as water gushed from his mouth. A blurry figure hovered over him, coming into perspective slowly, and his face burned again, this time on the right. Strong hands pulled Vernak up and heaved him onto his stomach. He puked more water and sludge, his stomach lurching inward and pushing up everything he had left. It felt horrible. But he was still alive. *Now this is something to complain about,* he thought, and slowly crawled his knees closer, arse sticking up to the sky.

'Are you crazy? Stupid bakghor! You better get out of Skalg before the wrong people see you, eh!' said a man in a thick common tongue, panting with his hands on his knees.

Strings of spit ran down Vernak's chin, causing small bubbles to form in the ankle-deep water he found himself in. 'Bakghor? I might be a foreigner, but don't think for a second that I can't speak your tongue.'

The man was very dark-skinned, with a bulging forehead and thick, bushy brows. His black hair was plastered against his scalp, yet the curls were already regaining their bounciness. 'I don't care if you understand my tongue or not. You are stupid.'

Vernak climbed to his feet and winced at his burning ankle, seeing all the cuts on his foot. The sword and the milky-stone sheath lay in the wet mud next to him, gently lapped by the receding water. He bent down and collected them, wiping the blade on his robes and washing out the scabbard in the water before sheathing the weapon. 'Thank you for saving me.' The man shook his head and sucked at his teeth, clicking his tongue as he walked away.

'Jorin!' Vernak shouted as he searched the surroundings, unsure which side of the moat he was on. He had drifted down quite a way, and the bridge stood a distance to the left, water rushing over the black top, making it shiny and no doubt slippery. 'Jorin! I've made it across! Where are you?' The water had receded a lot, but there was no sign of them.

12. Liars and Killers

Bellard stretched his eyes wider than he ever had before, hoping to see something, anything, in the pitch-black darkness, even the slightest grey edges of a nearing object, yet no outlines were visible to hint that his eyes had adjusted. He did not know how long he had been in this place, but he was hungry, and thirsty, and above all, dead tired. If they couldn't find their way out, this would be their grave. No burials for any of them.

He longed to use his eyes again, to see the beautiful lands of the north, the high trees swaying in the winds, the large open lands and green valleys. Most of all, he longed to see the blinding snow on a sunny day in Forgeholde, where they could climb the high mountains and hunt for elk. Where a good day's work offered ale and meat. They would gather in the hall of the adavey and feast until the sun rose the following day.

Nothing seemed real here. An illusive trap tugging at the strings of his sanity. Even so, every sound and every touch drilled into his very soul.

'I will not listen to any of you! Where are my friends? Mila!' he yelled, turning round and round, with the dagger held tight in his hand. *How big is this place? It feels like I've been walking for days on end.* Rumbling laughter sounded next to his ear, grating and forced, wheezing foul breath over him, and he jerked around, brandishing the blade, swishing it back and forth vigorously. A splatter of something wet and hot sprayed over his face, vanishing as fast as it appeared.

'You know me, Bellard. Why won't you trust me? I have been your friend since you were seven. I have stood by you, fought for you, bled for you, and made others bleed in the name of protecting you. You are a brother to me,' said the voice of Gallus. There was a tone of sadness there that Bellard just couldn't believe to be him.

'I've not known Gallus to be a snivelling, sad little whelp who cries about not being believed or trusted.' *Follow the voice you know and trust.* But who exactly was that? Surely, not his father's, and neither his mother's. Mila's voice had led him astray, cutting his fingers, yet he thought he trusted her. Even Cora had caused him harm, and now Gallus. He had ignored the previous call from his friend, not wanting to know if he could trust him or not. For this was not just a game of chance tricking you. This was working in your thoughts. In your mind. And it would tear you apart from the inside, make you doubt every single thing you believed in, every single person you thought you trusted.

'What's the matter, boy?' came a gentle voice, deep and full of life, and Bellard could not help but search for the source. 'You havin' a bad day, are you?'

'Opa?'

'Step right!' Bellard obeyed instinctively, and nothing happened except for a rush of wind flitting over him. 'Yes, it's me, Opa Anglard. I have been trying to get through to you, but the Ormaghs overwhelm us at night. It is when they are at their strongest. Dive forward!'

Something swooshed over his head, blowing wind in his face, and he hit the floor hard, nearly sticking the dagger into his own chest. 'What was that?' he demanded, crawling away on his hands and feet.

'On your feet! Move to your left!'

Bellard's nerves were finished. He trembled and twitched, his head bobbing from anxiousness, but he obeyed and scrambled to his left.

'Stab on your right!'

He thrust the blade out and felt it sink deep into flesh, a horrible growl reverberating through the blade and into his arm, and he yanked it out. 'What was that? What's going on?'

'No time to explain! Don't move! Be quiet.' Stuck halfway between his current and next step, his right foot dangled in the air, and his momentum drove him onward. His foot hit the floor with a gentle tap, and his back suddenly burned fiercely. Something had cut into him from behind, and he sprawled forward, flinging himself to the floor dismally, dropping his dagger. It clanged and skidded on the floor somewhere.

'I said don't move! Next time listen to me, or there might not be another chance.'

Bellard wasn't sure if this had been the last chance, thinking he was bleeding to death already. He could see in his mind's eye how his back mushroomed open, how flesh ballooned and blood sprayed, streaming down to the floor, forming deep puddles at his feet. It stung terribly, and thinking about it made it even worse.

'Get up, Bellard!' He scrambled up, stumbling forward, and kicked something. He heard a scraping sound drag out on the floor. *The dagger . . . Damn it.*

'To your left, slowly.'

Eyes searching through the darkness, Bellard reached out with his right hand, perpetually moving his left to his side and back, feeling for anything near him, and stepped left.

'That's it, follow my voice.'

'If you are the Usha that chose me to take up your crystal, tell me why. Why was I chosen and not someone like Gallus, who is brave and courageous? Why me? I'm afraid of everything . . .'

'I chose you exactly for those reasons, boy. Because you know what it's like to be afraid. Because bravery and courage cannot exist if you aren't terrified of something. And because, most of all, I was once like you.'

'You were like me? Really?'

'Yes, yes,' chuckled the voice. 'I was quite pathetic myself.'

'Hey! I never said I'm pathetic.'

'Oh, you didn't? Well, then. It's good to be enlightened, isn't it? Walk to your right.' Annoyed at the remark, Bellard frowned and held his tongue. A pregnant period of silence grew to an awkward affair, where just enough time had lapsed to make the first who spoke seem indignant. But someone had to break the silence, or this might never end.

'How much further do I still need to go?' asked Bellard, inching forward with another step, then jumped back with fists balled when cold, sharp edges pressed against his fingers. Even though he was sure the floor was flat, he couldn't help but swing his arms out for balance, trying his best not to fall, as though the section of floor he teetered on was a tightrope suspended over a heart-wrenching drop.

'We are here,' said the voice of Opa Anglard in reverie, fading away at the end, like his watch was finally done.

'What do I do?' whispered Bellard, fearing something else might be near. *One of these Ormaghs, perhaps.*

'Next, dear boy, you will take from me the last remaining breaths I have left. You will grasp my Pillar and forge a new alliance with it.'

'Wait, you will die?' he asked, mouth agape and retreating a few steps. 'I can't be the one who kills you!'

'Calm down, son. It is how things are.'

'No! I lost my Opa once already. I don't want to lose him again.'

'Bellard . . .' the voice pleaded gently. 'You know I am not really your Opa Anglard. I am the voice you trust. My time has finally come, and I am proud to have you bear my torch for the next while. I am not sad, and so you shouldn't be. Now, step forward and embrace your new path.'

Times of old came rushing through his mind. Times of when he was a young boy no more than twelve. When his father beat him and yelled at him for the slightest reason, when his mother stood there and said nothing, just grinning away like the imperious bitch she was. Until Opa Anglard kicked in the door one day after hearing the swearing and cussing and slapping around going on inside the house. He raged forward and grabbed Bellard's father by the neck, squeezing hard and shoving him up against the wall, a blaze of fury in his voice and eyes. Mother had tried to intervene, slapping her father on the back to drop her husband. But the backhand came swift and fierce, leaving an angry red handprint on her cheek that sent her stumbling over the dining room table and cracking into the chairs on the other side.

'You treat this boy like filth! No wonder he fears everything!' Opa Anglard had shouted while Bellard's father scratched with his fingers, hunting for a sensitive hole to stick them. But he would not find any. The gurgling groans of his father made the sweetest noises to Bellard back then, until Opa Anglard dropped him to the floor and smacked him with an open palm, right off his feet. 'This is the last time I am having this conversation with you, understand?' Opa had said to his father.

'The boy needs to toughen up!' spewed his father back, and he received a gut punch for his troubles.

'Father, stop this!' Mother intervened again, her filthy fingers stretched like claws as she raged.

'I will get to you soon! Stay out of this!' Opa shoved Bellard's father's face away, toppling the fool to the ground where he lay searching for air, then climbed over the scattered chairs after his daughter who fled from his fury, but she was too slow, too drunk. He grabbed her by the back of the neck, and she clawed him in the face with her long nails, leaving a long scar down his cheek, dripping blood to his tunic. Yet he did not strike her. He closed his fist a little tighter around her neck, waited for her to grow calm, and turned her around. 'I taught you better than this, love. Didn't we teach you kindness? You are to be the voice of reason in the house. Like your mother was in ours.'

Bellard ran from the house then, and stayed away for a good few days, hiding at Gallus's home until things settled down. The days seemed to get better after that, even if it was at the threat of Opa Anglard. Two years later, he passed away on a hunting expedition, and despite all the questions Bellard had asked back then, very little information was given to him. For those two blissful years, he had known peace.

A cold tear tickled his cheek, and Bellard quickly wiped it away, realising that this was supposed to happen. Here in this horrible place, where he could see naught but the bitter blackness of night, a ray of sunshine fell on his hand as he closed his fingers around the Pillar. The world opened up to him, birthing a glorious light in ripples of magic from his very being that filled the entire chamber, spreading out faster than he ever thought possible. Nightmarish creatures, dark and disfigured, fled from him in leaps and bounds, their hollow eyes seeking justice for their existence. Words he did not fully understand flooded his mind, images of possibilities and warnings, a deluge of feelings forming around his deepest secrets. A power resonated unto him, glorious and spectacular, seeping into his bosom and feeling terrifyingly good, where it would remain till the day of his final death. For a mage dies not once, but twice. Once in the mortal realm, and a second on the release of the Pillar.

The waves of light flowed back into him, having cleared the figurative scales covering his eyes. The Sacred Hall was not dark anymore. Light shone through from windows high in its angled ceiling, casting beams down all over where a great number of crystals stood on rows of shelves neatly carved into a maze of stacked stones reaching nearly eight feet high, preserved for the next in line to take them up. He stood with his Pillar in hand, a radiant crystal of sparkling dark amethyst the size of his dagger. So many others stood ripe for the taking, yet he didn't collide with them in all the time spent running around and jumping away from the beastly creatures he had seen in his mind.

He reached out to another Pillar, and a whisper crawled into his ear, 'Take me. Use me, and I will give you a power none other can comprehend. A power no one can amount to but you. Yes . . .' The voice snaked into his mind, a sinister thing, caressing the dark side we all harboured deep down. It was right there. He could have it all.

A pulse from the crystal in his hand snapped him out of it, and he jerked his hand back, breathing deep and fast as thoughts of war and power reigned in his mind. Grandàre Shevira's words came to him. '*Be ready and help the others.*' 'Oh no! Mila!' He ran through the maze of crystal-lined walls, jumping to see over the tops, but even he was not tall enough. 'Brethnar!' No answer came.

Round every corner he went, Bellard glimpsed the shadowy creatures following behind, biding their time to strike at the right opportunity, their long-clawed fingers shaking ash to the floor with every move, a sparkle of fiery embers seen underneath their smoky skin. Heart thumping, he ran faster. At least in the dark, he could only imagine them, making them seem like something that might only be that, his imagination. Now he really saw them, and it petrified him.

The walls were growing lower and lower, until he could finally see over them, where in the distance a range of steps ran up to a new level, with an altar of polished red crystal in the centre. Beautiful ornaments of gold and silver lay upon it, sparkling in the beams of the sun. He could not make out what they were, but they were a magnificent sight. *Why aren't they attacking me?* he thought, glimpsing another creature clinging to the top corner of a wall.

The flutter of a robe flashed in the corner of his eyes, and he twisted to it, dashing down the narrowing corridor. 'Valdor! Mila!' Again, the robes waved at the end of a corridor. 'Brethnar! Talk to me!' He raced to the right, following close behind, yet just out of reach. Feet drumming on the floor, he nearly slid into the wall, and turned left, skidding to a stop on his next step. 'Mila! I found you. Why don't you answer me? Mila?'

She did not turn back to him, and he glided by her, seeing the fear in her stretched eyes, her hands trembling, with sickles grasped tight, blood, new and old, covering the blades. He could see the tear streaks down her face as she whimpered with a trembling lip.

'Mila, I'm right here,' he said and stepped closer, seeing cuts on her arm and dark stains seeping through her robes near her shoulder. 'Mila! Are you okay?' Bellard rushed forward, wanting to help her, but she swung her sickles right at that instant, sobbing while cutting and stabbing. He leapt to the side all wide-eyed and crashed into the wall, stabbing himself on the pointy crystals, cutting his chest open. 'Argh! Damn, that hurt! Mila, why'd you do that?' he shouted, but she had walked on, guiding her sickles at her back and front, waiting for something to scrape the blades.

She was moving slowly now, jerking her head left and right, searching for something. *The voices! She can't see! Of course, you idiot.* Dark creatures crowded in from all over, clinging to the walls with their talons digging into the mortar, somehow missing each crystal, like nimble felines. They herded her, and Bellard heard the faint whispers he believed were meant for her, for it was a voice he didn't recognise.

'It has been such a long time, Frosty. Don't you want to get out of this place and visit me?'

'Yes, big brother! Please, get me out of here!' she shrieked, sweeping her white hair out of her face, stained with dried blood.

'No, no, no, no! Don't listen to them, Mila!' Bellard held up his crystal and walked forward into their midst. The creatures spun to him and hissed with their snakelike tongues, baring their fangs and crawling away into the darkness.

'Tarvo! Brother, where did you go?' she shouted, nearing collapse as her legs buckled from fatigue. Bellard wanted to help her, but he feared she would stab at him again.

'This is a dumb idea,' Bellard said to himself. He shuffled a little closer, reaching out carefully and watching her every move. There was a very real chance she might take a swipe at him again. He lay his hand on her shoulder and was about to speak, when the strangest feeling rushed through his body, making him go rigid as it flowed into Mila, calming her. Words formed in his mouth, yet he was not the one speaking. It felt strange and creepy, but Bellard did not fight it. He was a conduit for the Usha seeking to guide her.

He guided her along the corridors, like he himself knew where they were headed, talking to her about past failures and success in a voice he didn't know. They talked of what she wanted to do when she was older, and where she would travel. Of how someone named Raldo was doing, and Bellard realised he knew very little about Mila, and he felt ashamed of it. They entered a large circular room and walked to stand before the wall, and the voice inside him said, 'We are here. Take what is yours.'

She reached out cautiously, licking her lips, while her eyes roamed all over, trying her best to see. Bellard stepped back and watched her grab hold of a green gem, no bigger than a coin. *A perfect size for a pendant,* he thought. A mystical aura flowed around her in waves, like smoke circling a hungry fire, and she took great comfort in it, grinning and laughing deep from her stomach. He wished he could feel what she felt one last time, or that he could tell her to hold on to it. Once it was over, that feeling would not return.

Mila opened her eyes and looked around, jumping at the sight of him, and said, 'Bellard! You're here!' She embraced him happily and held him tight, not wanting to let go.

'Yes, I'm here.'

She pushed him back and slapped him across the face. 'Why didn't you answer me? I was worried sick! Thought it was real funny not saying anything to me, did you?' Mila scoffed and winced, pressing against her shoulder where the dark stain grew, dragging long streaks down her side to her waist.

'No, Mila! It was no game. I was in your position a short while back. It was pitch black all around me and no one answered me. I shouted and shouted, but nothing. Then I heard your voice, but it sounded strange, and something cut my hand. And, and . . .' Bellard watched her pull her robes back to reveal the wound and grew cold at the sight of it. *That looks eerily similar to my dagger's blade.* 'Mila,' he said, reaching out to her shoulder. 'I did this to you . . . I'm so sorry!' He turned away, and she gasped behind him.

'Bellard! Your back! Did I do this to you?' she said, dropping the sickles in a clangour to the ground.

He whirled around, wincing at the stinging pain from the cut. 'It doesn't matter. We have to find Brethnar and Valdor! They are still in danger. Follow me.'

'What's wrong?' she called, following behind him, eyeing the scampering Ormaghs.

'They are forcing us to fight each other.' They ran through the maze, turning left and right, dashing up and down the long passageways, shouting for Brethnar and Valdor. Time rushed by, and their legs grew tired. 'Wait. I hear something,' stated Mila, and she grabbed Bellard's arm to slow him. A faint whisper of sobs and sniffs sounded to their left somewhere.

'Yes, I hear it.' Their tiptoeing made nary a noise as they cautiously skirted the bend of the hallway, keeping well clear of the crystals lining the walls in their sparkling splendour, and Bellard's breath suddenly caught in his throat. He thrust out his arm, trying to keep Mila behind him, but she clawed her way through, pushing in under his arm to witness what had caused the shocked response from him.

Before them lay Brethnar, clutching Valdor's robe, shuddering sobs and sniffing with the unabated bawling, pressing his head against the man's chest where a crimson pool spread from underneath the blue robes. His sword lay off to the side on the floor, the rusty blade coated in blood.

Mila stepped closer, but Bellard couldn't move. He watched her with mounting fear that gripped his throat and heart. 'What happened?' she asked Brethnar with a trembling voice, and the man's head came up slowly, veins bulging on his red forehead as tears streamed down his cheeks. The man gave an involuntary shudder and bawled with renewed vigour. 'What did you do?' Mila pushed, her face glistening with wet, overflowing eyes.

Bellard sagged to the floor. The horror of what he had imagined had been made real. Brethnar reached out his red-stained hand and opened his palm, showing a finger-thick blue crystal to her, and said, 'I followed a voice in terrible darkness, but something attacked me from behind when I drew near.' Brethnar shuddered and slapped himself on the head, stabbing himself with the sharp edges of the crystal, until Mila caught his hand, holding it steady for him to continue, 'There were so many voices in my head, telling me to do this, do that, stab here, to fight! I didn't know what to believe. Something cut my leg, and that's when I stabbed . . .' He closed his eyes again and dropped his head onto Valdor's stiff body. 'I kept screaming your names, but he didn't answer me! Why didn't he answer me?' Mila threw herself at Brethnar, hugging the young man from his back, both of them sobbing uncontrollably. 'I couldn't see a thing until I grabbed my Pillar. But by then, it was too late! You have to believe me! I never wanted this to happen.'

'We know,' said Mila, cradling his head. 'I nearly killed Bellard, and he stabbed me as well. These voices are evil, corrupt things sent to cause us harm.'

'I killed him, Mila . . . I killed my best friend.'

Bellard sat with his hands in his hair, rocking back and forth, cradling his knees in his arms. 'It was not supposed to be this way,' he whispered. 'How could this have happened?'

13. Call the Dead

Jorin burst through the water's surface, spluttering and coughing, wiping his burning eyes. He dragged Jonas out of the water, sloshing waterfalls from his clothing until he reached dry ground, then hauled him further by the arms, scraping deep grooves into the sand and sediment. They dropped to the ground under a pale old tree with paper-thin leaves that barely kept the sun from them, and lay there panting for breath. Jorin eyed his father, hoping this was not all in vain.

Images of that dark beast clutching Jonas in his tremendous claws rampaged through his mind. He had swung the axe as hard as he could, felt it bite, but then the world spun, his body hurting all over. When he came to, his father had been like this, unresponsive and drooling spit. That was two days ago now, and he was only growing worse.

Jorin pulled the stopper from his canteen and shuffled closer to his father, lifting his head slightly and prying open his teeth before dripping water into his mouth. Soft groans and wheezes, sounds of suckling and coughing escaped Jonas as his body accepted the liquid, yet his eyes remained closed.

'Where are you, Vernak? What am I gonna do if you're dead?' Jorin had not the faintest idea of where to go or what to do with his father. Then there was still the problem of getting out of Skalg and travelling all the way to Barren Hollows, and with no coin, it would be a tough ask. No, he would need to gain the favour of some locals, find a job, and work to feed and care for them. And only when he had scraped enough together, then maybe they could venture home. He wondered how old his little one would be by the time he made it back home, if he made it back at all.

He had skill with his hands, doing fine work as a clocksmith, having meticulous patience and finesse to work with the smallest of cogs and springs and pins, placing them in just the right order with precision under the strict guidance of master clocksmith, Taronbhore Rimples. The old clocksmith used to glare at his work from over Jorin's shoulder through those thick glasses, curiously moving his hands and fingers as if he were a master puppeteer pulling on invisible threads to make Jorin do what he needed, mumbling instructions every few heartbeats. Maybe he could do the old clocksmith proud and work for someone here in Skalg. *We will have to wait for the water to recede before crossing that damn bridge again.*

Still thinking of what he might do to make some coin, he heard a call filter through the air. 'Jorin!' He sat up, scanning the flooded area for signs of the old man. 'Jorin!' It came again.

'Vernak! Over here,' he shouted and jumped up to run back into the water, shielding his eyes from the bright light. He had no choice but to leave Jonas on dry ground under the tree while he ran deeper and deeper into the water, searching the side roads for the old man. All around there were houses with damaged walls and debris that had drifted from one location to the next. It did not escape his attention that the houses on this side of the water were much bigger and built with a little more care and quality.

* * *

Vernak stomped through the water, cursing obscenities, when he stumbled over something concealed under the surface and nearly dived headfirst into the water. Arms flailing, he freed his leg just in time and righted himself. He turned back with a fierce gaze, seeking the object of his troubles, then he heard his name called.

'Vernak! Over here!' Jorin came round the corner a few hundred feet down the flooded street, waving his arms and shouting to be noticed.

'Damn fool of a child! Shout it to the world, why don't you? They'll know you're a foreigner if they hear you!' He listened to the calls for aid carried on the morning breeze, the wails of those that had lost much, then sighed.

'Eh? I can't hear you! Come closer.'

Vernak swallowed his words and marched closer, biting his lip and forcing his legs forward through the obstructive water, with a nagging feeling in the back of his mind that he would soon trip over the next bloody thing. A deep anger drove him up the street, his head boiling over with all the thoughts racing through his mind, the problems they would face and the struggles they'd need to endure. Images of a coming conversation with the Primarch played over and over in his head. How he would be imprisoned, at best, or be stripped of his powers and demoted to a Lichen for the sport of it, or altogether decapitated. *I guess it will all come down to the mood of the Primarch.*

Jorin ran up to Vernak, with knees lifting high out of the water, splashing and grinning like a fool, when a hard and bony palm smacked the grin off his face, planting him into the water. He had not expected that welcome. Jorin floundered in the water, struggling to find his footing, and crashed back into the water on his arse, using his hands to stop his fall. 'I said, why don't you call out to the whole of Skalg to announce our presence? Hmm? Maybe call a little more danger to us? You seem so adept at surviving on your own. I'm sure you'll do just fine fending off marauders and murderers.'

'I was just happy you're alive! Ungrateful bastard!'

Vernak found his emotions toying with him while he stared at the boy. Waves of sympathy washed over his red-hot anger, and for a second, he wanted to reach out to Jorin and pull him to his feet, but for some odd reason, his arms didn't move. 'Get up, we have to go,' he mumbled instead. 'Where is Jonas?'

'I left him under a tree over there, down that road.' He pointed to the intersecting street and set off.

This world is affecting me more and faster than I had hoped. I need to be more careful. People passed by them, slogging through the water while they searched for belongings washed from their homes, avoiding the bloated basimets, cats, and dogs, dragging the occasional corpse of a man or a woman from the waters for burial.

Vernak turned down the street, following Jorin at a distance, and tried to think of something to say to the boy, but it was too late for all that, he guessed.

They reached the edge of the water, where deep, churned mud made them slip and slide further up the road. Vernak used his cane for balance, stabbing it into the ground every time his feet shifted under him.

'He was here. What . . . ? Where is he?' he heard Jorin mumble, and Vernak jerked his head to where the boy stood under a tree. 'I dragged him up here.' There were indeed drag marks from the water to the tree, but no man. 'Could he have awakened and wandered off?' asked Jorin, scratching his head.

'No . . .' Vernak drawled the word out. 'Someone took him.' More footprints were stamped into the mud, with little effort applied to conceal their act.

'What?' shouted Jorin. 'Can we not have a day's rest?'

'The tracks lead up the road. I'd wager whoever has him is waiting for us,' he said, following the tracks.

Jorin's eyes grew large, and he stumbled over his words, sprinting to catch up. 'What . . . er, what do you mean, they are waiting for us?'

Vernak pulled the blade from his cane ever so slowly and turned down an alley, where three men rummaged through Jonas's clothes, tugging at them and turning them inside out, looking for items to loot while whispering to each other. One thief already had Jonas's shirt halfway off, and another was pulling at his boots, while the third patted down the pants.

'That man has nothing to offer you!' shouted Vernak, brandishing his blade. 'Let him go, with his clothes, or this might get uglier than it needs to be.'

'Ha,' laughed one man, still pulling on the shirt. 'Would you look at this? And just what are you going to do if we don't? You and your grandson over there, whimpering like the little girl bakghor he is.'

'Hey! I'm not afraid!' cried Jorin in a feeble attempt to sound brave, and the thieves only laughed harder, clutching their stomachs to make it that much more humiliating.

'We will strip him naked, and there's nothing you can do about it,' one said and rose, his grin disappearing.

They seemed like hard-working labourers, well built under their loose raggedy clothes, wearing cream turbans on their heads to blend in with the rest of the people in the streets, their dark skin glistening with sweat. 'Stay behind me!' Vernak warned Jorin and pushed the boy back. They took a step back, and again, as the three approached them.

'What you gonna do? Huh? Bloody old bakghor!' one said, spitting to the ground in disgust. 'What are you doing in our city, anyway? We will teach you not to go where you're not wanted!' He pulled a knife from a sheath and quickened his pace towards them. Jorin got startled and slipped in the mud, sprawling to the ground, dragging on Vernak as he fell.

Vernak yanked loose from the boy's grip and stepped up to meet the bigger man, sword clashing against knife. A fist sailed through his defences, rocking his face backwards, teeth rattling in his mouth, and blood pooled instantly. Lights exploded in his sight, and he saw the brass knuckles flashing around the man's fingers. *No wonder it hurt so much, bastard. Zorieèl will taste your blood today.*

Jorin pleaded behind him, then spluttered a cough of air, and another, taking a beating from another thug. Vernak leapt at the man with the knife. His long blade sliced into the thug's shoulder, and a wail was born, the sizzling smell of burning meat prevalent in the air.

'Enough of this!' called a voice from the rooftop of the building to the right. 'Leave them be or you will deal with me!' Orana made her way down a set of stairs on the outside, taking her time and glaring at the three men. Vernak stood ready with his sword, eyeing the knife-wielding thug who paced a few feet before him in frustration, rambling angrily to himself. The other two still held Jorin, ready to swing another fist at the boy.

'Orana? What are you doing here? This ain't your business! This is a fair haul. They are fair game,' said the one with the knife.

'Let's say I have a vested interest in these three. They are under my protection, so don't make me speak with Malick, understand?'

'You standing up for these pasty bastards is disgusting, Orana!'

'Work is work. Now move along and leave all of that man's belongings. Oh, and your knife,' she said, pointing to the one before Vernak. 'And your coins, I can hear them rattling in your pocket,' she said to the one holding Jorin. 'And just for the sake of it, your scarf. We might need it.'

'Are you mad! We're not giving you anything!' stormed one, looking to the other two for support, but their confidence was fading fast.

'Did you just raise you voice at me?' she asked, and the man fell silent. Orana stepped closer and held out her hand, waiting for them to place the items in her palm, then continued, 'Leave. Before I change my mind.' They shouldered past Vernak and Jorin and stomped down the road, angry looks turning to her.

'What—' Vernak and Jorin said together, and Orana cut them off with a single gesture of her finger.

She waited a while longer, making sure the three wouldn't return, then said, 'Come, let's get out of here, before they get any wiser or bolder. I told you Skalg would eat you up without me. Erechol is not far from here.' This time, Vernak did not argue.

* * *

Waves of heat rippled over the already-drying ground, caking the mud and immortalising footprints, grooves, and the slips and slides dug into them – until the next flood, that is. Skalg was a city of little colour, and here, where the road led them higher and higher, they left a sea of brown buildings behind them, white and yellow sheets used for shading flapping in the corners and crevices of structures.

'Who are you to them?' Orana heard Vernak ask over her shoulder. 'Why did they listen to you?'

'Does it matter? Is it not enough that I helped you? And that I'm still helping you, I might add.' The slog up the road was taking it out of the two, carrying Jonas up the hill slung between them. They sucked air with wheezing lungs and blew ragged breaths, with faces red as tomatoes in the heat.

'It does, yes. I need to know I can rely on you.' Jonas slipped from his hands and dropped to the cobbles, forcing Jorin to the ground while he tried to hold on.

'Vernak! What are you doing?' complained Jorin with a scowl, his head bent low in the awkward position under Jonas's slack arm.

'Stop for a moment, please. I have not the strength of a young man in me.'

Orana paused and glanced around. 'We don't have far to go. I'll carry your load until we get there.' She took Jonas's arm and draped it around her neck, locking in with Jorin on the other side, and said, 'Take my other hand at his back. We will lift him up easier.' She groaned as she straightened. 'No wonder you're tired. He is a heavy bastard! Come on, move it! I don't want to carry him forever. Up the road to the left. You will see the rows of palm trees leading to her villa.' Quick steps and trembling thighs made for difficult walking, but they managed up the hill and sighed with relief at the level ground.

Arms burning and muscles straining, their shoulders were being pulled from their sockets. She glanced over the limp form of Jonas, sitting in his royal fleshy chair, at Jorin, whose face had turned from red to purple, eyes bulging and twitching, while veins angrily throbbed in his temples, mouth pulled into a snarl. Spit dribbled from his chin in long, sticky strings to his clothes, and the worst sounds were coming from his mouth.

Orana dropped Jonas in a fit of laughter, and stood there, hands on her knees with her head low, shoulders shaking and snorting happily. Again, Jorin took the brunt of the drop, having to hold up Jonas as best he could while she wiped her face, not even trying to conceal her laughter.

'Hey! Come on! What gives?' asked Jorin with a frown.

Orana came up straight, hissing laughter through her teeth and clutching her stomach. She attempted to speak and burst out laughing again. Vernak stood confused, looking at Jorin, then at her. 'I'm sorry. Oh, my. But you look like you are about to answer nature's call while we're walking, Jorin.' She laughed again, and Vernak chuckled with her.

'He does have the look of a rather constipated fellow, doesn't he?'

'What? I do not!'

Orana snorted again, covering her mouth with the back of her hand. 'Oooh, stop it. Please. Or I will not make it to Erechol's.' *Laughter is one way to bring people closer – and make them like you. Trust you, even.* She hauled Jonas up again, and they set off, giggling away. They passed a long wall of large brown and grey rocks, nearing a black iron gate of frivolous swirls and twirls welded to the frame.

Vernak stuck his hand through the patterns and lifted the latch, swinging it open for the two carriers to shuffle through sideways, groaning at each other to walk faster or slower, to lift their end higher or to lower him. Great rows of palm trees greeted them, with saplings sprouting in between to narrow the gap. *Soon, those trees would be walls fighting for soil,* she thought.

Ahead, at the end of the road, stood a villa of grey bricks and white mortar, dirtied by the recent floods with an ankle-deep scum line running throughout. Servants were noisily cleaning the walls and floors, running around with brooms and rags, while one man sipped from a small steaming cup, waving his hands and shaking his fingers at the others, giving precise orders that should not be deviated from. Upon their groaning entrance, the man cast his eyes on them, suspiciously looking them up and down, then mocked and proclaimed, 'Orana, what dubious affiliations do you bring to our doorstep today?' Dark rings framed his dark eyes, fading to a sharp, tan face with long, whipping, black hair and an inch-thick black beard, combed neatly and oiled with perfumes.

'Maliketh, looking deathlier than ever. Is the lady of the house appropriate to receive guests?'

'Do you really expect me to allow this rabble into our home?' he asked, raising his thick, black brows. 'Erechol is not the only one who lives here. She is not master of this house.'

'And I don't have to be master of the house to receive guests, darling. So do not keep my dear Orana and her . . . . associates waiting.

Can't you see they bring interesting problems to our door?' said a woman with a thick bush of black hair, held at bay with a red leather band, her silvery eyes glittering red, blue, and purple with pixie dust and dark eyeshadow. Her supple purple lips glistened with oils where she stood in the window framed with dark wood. 'Come in, dear,' she continued, never taking her gaze off Maliketh, who casually sipped from his cup, their eyes locked in a contest of wills.

One servant decidedly made the mistake of slipping in the mud not yet dried under the shade of the trees, nearly crashing into the man, and collapsed right in front of him, pleading his forgiveness.

'Are you an imbecile?' Maliketh cried in a higher pitch. 'Chop, chop, get back to it!' Orana and the rest slipped into the home during this distraction, hoping to spare them of more debate.

Slathered in riches, the home felt more like a piece of art than a place to live. On the white walls hung items, from highly decorative weapons polished to perfection and shields that had never felt the burden of an axe swung at it, to pieces that had seen actual combat, their blades nicked and scratched. Some were rusted with years of neglect, while shields bore great cut marks where splinters of wood were missing, old dark stains soaked into the leather straps. Stands of armour welcomed them down the length of the corridor, where they shuffled ever closer to the back room through an arched doorway. Various flowers were arranged in pots at every corner.

'Seems the alchemy business is booming,' ventured Vernak, sweating under the load of Jonas, having taken over from Jorin to give the lad a break.

'Oh, these two dabble in more than just alchemy, though no one risks saying what exactly. They come and go as they please and are never bothered by the ungracious thieves that have settled in Skalg.'

'You are a thief, though, aren't you? That's why those three left us alone. They knew you,' said Jorin, squinting at her.

'I said, *ungracious* thieves . . . and learn some manners when a woman is talking.'

'A thief?' Vernak asked, surprised. Deep lines creased his forehead.

'A thief . . .'

'Hey, don't go getting on your high horse. We all need to make a living. Besides, you know nothing of me.'

'Oh, no. On the contrary, my dear.' Vernak paused in their shuffle. 'I believe we will need your services after all.'

Orana turned her head and thought, *That was easier than I thought it would be.*

They entered a room filled with smoking vials hanging over burners, a distinct metallic taste in the air that smelled like old eggs or unwashed feet. Orana wasn't sure which, but all the same, it stank profusely.

'Put him down here,' said Erechol, pointing to a cleared section of the long table. She looked just as stunning as through the window, except she now wore a dark-glassed pair of goggles that tucked her hair in at the back. 'What is the matter with him?' she asked, removing the goggles.

Jorin helped Vernak lift his father onto the table, and Orana struggled on. There was nothing worse than working with an unconscious person. Their limp bodies rolled and flopped all over, never wanting to go where you intended them, and just when you thought you had them, another part would drop away. Exactly like what happened with Jonas while they had him propped up on the table, moving his arms and legs into place, only for his upper body to flop to the side. It happened fast. There was no time to react, other than for Orana to press her face against Jonas's scraggly beard, smelling the stink from his unwashed skin, trying her best not to drop him. Muscles trembling, she thought about letting go, to just let him slip and play it off that she was but a girl who could not manage the weight of a man as big as Jonas. *Head cracked open against the sharp edge of the table, red mist spraying, body convulsing . . . I would not be popular at all then.* But she did not want to put their newfound relationship in jeopardy. She pushed him up with a groan and dunked him on the table with a thud, bouncing his head on the wooden top, and saw Jorin squirm at the sight of it. *Oops.*

'Before I answer that,' said Vernak, 'I take it that the lucrative aspect of your business is dabbling in necromancy?' It was a dark art that was frowned upon and, in some places, completely illegal. An art that could see your head rolling from the guillotine and into a bucket to be dumped in the moat and carried away by the floodwater. Erechol shot Orana a look of disapproval, and Vernak continued quickly, 'Please, do not blame her. I rather hoped this would be the case. It would make this so much easier if you knew what is needed.'

'Did you know about this?' Erechol asked Orana, storming up to her and forcing her back against the wall, rocking vials and beakers filled with liquids of various colours on the shelves, sending a few to the floor in a shattering hail of glass and strange substances. Jorin stood with mouth agape, not knowing what to do or say.

'Is everything all right in there?' they heard Maliketh call from outside.

Orana shook her head profusely, apologising as she pushed up against the wall. 'No, I swear it. I'm sorry, Erechol. You know I would never betray you.'

'Erechol?' Maliketh's voice filtered through the shutters again. Orana stared unblinking into those silvery eyes flicking left and right and held her breath.

'Please, Erechol. She said nothing.' Vernak approached slowly, hands raised slightly. 'I figured it out by the way you dressed your home and the smell in the air. There're two things that make that smell. Nightshade and leaves of the alibus, both ingredients needed for necromancy. We mean you no harm at all. I promise. We need your help.'

Erechol turned to them and called out, 'All is fine, my love. No need to worry. The clumsy boy knocked over a beaker, is all.' She backed away from Orana, giving her room to breathe, and a flash of steel glinted in her eye.

Orana sucked in air, seeing Erechol sheathe a blade in between the many folds of clothing, next to an assortment of small leather pouches and straps she wore. A thin silver chain jiggled in the sunlight cast from the window, and Orana noticed a thick leather-bound book strapped around her shoulder, with a silver latch keeping it closed. The woman was a walking, talking alchemist's workshop.

'Is he dead?' Erechol asked and poked Jonas in the ribs with her middle finger. Once, twice, and he moved slightly. 'Not dead then.'

'No, he is not dead. But he is rather soulless,' said Vernak, and cleared his throat with a shy glance at Orana.

'Soulless? How? You said he lost his fighting spirit!' stormed Orana, wanting to hurl a beaker over the table at his head.

'No, I said he lost his spirit. You assumed the fighting part.'

Erechol leaned closer to Jonas and whispered, 'Interesting. Never worked with a soulless before. I'm intrigued. I gather you know what is needed for this?'

'Yes,' said Vernak. 'There are a few ingredients we will have to prepare. It should not take long.'

'First, I need to know who is going to pay me?' They all turned to Orana, waiting for her to answer.

'What? No! No! Absolutely not! What would you have done if I weren't here? No!'

* * *

'Thank you. I don't know how I can repay you for all you've done.'

Orana tore the black skin from a large fruit where she waited under a tree in the yard, and spat it to the ground before sinking her teeth into the white flesh. Milky juices ran down her face, and she bellowed a mighty burp, giggling to herself. 'Yeah, don't sweat it, kid.' She rose and took another bite into the fruit, then said, 'You tell Vernak I will get all the gear and horses we require for the journey. Does he know how long this will take?'

'He said you might ask and that I should tell you we should be able to leave before the sun rises in two days.' Jorin eyed her with a lustful gaze.

'Good, I'll bring everything here.' Orana raised one brow and squinted at him. 'Why are you looking at me like that?'

Shaking his head, Jorin blinked and said, 'Oh, er . . . What is that fruit? It looks delicious.'

'Oh, it is. Grab one from the tree over there. It's called the calluwangoo. Beware, though, it makes you gassy.' Orana turned and left the villa, heading down the street and back to the city.

14. Unbridled Sorrow

The gigantic door to the Sacred Hall swung open with a loud groan, and Bellard walked out with his back to the waiting crowd of students and teachers. Everyone burst into cheers, dashing closer and throwing hats to the sky, celebrating the completed claiming. Then, the body of Valdor appeared, Bellard's hands hooked under his armpits, hands dragging in the grass, and Brethnar carrying the dangling legs at the back. Mila stumbled from the door, dishevelled, dirty, and her face streaked with tears.

The doors closed with an awful shudder, and she collapsed to the ground on her knees, unable to carry on. Students and teachers alike all froze in their spots, their smiles fading, and the mood turning sour.

'Help! Help us!' Bellard shouted over the sea of silence and stumbled backwards, his knees buckling under him as he went down, crumpling to the grass, with Valdor sprawled over him. Brethnar also sagged to the grass and raised a trembling hand, sobbing terribly, and yanked out the knife sheathed round Valdor's waist. He roared a heart-shattering wail and turned the blade on himself. Eyes closed, he cried to the heavens and stabbed the blade to his heart . . .

'No!' shouted Bellard, but he had not the strength to stop him, nor did Mila. A glare from the blade blinded him, and a crash and gurgle sounded. He did not want to look. He did not want to see another friend dead on the ground. He did not want to open his eyes.

A flurry of voices and shouts and people running towards them took over. Through the cacophony of sounds, he heard Brethnar crying and opened his eyes. Someone had tackled him to the ground, knocking the blade from his hands, and pinned him to the ground.

'Out of the way! Move! Out of the way, I said!' bellowed a stern voice, and from the gawking crowd of students, Grandàre Agoras pushed through, followed by Grandàre Shevira. They stared with slack mouths until Agoras continued, 'Good God. Get them to the infirmary immediately!'

'You piece of shit! This is all your fault!' shouted Brethnar from under a student, head propped up from the grass, his face in an angry scowl. 'Get off me!'

Grandàre Shevira pushed past and knelt by Valdor's body, looking for any sign of life, with mouth agape and eyes glistening wet. She turned to Agoras and shook her head sullenly.

Air hissed through Bellard's teeth, racing for victory against an invisible foe. He could not speak, nor did he want to. The flurry of activity around them seemed surreal, a great fuss made over them, and nothing made sense to him anymore. A gentle power drifted from Agoras, and his eyes became heavy. He was so tired, and it seemed so were Brethnar and Mila. He tried to stay awake, but it was a fight he could not win.

* * *

The infirmary smelled of honey and mint, waking Bellard to a growling stomach. A vacant, gloomy room came into focus and he worked his mouth and tongue, feeling it stick to his palate with no spit to ease his throat. He licked his teeth and swallowed the dryness, slogging saliva back into his mouth, constantly having to cough from the irritation in his throat. 'Mil—' It didn't help him when he tried to speak either, his voice coming out raspy and scarce.

His aching back burned with a stinging sensation when he pushed up on the bed, crawling backwards to sit against the wall, and flinched when it touched him. They had wrapped his hand in bandages, a piece of black thread sticking out at the bottom. *Stitches, then.* He reached back over his head with his other hand and worked his fingers down over more bandages wrapped around his chest. Two subtle ridges ran along the length of his back, intersected with tightly pulled thread, but he couldn't reach the end.

A woman walked by the door and glanced in, stopping in her quick stride to turn to him, and entered the room. Plastered on her face was a fake loving smile, forced to her lips to make him feel better about the situation. Her eyes told the truth, though. She might as well have been shouting it from the rooftops. How poor Bellard, Mila, and Brethnar would never be the same. They had been pummelled into the ground, destroyed from their very core, and if they were strong enough to rise, whatever they became would be something new.

Her short-cropped brown hair hid a small pink scar on the right of her forehead, which Bellard could not avoid staring at, and she quickly brushed the hair with her fingers to conceal it. 'How are you feeling?' she asked as she sat on the bed next to him.

How do you answer a question like that? I'm fine . . . Yeah, nothing to worry about over here. I just carried my dead friend for who knows how long through that bloody hall, looking into the eyes of another friend who I know killed him. I've stabbed Mila, and she could have easily died if it had been any lower. Not to mention they also tried to kill me, failing only because I was lucky, leaving me scarred and injured inside and out. Oh, yeah, I'm just great! Thank you for asking. 'I'll live,' he answered instead.

He shied away, wishing he had just blurted it all out, but he silently packed it all away into a neat little box and sealed the lid, hiding it deep inside. What could she have said that would make it any better? What great insight would she possibly have that could assuage the anguish he felt?

She smiled a little broader and reached for his face, then pulled away and rose. 'You have a deep cut on your back, but it is not dangerous other than for the risk of infection. Keep the wound clean and come in often during the next few weeks for us to change the bandages. Got it?' He nodded, and she continued, 'The cut on your hand missed all vital arteries, but the middle finger's functionality may be hampered. Our physician has stitched the nerves back together, but you will have to take it easy. He has left an exercise regime on the counter for you to follow. Adhere to it or you will lose that finger's use. Got it?' He nodded again.

'Where's Mila and Brethnar? What have you done with Valdor?' His eye began twitching, making him blink incessantly until he rubbed it with his bandaged hand.

She had not prepared for the question and fumbled over her words. 'I, uh, er . . . They took him to be cleaned and . . .'

'And what?' he asked, harsher than he wanted, and she flinched at his anger.

'. . . examined for the cause of his death.'

We know the cause of death. A rusted sword pushed through his gut, yanked out, tearing every organ it came in contact with. 'Where are my friends?' he asked again, this time in a barely audible whisper.

'Mila is with Brethnar, two rooms down. Their wounds are not as bad.'

'What about the stab wound below her shoulder?' He could not look up at her.

'She was lucky. There was minimal bleeding, and it didn't penetrate too deeply. She will recover well, with a faint scar maybe.'

Bellard leaned forward, groaning as he reached for the edge of the bed to pull himself near, swinging his legs to the side, when the nurse rushed forward, hands waving at him to stop.

'No, no, no! Where do you think you're going?'

'To my friends. They need me. And I need them.'

'You, mister, will get back in bed! All your belongings are over there, including your Pillar. I will call for them. You are in no condition to walk around.'

He lowered himself with some careful negotiations with the pillow and sheets, breathing a sigh of relief when his head settled on the soft feathers. He closed his eyes, instantly snoring again.

* * *

'Bellard? You awake?' he heard coming from the door, but he didn't open his eyes. It was Mila's voice, gentler than her usual self.

'I told you he wouldn't want to see me. And I don't blame him,'

137

came Brethnar's voice. 'This was a stupid idea, Mila. I'm going to leave. Tell him I'm sorry.'

Wait, Brethnar! Bellard wanted to call out, but he didn't. The door slammed shut, and he jumped, shaking the sheets with the startle.

'I know you're awake. You don't have to pretend anymore. Brethnar isn't here.'

Bellard turned with a groan and scratched his chest, wanting to get to the burning ache deep inside. Pain was a funny thing. You could stub your toe and feel it in your groin, or cut your arm and feel it in your shoulder. He guessed that this was no different. The cut on his back was hurting everywhere except on his back, where it itched.

'You could have said something, you know. He hurts as well. This is not easy for any of us. And you have no right to be angry.' She scowled at him, her eyes already wet again. She had her arm in a sling and a bandage wrapped around her shoulder, revealing a flowery arrangement of tattoos on her chest and arms. He had never seen them before now and was fascinated by the discovery. He could not look away from her heaving chest, veiled only by a thin green gown covering the rest of the ink on her skin. 'Did you hear me?'

'Yes.' He shook his head. 'You're right. I have no right to be angry at him, and I'm not. But that could have been you, Mila. I could have been the one to have killed you, and I damn sure nearly did.' He glanced at her bandaged shoulder and turned away. 'It's not about him. It's about how close I got to being him. Don't you see?'

'Yes, of course I see, and it's okay. That could have been me as well. We cannot blame ourselves for what happened in there.'

Bellard sighed and shook his head, wanting to believe it, yet deep down he knew he would always feel the guilt of that night. 'I don't know if I can forgive myself. But Brethnar shouldn't have to suffer because of me. I will speak to him.' He closed his eyes and felt her soft hands on his shoulder and nearly wept, biting his lip to stave off his tears.

'When, uh . . . when is the procession?' he asked, laying his hand on hers, and she stepped closer with shuddering cries. They embraced and cried for their friend, holding each other in this time of need.

'*Ahem.*'

Their heads came up, and Mila stepped aside. 'Grandàre Shevira.' Bellard did not greet her.

She slowly stepped closer, nervously digging her nails into her palms, and glanced between them. 'I'm so sorry for what happened, children. This claiming should never have been allowed.'

'We should never have had those weapons,' mumbled Bellard, wiping his face with the back of his hand.

'I had no idea . . . I only meant to protect you. When I did my claiming, it was in the day, and I was alone. It was so easy for me, I could not understand what all the fuss was about. There were voices, and they tried to steer me in endless loops, but I never thought in a hundred years that they would do this. That they would guide you to one another and, well, you know.'

'Yes, we know very well,' said Bellard. 'If you don't mind, Grandàre, I have to rest.'

A brief smile of sorrow and worry flickered over her face. 'Of course. I merely wanted to inform you that the procession will be tomorrow. So you might attend if you so wished.'

Mila glanced away, her eyes wet all over again, cheeks streaked with tears, and Bellard shied away, then said, 'Thank you, Grandàre. We will be there. Have his parents been told of what happened?'

She nodded subtly. 'They have been told that Valdor lost his life during his claiming. Nothing more. The council decided that to tell them all the details would unnecessarily sully the school's name.'

'Typical. As long as the school doesn't get a bad reputation . . . Is that why you're really here? To ensure we say nothing?' Bellard crawled closer on the bed, and snorted mocking laughter. 'Our friend's body is not even in the ground, and you already seek to buy our silence! And just what do we get, eh? Maybe some poison with our porridge in the morning?'

'Bellard! Enough!' shouted Mila, shocked at his outburst, and silencing his rage. 'I'm so sorry, Grandàre. We are still struggling with all that occurred.'

Shevira stretched her already enormous eyes even wider, making them look like they were about to pop from her head, and said, 'Quite all right, dear. I expected a little hostility. But I assure you both, we are not buying your silence. In fact, I have launched a formal inquisition into Grandàre Agoras for his role in this. But keep that to yourselves for now.'

Bellard looked at Mila, then said, 'Apologies for my outburst, Grandàre. We will keep quiet.'

15. Ambition

The blade lay on his finger, perfectly balanced just beyond the bronze cross guard, its dark, twisted, wooden hilt waiting to be grabbed, the polished blade yearning to be swung. To drink the blood of its enemies. A deadly and impressive weapon in the hands of a capable warrior.

But Calmantis was not a capable warrior.

It slipped from his finger, and he grabbed at it like a fool, missing it completely with his clumsy digits. It clattered to the ground with a tremendous clangour, chipping and cracking the corners of the intersecting red-and-white tiles. He kicked at the blade to stop it from making more noise, and sent it flying, cutting through his leather moccasin, nearly dismembering his big toe, and causing more of a ruckus when the blade hit the floor again a good ten feet away. The sharp reverberating clangour and screech echoed in his ears as he cringed and winced with every bounce, blade trembling and reflecting the sunlight cast through from the fluttering white curtains of the red-and-white training room.

'Ah, you have truly mastered the art of invisibility, I see.'

'What?' Calmantis drew in a sharp breath and spun to see Clairvoy Yeron strolling closer with his hands behind his back. A sudden loose bowel movement raced through his intestines, turning his stomach into knots. He tensed his muscles and clasped his sphincter shut, fearing that he might expel some distasteful excrement from his trousers. 'Er . . . Clairvoy! I didn't expect anyone to be here today.'

'And why is that?' asked Yeron, tilting his round face and scrunching up his virtually non-existent brows.

'Well, er . . . uh . . . With the World Storm and all the damage caused, I thought everyone would be too busy. You know, with fixing things.'

'So you sneaked away to play with some swords?'

'Exactly! I mean, no. Of course not. Not like that. It's just . . . well, me and . . . with them . . . You understand, don't you?' explained Calmantis, gesturing left and right, up and down, never getting his point across. He waited for the silent, staring clairvoy to answer, finding the floor extremely fascinating to look at.

'I think I do,' began the clairvoy.

'You do?' Calmantis jerked up with a creased forehead, pulling his mouth up on one side.

'You sound surprised,' Yeron stated with a chuckle. 'I'm under no illusions that you aren't a pathetic excuse for a human—'

'Hey!' stormed Calmantis, his filthy, ragged head of hair shaking a shimmer of dust to his shoulders.

'—but . . .'

'Oh, there's a but? Of course, there's a but,' he mumbled in a whisper, eyes slinking back to the floor. '*Ahem*. Please, continue.'

'*But*,' Yeron spat the word out in such a manner as not to be questioned again, 'we were all pathetic at some point. No matter your lineage or your wealth. Before Aztar, we are all pathetic little beings, trying to find some meagre purpose in this world, a certain belonging. Yet only he can truly give you your reason for living. And until our Lord, God Aztar, God of Life, the true father, has given you your purpose, we are all but grasping at straw in the wind.'

'So, you think there is hope for me yet?' Calmantis's face lit up.

'I do not judge. I merely prepare.' Yeron sauntered past him and kicked the blade up, grabbing it perfectly round the hilt. He turned the weapon, feeling the weight, and ran his hand down the length of the polished steel. 'Why did you choose this sword and not one of the other hundreds lined on the racks?'

Calmantis glanced towards the weapons racks lining the side of the training room. Great big stands, with various weapons, ranging from long bows to horse bows, swords great and small, spears with dark metal to polished, glistening steel. From hammers to axes, throwing knives to great daggers sharp as scalpels, scythes to other instruments with long curved blades running out in three directions from its centre. All looked serious and deadly. The blade in Yeron's hands was straight and long, double-edged, with a considerable weight to it. 'It looked nice . . .'

Yeron chuckled and shook his head. 'One does not select a weapon because it looks nice. And I promise you, the first time you swing it against another man, even the most beautiful blade will make your stomach churn. No, you choose them for their ability to kill, nothing more. This one, you have chosen wisely, though it was chosen in error. The blade of Argolis, an outstanding knight and brother of the Shadow Guard.'

'Wait. Where have I heard that name before?'

Yeron made sharp, diagonal cuts through the air, the blade singing with each pass. 'He died a long time ago in service to our Lord. He was a good man.'

'You talk as if you knew him personally.'

'I did. I'm a clairvoy. Aztar granted me the gift of a long life. For two hundred and thirty years I have roamed these lands, doing his bidding,' Yeron said and exhaled loudly.

'That sounds remarkable! Yet how is it you seem so sad about it?'

'Nothing is given freely, Cal. The sooner you learn that, the better.'

Calmantis followed the clairvoy to the centre of the room, gazing at the wooden and straw mannequins used for sparring, marred by great cuts and stabs, with large chunks of wood missing from their bodies, straw limbs lying on the floor next to them. He wanted to press on and ask what the clairvoy meant, except when he finally got the courage to talk, Yeron shoved the blade back into his hands, hilt first, and he nearly dropped the weapon again.

'Why do you want to become a Shadow Guard? What drives you so? You must see that you are not at a physical level as compared to many others,' Yeron asked, showing no signs of mockery. It sounded like a genuine question born of curiosity.

The wooden hilt in his hands never felt rougher or heavier than it did right then. Calmantis worked the dents in the wood with his thumbnail, pressing a splinter back into the old handle. 'You'd think me mad.'

'Just the same. That might be an even better reason for me to know.'

Calmantis shook his head, screwing up his face, and exhaled a deep lungful of air. 'When I was young, I used to be a handful—'

'When you were young, you say?' Yeron interrupted with a slight chuckle. 'From what I've heard, you are handful still. Please continue.'

Calmantis stared at the clairvoy for a while, considering his options, then said, 'Back then, my mother and father were important. Too important to keep watch over me the entire day, so they employed someone to fill their shoes.'

'You come from a wealthy family?'

'I told you, you would think me mad . . .' Yeron gestured with his hands apologetically, and Calmantis continued, 'Nobility might be in blood, but I damn well don't feel it. Never have. They wanted a puppet, someone they could groom for the family businesses.'

'What were the family businesses?'

'The Pale Horse, and Globe 'n Spice. Mother ran the transportation side, making The Pale Horse one of the biggest couriers and transportation businesses around. Father focused on the spice. I think that was his true love, more so than my mother, and definitely me.' He gazed at Yeron, searching for signs of mockery. There was none he could pick up on. The man still stood with his hands clasped atop each other before him.

'One morning, I was a particular handful, running circles around my caretaker, jumping on the furniture and evading capture. I was having fun. Though that fun suddenly ended. We were on the third floor, near the stairs, and I ran to grab the railing, knowing not that father had commissioned men to replace it.

'It snapped from the floor and dragged me over the edge. I remember the urgency in the caretaker's voice as she screamed for me, the horror on her face as she realised there was nothing she could do but watch. Walls raced by in grey and white, with occasional flashes of the red carpet. It felt like I was falling forever. For some reason, I sucked in all the air that I could and held my breath, as if I were about to fall into a pool of water. Still don't know why I did that. But then something happened.

'Then I hit what I thought was the ground with my back and head, and my little mind could see how every bone in my body shattered. But suddenly, I had to fight to breathe as water rushed over my face, my entire body, sucking me down. I kicked and swam, kicked and swam, until I breached the surface of a large pond. Enormous trees lined the sides, with beautiful walkways of silver and white. I did not know where I was or how I got there. That was not the strangest thing, though.'

Calmantis stared at Yeron, seeing the struggle to believe his words reflected on the man's face, yet he continued, 'People crowded a great dais at the end of the pond where someone spoke flamboyantly, passionately. With my interruption to their proceedings, he pointed to me in the pond and called out loud. I heard his booming voice in my head and in my ears, a roar of authority. They were gods, I swear it. I could feel it deep inside me. As one, everyone turned around and ran to me, but I was so tired, my legs could not keep kicking. Before they could reach me, the water took me again, and so did the darkness. When I came to, I was lying on the floor of our house, the bent railing next to me, water spilling from my lungs. The caretaker stood over me, rubbing my chest and sobbing. I thought I would die surely, but there I lay, with not even a scratch on me.'

'Huh. This is a lot to take in. What did this supposed god say to you?'

Calmantis glanced around and whispered, 'Intruder . . .'

'Very interesting. I will have to think about what you said, but for now, we are here to train.'

'So, you believe me? You don't think I'm crazy?'

Yeron stepped back a few feet. 'It remains to be seen, young Cal. I believe that you believe it to be true, and that's what matters right now. Let's begin. Try to cut me. The one who draws first blood wins.'

'But you have no weapon. I don't want to be the one that killed the 230-year-old clairvoy.'

'Odds of winning are in your favour then. Don't waste it.'

Feet planted wide, legs splayed out like a frog about to leap, he had both hands on the weapon, directing the steel, with curled tongue sticking from his mouth, and he lunged at the clairvoy, steel stabbing forward. He ground his teeth, feeling the weight of the sword drive his arms down. Yeron slapped the blade away with ease, spinning past and flicking his ear. 'Ow!' he shouted, and whirled around, arse sticking out like a proud baboon, arms stretched forward and sword dipping to the ground. Neck bent as far as it could go, he pressed his burning ear to his shoulder, working the pain from it.

Yeron stood a few feet away, calm and relaxed, hands resting on top of each other. 'You have poor form, and it seems you need to run to the bushes to relieve yourself. When did you last have a proper bowel movement? Relax. Let the blade flow with your momentum. Do not fight it. Guide it.'

Calmantis swung the sword in an arc and stepped in to meet Yeron, planting his big feet firmly on the ground. It seemed his body was reluctant to close the gap, where he swung the blade wildly before him, reaching with the tip for the clairvoy. The tendons around his neck were taut and stretched. His back and shoulders felt like they might pull apart from each other. One eye closed, he glanced with the other between swings, glimpsing only fluttering robes, before a solid fist thumped into his face.

The blade clattered to the floor, and Calmantis dropped on his backside, eyes leaking tears and nose streaming red. 'Argh! Ow!' he rolled over to his knees and blew sprays of red to the floor, making slight sounds of pain while caressing his nose with thumb and finger. 'You win! You win! I give up!'

'I think that might be a record. It's not broken, you'll be fine.'

'Easy for you to say. You didn't get a fist to the face.'

The tapping of footsteps reverberated through the vast training room, and Ackelides appeared, striding through the doorway towards them with a grace of movement, armour chinking and chafing. He carried his dented helm under his arm, the narrow T slit for his eyes, nose, and mouth accompanied by black crosses on the cheek flaps.

'Clairvoy Yeron,' he said with his approach, and bowed low, waiting for Yeron to acknowledge him. The man's golden hair shifted from his armour to cover his face, concealing his dark brows and blue eyes.

'Rise, Sir Ackelides. I have told you before. You need not bother with bowing to me. When I was younger, the idea of people bowing before me was exciting. It gives one a sense of power, but after a while, it gets pretty annoying. Look at our friend here. He isn't bowing to me.'

Calmantis was not even aware he needed to bow to the clairvoy and was now not sure if that remark was to enlighten him or humiliate him. He felt he had to do something, bow maybe, but how could he after the fact? Say something, but what? Apologise maybe? 'Yes, I, uh, er . . . There is my knee and all. Old injury and such. Didn't want to injure it further.' He chuckled nervously and saw the sneering glare from Ackelides. Calmantis quickly turned his chuckle into a clearing of the throat and glanced away to the high roof, following a big fat rat charging across the rafters, thick tail whipping with the jumps to the other beams. 'Bloody rat!'

'What did you call me?' stormed Ackelides, and gripped Calmantis by the collar of his shirt, metal fingers digging into his chest, his feet dragged from the ground.

'Nothing! I swear! I was talking about the rat in the roof! Up there!' he pointed to the skittering rodent. Its baleful arse dragged over the wood, depositing pellets of poop as he ran, squeaking and sniffing, whiskers wagging, tiny eyes glinting.

Ackelides dropped him and brushed the stretched and pulled shirt with his gloved hands, forcing a smile to his otherwise sneering face. 'Bloody rats, yes. We should get rid of the vermin. Will you see to it, Cal?'

It didn't sound like a request to him, more like a threat. He stared into the man's unblinking eyes and muttered, 'I will see to it.'

'Did you have a message for me, Ackelides?' asked Yeron, waiting patiently with hands behind his back.

'Yes. Apologies, Clairvoy Yeron. We got sidetracked by the rat. Lord

Latimus needs to see you in his chambers immediately.'

Yeron stepped away with a slight bow and walked from the hall, his bare feet not making any sound on the tiled floor. Calmantis fell in behind him, not wanting to be left alone with Ackelides.

An armoured arm shot out in front of him and pressed against his chest, halting him instantly, when he heard Ackelides's voice so close to his ear, 'I left a big, fat, steaming pile o' shit for you to clean up. Better get to it, the boys have been working overtime to keep you employed.' The man shoved him back, nearly planting him on his arse, and strode from the room.

* * *

'Stupid! Pompous! Arrogant! Arse! I'll show them! I'll show them all that I am worthy.' Calmantis stomped down the stairs, bony fists swinging by his sides. *Working overtime to keep me employed . . . Idiots don't realise we can't clear out the cesspits until the water has receded completely. They'll be walking in their filth for another week!* He stepped into the murky water and waded over the lawn, his moccasins getting stretched and ruined, nearing the point of coming undone. He curled his toes to hold on to them, clasping the leather tight and slowing his movements, working his legs forward with the grace of a sloth. Water still ran ankle-deep in most places, slowly receding from the temple grounds, where workers swept streams into the streets, churning up mud and clay.

Calmantis took a deep breath, shook his head, and chuckled. He dipped his hand into the water and washed his face, rubbing the now dried and crusty blood that had flowed over his mouth. There were better things to be than angry. Here he was, living at the temple and being trained by a clairvoy. Who else could say that? It felt like a silly thing to hold on to the negativity. What use could it possibly have to stay angry and rework the words over and over in your head, seeing them laugh at you in your mind, putting words in their mouths, their contorted faces hurling insult after insult, laughing at your misfortune?

He stopped to give his shoes a break, took another deep breath with eyes closed, and smiled, forcing the images from his mind. Something bumped into his calf, and he opened his eyes.

A thick turd rode his leg, wobbling back and forth in the choppy waters, embracing the freedom it had been given. The anger returned tenfold, and he kicked it away with a splash and a scream, swinging his fists. It sailed away to plop back into the water, slowly making its way back to him, just like the hurled insults he had received his entire life, always coming back for more.

He pushed through the water to the lawns of the Lord's Hall, its own moat filled with water. Trickles of run-off from the grass on the other side sparkled in the eyes of the sun, running over the edge as small waterfalls into the still water of the old moat. Wherever he looked, the wet grass shimmered back at him, a faint smell of petrichor in the air. He had always liked the smell of wet earth, but ever since his work started as a gongfermour, it had mostly eluded him. *It must be strong if I can smell it . . . I've forgotten how wonderful a scent it is. Or even that there are other scents besides that of human waste.* Guards stood at the front of the bridge, spears in their hands, shiny steel tips raised to the white puffs hovering above, coming and going with the push and pull of the wind.

'Hold on, Cal. Where do you think you're going?' asked one guard, hand raised to stop him before the gate.

'I need to go see the levels of the pits, or do you want *them* to walk around in the floating turds like us?'

'Whoa! What's with the hostility, Cal? I know some of the boys have been giving you grief, but that's just a bit of hazing. You can't take it personally.'

Teeth grinding over one another, jaw muscles bouncing, Calmantis's eyes shifted between them. 'Hazing? Do you call putting scorpions in my bed hazing? I have not been able to sleep for days, Tannis.'

The guards chuckled, glanced at one another, and Tannis said, 'They weren't venomous, Cal. Just a bit of harmless fun.'

Harmless fun, eh? 'Can I go now? I have plenty of chores to get done.'

The guard shook his head, doleful, pulling his mouth to one side, and said, 'Yeah, sure. Go on.'

* * *

Ever since this morning after the bath, his head had itched terribly. Tiny white flakes drifted to his shoulders and lodged under his nails whenever he scratched at his scalp. It was getting rather annoying having to contend with the irrational itching, especially with all the cleaners and other household staff leering at him. *How is it that the lowliest of servants in a rich abode have the audacity to sneer and judge those that enter the dwelling? I mean, it is not their wealth. They have no right to be uptight pricks.* With his late-night work, there had never really been a reason for him to walk around the corridors of the Lord's Hall. And he really had no need to do so now.

'Can we help you?' asked a woman with scornful contempt, her white apron perfectly aligned with the fold of her black dress, hiding her full bosom. She peered at him, with pale blue eyes darting up and down from under a white bonnet, a few strands of red-brown hair curling out at her temples and forehead. There was not an inkling of a smile on her thin-lipped face, nor that there had ever been one. *She must be the life of the party . . .*

Calmantis plied himself to his skill and smiled his warmest smile, standing up straight with his heels clicked together. 'Yes, yes, of course. Or rather, I hope you can. And please forgive my poor appearance here today. It seems the World Storm has destroyed all my clothing. You see, I'm a dear friend of Lord Latimus, wonderful man that he is. We were to meet tomorrow for brunch, but with all the damage caused by the storm, I daresay he will not have time for poor me.'

Confused, the woman let down her guard a little, mouth opening and closing, but no sounds came out. He waited a while for her to work through the thoughts in her head, then spoke before she could get a clear grasp on the matter. 'It's okay, my dear. I arrived rather unexpectedly, you see. Will you be a lamb and point me to his quarters? I shall wait for him there.' He started walking down the corridor as if he owned the place, taking big strides with authority, forcing her to keep up with him.

'Sir! Sorry, sir! You cannot just walk around here. There is protocol to the matter of attendance!'

'I'm sure there is. He will understand, I assure you.' He kept walking.

'Please, sir?' came her voice, higher than it had been only moments before.

Calmantis stopped and dropped his head, annoyed, and breathed a loud breath. 'What is your name, ma'am?'

She stopped in her tracks and stared at him with the eyes of a cornered deer. 'Melissa, sir. Please, I'm just doing my duty, sir.'

He gripped her by the arms, gently squeezing her, a sweet smile plastered on his face. 'All is well, dear. Just point me to his quarters and nothing further has to come of this unfortunate misunderstanding. You go your way, I'll go mine, eh?'

Palms cupped over her mouth, she looked around for support, but there was none in the gigantic construction that was the Lord's Hall. Great columns of polished black stone ran on both sides of every corridor, magnificent hangings of immeasurable value in between them on the white walls. It looked more like a palace than anything else. Calmantis's patience was wearing thin, and he emitted a loud sigh of exasperation in her direction, before turning and quickly striding away.

'Wait! Wait, sir,' she shouted, running to catch up. 'Head down this corridor and turn left at the first intersection. From there, you will go to the end of the hall where his chambers are. But you will have to wait for him to finish with the clairvoy. They are in discussions. There are some seats outside for your comfort. Would you like a cup of tea while you wait?'

He was rather thirsty, and the mere mention of tea made his throat even more parched than it was. But it would be just the thing that would get him caught. 'No, no. Thank you, my dear. I shan't be here for long. You have been a tremendous help. I've always wanted to meet a clairvoy. Maybe today is my lucky day.' All those times spent watching his father talk to investors had paid off. She smiled back at him and sauntered away. *That was close.*

When she disappeared round the corridor's corner, Calmantis glanced around for anyone else and jogged further until he reached a door with a plaque that read, "Dean of the House". *I've got this far, but what now? I need to know why Yeron was summoned. I need leverage. Wait a moment, we never used to lock our home with all the staff always around. Could it be this easy?*

He gripped the polished steel handle, squeezed his eyes shut, and very slowly pushed down on it, pulling slightly to keep it from making any noise. The handle lowered ever more until it would not move, and he silently breathed out as he pushed on the door. There was no resistance. They had not locked it. Calmantis had to smile and just shook his head.

Voices filtered through the home, getting louder the further he crept. The floor had turned to one of dark wood and subtle skirting of a lighter shade, flowing into the warmer off-white walls where copper sconces burned with glowing candles. Expensive lounge sets of deep red furnished the extravagant room, situated around a solid tea table of antique wood, looking blemished and grey, scarred with deep grooves in between the wood patterns. *Must be a sentimental piece.* Everything looked very staged, as though one was never meant to use any of the things on display. Bookshelves with old books, great and small, lined one wall, side tables with perfectly spread books, two or three on each. A side table stood between the lounge sets, a small box waiting on top, lid ajar, the cigars inside arrayed for all to see, with a polished glass bottle of golden liquor next to it. He heard the voices clearly now, coming from ahead to the left, the room just adjacent to the one he was in.

'There have been some questionable sightings to the east. I won't lie and say I don't wonder if it is at all related to what happened a while back in Barren Hollows.' It was Lord Latimus. His hard and grating voice was unmistakable.

'What sightings have you concerned?' Yeron asked, his voice calm and flat, soothing in its own right. There was a long pause, and Latimus sighed with a grunt.

'A good number of men, maybe bandits, camping or gathering, near the Black Mountains of Khormund-ur.'

Another pregnant moment grew between them before Yeron spoke. 'What are your orders, sir? Are we to confront these people? Chase them back to whatever hole they climbed from? And why us? Why not the king's men?'

'I don't like your tone, Clairvoy Yeron. You chose to be on the sidelines, to fight instead of lead. If you want to make decisions, you should have taken my seat a long time ago.'

The air was tense, and only getting worse. He never thought there could be hostility in the temple as he'd seen it these last few days. People didn't trust each other, nor liked each other. He'd always thought it would be a place where relative safety could be found, where respect and kindness would be forthright. But things seemed a little darker now.

'I don't want your seat, Lord Latimus. Although, I don't believe you should have it either. I will take some men to the mountains and see what they are up to. Is there anything else I should know?'

'Huh, and you should not be alive anymore, yet here you stand two hundred and thirty years later. Somehow, you have managed to live a very long life, making no strides up the ladder of power. Still the same old fool, training and fighting.' A cold sweat poured from Calmantis's forehead, wetting his brows, his knees weak. Lord Latimus continued, 'There have been rumours from travellers of strange noises in the area. Some say it sounded like the howls of a beast, while others are inclined to believe that it is the world being torn apart. Like stones grinding against each other, roots snapping under great strain, the earth being rended open. That sort of thing. Whatever it is, there's more than just the work of man involved.'

Calmantis slipped from the room, padding down the corridors and out of the Lord's Hall.

16. To Kill a God

Singed hair and skin left an awful smell in the gloom of Jonas's surroundings. Black char marred the grey rocks and brown dirt all the way to where an enormous beast sat on its throne. A flaming whip stretched from its gigantic, eternally burning claw to lash around Jonas's chest and arms, squeezing the life from him. His blood boiled, his flesh becoming mangled and grotesque. His mind was on fire, and wherever he looked, flames raged to the beckoning of the terrifying beast, its roaring breath and smoke-billowing eyes a promise of torment.

There were scarce moments of reprieve, short ones barely long enough for a deep breath, but they were all he lived for at this moment. Moments when the beast toyed with him, giving him enough slack on the whip to breathe a few quick breaths, and always straight after, the claws would tighten on the fiery rein, squeezing harder than before to crush his chest a little more.

Jonas screamed for someone to help, but there was no one there. *Why would there be anyone in the lair of this beast?* All he could do was hope. Hope that the beast tired, which seemed all the more unlikely, or that someone would free him, which seemed even more ridiculous.

Head hung low, he did nothing but accept the punishment, waiting for his body to become ash, but it was taking an awfully long time. *It's always best to get things done.* That was what his father used to say. *You can't live in fear's shadow, biding your time until maybe, just maybe, someone else does something for you. If you want to survive, you have to act.* The heat was tremendous, with the flames roaring aloud, sounds of snapping and crackling jumped in his ears, stones and twigs suffering from the blaze.

Thirsty beyond comprehension, hot air flowed from his mouth, his throat feeling scratchy and parched. Jonas wanted to go home. 'What do you want from me?' he wheezed to the beast, and wondered if it understood anything. Vernak had called it a darcöle, some kind of hunter. Of what, he could only guess it wanted souls. It leered at him, dark slits narrowed on his, judging, head tilted in wonder, but it made no sound that could be mistaken for speech.

A loud creak sounded to the far left, and light poured into the burning lair, beaming like a bright sun, and a figure stepped through, bending low to clear its head before rising. The flames died as the figure squelched across them, sizzling angrily, as if water poured from the figure to douse the fires, trails of smoke left riding its wake.

The figure approached from the inferno, hood lowered to hide her face, but he could see her jawline, her red lips, so feminine and soft. Dark curls hung from beneath her hood. She walked in the path of the dying fires until only a few feet from him, never raising her head. The surrounding heat lowered considerably, and for the first time, a cool breeze caressed his face, left him yearning for more. He searched for it with his head, panting, eyes rolling.

'Voidwalker . . .' Her voice sounded harder, more authoritative than he'd judged her. 'You should have accepted my offer.'

'Danu . . . I should have guessed you would be behind this. Is your pet still alive? Or did we stick him good and proper?'

'Your consciousness is still attached to your soul. How wonderful! Painful, isn't it? Being torn from your body like that.' A twitch of a smirk flashed on her lips, and she stated, 'Ortis lives, which is more than I can say about you. Though, another failure like that, and I can't say the same.'

'Let me go or end this. Stop playing games.'

'Oh, as much as I'd like to end this, I do not have the power to kill through the Fold, merely to wound and torture. Aztar would take affront for my even attempting something like that. And I need to lie low, for now.'

'You gods are all the same: pathetic, whining beings given powers you don't deserve. All you do is manipulate the world of man, playing puppetmaster while we suffer for your entertainment. What makes you worthy, anyway?'

'What makes me worthy?' she asked, stepping closer and bunching her fists. 'Without me, the unchained winds would blow the roofs from your homes, would sweep across the plains like the whirlwinds of the World Storms. It would cause havoc and destruction, without ease, without serenity. I keep the world safe and so do many others of our kind. What is our worth? Without us, you would cease to exist.'

The flaming whip had simmered to a thick wrap of heated leather, and breathing became easier, though his life was not about easy. Jonas worked his fingers through the tight bindings, the blisters on his hands popping and expunging the foul pus within, tearing skin and burning profusely. He wanted to scream from the pain, but he could not give away his efforts. His right hand slipped out with a splash of blood and pus, arm snaking out fast and furious to grab Danu by the throat, squeezing as hard as he could. 'Worth! You, bitch, are worth nothing!' Hard fingers strangled her, calloused, an old friend to pain, doing their best to rid this world of her. He screamed, and so did she, thrashing and clawing at his arm with long nails, tearing out strips of flesh until the whip burst into flames again, searing his skin anew.

Jonas dropped her and yanked his arm back, the flames turning blue at the base, gradually growing from purple, yellow, orange, to a near red. Danu had dropped to her knees, coughing and rubbing her neck, then slowly rose, not a mark on her flesh. It took some time for her to regain her composure, standing with parted lips, breath hissing between her teeth. Jonas had glimpsed her bright blue eyes, saw the possibility of fear that crouched within.

Danu licked her lips and said, 'Did you really think you could hurt me?' She shook her head disapprovingly. 'Your wife prayed to Erua, right? The moon goddess?' Jonas's head jerked to her, and he clenched his jaw. *Never show your enemy they have wounded you. Never show them they have leverage.* His father had taught him many things, but that didn't make him infallible. She smiled sadistically and continued, 'Maybe I should pay Erua a visit, persuade her to hand over your precious Ayla to me. We would have so much fun together. It would be a bloody sight indeed.' Danu turned and sauntered from the lair, the fires jumping back to life behind her.

'I will find a way, Danu. I will kill you! Remember that!' The bright flash of her blue eyes locked to his one last time before she slammed the door shut.

* * *

'Hey, ugly! Think I can get a drink of water?' Jonas called to his captor, but the beast barely looked at him and adjusted its gigantic frame on the stone throne beneath it. 'Didn't think so . . .' At least he wasn't in the grasp of the burning whip anymore. He stretched his sore back and gently leaned with his shoulder against one of the thick iron bars of his cage. With eyes closed, he dropped his head against the solid bar and thought of his Ayla, wishing he could see her one last time.

The thought of her dancing, as she always did in the wee hours of the morning, came to him. The way she swayed her hips to imagined music, the way she hummed with the rhythm of an imagined band. Her sweet fragrance filled his nose and swallowed his inhibitions, relaxing his tormented mind. A shudder raced through him, and his chest heaved with a gasp of air, lips trembling, face screwed to a frown.

'Real men don't cry!' he remembered his father telling him whenever his lips began to quiver while he was but a young boy. They were warriors, after all. The men of the North. Not like the soft-bellied city dwellers of Yahrska. They were hard men, with a hard life, fending off the deadly elements alongside the continued raids from other clans. Yet, all the pain in the world paled in comparison to losing his Ayla. With bleeding hands, he pulled at his hair, hoping the pain would lug him back to reality, yet it failed miserably. His feet scraped over rough pumice, porous and warmed by the fires ever burning, making the lair so much more unbearable for one used to the fresh air. *Oh, the fresh air . . . up in the forests near Barren Hollows. I could work my anger out on a few of those logs right now.*

Ayla glided over the floor, white gown having a certain translucence, revealing her body beneath ever so slightly when the sun hit at just the right angle, taking Jonas's breath away. 'What are you doing?' he asked her, setting down his axe near the front door, and leaned on the wall with his shoulder. She twirled around in the dying light of the day, soft beams of light flickering through the drapes, and swung her long blonde hair into his face with a flick of the head, laughing at his shock. 'Hey, what gives?' he spat out, flinging her hair aside, only to see her in his face, and felt her nails grasp the back of his head. She yanked him closer and planted her full red lips to his, ignoring the plea for breath he desperately needed. She fondled his goods, and his breath drifted further away. *Then again, this is not so bad either . . .* He could hold out a little longer. She finally released him and stared at him with a certain animalism reflected in her beautiful blue eyes, lips parted ever so slightly. 'Well, good day to you too, Missus Creed.' She laughed and spun away from him, dancing to the far side of the corridor with grace.

'Oi!' he called, hot flushes of embarrassment making him blush while he adjusted his pants. 'You better finish what you started!' Jonas ran after her, following her giggles, running his fingertips along the old wooden wall, crumbling the peeling white paint from them to the floor. Sharp cracks sounded from beneath his fingers all the way to the room, where he turned into and stopped, staring down at her lithe form, naked and curled between the stretched bedding.

'You sly minx . . .' Jonas said with a smirk, and made to sit on the bed, finding the floor instead with a thud on his arse. It vanished with Ayla and the rest of the furniture, leaving only a vacant room, where he lay on the floor, surprised and shocked.

'Ayla!' he called, and ran from the room, scanning the others as he passed from the corridor. All were empty. He rushed forward, breath racing through his teeth, and turned into the lounge, gasping for air as the world shifted beneath his feet, and suddenly, he sat up on the couch, eyes wide and heart pounding, muscles tense, hands bound in fists, ready for a fight.

'Yes?' came a soft voice, lovingly annoyed. 'Why'd you have to wake me like that?' Ayla rubbed the grains from her eyes, rolling the sleepiness from them with her head in his lap. She got up and yawned a long sigh. Her hair was dishevelled, and deep prints lined the side of her face. The folds of his pants had left their mark on her. She smiled at him and tugged on his beard. 'You seem burdened of late. More so than your usual self. What has your mind racing? Is Yurgassun giving you grief at the site again?'

Jonas could not stop looking at her. *How did she get here? Is this a dream? It all feels so real.* 'Yurgassun? Er . . . Huh . . . No. Just havin' a bad dream is all, my love.'

'Good,' she said, and yawned again. 'It does not help to dwell on past mistakes.'

'Mistakes?'

'Mpf,' she let out a long thoughtful breath and caressed his bristly cheek. 'Our son's death was not your fault, but you keep calling it your mistake.'

'What?' Jonas shouted and jumped up from the couch. 'Jorin is not dead! I was just with him.'

'Yes, you were at his grave only this morning.' Ayla stood and reached for his face, but he pulled away.

'No! This isn't true. I can't believe what I'm hearing from you!'

'We are coming for you . . .' An old voice drifted around the home. Jonas scanned the corners of the room, searching for its origin, seeing nothing, yet Ayla seemed undisturbed by it.

'Did you hear that?' he asked her.

'Hear what? Stop ignoring this conversation, Jonas! You can't keep running away from it.'

'I'm not running away! It simply isn't true!'

'Jonas Creed! Be ready!' The old voice filtered through again. *Ready for what?* he thought.

He turned around and called up to no one, 'Who are you? What must I be ready for? Show yourself!'

'Fine! Ignore me then. Make a fool of me! I will not have it.' Ayla stormed from the room, pulling her arm from Jonas's grasp.

'Ayla! Wait!' Jonas ran after her, grabbing hold of the wall to steer round the corner, when the ground gave way under him to a bottomless pit of grey stone, growing deeper the further he fell. He screamed for help and stretched his fingers to the side of the wall, where black sconces with small flickering candles raced by in front and behind, far from his reach, their red-orange glow reflecting on something far below.

There was nothing to do but wait for the rushing floor to do its job. Jonas screamed and swam in the air, kicking and fighting to reach the sconces, hoping to grab on to one, even if it meant breaking his arm. His clothes fluttered in the push of the wind, his face getting flattened with the ripples of skin pulled taut. He was not going to make it.

The floor rushed at him, and he shielded his face with his arms in a scream of defiance.

* * *

A snort of shocked surprise snapped Jonas's head up, eyes hunting, scanning the gloomy lair. He wiped the string of drool from his mouth and beard, coughed and spat through the cage to hear the ball of phlegm sizzle on the hot stones where it fell, a sticky goo. *Just a dream, then . . .*

The burns on his naked arms and chest seemed to have healed a lot in the short span of time he had slept. No more blood flowed from pus-filled boils. Scabs caked him, a layer of crusty dried blood, filthy and sore. *If I could only heal like this in the real world. Then maybe I could get all the demons out of my head.* He sighed and closed his eyes again.

17. Only so Much

'I told you to use more Devil's Snare! We need to break through the Fold! I don't even know if he heard me.' Vernak tossed the thick leather-bound book on the table with a loud clap.

'More? I have given you more than most can handle safely. And even if *you* could handle more, who's to say he can?' Erechol stated, pointing at Jonas's constantly murmuring body. The muffled sounds escaping his cracked and bleeding lips, groans of indistinctness.

'He can handle it! He must . . . and so can I. Now, double the dosage for both of us.'

The alchemist turned to her husband, seeking support, evidently getting less than she expected, and swung back, mouth agape. 'Well, if one of you dies, I better make sure we are not held accountable.' She stuck out her arm and snapped her fingers without a glance at Maliketh, who slid a sheet of papyrus into her hand, and she extended it to Vernak. 'Sign it!'

'What is this?' Vernak leered down at the paper and took it from her.

'Safety. Mine and Maliketh's. It states we are not to be blamed if either of you kicks the proverbial bucket. There's a quill on the stand over there, inkwell next to it.' The light in the house had faded a while back to little more than darkness, trying its best to swallow the vestigial memory of what once was. A memory now shared between multiple candles, tongues dancing to silent music, smoke drifting with momentary flickers. The moon was obscured tonight, hidden behind thick clouds hovering up high, a moonlit backdrop with the occasional thinning of cover.

Vernak glowered at the two, then said, 'Jorin, fetch the quill and ink. I have a suspicion they'll want you to sign as well.'

'You assume correctly,' said Erechol, 'You can't be too careful in our line of business.'

'Is this safe?' Jorin asked as he handed the quill and inkwell to Vernak, eyeing the two alchemists.

'My goodness, no! Not unless he was already dead. In which case, yes, it is safe. Can't really get any worse than that, can it?' Maliketh chuckled, oily black beard glistening in the light of the flames.

'Jorin, we have no other option. We need him awake.' Vernak reached out to the boy and held him by the shoulders. 'I know you are young. You probably never thought you would be in this position, having to sign away your father's life like it was nothing more than rotten cheese to be cast in a bin, making choices that could possibly haunt you for the rest of your life. But this is what growing up is, making hard choices, my boy. You know I'm right. And believe me, where he is at the moment is no picnic either. You can't leave him there.'

Jorin looked between the three of them and sighed, clenching his jaw, his fists bulging. He nodded and waited for Vernak to sign the piece of paper. 'Here you go, lad. Sign right there.'

They all stood silently, waiting for young Jorin to finish scribbling on the paper. Erechol glanced over his shoulder and plucked the paper from the table as soon as he lifted the quill, and said, 'Excellent. Now we can continue. Double the dosage, you said?'

Now, with the acceptance of his needs, Vernak struggled to answer and cleared his throat. '*Ahem* . . . Yes, double. Let's get started.' He flicked his raggedy cape aside and sat in the chair next to Jonas, leaning on the wooden slab of the table. 'Jorin, wait outside. It's getting a little crowded in here. Don't want you being in their way when they need to work.'

'But I cannot—' Jorin started, quickly cut off by Vernak's stare and icy tone.

'Wait outside.'

An angry growl rushed from Jorin's mouth. He squeezed his father's hand, then left the room.

'You have your work cut out with that one,' said Erechol, rubbing an ointment on her hands that stank of heated honey. 'Is he your grandchild?'

'No. But I am responsible for him, nonetheless. Sixteen years old and on his way to becoming a father. Now he thinks he knows everything.'

'Oh, don't be too hard on him. We were all there at one stage, thinking ourselves better than the gods.'

Vernak spun his head to her, eyes narrowed, searching for hidden meanings in her words and finding none. Not a smirk or a twitch of the mouth, not a sparkle in the eye, not even a lingering stare. She merely continued rubbing the ointment on herself, then moved over to Maliketh, doing the same. 'Yes, I guess we all were. And to what god do you pray now?'

'None. I fear they would not be too thrilled with our line of work, wouldn't you say? Stealing people back from the dead. We keep our distance far and clear of anything god-related.' *No, I guess* they *would not,* Vernak thought and watched her tilt her head as she asked, 'You say his soul is not free to roam. How do you know this?'

Hmm, the question I've been hoping to avoid. 'I have my suspicions.'

'Look, honey. If your *suspicions* are off, then this will never work, and you would be putting all of us in danger. So you better be sure.'

Vernak shifted his dull eyes to Maliketh, who sipped more of his steaming drink, and said, 'I'm sure.'

'Okay then. Be ready to grab his soul once we're there. It will be a fleeting moment that we will have to get it all done. If we miss this, we are not going back. Do you understand?'

'I do.'

'So be it.'

The room stank, smelling sour and acrid, to where Vernak could taste the scents on his tongue, on his gums, and in the back of his throat. The bitterness pulled at his jaw. He swallowed the dry and sticky saliva, hoping to coat his throat, but it only made it worse, turning the bitterness into a sour musk. With his jaw clenched, teeth grinding and face tense, he gripped Jonas's hand while Erechol and Maliketh mixed the ingredients, grinding them to a thick grey paste. It took a powerful sorcerer to open the gates between realms, even for a fluttering heartbeat. He only hoped they were up to the task.

'Drink, all of it,' Maliketh said, handing a small brown bowl to Vernak, while Erechol pried open Jonas's mouth, scooping the foul contents of another bowl down his throat. She held his mouth closed, forcing him to swallow it. The man spluttered and choked, arms flailing and legs kicking, yet his mind was not in control. She mouthed words Vernak could not hear, her prominent eyes closed, dark face glistening with sweat. Her full bosom and round bottom pushed at her black dress, stretching the material as she bent over Jonas, heads locked together.

The world became like distorted glass and misshapen mirrors, changing everything around him. Vernak had never thought that he might feel the effects of a drug such as this in his life. Yet, here he was, snared by the potions blended together, and his mind was absolutely swimming. Fingers smelling of strong tea gripped his face, forced more of the concoction down his throat, and a rush of overpowering ecstasy dragged him down. The room exploded into a million colours, the myriad candles' flames bursting into fanned fire, their tongues reaching for the roof, burning harsh and discordant, unlike any he had ever seen. Their heat transferred onto him with something pressed against his head, an utterly cold thing, dripping salty sweat onto his lips. His mind vomited, but his body was not allowed. *Double the dosage . . . shit.*

His guard was down and his mind slow to react. The world spun faster and faster, changing locations quicker than he could blink. 'What's going on?' he heard a man shout but was not sure who it was.

'His mind is being devoured. I told him it's too much! Stupid bakghor!'

* * *

'Hey, kid, couldn't stay away from the calluwangoo, could you?' Orana called from the front of a wagon loaded with supplies, drawn by four strong Percherons. Their long manes flicked with annoyance at silhouettes in the darkness, pulling at the bits in their mouths, snorting and neighing to show their displeasure. She had nearly not seen him at all where he sat under the tree, but his loud slurping of the juicy fruit gave him away.

'Wow! Where did you get all of this?' Jorin asked and wiped the glistening stains from his face, burping loudly.

'I have friends,' she mocked and jumped from the wagon. 'We will need enough supplies to last us a while. It's quite a trek to Baldor, you know.' Orana looked around the garden and pulled a face. 'Why haven't they lit any of the lamp posts? I can barely see two feet in front of me.'

'Maliketh sent the servants away. Think it's about what we're doing here.'

'More likely what they are doing in there,' she said, pointing to a window on the left, an orange glow flickering through the closed drapes. She narrowed her gaze to make out Jorin, but the murkiness swallowed up her vision, giving her only contours and dark silhouettes against a shadowy backdrop, the faint glimmer not enough for her to adequately see him, and she wanted to gauge his expressions. 'Say, what happened to you three? How did your father end up without his soul, and who is Vernak to you?'

A long moment of silence stretched between them. Jorin sat on a root of the tree, hugging his knees, head drawn up close to his arms, and muttered, 'I don't want to talk about it.'

'Yeah, I guess I wouldn't want to talk about it either if my father was crooked. Safer that way.'

'What?' Jorin shouted, his voice turning shrill as he jumped up. 'My father is a good man! He saved me! It was my fault. All of it.'

'Saved you, did he? From what? Or from whom? What did you do?' Jorin's mouth moved with the words held back in his throat, his eyes turning watery. 'It's okay, kid. I'm not here to cause you troubles. Forget we talked. We have a long road with late nights around campfires ahead of us. We'll talk when you are more at ease, with your father around.'

Jorin clasped his hands tight, rubbing his knuckles nervously, and sat down, staring at the dark ground. 'You think he will be okay?'

She sat down next to him with a sigh. 'It's hard to say. He looks like a hard man, willing to fight. It will be up to him. He has you to fight for . . .'

'I'm not sure that means anything.'

Orana didn't know why, but those words hurt her at some level, upsetting her. Or maybe she knew after all, but the will to be honest with oneself sometimes lacked the courage to speak out. 'I'm sure it means more than you think.' She turned back to the window and continued, 'How long have they been at it?'

'They started before dusk, but the mixtures were wrong. Vernak shouted at them. They shouted back. Then they made us sign a form so they can't be blamed if my father or Vernak die.'

'I'm sure they are just being cautious. They are taking a colossal risk trying to help you.'

'I know. I'm just not sure they can.'

* * *

Vernak's head bobbed around, drool spilling to his robes, muttering nonsense to a crowd deep in his head, 'I'm a god! Don't you talk to me . . . about your pestilence and woes. Be gone, I tell you!' He chuckled softly, shaking his head to focus his mind. 'What was I saying? Where am I?'

A soft hand rocked his head to the left, his face burning shortly after. 'I'll tear your balls off! The insolence!' His mind was suddenly more focused. Maliketh stood before him with a deep scowl.

'We have to get this done! Get yourself together!' The world turned slower, and from the corner of his eye, where Erechol hovered over Jonas, a swirling black ring came into existence, growing larger where it spun in the air, gusting breaths of wildfire beyond, embers drifting from the perilous plane. 'You have to reach out and grab him, pull him to this side! We are losing time!'

Everything Vernak touched had a certain beauty to it, even in this darkness that shrouded them, giving off a specific sense of wonder. The material on the chair seemed more than life itself, the shallow bumps and ridges of the stitching a sensual pleasure to rub, the material so soft and velvety, like the face of a newborn and he was its mother, nurturing it, letting it know that it was safe in his arms, his hands protecting it from the very real world.

The world bloomed around him, spreading outward with fields of green, purple, yellow, and white, rolling meadows with cloud-scraping mountains, an old home of wood perched on the face, smoke drifting to the sky. 'I know this place,' he mumbled. 'I cannot be here.'

'What's happening, Erechol? This is not normal!' he heard someone shout.

'I don't know!' he heard again. A woman's voice, high-pitched and worried. Footsteps echoed on a wooden floor, yet he was sure they stood in the meadow.

'Well, we did give them enough to kill three men three times over . . .'

'Shut up and come here. Look after him. I will work on Vernak.'

'I need no working on!' Vernak shouted, swinging his arms, his eyes wild, scanning the fields but seeing nothing around him. The world shuddered and rocked, quaking with roaring rumbles, calling out its misery. His face burned with a flash of a hand, then another, and another, before a blinding light burned his eyes. When his sight came back, the somewhat corpulent form of the sorceress Erechol stood before him, his head gripped between her palms, the cleavage of her great breasts a dark valley between dark mountains where lay a precious gem, glittering red on a necklace of gold.

All sound, even her voice coming from her flapping lips, reached his ears muffled, stifled, softened to the velvety chair he still rubbed. Vernak focused on her lips, trying to read what she was saying.

'Call out to him! We're running out of time!'

He was so tired. His eyes felt like iron, pulling closed and wanting to remain so with every blink. He was back in the house, but everything lay sideways. Even Jonas stood upright, with his back against what looked like a wall, but then Erechol picked him up, the world swinging around until Jonas lay flat on his back again. Vernak grew restless, pushing and shoving Erechol out of the way, then leaned over, spilling his guts to the floor.

The home's plaster tore from the walls, ripping out beams of wood and bricks of stone, and all joined the swirling mass of black. A loud roar escaped the swirl, followed by a growing heat.

* * *

'So you are to become a father at your age, eh? Wow. That must be a terrible burden . . . for one so young.' The night air had brought a soft, cool breeze with it, and Orana cherished it. She knew just how hot the city could get.

'It's not a burden! And I'm not so young!' stormed Jorin, scowling up at Orana, where she giggled.

'How old do you think Vernak is?'

'I don't know. Fifty, maybe?'

Orana burst out laughing. 'I reckon he's more like seventy.' She watched him register the age, shaking his head in confusion.

'What? Can you even get that old?'

'Some do. So you see, you have many lifetimes ahead of you still. You are very young.'

'Well, how old are you? I'm guessing—'

'No! No, no, no, no. We are not playing this game with me.' She laughed, wagging her finger at him. 'I don't grow older, I merely grow wiser and more graceful.'

'Oh yeah? Hopefully, my Tunisia grows older then. I don't need her getting any wiser.'

Orana caught her laughter in the cup of her hand. 'Little wise-arse.'

The ground quaked beneath them, rumbling like a thing displeased. Again the world lurched, throwing them from their feet, while fear-filled screams from neighbouring homes went up. The tree above them shook violently, dropping the calluwangoo to the ground, splattering them to spill their slippery sustenance all over. 'Quickly! Get to the open ground!'

'No! I have to get to my father!' Jorin ran for the door, legs swaying, arms low to the ground, hands waiting to stop his fall should the world be ripped out from under him.

'It's too dangerous!' She grabbed him from behind and dragged him to the ground moments before the right column of the arched doorway to the foyer collapsed in a hail of grey dust, splitting the door down its middle. In the darkness, while they cowered on the ground, waiting for it to end, they could not tell the extent of the ongoing damage.

When it became clear to Orana that it was not about to end soon, she crawled away from the house and trees, dragging the screaming Jorin by the scruff of his neck. 'Stop fighting me!'

'Let me go! Father!'

18. Mourning and Anger

The day was a bitter one. Flecks of snow drifted down, the winds forcing them to swirl endlessly over the frozen grass. A dark mood besieged Kunia, with dark clouds, and dark times as company. Bellard sat alone in the courtyard's corner, his back turned to everyone, hearing the snide comments whispered as students passed. He could not care what they thought, he couldn't care what anybody thought. Just this morning he had said his final farewell to his friend, and people were already continuing with their lives, shaking off and putting to rest what had happened.

The procession was over so quickly. Don't know what I expected, but I expected more.

All the students of the arcane and all grandàres had gathered at Flach's End before sunrise, all wearing black robes with a red ribbon strapped round their right arms, waiting for first light to arrive. He had found himself amid the milling crowds, pushing through the darkness to get to the front line. Flach's End was a grassy outcrop high above Khorvellen, overlooking the city, and Kunia in the distance. It was used as a beacon to warn the city guard of approaching enemies, with a tall tower having a 360-degree view.

Today they would use it for something else.

His hand itched fiercely beneath the bandages, and he desperately wanted to scratch it, but having to redo the bandage with only one hand if it came loose sounded like a load of inconvenience he didn't need. 'Bellard?' came a voice from his left. A voice of someone he wasn't sure if he was ready to speak to.

'Brethnar . . .' Bellard dragged the words from his mouth, sounding bitter and angry. He could only see the grey outlines and rough features in the darkness, but he could tell the sadness in his friend's voice. His back twitched, and the stitches pulled at his skin, stinging with every movement.

Brethnar gave way to a sigh and turned away as he said, 'Never mind
. . . You will never forgive me.'

'Wait, Brethnar. Please.' He reached out to his friend, grabbing the
folds of his robe around his wrist. 'Look, I'm sorry. I'm just angry. Angry
at everything and everyone, but it has nothing to do with you. I
promise.'

Brethnar relaxed, and Bellard turned to the faint outlines of a
funeral pyre overlooking the long drop to the valley basement, a body
wrapped in white sheets lying on top. It was always quietest before
sunrise. The winds all slept while the weather yawned, getting ready to
do its duty for the day. An awkwardness lingered between the two, a
tension that had never been there and now made it hard to speak.

The crowds spread out over rocks and mounds, taking their places
to get a better view, whispering in hushed tones to each other. Bellard
glanced sidelong at Brethnar and asked, 'Have you seen Mila?' He
received only a cursory nod before Brethnar pointed past him.

Mila's white hair flowed out from under her hood, stark green eyes
glimmering unnaturally from where she approached, surefooted,
walking over a treacherous terrain as though in daylight, right arm
swinging in the sling. 'You sure it's a good idea to use magic right now?'
he asked her.

'Why not? It is, after all, what we are. We bled for this. Why not use
it? Besides, why should I stumble like an idiot if there's something I can
do about it?'

'It's just . . . It feels wrong.'

'I would argue that it would be wrong if we didn't use it. Do you
really think Valdor would want us never to use our gifts?'

'Er . . . Well. Uhm. No, not like that. No, I guess he'd want us to
use it.'

'He wanted to be a mage more than any of us. Its use would not
offend him.'

'Yeah, you're right, Mila. You're always right.'

A figure walked up to the stand before the pyre, hands clasped at the front. Bellard couldn't tell who it was, but with Agoras being the head grandàre, it was sure to be him, and the thought of that made his blood boil. Fists bunched, teeth clenched, he took a step forward. It came as a bit of a shock when it was Grandàre Shevira who cleared her throat and spoke instead, stopping Bellard in his tracks.

'I am sure it will shock some of you to see me standing up here and not Agoras.' Bellard noticed she neglected to call him Grandàre. 'So let this be a formal notice that we have dismissed Mister Agoras from the academy. Forthright, he will have no connection to this school any longer. All contact with him is to cease immediately. I have cast my hat into the ring for the nomination as his replacement, and as such, I stand before you this very early morning, taking on this terrible burden of laying to rest a dear student after a terrible error was made. This life could have been spared if only Agoras could let go of his ego. I know we all played a part, and we should have spoken up, screamed it from the rooftops, but it is always easier to see the mistakes made after the fact.' Grandàre Shevira gazed over the crowd, eyes scanning until she found Bellard, Mila, and Brethnar. 'I know this is not enough for what you three endured in the Sacred Hall, but I hope it is a start. Please join me as we say goodbye to Valdor Treyphus, a wonderful soul.' She beckoned them closer with a wave of the hand, and all attention spun to them. Every eye focused on them, waiting. 'Come.'

Forced to be the centre of attention, they crept forward nervously, glancing at one another sheepishly, edging towards the pyre.

'Come. It's all right.' The pyre grew larger the closer they got, a smell of pungent oil heavy in the air. Shevira's enormous eyes stretched wider with a loving smile. 'You all know how to summon fire. I taught you myself, and I know your worth. Only now we will add a little twist to it.' She saw Mila's arm in the sling and asked, 'Will you manage, my dear?' Mila nodded, and she continued, 'Good. Each of you take up a corner and stand a few feet back. Follow my lead.'

Bellard gazed back to the crowd staring at them, their glistening faces filled with sorrow and heartache. People he had never seen cried their hearts out, hugging each other. People he'd never seen talking to

Valdor now had their worlds ripped out from under them, as if they had been friends their entire lives. And he grew angry again. There was no reason for it. And he knew it was stupid, but it felt wrong of them, as though they were pretending, taking *their* hurt and making it their own.

He looked up at his friend lying on the pile of wood, tracing the form of Valdor's face and body hidden beneath the sheets with his eyes, while Grandàre Shevira kept talking to the crowd. *I will miss you, my friend. Forgive us for the part we played in your death. If there was anything we could've done, we would've. I am sorry things turned out this way. Above all, forgive Brethnar if there's anything to forgive.* Bellard looked for Mila and Brethnar, only seeing Mila on his right at the back of the pyre. She was saying her last goodbyes as well, reaching out her hand to touch the logs, arm trembling where she lay her palm, then pulled away. *Go now, in peace.*

'. . . and we are reminded that life is fragile. Something to be celebrated every day. Somewhere along the way, as we get older, I think we forget that, until a harsh reminder like this comes along to put us back in our place. I have often wondered if this is the gods' way to get our attention, to give us a good kickin' under the old rump. Whatever it is, it is a call to wake up.' Shevira turned to the pyre as the sun peeked over the rim of the world, and took up the corner on Bellard's left, then nodded to him. She rolled her hands over one another and a blue ball of fire grew in her palms, the heat rippling the air around her hands. With a last nod to Valdor's body, she cast the blue ball of flames into the pyre's base, followed by Bellard, Mila, and Brethnar. From each corner of the great watch tower, streams of blue flame rose to its beacon up high, lighting the logs to burn a brilliant blue.

Now, here in the courtyard, alone with his thoughts, Bellard felt neither the need, nor the want, he'd always had to study magic. Dark and shiny, his Pillar lay in his hands, an object unhindered by emotions. He closed his fist around the amethyst gem, clenching his teeth and squeezing as hard as he could, hoping it might just shatter in his hands. Stolid, it lay waiting when he opened his hand, untouched, except for the few drops of blood from cuts on his hand. He didn't think that the raw crystal's edges could be so sharp.

It was quiet around him. The students had all drifted back to class, leaving him truly alone, and it was blissful. It wasn't long before his solitude was interrupted.

Mila headed towards him, walking next to the building on the gravel path, feet crunching on the rocks. 'I've been looking all over for you. Aren't you coming to say goodbye?'

Bellard looked up, squinting with one eye against the bright sunlight. 'Say goodbye? Where are you off to?'

'Not me, you idiot. Brethnar. He is leaving the school and heading back home to Velorine,' said Mila, standing with her hands on her hips.

'He's leaving the school?' Bellard asked, dumbstruck.

'That's what I said! His parents arrived this morning and are forcing him to go back with them.'

'He can't leave!'

'That's what I said,' she mumbled. 'But I don't think his folks are going to listen to us.'

Bellard jumped up and asked, 'Well, where is he?' Before she could answer, he already started running across the quadrangle, sprinting to nowhere in particular.

'You're running in the wrong direction! This way!'

Grass flew from under his boot, kicked to the air as he slid over the immaculate lawns, bandaged hand scraping dirt to steady himself.

They ran through the main doors into the foyer, where an angry old woman jumped from her chair and shouted at them. 'No running in the school!' There was more she shouted, but they didn't hear or care.

They crashed through a back door and ran onto the gravel road, harsh and discordant crunching assaulting their ears, while they sprinted after a wagon in the distance, dust drifting from its rolling wheels, more kicked up by the horses' hoofs.

'Wait! Brethnar! Mister and Missus . . .' Bellard realised he had never asked their names. 'Brethnar!'

'Brethnar!' Mila shouted next to him, but the wagon didn't stop.

Bellard reached out his good hand, focusing on the wagon's wheel, visualising it shattering, feeling the force move out from him to wrap around the wooden spokes as he closed his hand.

'What are you doing?' demanded Mila, and she grabbed his arm. 'It's too far. You can hurt them.'

'I can stop them!' He shook her off and reached out again, grabbing hold of the force inside. He felt his hands wrap around the structure of the wheel, starting to pull it apart with sheer power, forcing it to crack and splinter.

'No! You will hurt them! It's too risky!' Mila slapped him across the face, and he saw the wagon buckle slightly to one side, but it kept going, disappearing round the corner in the distance.

He rounded on Mila and grabbed her wildly swinging arm. 'Why'd you go and do that? I could've stopped them.'

'Or killed them! What then?'

'I'm only using my gifts, as you said we should. Remember? We bled for them, after all . . .'

Her face went slack, her breathing quickened, and she yanked her hand from his grip. 'Oh, you arsehole.' Mila spun around and stomped away, turning back once to glare at him, before slamming the door shut behind her.

Head shaking, he rubbed his eyes, calming his mind. Bellard knew instantly he was in the wrong. He should never have said that. 'Way to go, Bellard.'

* * *

Everyone is leaving me again. Just like they always do. Except this time, it truly is my fault. If I hadn't been so self-absorbed, I would've seen this coming, been able to do something about it, or at least been prepared for it. But no, I had to cower away and hide behind a wall of self-loathing. How pathetic. Bellard shook his head with a mocking chuckle. *And here I'm doing it again.*

He traced his finger over the underside of the bed above him and closed his eyes when dust fell on his face, tickling his nose. A mighty sneeze rocked him, and his crossed legs sticking out from under the bed splayed wide, kicking to the air again and again, with more sneezes abusing him. The more he sneezed, the more dust got loosened to drift down. Hands cupped over his face, he sneezed into his palms, wetting them with snot and saliva.

Bellard had always felt so comfortable under the bed. It was something solid, always there to protect him from an angry father or mother ready to hand out a proper whipping he thought he didn't deserve. A place where he could hide and be himself, even if it was mostly in his head. The bouts of sneezing lessened, and he thought he had it under control, pulling his eyes wide and wriggling his nose, when out of nowhere, another sneeze jerked his head up, knocking it on the underside of the bed, rocking him with the hit. 'Ow! Bastard!' he cussed, and he wiggled out from under the bed, quickly rising to put distance between him and the dust.

'What are you doing?' came an unexpected voice from his left. He hadn't even heard the door swing open, nor her footsteps. Yet, here she stood, arm in a sling, lips trembling and eyes teary. Her eyes were always teary the last few days. And who could blame her? Definitely not Bellard, that was for sure.

'Er . . . I was actually on my way to find ymm—' What he didn't expect was how fast she moved. He had no time to react. She was on top of him in an instant, her salty, wet lips locked to his, tongue snaking and hunting like a thing possessed. Wearing nothing but a thin silky gown, other than the sling holding up her exposed right arm while the left was wrapped in the folds of the material, it wasn't hard to pick up on her motives. Her soft skin prickled with pleasure, goosebumps riding her arms and breasts, her nipples becoming hard, pressed up against his chest. Her vanilla scent filled the room, and with it, a lust that had been kept chained for a long time. It felt good kissing her, though he wasn't sure what he was doing, to be honest.

His pants were becoming an unbearable place as space continued to evaporate, getting smaller and smaller the more things grew. He fumbled at her dress with his bandaged hand, trying not to hurt her arm, but the darn straps were a conglomerate of evil, snaring his clumsy fingers at every turn, where hundreds of the things crisscrossed her back. Whenever he thought he pulled the right one, it would just tighten another. Bellard was on the verge of ripping them apart or biting them off with grinding teeth, when she stepped back with a giggle and merely lifted the gown over her head, leaving only her green Pillar clutched in the arms of a silver necklace.

Bellard was speechless.

There she stood, white hair bristling, exposed to the world in utter vulnerability, skin like milk, so soft and tender. She approached him more slowly, gauging his reaction, and he complied. It was cold outside, but they didn't care. They had each other's warmth. She guided him back to fall on the bed, going down with him in a fell swoop, giggling briefly. Her green eyes seemed brighter than ever while she tugged at his tunic, pulling it over his head and setting to work on his trousers. *The one day I don't wear a robe, and this happens . . . Maybe I should wear trousers more often. It never seemed to work before, though.*

He reached for the goods, having heard that a bit of work beforehand pays off in the long run, so he set out to discover for himself. An adventure was only an adventure if you partook in it, after all. And this was an adventure for him. She was so wet.

This had never happened to Bellard. Women had never made moves towards him, other than to mock and laugh at him. Always being shy, guarded, cautious, and afraid, very little happened that he could count as an adventure, especially a good one.

She stroked his pride and gnawed on his earlobe, kissing the side of his face until reaching his mouth. Gentle, yet urgent fingers clasped his back, then buttocks, sharp nails digging into his skin. His injured back didn't seem so important right now. They could always re-stitch it. They swapped saliva and groans of pleasure, his hand becoming numb and tired, the cramps getting harsher. Bellard kissed her neck and worked his way down to her breast, nibbling and tonguing her teat.

'Ow!' she squealed, and he stiffened, unsure of what to do. 'Just a little softer,' she continued, grabbing hold of his hair and pressing his face down between her breasts.

There was only one thing left to do . . .

* * *

He didn't know how much he needed that until now. And he assumed so did she. 'Well, that happened . . .' Bellard whispered, hoping for any response from her. She had been lying next to him without a word, unmoving. The sheets covered her rump and part of her back, her shoulder blade pushed up where she lay on her arm, forming a ridge that looked like a mountain, and Bellard could only imagine there to be the most beautiful valley at its feet. He traced his fingers over the ridge and felt her stir. 'Are you okay?' Instinctive thoughts of her regret flashed a sheen of sweat on his forehead. *Why wouldn't she regret it? It's me, after all.* The relaxed atmosphere he thought roamed in the room, turned to one of tension, awkwardness. 'I'm sorry, if I did—'

'No, it's not like that,' she whispered, face kept turned away. 'It's just . . . I hope this doesn't ruin our friendship.'

Friendship, yes . . . What did I think this was? He begrudgingly pulled his hand away, teeth clenched. 'We won't let it,' Bellard said in his calmest, gentlest voice.

19. The Stowaway

Many of the Shadow Guard were readying their gear, loading a queue of wagons with large barrels of water, taking three men to lift each to the bed, crates of food, pots, and pans. Another brought the rolled-up tarps for tents and shovels to dig latrines and other necessary earthwork. *It seems they are planning to be away for a while. Whatever these travellers have noticed has Lord Latimus's head on a swivel.*

The hastily gathered gear in the pack was pushing hard, sharp ends into Calmantis's back, dragging at his shoulders, overweight and out of line. He wobbled forward, keeping an eye on the patrolling guards near the entrance of the temple. The front wagon, covered with a white tarp, seemed to be loaded to the brim. *Second from the front still has space on the right, next to the crate of swords,* he judged. *But it's too close to the guards still packing.* It had to be the third in line. A tarp lay half covering the items within; extra boots and uniforms were all he could see sticking out.

Calmantis moved to a tree, taking cover behind its trunk. There were twenty guards he could see, and more manned the gates. Harsh sun leered at him, burning big white balls into his vision, dragging long threads every time he adjusted his eyes. Men vanished behind those balls. Even when he closed his eyes, they remained unchanged, their bright silhouettes burned into his lids. He squeezed his eyes shut and rubbed them hard with finger and thumb, hoping to regain his sight soon.

'Oi! What are you doing with that?' a voice shouted from close-by, startling him into a run.

He did not get very far.

Pain shot through his right foot as he stubbed his big toe against what must have been a bastard of a root sticking up from the ground, tripping him to plant face first into the grass, a splash of wetness sloshing over him, backpack digging into his side. Spitting out wet leaves and tufts of grass, he gagged a little, smelling stale water, when a pair of boots came into view.

'What do we have here? Cal, just where do you think you're going now?' Calmantis jumped up and gave his face a good wipe, flicking off the excess grass and water. He stared into the eyes of a pale-faced Shadow Guard, freckles covering his stubby nose and cheeks, red hair curling in all directions.

'Er . . . Just needed to get some fresh air, Tannis. Why are you everywhere I turn lately? Feels like I can't take a shit in private without you watching over my shoulder, waiting for the plop to drop. You stalking me?'

'I don't have time for this. Get back to your duties. I'm sure there's plenty to do.' Tannis strode off to the sandstone building on his right, where Norai was busy preparing lunch for them.

Calmantis's stomach growled at the thought of food, and he saw more guards make their way to the kitchen. This was his chance to get onto the wagon, but that meant not getting any food. *For the greater good then . . .* He ran across the lawn and leapt onto the bed of the wagon, quickly drawing the tarp closed, working his fingers to hook the ropes around the catches on the side.

Damn, it's hot in here. No air flowed under the tarp, and even in the shade of the trees where the wagons waited, the heat was oppressive today. His stomach lurched and growled, rumbling and feeling thin. He had known hunger before, during the months of struggling to find work, struggling to make ends meet. Sure, he could go home to his parents and ask for coin, but the thought never even crossed his mind. He was his own man, reaching for his own goals, however strange they might appear to some.

Wedged in between the boxes, he wished he had taken a food cart instead, one with some water on. He was getting mightily thirsty. *Maybe I can sneak back out and jump into one of the other wagons.* He wiggled his backside down the wagon, working his way to the tailgate, when the kitchen door was flung open, banging against the sandstone wall, no doubt leaving a nasty chip in it. He quickly scampered back into place, lying down and clutching his pack in front of his chest.

'Are we ready to set out, Knight-Marshall Rechker?' asked the clairvoy, the sound of his sandals dragging over the paving near the wagon.

'Yes, sir. We have loaded the wagons, and the men have eaten their fill. Once we get going, we won't stop until late tonight to make camp.'

'Good. The sooner we can leave and find out what has Lord Latimus so worried, the sooner we can come back.'

'Couldn't agree more, sir.' Rechker's voice sounded hoarse, as if he had been fighting a cold, and the cold was winning. He was not Calmantis's biggest fan, not even close, but he was an honourable man.

* * *

He needed to pee so badly . . .

The more Calmantis struggled not to think about urinating, the more it seemed to head in that direction. *Dry bread. Dry dread, dry bread for breakfast . . . served with a pitcher of cold, refreshing wine – No!* His eyes flared wide, and he held it in, forcing the flow to come to a begrudging stop. A sharp pain shot through his groin, and he nearly let the flow continue.

They had trudged up steep hills on one side and down the other the entire day, non-stop, legs working autonomously, groaning about fiercely burning muscles. Even the horses were complaining, neighing, and snorting contemptuously at their riders. Of course, this would not bother Calmantis in the least, lying comfortably in the back of the wagon on a pile of uniforms he had pulled from the crate on his right. Now, though, it had got to where every move he made felt like his bladder was about to burst, and the jostling road did not help things at all. The wagon kicked him in the back and hurled him into the air to thud back down on the bed with little sympathy. He was sure a little urine escaped with the hit.

'Ow! Damn. Fine. I can't take it anymore.' Calmantis wrestled with the tarp, swinging his arms until he finally loosened a rope enough for him to poke his head out, drawing a big breath of fresh air. A train of loud shouts brought the wagons to a stop, and guards assembled from all corners, swords and spears held at the ready. Angry horses' faces glared at him from above, their riders scowling in contempt. 'It's just me! Calmantis.'

Strong, metal-clad hands mercilessly pulled him from the wagon and flung him over the side. He clung and scratched and clawed at the arms not to be cast to the ground like a common piece of rubbish, but it all happened so fast. Calmantis hit the ground with a great expulsion of air, arching his back from the pain of the blow, face screwed to a scowl. Could it be that he'd underestimated their annoyance? Quite possibly. Through his tear-filled struggle for breath, gasps of air raced to his lungs that felt like they would never reach their goal, and he heard a soldier shout next to him.

'What in the underworld are you doing here, Cal?'

The gasps continued, aided by harsh coughing that hurt his throat. 'I think I swallowed my spleen.' He could not hold it any longer. A warmth spread from his groin, the blissful release from what had plagued him for so long, now stained his pants, spreading dark and wet.

'Ah, f—' The guard caught himself. 'Cal, you sick bastard! Why couldn't you hold it in? The bush is right there.'

'Ahh,' Calmantis groaned. 'It's too late. I couldn't. Couldn't keep it in any longer.' The words came as sporadic spurts while he rolled on the ground, kicking his right leg like an angry mule to free some of the urine trapped in his pants. A dark steel gauntlet gripped his shoulder again, and the world spun around him, his back hitting the wagon's side wall with a crack.

'You are not supposed to be here!' stormed Ackelides, drawing his helm off, his hair looking dark and sticky under the mail coif covering his head. 'You are putting all our lives at risk by being here! Start walking! Go back to Baldor!'

'But I just wanted to prove—'

'I don't care what you want! Walk!'

'Hold on, Captain. We are too far from the city. He will not make it back on foot without supplies,' said Clairvoy Yeron, and he sauntered closer, wearing only leather armour around his chest, arms, legs, and groin, a fluff of brown and white from the padding and tunic sticking out underneath.

The veins on Ackelides's forehead pulsed angrily, his eyes becoming wild with anger. 'I don't care. I will not risk my men because of him.' He stepped in front of Yeron, staring down at the shorter man.

'I have no love for this man, any more than you do.' Calmantis's mouth dropped open. And he wanted to say something, but Yeron was already continuing. 'But if someone so - apologies, Calmantis - *deplorable* could cause danger to all of you, then I think it is time to re-evaluate your position as part of the Shadow Guard, wouldn't you agree?'

Calmantis rolled his head back to lean against the wagon, eyes fixed to the sky. *Deplorable* . . . Words hurt, no matter if there was an apology or not. And Calmantis'd had his fill throughout his life, being called all kinds of names, from all kinds of people. All thinking they were better than him. *More words, more sticks, more stones.* He could've worked alongside his parents, taking up ownership to continue their legacy, but Calmantis wanted a legacy of his own.

A black stain in the blue sky swerved and glided up high, catching his eye. It was too far away to say what it was. *Maybe a sheet that got taken by the winds, or a large odd-looking bird of some sort.* It gradually grew, and he squinted, face pulling into a sneer, trying to bring it into focus.

A hard hand shoved him in the chest, back against the wagon's wall, and Ackelides demanded, 'What are you leering at, buffoon? Say something!'

The hit had knocked the air from his lungs, and Calmantis coughed and spat, sucking in air in a rasp. 'I was looking at that thing in the sky.' Soldiers turned their heads, searching the air.

'What are you talking about?' asked Tannis, hand cupped over his eyes.

He coughed again and searched for the blotch. 'There.' It appeared from behind a lonely cloud, a triangular mass with wings in tatters that seemed to shed pieces of itself as it flew, tearing off in its wake to burn away before they ever reached the ground. It was sporadic in its movements, diving to a skein of geese flapping their wings to get away from it, clucking and moaning in fear. The gigantic blotch rushed into the fleeing geese a few hundred feet over a pond, ripping into them with a spray of blood and feathers.

The guards jumped back with a start, and Tannis made the protective sign of the Order of the Eternal Sacrament, drawing a circle with a cross on his forehead. 'What is that?' he shouted, and the beast swung to them, his outburst having drawn its attention.

'Take cover!' Ackelides shouted, and everyone ran to cower behind the wagons. But the horses got spooked, stamping their feet and crying in fear, and started pulling the wagons forward while the drivers fought to calm them. Those on their mounts dashed away to pull the creature's attention from the slower wagons, swinging arms and belting, but the beast did not waver. It drew near with an ungodly shriek, a scream that sounded like the dying of a thousand children. Its blackened fangs were revealed behind a gaping maw, small beady eyes darting crazily, its tattered wings like black fire sucking the light from around it as if stealing the very sun and the life it brings.

Calmantis had dived under the wagon, heart racing, piss pumping. He did not know there could be so much urine inside of him, and at this stage, he wasn't sure if it was just because of the amount itself or out of fear, that it was flowing like a gushing waterfall. The beast pulled up and collided with the wagon, shearing off the top rails and stripping the tarp, tearing long white strands with its claws and rocking the wagon on two wheels. Calmantis was briefly exposed before it fell back on its other wheels with a shatter of wood, splinters flying, beams cracking. Luckily, the beast had gone past too fast to notice him at the bottom.

The men that cowered behind the wagon screamed and slashed with their swords, brandishing their weapons to kill the beast. When the wagon tipped, they had all grabbed at it, pushing it away to fall back on its wheels. Having limited supplies, they could not lose too much, and the thought alone of being crushed under its weight was reason enough for them to act swiftly.

'Where's Otrah?' one shouted, searching left and right. 'Where's my brother? What in the name of Aztar was that?'

'Dear god,' someone muttered. 'Over there!' Calmantis couldn't see. The wagon's wheel was in his way. On his elbows and knees, he crawled out and saw a limp pair of legs flailing from the beast's mouth, moments before they were gobbled up with a shake of its head.

'No! No! Otrah! No!' The guard dropped on the ground, wallowing in anguish, crying his heart out. 'What will I tell our mother?' The beast banked before the sun, its wings blocking out the rays, sucking the light away. 'I will avenge you, Brother!' the soldier screamed, casting his helm to the ground, and ran at the charging beast, when Ackelides intercepted the man, cutting him off with his armoured horse.

'Get back in line, Embra! That's an order!'

'To the underworld with your orders! That's my brother!'

'Get down!' Ackelides shouted and leapt from his horse, crashing into Embra and taking him to the ground as the beast crushed the horse's armour, snapping bones with the hit. It flung the horse off its feet and over the two men, colliding with the earth in a spray of dirt and blood.

Calmantis had his hands before his eyes, fingers spread open so he could still see, although everything in his body told him to look away. 'Ride! Go now!' shouted Ackelides from somewhere beyond the beast as it scanned the broken horse with its glistening eyes, like it was trying to understand what it was. Then it snapped out its shadowy neck and tore into the dying animal with little remorse. It all happened so fast.

Wagons lurched forward, and they left Calmantis by the wayside while he stood dumbfounded at what he was bearing witness to. 'Hey, wait for me!' he shouted, and sprinted with his long legs scything through the air to catch up, eating dust from the back of the wagon, not wanting to be left in the field alone with that thing so close-by. He jumped on the last wagon, crashing into the supplies. Splintered wheels creaked and groaned, wobbling under the weight of the load.

'Get the wagons out of here!' shouted Clairvoy Yeron from astride his horse, galloping next to Calmantis before veering away and pulling most of the mounted guards with him back in the beast's direction. 'Head for the mountains! We will find you!'

Calmantis could still see the beast in the distance, standing only a few feet from Ackelides and Embra, their swords at the ready. Yeron and ten others pushed their mounts across the field, dragging dark lines through the tall grass. The wagons were at the rise's top, and soon his view diminished, taken from him by the drop of the land. 'Yah!' he heard the wagon drivers urge on the horses, leads lashing, whips cracking, wild-eyed mounts pushing their hearts to the limit of bursting.

He remembered a day when his father took him hunting. A tremendous event with bows and arrows, wine and more wine. They had come to hunt deer, hoping to smoke-dry the meats, a delicious treat. *'A father-and-son excursion,'* he had said it was. An opportunity for them to bond. *It seemed more like an opportunity for him to drink without Mother nagging in his ear. Not that she was some sort of saint.*

For the first half of the day, his father had sat on a rock, washing his mouth out with wine, gulping one large drink after another. 'Know when to be a man! Cal . . . Can't always be a-a child. You know. We—' The hiccups assailed his father, long combed hair slipping out from behind his ears to fall over his face, wet and unclean. 'Can't be made a fool of, my boy! You know.' Another hiccup, sounding painful, and his father clutched his chest. 'Damn annoying, bloody hiccups. Just the devil's work this, you know. Giving honest men a taste of torture.'

'Yes, Father,' he muttered, wishing he could go home to play with Nestra, a friend he had made one morning on their way to the market. A poor boy. Too poor to be seen with them, according to his parents. But in Cal's eyes, Nestra was richer than anyone. He had the freedom to do what he wanted, and didn't care who he was friends with, to go where he pleased.

'Come, boy! It's time I showed you how to be a man,' his father said, and gained momentum, rocking back and forth to get up from the boulder, arms held out in front of his pot-bellied show of richness, the finest silk shirt glinting in the sun. 'Ah, there we go. Here, take this,' he slurred, handing Calmantis a bow and quiver stuck with arrows. 'How old are you now, Cal?' His father rounded on him. 'Nine, is it?'

'Eleven.'

'No need to be snotty about it.' His father stumbled over to the horse and planted his foot in the stirrup, but his stomach impeded his knee, expelling the air from his lungs with a wheeze as he reached for the horn to pull himself up. It took a few tries, but he eventually managed, and reached down to pull Calmantis from the ground, scraping his tiny legs against the saddle's rough leather and buckles. *What a wonderful day . . .*

They had walked the poor horse up the valley and down to the ravine, across great fields and up more steep hills, searching for a proper deer, having no luck at all. Night-time was crawling closer, taking the colour from the day, changing perspectives, and bringing an unease with it. It wasn't until they'd reached the riverside that Calmantis saw the most magnificent black stag he had ever seen, drinking from the river. Its horns were a feasting honey locust tree, spreading wild and wonderful, the colour of bark, blending in with its dark pelt. It had the most amazing white marks under its gentle eyes, looking like flowing tears down to a hairy mane.

Sure enough, his father saw it too. 'Will you look at that . . . We have been blessed, my boy. We can't let it get away.' His loud voice spooked the animal, and it bucked and ran, crashing through the shrubs in the forest. 'Damn it! See what you've done! Hold tight!' They gave chase, pushing the horse hard to catch up with the stag, galloping to their right skilfully like a practised master, leaping over a fallen tree. Calmantis clutched the bow and horn, crying not to be thrown from the racing horse, the earth never slowing beneath them. They were gaining on it. Hoofs splashed in the water of the shallow river and out the other side with a long jump, the horse snorting and blowing loudly. Ahead of them, through the bog, the stag veered right, heading up the rapidly rising valley floor.

'Cal! At the next corner, you shoot! Okay?' He had never even pulled a bowstring. He did not know what to do, but as it happened, he didn't need to know. The horse snorted and sucked in air, rasping breaths coming out in stutters. Its muscles tensed and froze up, squeals of pain riding up its throat, throwing its head back, and it collapsed under them. Dead.

Calmantis was flung over the horse's head, and his father over him. The ground rushed at them, and the stag got away. He was glad about the way it turned out, and even a little broken arm wouldn't change that. He never forgot those enormous eyes of the horse where it lay snorting its last breaths.

'Slow the horses!' Calmantis shouted, coming back to reality. 'Let them breathe!' The beasts kept thundering over the hard trodden road, yellow-brown grass fields whisking by. 'I said slow the horses!' The wagon bounced from a rut in the road, and he was thrown against the railings, smashing into crates filled with pots and pans. Gear clattered on the dirt road, whirling in the dust behind them, flashing in the light of the day. They could not see the beast, nor the clairvoy and his Shadow Guard. 'Stop or I'll jump!'

'There's no way I'm stopping this wagon!'

For all his faults, one thing was certain: Calmantis was no coward. Not in his mind, that was. That didn't make him smart, but it certainly made him stubborn. Light brown earth sped by, with dark patches glinting back, spraying water whenever the wheels hit them, the grinding of wood on soil never silent. He jumped . . .

Would it become surprising to realise a little too late that the ground indeed was rushing by quite fast? Calmantis found out halfway between the wagon and the ground, while the driver reached back to grab him from behind. It was a vain effort. His teeth clattered with the hit, immediately tasting blood when his feet got pulled out from under him. He had the good sense to tuck his arms over his head and felt as abused as the wagon wheels while he tumbled head over heels, arse over face, until coming to a standstill. *Why on earth did I think that my jumping would make him stop the wagon? That was as dull an idea as my mother's cooking.*

'Argh!' Calmantis howled, face planted in a patch of wet dirt he hadn't seen coming. There was silence all around him, the long grass waving in the winds, and not much else. No wagons with angry guards, no beast bearing down on him, no winding road. 'What happened? Where am I?' He wiped the muck from his face with his sleeve and shook his head, and a big ball of spit choked his airway momentarily, restricting his breath for a terrifying heartbeat. Then he blinked, and the wagons were suddenly there again, the air tense and urgent.

'Cal! Where are you? What are you doing, man? We've got to get out of here, before that thing comes for us!' the driver yelled, drawing on the reins and forcing the rest of them to stop the other carts.

His elbows hurt, and he bled from multiple scrapes on his arms, hands, legs, and head, a layer of dirt concealing their whereabouts. '*Ahem.*' He coughed and spat some red mucus on the ground, drawing an uneasy breath. 'That hurt.'

'Nah, really? Get on the wagon!'

Arguing seemed less important now. He felt he had made his point. *Why argue when you've won, right?* Right arm folded in under him like a chicken's wing, he hobbled to the wagon and climbed up the side, dropping to the heap of clothes.

20. Heads or Tails

His eyes were burning and watery, and all he wanted to do was sleep for a while. Jonas couldn't understand how all this worked, how his soul could be disconnected from his body, when he was still supposedly alive, and with this new information that his body didn't possess his consciousness, he was even more confused. Then again, he was a simple tree feller. His days of adventure were long since passed. Or so he hoped. It was a rarity these days to get what you hoped for, though. He should have known that. He squeezed his eyes closed and pulled at his mouth, felt the torn corners splitting open, his scabbed lip tearing with the strain. His tunic came away with drops of blood as he dabbed at it.

A thought popped into his head, and he palmed his clothes urgently, searching, and felt the coin in his breast pocket. He thought he'd lost it. Fingers and hands wrapped in torn cloth, he pulled the silver coin from his pocket, smiling as he did. This little item that had given him so much pain and suffering, yet was an endearing companion for so very long, truly knew the meaning of friendship, or so Jonas thought. It always told him what he needed to hear, especially when the risks were high.

How many times had he rubbed the coin, wearing the symbol down to an indistinct memory: the crown of Westopher Ogiffe, king of kings. The Great North's failed uniter. For all his promises of fame and glory, the North was set to rise again. To crawl from the ashes to become the great nation it once was in the time of old. So many Northerners flocked to him, taking refuge under his guiding wings of steel and blood, but so did his enemies . . . And they got a step closer than they should have. Wolves in sheep's clothing, they accepted his rulership, only to slit his throat while he slept soundly.

A half-hearted cough of laughter escaped him as he rubbed the coin, feeling the smooth bottom, and Jonas called out, 'Tails.' He watched it spin in the air, glimmering red from the low fires, and snatched it from the air, slamming it on the top of his left hand. He removed his hand and stared at the crown on the coin. *Heads . . .* 'Guess I'm doing this then.' Jonas tilted his head up and stared at his cage.

Subjected to the tremendous amount of heat over a very long period, the metal bars of the cage had melted over time, dripping like wax from burning candles, streaming down the sides at a snail's pace, thinning the tops to thick rusted bastions. One bar in particular seemed to have taken the beatings worse than the others, having sheared down its centre, leaving the frail and weathered tops to buckle under the pressure. Jonas placed his bare feet on the rusted bars, the filthy sharp edges cutting into his soles while he climbed for the top, arms pulling, feet pushing, to lift his body with a wince and a groan. He had to be quiet and bear with the pain.

On a patch of blackened rock not far away lay the darcöle. Its flaming body had morphed into a soft glow of blue, a deep bearlike gurgle drifting from its sleeping form, thick, muscular arms tucked under its head.

The bars were old and worn, turned orange from the rust. A lifetime of neglect that would serve him well today. He reached the top of the cage and grabbed hold of the crossbar above him with one hand, pushing and pulling with the other on the neglected bar, working the stubborn iron back and forth with minimal movement. The metal edges scraped over each other, a screeching sound deafening to him. For a moment, he thought he saw movement from the beast, and stopped, anxiously glancing at it, waiting for it to rise with that dreadful whip, yet time stretched and nothing happened. It lay snoring with eyes closed, unaware of the activity from the cage.

Come on! Break, damn it! Jonas grunted, clenching his aching jaw while he pushed on the shard of metal, bending it until it snapped with a loud clangour reverberating through the structure. His foot slipped, metal cutting deeper into him. Head bouncing off the rails, he tried to grip them to stop his fall, fingers slipping from the rough iron, knees buckling from the impact on the floor. He lay there on his back, groaning in agony, and heard the beast awaken with a soft bellow, its eyes scanning him where he lay.

It rose, carefully gauging Jonas from afar, and steadily made its way closer. A crown of fire blazed above its head like a violent halo, fire coursing through its very veins in such magnitude that its dark-charred scales and flesh could not contain it. A scalding slime simmered over its entire being, volatile and angry, igniting with the touch of air.

Jonas lay on his back and pressed up to his elbows, working his way to a sitting position, eyes locked on it. There was a certain intelligence behind those dead eyes. It was not a mindless beast. *How did they get you to do their bidding?*

It rumbled a few words in a language that sounded like rocks being shattered by hundreds of gigantic hammers pounding away. Jonas gripped his head, clasping his hands over his ears to find relief in blocking out the noise. And though it only helped to a degree, it was better than nothing. He glimpsed the rusted rod at his feet and slowly bent to pick it up, hiding it behind his back. You didn't have to like something to have respect for it, and this creature deserved some. After the torturous conversation, the darcöle blew a puff of black smoke through its cavernous nostrils and bent down low to leer into the cage at him.

There was no thought to it. Jonas moved fast, running and jumping from the ground with the sharp shard of metal in his hands, driving it with all his strength into the head of the beast, then quickly jumped back. Cries and roars of pain and fury echoed through the chambers as the beast thrashed about, the rod protruding from its head, scraping the ceiling and walls, sending sparks flying all over. Flames exploded from the beast, and it crashed into the cage with its tremendous weight, rocking it up and to the side, then swiped its claw into the cage. Jonas dropped to the floor, keeping away from the searing heat radiating from the claw.

The old metal bars couldn't take much more of the abuse. They groaned and bent under the weight of the beast, lowering the heated ceiling closer and closer to Jonas's face. The cage rocked, and the darcöle slammed its fists on its roof, again and again, forcing it to the ground, mangling the iron. The creature unleashed a roar of anger as it stumbled away, claws hunting for the tip of the shard.

'Come on! Just die!' Jonas screamed where he sat on his haunches, watching it thrash about.

It grasped the iron shard and dragged it out, a tremendous roar erupting from its maw, gigantic black fangs that seemed to steal the night flashing between the fire living within. 'Just die already!' The shard peeled from its head, and its legs nearly buckled, a fountain of red and fire spraying up moments before the flaming whip came into view, harsher than ever before. Smoke and streaks of fire burned wherever it touched, cutting grooves into the rock walls and floor.

Then it came at him. *Oh shit!*

The metal around him stood no chance. The whip cut through the bars like a warm knife through butter, never even registering that something tried to stop it. Jonas jumped to his left, avoiding the wild swing, landing face first and scraping his forehead on the jagged floor. He felt the coin press into his chest and rolled his eyes. 'Bloody heads . . .'

Half of the cage careened away with a diagonal cut of the whip, the white-hot rails sizzling furiously, and Jonas jerked away from the cacophony of sounds and sights of spraying red-hot metal, protecting his head with his arms. Showered by the hot shavings, the hairs on his arms and legs melted away, while sharp-tipped metal rods crashed to the ground around him.

What I wouldn't do for a glass of cool water. I would definitely sell my soul for a pint of ale. If Danu had any brains at all, that's how she would've turned me . . .

The darcöle shook its head dizzily, the gaping hole in its skull sloshing burning liquids from above to stream down its gruesome face. It had no nose to speak of, just the flaring nostrils. It was struggling to aim the whip, snapping it down again to cut a section of the cage open, metal bars grinding over each other horribly, collapsing towards Jonas with spiked shards coming in fast and furious. He dived to the right, missing most, but one spike drove into his right biceps, slicing deep and burning utterly, grinding to a halt on the bone. 'Aaaagh! Bastard!'

On the floor, with the bar still in his arm, Jonas was in an awkward position where he was lying on his stomach. His plan had almost worked. The cage was destroyed, sheared open right before him, but he could not get out from under the collapsed roof. Every move he made saw the metal rod grind against his bone, tearing the muscle further. It hurt tremendously. His other hand was in no position to push the rod out, he had no leverage. Rocks fell from up high while the beast thrashed in anger, bouncing off the cage, sagging it closer to his head, metal rod ripping into his arm. 'Argh!' Dust drifted down, obscuring his view, yet he could still see the orange glow of the beast crashing into the sides and the swinging whip.

He brought his left arm up as far as he could and pushed on the ground, trying to lift the roof, grinding the rusted metal rod deeper into him, which set him screaming in pain.

It would not budge.

The beast grew suddenly quiet, its heavy breathing an excellent sign that it hadn't died. 'Shit . . .' Jonas squirmed under the iron, tearing the rod through his flesh as fast as he could bear. But flesh was quite resistant to tearing when used with a blunt object, Jonas could vouch for it.

The floor shook with every footstep as the beast drew closer, a fierce glow of orange and red getting brighter through the heavy dust and smoke. The whip cracked next to the cage, sparks flying, with a snap like lightning. He knew the beast was toying with him now. Jonas was dizzy and scared. This was not a good idea. He could heal from a torn muscle. He was not so sure if he could survive being torn in half.

All Jonas had ever wanted to do was settle down with his wife Ayla, raise their boy to see him become a man, and grow old drinking too much ale. And for a time, he really thought that it might've been possible, that his old days of warring were behind him. It seemed now he was mistaken. Ayla had so much hope for him, even knowing what he had done, what brutal life he had led. She was so sure that he could change that she paid the ultimate price for it, and he would never forgive himself. One thing he was sure of, though. He would take every single one that was involved with her murder down with him. He pulled his arm, slowly tearing the rod out sideways, destroying his biceps.

The beast was getting close now, the warmth of its ever-burning fires raging bright through the dust. The disgusting smell getting stronger, becoming palpable. He really thought he could do it, tear the rod from his arm and scamper from the cave, avoid the beast and get away somehow. But the pain was greater than he could endure. Black spots appeared in his vision, and nausea overtook him, the world darkening around him, night swiftly closing in.

Faint sounds brushed his ears, a drumming, a beating, scraping, and snapping, a crack of the whip, waking him to the vile taste in his mouth. He spat out the last bits of vomit and pulled his arm further, getting dizzy once again. *Ya weak bastard! Push through it!*

A light exploded in his sight, and he was sure he had passed out again, but it was the strangest dream. He was still in the lair, still pinned by the cage, but in the light before him, he saw Vernak's old face, calling out to him and waving for him to run to them. There was a sense of urgency in the old one's face. 'I'm stuck,' he heard himself mutter and saw the anger reflected in Vernak's dull eyes.

What a strange dream. You have to wake up, Jonas! he thought. A big woman, with dark skin and a full bush of black hair bouncing on her head, followed Vernak from the light, a scared look on her face.

'We should not be here!' she said, glancing around. 'We have to go!' The whip snapped from the dust, cracking against the cage at the back, and the rumbling through the earth quickened. If the beast had been toying with him before, it was about to end. She fell against the rails of the cage, covering her face as she screamed in Vernak's ear.

Jonas reached for her foot and touched it, feeling the leather of her sandals brush his fingers, her cool body as he ran his hand up her calf. 'You're real?' he asked, stunned, wanting to believe it. 'Well, get me out of here!' he shouted at Vernak, greeted by an icy stare, humourless and unsympathetic.

'If we can't get his soul, get his consciousness. We will have to come back for it later,' said Vernak as he turned to the darcöle. 'I can't hold this thing away for long. Get it done!'

'This is not what I signed up for!' the woman screamed, her fear so close to the surface.

'I said get it done!' Vernak changed, seemed bigger somehow, authority flooding from him in thick waves, yet he looked the same to Jonas. Ripples of power flowed over him, his calm old face set stern in the face of danger. 'I am your superior! You, Malgor, answer to all of us! Stop this now or pay with your life!'

The darcöle stopped its advance and glared at Vernak, with the gigantic flaming whip and axe in hand, massive tail flicking at the back. It pointed at Jonas, then at its head, making the strange noise that must have been its language.

'What's he doing?' asked the woman, mania in her eyes, rubbing her palms together and placing them on Jonas's arm and the rod. She started pulling on both, heaving her impressive bosom and behind, worming backwards to bend the rod.

'Argh! I don't know, but we don't have long. Hurry,' Jonas slurred, nearing the point of fainting again. He bit his lip and pushed as hard as he could, hearing the tendons snap under the pressure. Jolting pain like when you hit your elbow just right shot through his arm, only a thousand times worse. 'Stop! Please! Just stop this!' he yelled and vomited. The yellow bile flowed to pool under him, adding to the stench in the lair.

'It wants you to pay for what you did. It calls you without honour. Says you are a snake. You hurt him badly with the metal.'

'You can talk with that thing?' Jonas and the woman asked together.

A great roar sounded, and the beast charged, whip and axe swinging, not giving Vernak a chance to respond. The old man retreated a few steps, waving his arms, and a great sphere of thick air enveloped the creature, swirling around it in a mass that flowed like liquid. Malgor fought with it, struggling for breath as the fire from his body was pulled into a blazing inferno around him, sucking out the oxygen.

'Hurry!' shouted Jonas, and the woman nodded fiercely. Her hands were strangely cold in this fiery place, her palms caressing his hot cheeks.

'I can't get your soul out. I'm sorry.'

Survive to fight another day . . . Jonas nodded and felt his head turn hot, his cheeks and teeth burning from the inside. A great howl came from within the swirling mass, and the darcöle broke free, dissipating the air and immediately getting buffeted by powerful gusts.

'Quickly now!' Vernak shouted. It was gaining ground, snapping the whip at them, and Vernak had to dive out of the way not to get hit by the iron-melting weapon. Malgor cleaved the axe into the ground and dragged itself closer with a burning vengeance.

'You have to let go, Jonas! I can't make you leave your soul. It has to be your choice,' said the woman, sweat pouring down her chubby round face, eyes flicking back to the beast. 'And whatever you do, please touch nothing.'

For once, he would like it if something wasn't his choice. That someone else made the decisions, and he could just follow their lead. Some had called him a born leader, others a ruthless killer, all thanks to the choices he'd made. He had learned from a young age that not everyone could be pleased, no matter what you did for them. And so, he had stopped trying. He closed his mind to what was happening around him, focused on his own problems, and felt the embrace of his soul, begging him to stay. It would be a lot easier to die right here and join his Ayla. Yet he knew she would not forgive him if he were to leave their son to fend for himself. 'I have to go.'

It felt strange getting separated. Being cut away from the thing that made you human, the thing that kept you in check. His effigy gripped him with all its power, holding tight to the last bits it knew to be mortal, pleading with him not to leave. In his mind he saw his own terrified face, afraid of what was to come. Especially now with Malgor so angry. 'If we are to survive, you have to let me go. I will come back for you, I promise.'

The effigy let go of him, and the world dragged him into inky blackness while the woman called to him.

* * *

All around him, the stars flashed and sparkled, and the smell of wet grass reached for his nose, calming his frayed nerves. Before him stood a lake, reflecting the sky above, winding far and wide past the gigantic dark shapes of mountains, and trees swaying gently in the breeze. He stood on the only patch of grass, no larger than a barrow in the centre of the lake; the shore being lapped by small waves far in the distance. Jonas could not see it, but he could hear the water rolling over small rocks and pebbles.

'Touch nothing?' Jonas pondered, scratching his head. 'There's nothing to touch . . .' He reached down into the cool water, splashing it over his face, and saw the stars move with the ripples of the water. Head tilted, he reached down again slowly, trying not to disturb the water, until tiny pebbles scraped against his fingers. Hand cupped, he carefully withdrew, his hand lined with a profusion of glittering stars, hundreds of them, all just in his palm. One dropped from his hand and splashed into the lake, birthing a gigantic ripple that spread far and wide, before a vision appeared in the water. Jonas jumped back, clasping his hand shut not to drop any more.

It was the big woman but younger, and her figure was not as rounded yet. She sat on the edge of a wharf, feet dangling over the side, while she mumbled songs with a sweet youthful voice, a fishing pole in her hands, with some line dangling in the water. She was the only one there, enjoying the early sun rising over the water, fish leaping out in flashes of silver.

'Ugh! I'm so bored. These fish don't want to eat anything,' she muttered, kicking her toe through the water and flicking up a spray into the air. The sun beetles sang their songs, loud and proud, a shrill cry for attention. Crickets and frogs chirped and croaked the day away, while the woman continued her pursuit of fish. She turned around, searching the forest behind her, and seeing no one, laid her pole down.

She turned to lie flat on her stomach and reached for the water, slipping her hands under the murkiness. Eyes closed, she started to giggle and laugh, like she was being tickled, her mouth stretching wide with joy, goosebumps riding her skin. All around her, the water came alive, white foam forming on the choppy tops, a whirlpool of aggravated fish getting closer. Fish jumped from all over, leaping onto the wooden deck and knocking into the girl. At first there was joy, with the abundance of food suddenly available, but then it turned into a disturbance in their nature. Fish of all sizes and forms crashed into the platform, rocking it violently, and even after the girl yanked her hands from the water, they did not stop.

A screech of terror escaped her as she grabbed the rod and net from the ground and ran for the land, arms flailing to keep her balance on the rickety old deck. A large fish sailed from the water, teeth snapping, its body writhing through the air and cracking her in the face. She dropped to the ground and crawled the rest of the way to reach land. On the edge of the water, she watched the carnage take place.

The platform groaned and creaked, rocked and shook, until finally, its columns cracked and broke, ripping it off the side to be dragged into the water. While it sank to its grave, something tugged on the line, and the girl held tight to the rod, carefully pulling it in. A fish leaped from the water, hooked, thrashing about angrily, but she had him well and done, dragging it close to land it with the net. It would be a good meal for her family today, and she smiled, until a shout came from behind.

'Erechol!' A man ran at her, waving his finger angrily. 'What have I told you about using your abilities?' He grabbed the net with the thrashing fish inside and killed it with a rock he carried.

'I'm sorry, Papa! But the fish weren't biting, and we are so hungry.'

'Erechol! You know it's unwise to use your gifts without the focus of a Pillar. You are too young! Just look at what you have done! How will we fish now? Huh? Stupid girl . . . You could have been hurt!'

'I'm sorry, Papa!' Erechol cried, mouth curling into a frown while tears streamed down her round cheeks. Her father shook his head and rubbed his eyes with a great sigh, breathing deep to calm himself.

'Okay, okay. Come, we will figure this out. Important thing is you're safe and we can eat today.' He wiped her tears and took the rod from her, leading her away into the forest.

The vision faded as fast as it appeared, and the lake before Jonas turned calm once more. He glanced over the water and thought, *There must be millions of these in here.* With a steady hand, he slowly lowered the rest back into the water and backed away from the edge.

'Oof!' Breath exploded from his mouth with an invisible gut punch, doubling him over in search of air. He dropped to his knees, clutching his stomach, and sighed with the tumbling world, getting yanked off his feet. He crashed into the invisible walls of this domain, rolling around, getting battered and bruised, until a light appeared at a far end, growing closer at a rapid rate.

There was no time to react.

Jonas was propelled out of this unfamiliar place and hurtled through the vast expanse of space and time. The wind howled past him, whipping his hair wildly around his face. There was no time to scream, and no one to hear him anyway. The brilliant light gradually dimmed, blending with the rising sun as Jonas landed on the table with a thud, snapping its legs, his body jerking from the impact.

A gaping hole in the wall served as a frame for the scene before him. Bricks, a table's legs, shards of wood, and shattered vials of various hues, herbs and other debris littered the ground around him. Sounds of crying and shouting, cursing and ranting assaulted him. Smoke drifted up from a smouldering curtain that lay in tatters on the ground. Jonas heard a cough to his right and turned to see pots, vases, and other shattered decorations roll closer. His eyes caught sight of a tan foot wearing a sandal, then a leg, wrapped in loose pants smeared black and red, the material flapping in distress. An unfamiliar man with dark eyes and dark hair stumbled past, falling over the debris on the ground. It was his leg he had seen. He waved his arms about to dissipate the dust, struggling for breath as he did.

'Agh!' Jonas coughed and clutched his side, struggling to comprehend what had just occurred. 'What happened?' he croaked.

'Jonas?' came a groggy voice from behind, moments before Vernak's soot-blackened face popped into view. Jonas was back in the mortal realm. Thick smoke hung low, burning his nose. He lifted his hands, opened and closed them, bent his feet up and down, wiggled his toes. Everything still hurt, everything still moved. That was a good sign.

'Vernak? I'm alive?'

'It would seem so. Thanks to the help we received.'

Jonas reached up and took hold of the old one's hand, who pulled him up with care. The room was an utter mess. Broad cracks ran through the foundation and up the walls and ceiling. The ground was unsettled, growling warnings of tremors and aftershocks, an unwelcome gift from an earlier earthquake. In the room's corner, near a broken window, sat Erechol, hands in her hair, crying while her plump body shook, shoulders bouncing to the rhythm of her melancholy.

He glanced at Vernak, who pinched his lips and raised his brows. 'Did I cause all of this?'

'I fear it was the process, yes.' They waded through the destruction. Shelves he assumed were on the wall before now lay on the ground, broken or damaged, their carried jars, vials, and containers lying next to them, bleeding away, liquids leaking on the floor.

'Lady Erechol?' Jonas started. 'Thank you—'

'Get out,' she whispered back. 'Get out of my house.'

Taken aback, Vernak shook his head at Jonas and said, 'Erechol. We are—'

'I said get out of my house! Just look at what you have done! All of it! You! Bastard of a man. Double the dosage! Pah!' she spat, rising from her limp chair to shove her finger into Vernak's chest. 'What was that, eh? You should have died! Not caused all this destruction.'

'Well, I . . . don't know. I can't predict when an earthquake will hit,' lied Vernak, hands before him, all apologetic.

'Lies!' she stormed and picked up a wooden ashtray on the broken table behind her, throwing it angrily at Vernak's head, splitting it in two against the wall above as he dropped to the floor. 'I know when something is created! And that earthquake was created, damn you!'

'Father!' Jorin shouted from outside, pushing through the rubble to get in. 'Father! You're alive!' Erechol stopped her shouting and stared at the boy, arms shaking in anger.

'Jorin, my boy! Ha!' Jonas laughed and grabbed his son, embracing him. 'I'm okay.' The reunion of father and son seemed to cool her burning rage, subdue her anger, and she opened her bunched fists, breathing deep to calm herself. Jonas pushed Jorin away by his shoulders and said, 'I'll be outside soon. Let me finish in here, okay?' The boy nodded and smiled at Erechol.

'You have given me a magnificent gift today. I will be forever grateful to you for this,' Jorin said, and waited until her heaving chest slowed, watched her acknowledge him with a nod, then turned to leave through the broken wall.

Jonas smiled after his son and turned to Erechol. 'He is right. We will not forget what you did here. Thank you for saving me. I owe you a great debt.'

Erechol waited until Jorin was at the carriage, then she said, 'Take your things and get out of here. I don't want to be a part of this. Leave our city and never come back.'

'Erechol . . .' Vernak pleaded.

She stood before them, thumbs rubbing her forefingers anxiously, then pushed past and rummaged through the debris, righted a table, and started combing through broken vials and silver sachets containing different herbs.

'You are not whole,' she continued. 'You will need . . . *help* until you can get your soul back.'

'What do you mean?' asked Jonas, a note of concern in his voice.

'Your mind will slip, and you may become . . . distant, uncaring. To what extent, I don't know. Take these whenever you start to feel unlike yourself.' She handed him a brown leather pouch and undid the strings, unrolling the leather to reveal a few vials of dark orange, the glass stained by the contents inside, and a pocket filled with silver sachets.

He smelled it and jerked away, pulling a face, and asked, 'What is this?'

'It's the seed of the bulgar fig. Alone as in the sachet, you can drink them as a tea. It will help some, but the liquid version is mixed with the urine of a black stag. They have a very potent acidity that brings out the power of the seed.'

'Ah shit! I'm not drinking that.' Jonas curled his lip in disgust.

'Suit yourself. I have helped you as much as I can. Now leave. We have loads of work to do, thanks to you.'

With a nod, he turned and made his way outside, seeing the deep cracks in the earth spread out from the house, running far and wide through the city where homes lay in ruin, the wails of their occupants reaching for the clouds above.

'This is Orana, Father. She will be our guide.'

'That so?' Jonas twisted his back and stretched his legs, working the pain and stiffness from them. She was scraped up, her face swollen and bloody. Her lips were bruised from a proper beating. *Someone was unhappy with her. Tough girl. Wonder what she is fleeing . . .* He eyed her and extended his hand, wincing at the stitches pulling at his shoulder and arm. *Pain, my old friend, you taunt me yet again.* 'Good to meet you, I'm Jonas.'

'I know. Get on. Daylight is being wasted.' There was little humour in her voice, her stare as cold as ice.

He climbed up next to her, groaning like an old dog, and waited for Vernak to climb up at the back.

'Pull your hoods down low. You two in the back have seen how little Skalg likes your kind. Say nothing and let me do all the talking if we are stopped. Got it?'

Everyone was quiet. 'Good, then. Let's go.' Orana whipped the horses, and the wagon rocked forward.

21. A Long Road

A certain stillness took a city by storm in the early hours of the morning before men and women made ready for their day, a calmness that cleansed the day from the previous sins. Smoke drifted from brick and clay chimneys upon the roofs of many houses, food being prepared to give strength for a long day ahead. The crisp air sent shivers down Orana's spine, and she pulled her long jacket tight.

'Damn, it's cold here. Do we have spare clothes?' Jonas asked, rubbing his naked forearms. 'My boy is freezing, and Vernak is too proud to ask for anything.'

'You sure it's for the kid? Or you?' Orana sneered at him.

'Huh. You always this friendly? Or is today just special?'

She turned her focus back to the road and the people emerging from their homes. 'There's spare clothing in the trunk behind us. I took what I could get hold of, so you'll have to see what fits.' *I have lost too many days saving you to care about being nice.* 'You won't need them for long. It will get hot soon. Living so close to the desert, the weather changes rapidly.'

'Huh,' he grunted, rummaging through the trunk, lifting robes, tunics, trousers, sheets, and all other materials. 'Jorin, take this. Vernak, see if this fits.' He handed them thick robes made of a dark wool and draped one around his own broad shoulders before taking his seat again.

'I said, draw your hood over your face,' Orana whined. 'The guards won't think twice before ransacking our wagon and tossing everything to the road. And we will not get it back. Then they'll take you three into custody, probably torture you for being spies, and dump what remains on the outskirts of the city.' Jonas drew his hood low, clearing his throat with a growl, and reluctantly sat back.

'What are guards called in your tongue?'

'Why?'

'Call me curious . . .'

Orana cursed and mutter, 'Selkath.'

'Huh,' Jonas grumbled and turned away.

Groans of reluctance echoed while a pair of men yawned from the side of the road, sleepily dragging on their boots and fumbling with tools. One grabbed a wheelbarrow and started down the street, moving in the same direction as they were. Orana kept her eyes on the man as they slowly crept by him, his stubbled chin moving up and down with the low tunes that glided from his mouth. An old song Orana remembered from her childhood. It brought a slight smile to her otherwise unhappy face.

More doors creaked open the further they went, and the city started getting a life to it. They stayed on the outer rim, taking the long way to the gate, not wanting to struggle with the flooding or mud. Most had subsided by now, but the terrain would be slippery, and getting stuck was not an option. They couldn't afford to be identified as foreigners by some good citizen's act of kindness.

Jonas turned to the back and asked, 'What happened to me, Vernak? Why did my, uhm . . . consciousness end up in my soul and not my body, like before?'

'I used a scalpel,' whispered Vernak, and Orana saw his dirty white fingers appear on the rail behind her, grasping the wood from between the folds of his robe. 'The darcöle used an axe and its claws. It tore you apart with little concern for your wellbeing.'

'Stay down!' Orana stormed under her breath. 'How many times do I have to say this?' The hand slipped away, and Vernak spoke from behind the railing.

'Apologies, Orana. We will keep quiet until we get out of the city.'

Small, dilapidated ruins of homes spread far and wide where they were at the city's outskirts, dwarfed by the brown wall a few hundred feet away, stretching all around the city, the red pitched roofs of the watchtowers a common place for waiting archers. They followed the road's natural curve, bringing into view the enormous gates ahead, patrolled by guards Orana hoped were still sleepy and not overzealous to perform their duties.

One leaned back against the wall near a door leading to an office on the right, basking in the low-hanging sun as its rays crept over the buildings. A great set of stairs led up to the top of the wall on his left, where Orana could already see in her mind how dozens of armed guards would charge down with weapons drawn. Another guard sat on a low retaining wall, sucking on a floppily rolled tarang-weed smoke, thick white clouds puffing from his mouth. She could smell the sweet scent as they drew closer. People milled about, some entering and exiting the gates unaccosted by the guards, but most were on foot, not in a wagon loaded with supplies that had plenty of value, with three foreigners looking mightily suspicious. Orana doubted the efficacy of this plan.

Maybe there was still time to jump off, proclaim her ignorance to the knowledge of these foreigners. Just maybe, she could still slip away unnoticed and make her own way to Baldor to search for the merchant. Long cutlasses dangled from the guards' belts, thick and sturdy weapons, sharp and ready to cut the heads or arms off traitors, like cleavers in a butchery. Her heart beat faster the closer they got to the gate. Her mind was telling her to flee. Run and don't look back. She could make another plan.

Orana shifted her buttocks, dangling half of it over the side, her right leg getting ready to push off. Jonas still sat with the hood drawn low, his face a mask of darkness, the thick woollen robe covering his arms and chest. He was unaware of her plans. The time was now or never.

'Oi! Selkath!' called Jonas next to her, and the guard sitting on the retaining wall swung his head up, rose to his feet, and approached them. It was too late. He had already seen her on the wagon. *Shit! Bastard! What are you doing?*

Jonas waved his arm, gesturing him closer. Ideas surged into her head of how to escape this, but the most obvious one stood out – just run them over with the four massive Percherons and wagon. They might get away. But Jonas calmly grabbed her left hand and rein, shaking his head slightly.

'My friend,' Jonas said in the common tongue, and the guard frowned up, hand drifting to the cutlass. 'Do you mind if I speaking in this foul tongue?' he said, adding a terrible accent. 'I need to practise because I running to the bastard East to trade with them.'

The guard glared at them with bloodshot eyes, the waft of weed trailing in his wake, and he nodded, dropping his hand from the sword. 'Not running,' he answered, 'travelling . . . You are travelling to the bastard East.'

'Argh! You see. I need all the help. To repay, I roll proper smoke for you.' He reached out with his filthy fingers, charred and smeared with muck. The guard eyed him for a while, swaying slightly, head bobbing to see Jonas's face under the hood, then handed him the weed and some paper. 'We help each other.' Orana sat with a fake smile plastered on her face, sweat streaming down her chilly back, not at all curious about what he was doing.

On his filthy lap, he had the small piece of paper between his fingers, holding it tight to add the brown weed, spreading it out evenly across the length, and started rolling it. He added a little more weed at the tip and licked the ends to make it stick. 'I learn language, you learn roll.' He handed a perfectly stiff rolled smoke back to the guard. The guard grinned as he walked to the fire at the side of the gate and dragged a burning twig out. He lit the smoke and walked back to them, bouncing his head up and down to test it. 'Secret is in tension. Always keep tension.' Jonas chuckled with his coarse voice and slapped him on the shoulder.

The guard made eye contact with Orana, and she laughed with them, forcing the sounds from her mouth, wanting to punch Jonas in the face. It took an awfully long time before the guard waved them on, dragging hard on the smoke, clouds billowing up around him. The wagon crawled through the gates, and Orana leaned to Jonas. 'What the heck was that? Are you crazy? That could have ended badly.'

'Oh, relax. The best way to stay unnoticed is not to be afraid of being seen.'

'What does that mean?' Orana stormed, ready to jam her fist into his nose.

'If you act suspicious, trying to hide from them, they will notice you.'

* * *

Had she made a mistake to travel with this bunch? Not having any real idea who they were, or what they had done to be caught in Skalg like that. All the strange things that had already occurred around them. They had travelled the entire morning with little conversation, other than Jorin continually speaking with his father. The sun was high and deadly, a wafting heat haze obscuring the endless plain, baking everything and everyone into a stupor of laziness. They had shed their robes a long time ago and now used them for shade, spreading them over the supplies and themselves at the back, pinning them down with heavy crates. The little shade they gave was a blessing, letting them hide away from the harsh heat. A curved wooden column fastened to the bed of the wagon on each side extended past the front seat with a flapping white sheet pulled up over the arms to give the drivers some shade. Orana and Jonas leaned back against the sheet, sweat dripping from their heads.

'Pull up under that tree, would you?' asked Vernak, pointing to the fork in the road, and fanned his face to cool down.

'Yeah, we need to rest the horses. This heat is terrible for them,' added Jonas, glancing at her from a sweat-stained face. 'If we are to reach Keltorison, we best treat them well, eh?'

'Keltorison?' Orana shouted, spitting the word out with a spray of saliva, and drew on the reins, bringing the wagon to a dust-swirled stop. 'That was not the deal! You said we were going to Baldor! Keltorison is a month away!' Orana shook her head, fists bunched where she stood at the driver's seat. 'I can't go there. I need to go to Baldor.'

'I'm sorry, dear,' said Vernak as he rose to meet her, staring over the sheet with Jorin at his side. 'We were unsuccessful in drawing Jonas's soul back. We have to get it physically.'

'What does that even mean!' she screamed, arms flailing about like a madwoman. 'He's talking, walking, joking, annoying, stinking the front seat up with me!'

'Calm down, Orana. I know this is hard to understand. I don't fully understand it either,' said Jonas, shaking his head. 'They pulled my consciousness back into my body when they couldn't get my soul, so I can at least function.'

'Don't you tell me to calm down! You bastards used me! Lied to my face so I could help you get out of the city.'

'Not completely so,' said Jonas. 'I could've got us out, but with you it was easier, and we have horses and supplies.'

'Don't you even dare . . .' Orana glared at him sidelong.

'You know why *we* need to get to Keltorison. Why do *you* need to get to Baldor so badly?' She had overplayed her hand. Shared too much. *Damn!* 'Whatever it is, we can help you. Protect you.'

Her head came up at the last words, eyes big and wide. 'I, *ahem* . . . No.' She sat down on the seat, thumb rubbing her itching palm.

'You stole something, and someone wants payback? That about right?'

'Leave her alone!' shouted Jorin. 'She has done nothing but help us.'

'Oh, Jorin. Wake up, lad,' Vernak chimed in from the side. 'She's not the only one that was used. Who do you think sent those thugs after us in the first place?' Orana's head jerked up to stare at him.

'No! She saved us.'

'Exactly,' stated Vernak. 'And she knew we couldn't resist her offer for help after that.'

'Fine! I did it . . . How'd you find out, old man? I was very careful.'

Vernak released a long-drawn sigh and said, 'I have a keen sense in these things. Let's move the horses under the shade, then we can talk.'

Orana saw the look on Jorin's face and swung her head away to leer at the ground. 'What do you want from me, kid? I have to look after myself.'

'I thought we could be friends,' he muttered as he sat back down, cradling his knees in his arms.

'Ha. Friends? Be glad then, kid. I have taught you a valuable lesson. Real friends are scarce. I would say almost a myth. We all just want to survive. People feed off each other, using each other until there's no worth left, then they move on to their next *friend*.'

Jonas stared at her sidelong, not saying a word, and jumped off the wagon. He sauntered up to the horses and grabbed the lead, walking them to the shade.

Keltorison . . . I have three weeks to get the stones back. Or I'm dead. Orana watched the slow-rolling soil disappear below the wagon, sitting sideways on the seat, not wanting to look at Jorin.

'We could really use your help, Orana.' Vernak lowered the sheet and climbed over the railing to sit next to her. 'And you could use ours. So let's be friends, until the worth has run out, as you say.'

'Why would you risk your lives to protect me?'

'It's in our interest. We will need someone with your talents to sneak in and liberate his soul.'

The wind howled through the few acacia trees standing their ground against the arid lands, dry shrubs rustling with a gust of warm air sailing over them. 'I have three weeks before they come for me. I need to keep his men off me until I retrieve the items I stole.'

'If it will make you feel better, let's call this a business arrangement. You help get his soul, and we'll help you get the items and keep you safe. Deal?'

She stared at the old man for some time, weighing her options, then stuck out her hand, waiting for him to grasp it. 'Deal.'

'Good. Let's wait out this heat before we continue. I could really use a nap under the tree.'

Orana rummaged through a pack at her feet and pulled out a map, unfurling it on her lap. 'We can turn south, to Dragons Rest, and board a ship from there. It'll be the fastest way. It's a port city, so they will be used to foreigners.'

'No! We go by land as far as we can,' Jonas called from the front of the wagon, stroking the neck of the black Percheron.

'Why? It will take much longer!' Orana turned to Vernak, hoping to get support from him, but he just shrugged and pinched his mouth shut.

'We go by land! There's a bridge at Pikeridge we can—'

'I know there's a bridge! That thing was built ages ago by buffoons trying to cross the largest river ever seen. All for what? To conquer the West. Well, you learnt a harsh lesson in that war. Who's to say it won't collapse under us, eh? Send us to the depths of the River Parth?'

'We are not from Yahrska. Don't misplace your anger,' muttered Jonas, and he sat back against the tree. 'I lost my bloody hat . . .' he mumbled, blinking the sun from his eyes as it shone through the waving leaves, and spat when a fly nearly flew into his mouth. 'Hey, Jorin, be a good lad and make a fire. Get rid of these blasted flies, maybe cook us something to eat, eh?'

The wagon rocked left and right while Jorin walked to the rear and dropped off, gravel crunching underfoot. 'Sure thing, Father.'

'Where'd you come from then?' she asked, her interest piqued.

'North.' Jonas leaned back, head tilted against the bole. 'Far north.'

'So why would ya be going to Baldor?'

'You ask a lot of bloody questions.' Jonas scowled at her and leaned back again. 'We're not. Or we weren't. Been living in Barren Hollows for a few years, so we will go there to drop off Jorin. Then we will head to Baldor to resupply. There's someone I need some information on. I'm hoping to find it in Baldor.' His voice had turned cold and coarse, having an edge to it. A warning not to continue prodding. Orana jumped down and stretched her legs, scanning the flat plains for signs of life. Small black dots grazed in the distance on a hill lined with streaks of green and brown, their movements difficult to see over the rippling heat.

'I guess we go by land then.'

22. An Olive Branch

'Can I get a volunteer, please?' drawled Grandàre Larison Darklemayer, twice blessed, thrice cursed, watching both the windows and door, one with each eye. Some said that her cross-eyedness resulted from a mistimed spell. Bellard wasn't sure about the theory. She had the eyes of a praying mantis or a chameleon, and there was no doubt that she looked crazy, with her dishevelled black hair and black lips, robes all tattered and worn. He glanced down, not at all surprised that she wore no shoes again, seeing her feet all crusted in mud. There must be a freedom to being a sorcerer he wasn't yet aware of, to dress and act the way you wanted and not have it questioned. Her eyes flittered and jerked, jumped to anything that moved, and Bellard wondered if this was not by design; her design. No one raised their hands. They all just sat in their chairs like watchful gargoyles. 'How about you, Bellard? Care to step forward?'

A wave of heads turned his way, eyes glittering, judging. Students never wanted to be the one called on by the teacher, especially not to perform something in front of the group. It was just too easy to be made a pariah. *No, leave me alone so I can get through my last few days of the year,* was what he wanted to say. Instead, he just rose from his chair and made his way forward, walking between the rows of baleful students. He tried his best to imagine an empty room, peaceful and calm, yet now, the desks grew immensely large, the old wood creaking and groaning, pressing in from all sides, making the room feel claustrophobic. His mouth was dry, tongue clinging to his palate, and he could not remember when last he'd had a drink of water.

'Thank you, Bellard. Please remove your Pillar,' she beckoned with her hand, 'and place it in the box on my table.'

Heads jerked towards her from all over the classroom, and Bellard blurted, 'But, Miss, we are not supposed to take off our Pillars. It is forbidden.'

'Oh, don't be so dramatic. It is not forbidden. It is strongly recommended by all teachers that you do not remove them. Not forbidden. There's a difference. A difference. A difference . . .' She struggled to let go of the words and noticed their attention on her. 'Besides, we are not doing anything dangerous here.' All around, the room became a buzz of activity, students conversing in hushed tones, questioning what they were witnessing. 'Silence!' Her voice filled the room, growing from all directions like a snake twisting through your mind, and all conversations died instantly, mouths shut in shock. The grandàre gestured to the dark wooden box glimmering with oil, archaic symbols drawn in wax dripping over the sides and top. He lifted the lid. A pungent smell of weed drifted from a bed of dried grass.

Bellard stuck three fingers into a pocket and lifted the Pillar free, and with it all the memories of what they'd endured for them. For a time, he stood there, holding it in his hands, frozen in time, until he glimpsed a beige object in the corner of his eye hurtling towards him. It hit him square in the face, and the scrunched-up parchment bounced away with a gentle crunch on the floor at his feet. The students all laughed at him, their stupid faces cackling and fingers pointing. 'Enough!' shouted the grandàre, and Bellard quickly placed his Pillar in the box, snapping the lid shut.

'Good. Now, everyone move to the back of the class. Except you, Bellard. You stay right there.' Grandàre Larison followed the students to the back of the class, urging them on with waving hands. 'Quickly now! That's it.' He felt like the lamb being led to the slaughter, feeling naked and unsure what to cover up first, his hands drifting from one area of his body to the next.

'I want you to do something simple, like create a rose, or make it snow in the classroom, or turn a moth into a butterfly. You can choose, just don't make it complicated. Remember, without the Pillar your focus will be scattered. And if it gets too rough, I want you to stop, got it?'

He nodded dumbly and took a step back, trying to think of what he wanted to create, but his mind was a blank slate. *What am I going to do?*

Come on! Think of something! They are staring at you, waiting for you to perform. Talking book? Talking desk? Sand? Sand on what? Don't be ridiculous. Clean something? Break something? Mend something?

'Come on, we don't have all day!' shouted a student, and a murmur of laughter rose, causing him to blush, the hot flash racing over his face with a deep redness to follow. *Ah, got it.*

Bellard took the blue feathered quill from the grandàre's desk and held it out in front of him, focusing on what he wanted to achieve. He could feel the build-up of power within him, the source running wild in search of the Pillar, finding none. The world around him grew hot, and the quill in his hands even hotter, like it was growing spikes and digging into his palms. A wave of black smoke and burning embers rose from the desk before him in hammered sparks, until it burst into flames. Blue-red fire roved in a spiral at his feet, burning the floor to a black char. His mind grew numb, and chaos reigned within, unfocused, unwilling to bend the knee. A hard knock, like that of a hammer on a door, sounded in his ears, the smell of burning wood rising. He was lost to the magic inside, taken from the classroom and shoved inside himself, buried in the chaos. A world floated around him, of clock components, images of distant worlds, of beasts that should not be. 'Hello!' he shouted, and cupped his hand over his eyes, seeing in the distance a door on the crest of a hill, the field surrounding it, arid soil cracked from the harsh sun.

Bellard heard the loud knocks again, feeling a sense of urgency push him towards the door, yet his legs were weak, wobbling from exertion as though he had already climbed a mountain. *'Please help!'* He heard a man's voice on his right. *'I can't carry this alone . . .'* There was nothing there except the barren field. He stumbled over rocks and loose gravel, dragging his limbs up the hill, and a tremendous weight pushed down on him, nearly breaking his ankles. He wanted to scream, but his mouth was sewn shut, fear overwhelming him.

Who is doing this to me? Only a few feet from the door now, yet it was only getting harder to move. He groaned and blew harsh gasps through his nose, stretching his sewn mouth to tear the threads, but they would not give. He scrambled forth, dragging himself across hot stones on all fours, and reached for the handle. A shiny, unfitting piece of silver, completely out of place, unmarred and polished to perfection. And in its reflection, he saw himself lying there on the ground, hand stretched out to it, blue eyes streaming tears down filthy cheeks. His hand closed on cold metal, and he pulled it down, collapsing through the opening door.

'Stop! Stop, Mister Bellard! That's enough!' Grandàre Larison shouted. Through the haze of what occurred, he saw her beyond a wall of roving flames, kept at bay by her abilities, a whirlwind of fire containing the blaze, sucking it out of him.

Bellard dropped the quill, and the blaze instantly froze up. All the windows in the class banged open at once with a flick of the grandàre's hand, and flames shot out in a burst of glory, howling and clawing, a desperate spirit in search of burning.

He stared at his trembling hands, blackened by ink. His breathing was ragged and his mind numb. There was an awful taste in his mouth, a metallic one, cold and nauseating. His bowels pulled into knots, and all he could think of was where he was going to throw up. He ran to a bucket in the corner and dropped to the ground, clutching the sides of the metal bin, and hurled fiercely.

Grandàre Larison ran over to her desk and opened the box, then ran to him and shoved it into his hands during a break of the disgusting display. 'Take it, quickly! It will help with what you are feeling right now.'

The world spun, and his head bobbed around aimlessly, eyes searching for the bucket, hands reaching for the Pillar. He grabbed hold of the dark amethyst crystal, and a cool breeze swaddled him, spreading over his body and mind, easing his ailments like water poured over fire. Bellard spat the last bits of filth from his mouth and wiped his face with a rag given by the grandàre. The students were all quiet, wide-eyed, afraid.

'Maybe in hindsight it was not the best idea to ask you to volunteer after the traumatic experience you had encountered, Mister Bellard. I apologise for that,' stated the grandàre, pulling him up from the ground by the arm. 'But what were you thinking? What were you trying to create?'

'Nothing big,' he mumbled. 'I wanted to make your quill become unruly if your intention was to grade us poorly.'

The students burst out laughing and clapping, their mood suddenly uplifted. Until the grandàre swung on them and shouted, 'Quiet!' She turned back to Bellard with a scowl. 'You tried to make the quill sentient?' He looked at her, confused about what the word meant, and she continued, 'Cognisant?' Still nothing. 'Oh my, oh my! We should have started with language, it seems. Able to recognise, as in becoming alive, intelligent! Buffoon! You are not ready to create life. Only the very astute try that, and they are very careful with it, not to mention you doing it without a Pillar.'

'Sorry, I didn't know,' he begged while she dragged him by the arm back to the centre of the room and left him there. She walked to the back of the room, mumbling her disapproval. 'Come on. Try something small, now, with your Pillar in hand. And try not to blow up the school, eh?'

Something small . . . Got it. He held the crystal near his chest and felt his power awaken, guiding his thoughts, focusing on the end product. A soft breeze blew cold air over his skin, and a calm voice filtered through. *You have done enough.* The crack of a slap sounded, and one girl stomped away to stand on the other side of the group and shouted, 'You pig!' while one boy rubbed his face, a red handprint on his cheek. Other students were smiling, some confused, some crying, and some strangely unsure of what had occurred.

'What did I do?' the boy exclaimed, getting only viper's stares from her.

'Ah, the voice in the wind. Well done, Mister Bellard. You even gave me something to smile about,' said the grandàre. She turned to all the students and asked, 'Did all of you hear something in the wind?' She pointed to the angry girl who'd slapped the boy.

'I heard a voice saying how he wanted to . . . you know. I thought it was Kalrin. You mean it wasn't him?' The girl pulled her face and stretched her eyes, staring at the boy.

'No, it wasn't him. It was the voice in your head made real. A very useful tool in a sorcerer's arsenal. Especially if you learn to manipulate it. But that is not the lesson today.

'Chaos magic . . . Today I wanted to make it very clear why you should never try to perform magic if your Pillar is not on you, or very close-by. It could destroy not only the surroundings, but the bearer as well. And it has a terrible effect on your body, taking a toll on you physically and mentally. Mister Braxious can attest to this very well, I assume. Tell us, Bellard, what did you see? What did you feel when you performed magic without your Pillar?' Her stare felt creepy, a sense of longing, near desperation, seeping from her crazy eyes.

'I saw flashes of a distant world, a hot and dry place far away, and heard a man in trouble. A doorway on a hill. It was terrible. I couldn't walk. My ankles felt like they had shattered, my legs felt like logs. There was so much going on. I don't know. It was tearing me apart.' The bell rang, and students started for the door.

'There you have it. Stay true to your teachings,' Grandàre Larison called after them. 'Mister Braxious! Hold on for a moment, please.' Bellard was already halfway out the door, eager to leave the recent event behind him, and got pushed out of the way by the stampeding students when he tried to turn. 'Won't be but a moment.'

He waited for them to clear out before heading back in and approached the grandàre. The entire morning had been class after class, with no breaks in between, and he had hoped to see Mila during lunch, not called back by the grandàre to waste what little time he had.

'Your Pillar, Bellard. You can't simply keep it in your pocket like that. It is an unbearable item to carry around, dragging at your clothes. And you don't have to.'

The crystal was still in his hands, big and heavy, a clumsy piece of equipment he needed at all times. 'What do you mean, Grandàre?'

'There's an enchanter that lives in the mountains outside Khorvellen, near where the water meets the shore. He is an exceptional individual, with the ability to meld your Pillar with an object of your choosing, though he usually prefers steel. His name is Yosphore Blackstain.'

'I have nothing to pay with, Grandàre. He would surely not do it for free.'

'No one works for free, Mister Braxious. Tell him I sent you and the price might go down significantly.' She turned away slightly, and whispered, 'Lord knows he owes me.' It was said louder than she thought.

'Ma'am, why are you helping me with this? And not the others?'

Grandàre Larison twirled her black hair on her finger, her crazy eyes looking everywhere except at Bellard. 'They can speak to the local artisans to make necklaces or rings with their Pillars. Yours . . .' she tapped the crystal in his hands, '. . . would not really work on your finger. In a few days, you will finish school for the year. There will be ample time to get it done. But be careful on your journey. I haven't been up those mountains in a long time. Dangerous animals roam there, and so do thugs, you hear?'

Bellard nodded and stowed his crystal. 'Thank you, Grandàre.' He started for the door when she spoke again from behind.

'One more thing, Mister Braxious. Those flashes you saw during your chaos magic stint, do not dismiss them as hogwash your mind made up. Chaos magic may be dangerous and corrosive, but it is still powerful.'

He nodded and left her classroom, needing to see Mila.

* * *

Hungry students filled the mess hall like a pack of wild animals, all wanting to get to the smoked fish and mashed potatoes for lunch. Instead of queues, some formed a disorderly mob, all too afraid they might not get some of the delicious meat. Others already sat at the long tables, talking, eating, laughing, and joking; the world of the ignorant student, blissful and content.

'Mila!' Bellard called, looking for her amid the throng of bodies, seeing a few faces glance up at him, girls whispering under their breaths before looking away. He saw her white hair at the back of the hall and made his way to her table. Everywhere he turned, there were students blocking his path, so he squeezed through between the benches, smelling sweat and fish drifting around. He lifted his leg to climb over a bench and kneed another student in the back. Pink juice – probably from the kendar fruit – rushed from the cup in the red-haired student's hands, spilling juice over his face and down his throat, briefly choking him. The man jumped up and shoved Bellard back, nearly sending him to the ground if it wasn't for all the students walking behind him. 'I'm sorry. Really, I am!'

'Watch where you're going!' the man said, wiping juice from his face.

Those around him laughed and pointed. *Just like they always have.* He couldn't wait to be done with it all. To go where he wanted and do what he pleased. Become his own man. Luckily for him, those who attended the school, especially those who didn't have the gift of magic, were more of the scholarly sort, not the warrior type. He brushed the man's shirt and dabbed his sleeves over the dark stains on the tunic, apologising over and over. It wasn't long before the man brushed him off.

'It's fine! Just leave it.'

'Thank you. Sorry again,' he mumbled and climbed over to where Mila awaited, giggling at him.

'Making friends, I see.'

'Ha. Hilarious. You should become a court jester, you know, juggle some balls maybe, stroke some egos . . .' he said mockingly, mouth curled to a smile.

'Ah, and here I am in the company of another jester. I see what you did there. Perhaps you will stay hungry for the day?' She pushed a second plate closer, only to drag it away with one finger when he reached for it. 'Nah-ah-ah. The court jester only gets fed after the queen has eaten. Or not at all.'

'Oh, come now, Mila. I'm starving.'

'No compliment, no food.' She dragged the plate further away, watching the queue only grow at the canteen. 'I'm sure there's plenty who'd want this.'

'Really?' he asked, looking around, embarrassed.

'Really.'

Bellard still looked around, seeing if anyone was paying them any attention, then mumbled under his breath, not even moving his lips, 'You loo good this horning.'

'I what this when now?'

Just get it over with, nobody is even listening. 'You look beautiful today!' Just as he said it, the buzzing all fell silent, making his voice the only one to bounce off the walls of the hall. Students everywhere turned and laughed at him. And at first, he wanted to be angry, to smash the plate on the ground and storm from the hall, but seeing her giggle with them just made him chuckle and shake his head. 'That was cruel.'

'It worked out better than I could've hoped. All I wanted was a compliment.' She pushed the plate closer, and he sat down, taking a big bite from the salty fish, dragging pink flesh off tiny bones, carefully sifting through the meat in his mouth for more lurkers.

'Hey, I have been meaning to ask what you will do for the break?' he asked.

She turned her head, eyeing him sidelong, and asked, 'Why? You planning on running away? You want me to be your faithful companion, is that it?'

'Something like that, yes.' Her face went rigid, her mouth half open. She realised he wasn't playing anymore. 'I want you to go to the mountains behind Khorvellen with me, and from there, we'd go to Forgeholde until next semester, or until you've had enough of me. What d'ya say?'

'Uhm . . . Er, this is all very sudden. And you have your friends to keep you company there. I will just be in the way.'

'Nonsense. You are never in the way.' He saw her hesitation and grabbed her hand. Her soft skin brought back memories of their lust-filled evening. 'I promise.' The silence lingered, her eyes drifting to his hands.

'Fine, I will come with you, but you have to get rid of that ridiculous moustache. It makes you look creepy. And I will not be in the company of creepy men.' He had been growing it steadily for the last few days, grooming it every so often, thinking it made him look older.

'If you come with me, I'll shave it tonight.'

23. Dreams and Illusions

Calmantis sat at the fire, staring at the crevices between the rocks, following the grey-green lichen where it spread over the surfaces, and listened to the men argue, each one trying their best to raise their voices higher than the other. Four of the twenty guards were present and accounted for, three of which drove the wagons, one additional to safeguard them all on horseback. And Calmantis, the liability.

They had got to the cave a short while back, horses panting and snorting, their flanks caked in white salt, eyes wild. He felt like a coward, having left the rest of the guards back there with that beast, knowing one was already dead; Otrah had been killed, and it was very possible that Embra was lying beside him. *How many more, maybe all of them?*

'We should go back! We can't just leave them there,' Tannis shouted. 'Even if . . .'

'Even if what, eh? What were you about to say?' stormed Killan.

'Even if they're dead! We have to go to them!' Tannis yanked his helm from his head and tossed it to the ground, metal clanging and bouncing over the rocks.

'We have orders!' shouted a guard Calmantis did not know the name of, who shoved Tannis back. He was a big man, with crazy eyes, their steel grey bright against his dark hair.

'And what? Should we stay here for the rest of our lives? They could all be dead!' shouted Tannis.

'Calluric is right,' said Lothrain, climbing down from a wagon to make his way to them. 'We have orders. They would've retreated before it's too late. Ackelides will not allow all his men to be killed. And they had the clairvoy with them.' Now he knew the fourth's name.

'Oh, please! How do you fight that thing? It is pure evil.'

'With your help, mortal, we can,' came a powerful voice from the corner of the cave, and a dark figure appeared from the gloom, face hidden in the shadows. The guards all jumped around, drawing their blades, and formed a wall of shields, steel and wood their defenders. 'We can fight them all,' the figure continued, sauntering closer, hands clasped before him.

'Who are you? State your business here!' shouted Lothrain with axe in hand.

For all the tension in the air, Calmantis was sure he needed to be more afraid, more cautious, but the presence of this intruder didn't seem all that worrying to him. He felt at ease, calm even, where he still sat on his rock midway between them.

The stranger stepped into the light, bending down not to hit his head against the jutting rocks. His eyes had a faint red glow to them, and deep, dark, old lines coursed across his forehead, set in a permanently angry scowl. Strange golden formations grew from his forehead to sit between his silvery white hair as a crown on his head, spiked ears protruding from the sides. The man stroked his big white beard, gold and black armour pieces chafing over each other. Calmantis couldn't help but stare at the enormous spikes on the man's shoulder guards, wondering what had teeth like that.

'I am Ostarra, god of storms, and I am here for that creature you speak of.' A warmth spread throughout Calmantis, and he smiled, quickly checking that he wasn't urinating again. The guards shuffled back as if hit by an invisible force, stumbling with their shields, the wall crumbling before them.

'A god?' Calmantis whispered, swaying back and forth on the rock with manic glee, glancing between the guards and the stranger, finger pointing aimlessly as tears streamed down his face. 'A god . . .'

'That's a crock o' shite if I ever heard any!' shouted Calluric. 'Prove it! Prove that you are a god!'

'Do I look like a common mortal to you, boy?' The self-proclaimed god imperiously sauntered past Calmantis, thick muscular legs trembling with each step. 'Look at me! I am not here to cause you harm. I am here to help. Besides, I care not if you believe what I say. I care only about the outcome.'

'We serve only Lord Aztar! No false gods!'

'We all serve Aztar,' growled the god in a whisper. 'I don't want your servitude. I want to save your friends and kill the beast, but first, I need him to agree to my terms.' Ostarra pointed at Calmantis. *Me? Really?*

'Him? Why him?' asked Calluric, face pulled into a sneer. 'He's nothing, a nobody.'

Offended and hurt, Calmantis jumped up, angrily waving his finger at the guard, who only shrugged. 'Hey! What did I ever do to you?'

Ostarra turned to face Calmantis and said, 'Yes, but this nobody understands that by helping any god, he *is* serving Aztar. And he also has an invaluable gift. A gift none of you possess. A gift that makes him truly special. There are very few in the world that possess it, and even fewer that know how to use it. He is a Voidwalker.'

That warm and fuzzy feeling that had spread throughout his body turned ice-cold, his tongue becoming heavy and numb. *I have a title? I am a somebody? Not a nobody!* 'Ha! In your face, Calluric! In your face, and your face, and your face!' he shouted, pointing to them all, dancing a jig, snapping his fingers and swinging his arse. 'I am important, and you are a dog's arse. I am important, and you are a dog's arse,' Calmantis sang in a rhythmic tune, flapping his arms like a chicken's, being silly and annoying, his usual self.

'Cut that out this instant,' one guard roared, and Calmantis tripped with a start over a rock, flattening his face against Ostarra's blackened thigh guard. His teeth rattled in his skull, grinding over each other, his head rocking back as though he'd run into a solid stone wall. The god barely moved at all, just stared at him from above, white hair hiding his face in the darkness, only his eyes gleaming red. Calmantis scrambled back a few steps, rubbing his painful face. He got back to his feet and bent over, letting a long strand of red drool run out of his mouth onto the stones.

'You are lucky I was close-by to sense your brief journey to Tenthis. I would never have found you otherwise. Your friends' time is running out. Do you accept my terms, mortal? You have a chance to mean something here. To become more than you are. Will you do as I ask?'

'We are the Shadow Guard, we serve only Aztar!' Calluric charged with sword gleaming, swinging it at Ostarra's head.

'No! Stop!' shouted Calmantis, seeing the other guards frozen in disbelief, their arms outstretched, trying to catch their fellow Shadow Guard, but they were too late. The god stepped back, Calluric's blade swishing harmlessly past his throat. Ostarra's enormous fist came from below, arching up in an uppercut. The crunch and snap of Calluric's arm was gut-wrenching. Splintered bones tore through his skin, spraying blood over Calmantis and Ostarra. A scream of pain filled the room, then was replaced by a gurgle as the god wrapped his fingers around Calluric's throat, squeezing, bulging the guard's eyes, turning his face red, toes scraping the stones. The effort it took Ostarra to lift the man and squeeze the life from him didn't seem to affect him much at all, tilting his head and scanning Calluric's body, as if searching his soul.

Only now could Calmantis see how big Ostarra really was, towering a few feet over them all. 'No! Please! No! Let him go!' The guards were about to rush in, and the god had not a care in the world. He was fixed on the sufferance of the guard in his grasp.

'You dare to charge at me? You are nothing, an ant beneath my foot . . . a nobody, as you so arrogantly put it.'

'I'll do it! Just let him go! You have my word, Lord Ostarra.'

The god dropped the guard and stepped back, eyeing Calmantis, his white beard sprayed with drops of red. 'You have made a wise decision.'

Power and authority flowed from Ostarra in thick waves, great tides of it flooding over Calmantis. Movement was a chore in his presence, though it seemed his muscles responded all the same. He wanted to weep, staring at the god, and had to hold himself back with a stutter, a catch in his throat. He felt out of place, out of his depth, and most of all, he felt he had no idea what this Voidwalker was. A problematic situation if that was why he was recruited in the first place.

Ostarra left the coughing, crying Calluric on the ground and climbed onto the back of a wagon, the wood groaning and bending with his substantial weight. 'We leave now, or your friends are doomed.'

'Tannis! Are you coming?' Calmantis called and crept onto the same wagon. He took up the reins at the front, watching the shocked guards carry their brother in arms to another wagon, tying his arm off with rags to stop the flow of blood. They had no choice but to follow. Tannis leapt to their wagon's front seat and called for the soldiers to hold on.

Calmantis whipped the horses into action, and the beasts lurched forward, with the god standing at the back between the supplies, arms folded with not a care in the world.

* * *

How do you speak to a god? Calmantis wondered. *Do you change your voice, your tone, to sound more respectful? Do you feign who you truly are, hoping to find favouritism, or do they already know the true you? Have they already seen your entire life before you've lived it? Or should you just be yourself and hope that they don't know all your past transgressions, your misdeeds, your failures?* Calmantis whipped the horses again, a cloud of dust kicked up behind them by the wheels and hoofs of the horses thundering over the road. 'So, er . . . This Voidwalker business, eh? Uh, what's that all about?' *It seems I went for the bumbling buffoon.* He shied away, biting on his lip, cussing at himself.

'You do not know how to Void walk?' There was an edge to Ostarra's voice. 'Have I made a mistake coming for you?'

'No, no, no. Not at all. But yes, I don't know how to Void walk as much as I don't even know what a Voidwalker is.' There was an uncomfortably long pause of silence, and when he turned to look at Ostarra, he saw the anger permeating from the being, face muscles tense and hard, a flush of redness enveloping his head. He could hear the other wagons behind them, being pushed hard, catching glimpses of wide-eyed beasts between the swirling dust. *Was this a deal-breaker? Did I just doom us all with one of my inept responses? Such an idiot . . .*

'Where do you think the realm of the gods is? Up there?' he pointed to a gathering of grey and blue clouds. 'Where we fly with our little wings from cloud to cloud, pissing down on you mortals, giving you the water you so desperately need?'

'When you say it like that . . . I guess it makes sense—'

'No!' Ostarra's angry growl made Calmantis jump on the seat, swinging the wagon left and right, nearly tipping them over. Even Ostarra had to grab onto the rails for an instant. 'It makes no sense!'

'Oh, good, cause I was just being polite. You know, you being a god and all.' Calmantis watched the fuming god and cleared his throat, then turned back to watch the road.

'Tenthis, our world, is around us where we are now. It's everywhere. Normal mortals just cannot perceive it or reach it – until they die, that is. You, however, are not a normal mortal. You can come and go from Tenthis just like we can.'

'So, am I a god?' Calmantis asked, eyes wide, voice taking on a high pitch.

'That's the most ridiculous thing I've ever heard. No. You're not a god, but you are special.'

'What am I then?'

'We aren't exactly sure. And that scares some gods. Some feel you should be put down, but I think they are short-sighted. They just don't see the value in you as I do.'

'They want to kill me? And others like me?' Calmantis whirled around, the wagon swinging wildly on the road.

'Watch where you're going! Some do, yes.'

More, like me? How many? Where are they? Ooh, maybe we can start our very own guild . . . Become the emissaries of the mortal world. His mind raced with the possibilities. He steadied the horses and asked, 'Why kill us? What did we ever do to them?'

Ostarra cleared his throat and said, 'You are to us as what we were to the Eyavare, our gods. And because they did not like what they saw with us, they wanted to wipe us all out, but they didn't count on our power, our determination to live. For centuries we fought, killing each other until there was no one left to kill. In the end, we were the ones left standing.'

Mouth agape, Calmantis shook his head, not sure if he was daydreaming, but the god was still there, arms folded, eyes gleaming red. *The gods had gods . . . Who'd have thunk it?* Calmantis wondered how long the cycle had continued, how many more generations of gods were there? *And did they all start out as something small? Something misunderstood, perhaps?*

'What I am saying to you is, you can be glad it was I that found you and not some other god, like Aztar.'

'Aztar wants me dead?' Calmantis demanded, eyes wide with worry, forehead wrinkled with creases.

'You have to be careful with your gifts.'

'Dear god, man.' He cringed and amended, 'I mean, dear me, god.' That just sounded wrong to him. 'Apologies, I mean, I just don't know how to address you.'

'Call me Ostarra. I've never been concerned with titles.'

'I'm on a first-name basis with a god? How delightful.' Calmantis heard his father in his words and nearly slapped himself.

'There it is, in the sky. We are getting close. The foul beast will not live long now. Let's hope your friends still live.'

Fear gripped Calmantis's heart when he saw the beast again, its menacingly fast movements sweeping across the skies. There was something different to it, though. It seemed slower, hurt, dipping from time to time as it swooped to the earth. They could not see over the rise just yet, but hope surged through him, knowing it was swooping towards something, or someone. He whipped the horses and shouted, 'Yah! Yah!' There was only one thought raging in his mind.

He was so hungry.

Curse my mind for being the way it is. How can I be thinking of food at a time like this? How good would a butter-baked scone be right now, though? Maybe some bacon and cheese to go with it. A glass of fine wine and some grapes. Yes, definitely some grapes. A fearsome cry, shrill and loud, split his ears, and he saw figures running on the ground as they crested the rise. They took cover behind a large rock, and arrows sailed up to the beast, vanishing into its body.

'Keep the wagon steady,' Ostarra said and closed his eyes, raising his hands to the heavens, with an aura of godliness surrounding him. The clouds pulled together, growing dark and angry, thunder sounding, lightning flashing. One bolt arced down onto the beast with a tremendous crack, sparks flying, beast screeching. 'That's far enough. Stop the wagon here.'

The wind howled, and powerful gusts pushed at them, but they pushed even harder against the beast as it turned towards them. It flapped its black wings, fighting the wind to get to them, while Ostarra dropped from the wagon and sauntered a distance away, pulling the attention of the beast.

Calmantis jumped from the wagon and hid behind it, glancing around the corner to see what was happening. In the field ahead, armoured men dropped to the ground, fatigued, injured, exhausted, crawling away to find cover behind the rocks. Clairvoy Yeron was running towards him, his robe fluttering in the wind, smeared with streaks of red-and-black gore, panicked and limping, leather armour in tatters. Five guards followed at his back. *How can that old fool be so fit?*

The ground shook with the crack of lightning, and the horses became skittish, pulling at their bits, throwing their heads, ears pinned back. Calmantis grabbed the lead and patted the front horse, stroking its neck while moving them away from the danger. A squeal from the beast sounded as it hit the ground, kicking up a wave of dark soil in front of Ostarra, covering the god in it. It lashed out with its talons and blew a hail of darkness over the god, who stepped back and braced for the impact. The foul nature of the beast cocooned Ostarra, crawling over his armour until two bright flashes from above wrapped around the beast, burning it all over.

It took to the sky, circling them with a trail of darkness, and swooped back down, swiping talons. The god jumped away, blade flashing, and the beast cried in pain as one paw flopped to the ground.

'What are you doing back here?' screamed Yeron, panting and coughing as he arrived. 'And who is that?'

'We brought help. That is a, uhm . . . Ostarra . . . a god.'

Yeron's face went red. 'Heresy! The Order will have your tongue for this!'

'I'm not lying! Just look.'

Great talons split the earth open, the beast writhing under coursing lightning. Focused gales tore at the damned demon, shearing its wings away and snapping its front limbs. Ostarra stood before it and unsheathed a blade, then trudged up to the lightning-bound beast. Thick arcs obscured their view, giving only glimpses of the god and his fight. But Calmantis saw the death stroke clear as day. Ostarra swung the sword down mightily, pinning the blade in the beast's skull and dropping it dead at his feet with a shudder of the world.

'We are not done with this conversation,' Yeron said, glaring at Calmantis, and crept towards the beast, eyes on the creature where it breathed its last gurgling breaths. Its chest heaved up and down in quick rasps, its head pinned to the ground with the blade through from the top.

The lightning ceased, and the wind died down, the thick zapping bolts fading away to nothingness. Lying on the ground, the creature's back ridge was nearly the height of Ackelides, and a black goo oozed from its injuries, burning the ground where it lay. 'What is this foul thing?' asked Embra, clutching a bleeding arm, and he spat at the creature in disgust.

'It is called, an Aleagahr. It escaped from the underworld,' said Ostarra as he dragged the sword from the beast's head with a slosh. 'We have to go, mortal.'

'My name is Calmantis, sir. But you can call me Cal,' he said, nervously picking at the scabs on his fingers. The god nodded and walked away.

'Wait a moment,' called Yeron, with the rest of the guards approaching at the rear. 'Who are you? Cal says you're a god. But that can't be true. What vain sorcerer are you? What is your real name? And why does Calmantis need to go with you?'

Ostarra gestured for Calmantis to join him and sheathed his blade.

'Ah, Aztar's chosen . . . I do not need to prove who I am to you, mortal. I did what was asked of me, and I shall now get what I asked in return: The service of this man.'

Calmantis glanced back and forth between the soldiers, Yeron, and Ostarra as he reached the god and felt the slightest ripple rush through him. In the blink of an eye, the beast was gone, and so was the stench. There was no sign of Yeron, the soldiers, nor the wagons. They stood in the field as he remembered it for those brief heartbeats, heavy hands pressing on his shoulders. 'We have work to do.'

PART TWO

"A conqueror knows only war. Peace will always be temporary."

Anonymous

24. A Bridge Between

The night wind was peaceful. Sounds of crickets chirping and frogs croaking livened their surroundings. Jonas turned his head to a small critter scampering through the dried grass, rustling the stalks, and saw a long tail whip out, quickly disappearing into the field. His head was abuzz with thoughts and feelings, most of them angry, a constant humming never giving him the chance to rest.

He was the only one awake. The others lay around the fire, keeping warm, feeling a sense of security so close to the light. Not that it would help any if they were attacked, but he guessed it kept their demons at bay. Jorin was on the far side of the flames, tucked between Vernak and Orana, who had got increasingly more upset as the days progressed while Vernak ignored her not-so-silent rants, never giving her the information she requested.

Muscles twinging, Jonas groaned and drew a knife from a sheath round his belt. If it weren't for Orana's generosity, buying knives and axes, even a bow and some arrows, they would have starved through this journey. Now they had the tools to go hunting. He glanced at the strips of meat drying over the fire and rubbed his stomach, felt it rumbling for more food. 'Quiet you . . .'

Jonas had always fancied himself a pretty good shot, but during the previous day's hunting expedition, Orana had humbled him. They had ventured off in search of good game to fill their bags with dried meat, hoping to last them a good while. They had stalked through the bushes on foot and found the tracks from a herd of deer, the ground trodden with their twin-teardrop prints. It wouldn't be long before they would find their target, for the flat plains had few hiding spots to cower away. They had followed the tracks through the bushes, spying small hills and gullies in the distance, the fields becoming crooked, a good place for deer to wander unseen.

To keep themselves hidden, they stayed upwind, slowly making their way closer, smelling water in the air, and Orana thrust out her arm, stopping him from moving. She brought her finger to her lips and pointed to the waving tall grass. A group of does lay hidden beyond, one buck's horns seen turning above the dried grass. Jonas pulled the bow and an arrow from his back and lined up the shot, drawing the string back to kiss his chin and cheek. He breathed deep and slow, steady and relaxed, calming his heart.

A fly flew up his nose and he twitched, sending the arrow off to the right, narrowly missing Orana's head as she dropped to the ground. The deer jumped up, snorting and grunting, sounding like an orchestra of sneezes, and dashed to get away. Jonas was still in his fight with the fly, disgusting sounds coming from his nose, snot flying to the ground, when Orana grabbed the bow from him, nocking an arrow and letting it fly swift and precise. A bleating grunt sounded, and a doe collapsed in the thick of the grass.

Orana had clicked her tongue at him with a scowl. 'Quickly. It is suffering. Can you manage walking through the grass without hurting yourself?'

Jonas didn't respond. He just shook his head and followed her, jogging behind to catch up. The doe thrashed its numb and weak limbs, smearing the grass with its blood. The bolt had lodged through the chest and shoulders, slicing through its lungs, and possibly the heart as well, judging by the amount of blood quickly pooling underneath. A clean kill. She was definitely the better archer.

'I got it,' he said and dragged his knife free, quickly slitting the animal's throat, letting it bleed out. His father always said, *If you don't kill it, you drag it home. Everyone has a part to play.'* And he was going to do his part. With a few precise cuts, Jonas had exposed the sinews at the joints of the front legs and stuck them through holes he made in the back legs, making a backpack of the animal. He had wormed into position, and rose with a grunt, keeping the bleeding neck to the side while he walked back to camp.

Dried salty meat had always been a favourite of his. He cut a small bit from a strip hanging over the fire, chewing it slowly, savouring the taste. Jonas's breath came out as a mass of billowing white smoke, and he drew his shirt over his head. The cold gripped him, pulling his skin tight, causing the stitches to stretch. They needed to come out.

This wasn't the best of knives, but it would have to do. The blade felt loose and weak after only a few days' use, and rust was already showing around the cross guard, which also shifted around. Jonas slipped the knife's tip under the thread of the first stitch, struggling to cut through with the dull blade. 'Huh,' he groaned when the icy metal touched his naked back. He shook his head, clenching his teeth as the stitch pulled up, stretching his skin, and sawed it from the bottom slowly, working it back and forth until it finally snapped, then moved to the next one.

To their right, a few hundred feet into the bush, he could hear a pack of wild dogs barking and snarling, fighting for the biggest piece of meat left on the bones of the cleaned carcass he had tossed the previous night. He had made sure to leave some meat on the bones to let them feast, rather than them getting hungry and brave enough to enter their camp while they slept.

A sharp pain shot through his shoulder with an accidental jerk of the knife, tearing one suture through a bit of skin, and Jonas winced. The suture slipped back down, and he reached for the bottle of potent liquor on the ground beside him. He dragged in a mouthful, feeling it burn as it rushed down his throat, warming him, dulling his senses. He was thankful for all the supplies Orana had gathered for their journey, but not in the least as much as for the booze she had stashed in one crate.

'I can help you with that,' came a voice from behind, and Jonas swung around to stare at Jorin, all wrapped up in a blanket, shivering from the cold. The surrounding landscape had changed from a dark outline to light grey, quickly putting colour into the patchwork of green and brown. He handed Jorin the knife and leaned against the wagon, taking another swig before lowering to his knee.

The boy's eyes were dark, but not from the beatings he'd received.

No, those had already healed up, the cut wounds on his arms and legs only scabs now. This was tiredness. 'You sleeping?'

'Yeah, sure,' Jorin said offhandedly, avoiding the subject.

'Huh.' The edge of the icy blade pressed on his skin, and he felt the boy carefully sliding it back and forth on the thread. 'Cut it from the bottom, not the top.'

'Wait, I've got it.' Jorin worked the blade to the left, hunting for the threat in the gloomy light.

'Listen to me.'

'Almost . . .' The blade slipped from the thread and sliced into Jonas's shoulder, leaving a fresh wound.

'Argh! I told you to cut from the bottom! Give me the knife and go wake those other two. Start packing!' Jonas's hand trembled around the bottle. He had got so close to smacking Jorin on the head with it.

'Sorry, Father! Sorry!'

Jonas cleared his throat and muttered, 'It's okay. Just . . . go get them ready for the day.' He squeezed the new cut, feeling the trickle of blood run down his chest, and sighed. It was not deep.

* * *

The River Parth rushed below the bridge, the force of the water making the entire structure shake. Jonas had forgotten just how big the bridge was, spanning the great width of the old river with room for three carts to pass one another. Originally built as a means to conquer Tolomene, it now stood as a pathway for merchants and travellers, but few took the journey.

Jorin sauntered beside him with mouth agape, marvelling at the tremendous structure as the wagon creaked and rolled steadily behind. To relieve the horses from some unnecessary weight, they had climbed off, taking this time to stretch their legs. 'I had thought the flooded bridge in Skalg was big, but this . . . this is madness. How long did it take to build this?' the boy asked.

'A long time, kid. A very long time,' Orana called from the wagon.

'The war between Tolomene and Yahrska ended on that side of the river.' She pointed towards Yahrska. 'They had thought Tolomene was asleep to their plans of conquest, but an entire army was floated across the river at night, barges going back and forth over the mass of water, upstream from Yahrska's position, and we struck fiercely, putting an end to their plans. We had captured the King of Baldor's only son, Mathias the Second. Held him for ransom until the king called a truce.'

'So who finished it then?' Jorin asked and glanced down the side of the bridge, leaning over the rail, with Jonas next to him. Great columns of grey stone, each the width of two men tall, ran the length of the bridge and vanished under the murky waters. Jorin took an uneasy step back, shaking his head as if dizzy.

'We did. And Yahrska. We came to an agreement to trade instead of fight. Just because we don't like each other doesn't mean we shouldn't benefit from each other's culture.'

'You came like thieves in the night, almost,' mocked Vernak from next to Orana, setting off another shouting match between the two, but Jonas couldn't care enough about their squabble to keep listening.

'Hey, you okay?' asked Jonas, reaching out to steady Jorin, but the boy stepped back.

'I'm fine, just a little dizzy from the height.'

'Huh. I know you're not sleeping. What haunts your dreams so?'

Jorin looked away at the rushing water, biting his lower lip anxiously, and said, 'I . . .'

'It's okay. Talk to me,' Jonas stated, reassuring the boy with a gentle grip on his shoulder.

'I don't want to be asleep if someone or something comes for us again. I know, it's stupid.'

'No, it's not. I know the feeling.'

Jorin swung his head back to Jonas. 'You do? But I've never seen you worry.'

'Oh, I worry a lot more than you might think. But it doesn't help in the end. You do what you can, prepare as best you can. The burden here is not on you alone, Jorin.' The boy nodded his thanks with lips pursed and continued walking. Jonas stood for a bit on the bridge, gazing from Tolomene to Yahrska, seeing the stark difference between the two lands. One side lay pale and barren, covered with hard brown grass stalks and shrubs, few trees scattered over the tundra. On the other side, it was a sea of green, waves of different trees packed close together to form the Elderforest. The landscape rolled, undulated for miles on end, valleys and small mountains, growing larger in the distance towards Yuronia.

'It will take us a good while to navigate the Elderforest to get to Yuronia, then down to Winterbourne to find a ship bound for Keltorison. Maybe we should drop Jorin off before we head any further?'

His question ceased the ranting of the two on the wagon, and Vernak turned to him. 'I'm sorry, Jonas, but time is not on our side. We can't be making detours. Unless we travel to—'

'No! I hate that . . . place. And they would see us coming from miles away. It would never work. We'd be dead long before we even set foot close to the lair.'

'But I can get us there so much quicker.'

'No! I'm not going back to that place until I absolutely have to.'

Orana shook her head in confusion and demanded, 'Wait. There's a faster way to get there than lugging all these supplies across the country? How? And why don't we take it?'

'Because I said so! You wouldn't understand,' Jonas growled and quickened his step, walking down the last section of the bridge.

'The only reason I wouldn't understand is because you two are not telling me anything. What are you hiding from me? All I know is we are headed to Keltorison to retrieve your soul. How does that even work? Why would your soul be there? It makes no sense!'

No, it makes perfect sense, if you knew the truth. 'We need to stop at Pikeridge for some food supplies,' said Jonas, forcing a change in subject. 'We need more fruits and vegetables. We can't live off meat alone.'

'And who will pay for these, eh? I have a limit to my generosity, you know!' demanded Orana, guiding the horses down the angled foot of the bridge. She received no answer from any of them.

The green grass smelled fresh and wet, the soil soft and slippery where the wagon pushed through, wheels digging into the mud, churning up the soil. 'Yah!' she shouted, whipping the horses, and they jumped forward, yanking on the ropes to pull the wagon out, struggling with the stickiness of the mud.

'Jorin, come here, quickly!' Jonas gestured and ran to the back of the wagon to push from behind, heaving it forward slowly with his uninjured shoulder, feet slipping in the mud underneath.

The horses snorted and cried, and the wheels slipped around, garnering thick clumps of the dark mud between the spokes. His son turned red in the face next to him, pushing hard to move it forward, gritting his teeth in a fierce scowl. Jonas couldn't help but feel guilty for the torment his son had gone through and stared at the nearly healed slash across his lip and chin, giving Jorin a much harder, more terrifying look, making him appear older than he was.

The wagon launched forward suddenly, giving way under Jonas. He stumbled and slipped, arms flailing, legs searching for balance, sliding across the mud when a sloshing splash sounded behind him. He twisted around in his throes and saw Jorin face down in the mud, covered in the brown filth all over. Spitting grit and sand from his mouth, Jorin's green eyes and surrounding whites were the only pieces left unblemished, his embarrassment clear on his face. Jonas burst out laughing, barely finding his footing on the slippery surface.

'It's not funny!' scowled Jorin, shaking the mud from his clothes and face.

'Yes, it is!' Jonas slapped his thigh and bent over, laughing even harder. Orana had pulled the wagon to a stop, watching them from the front, joining Jonas's laughter while Vernak sat all serious next to her.

'It's not *that* funny . . .' Jorin said again and chuckled slightly, flinging dirt to the ground.

'Go to the river and get yourself cleaned up. We'll wait here,' Jonas said, and turned to Orana on the wagon, hearing his son's mumbled curses as he walked down the bank. 'I know it seems like we aren't telling you everything, and you're right, we're not. Understand that we do not know if we can trust you yet.'

'And just how should I trust you if I know I'm being kept in the dark? It goes both ways. And if you want my help, I need information. Think about it. I'm going for a quick stroll in the forest. Do not come peeping to catch a glimpse, eh? You men have it so much easier with this stuff.' She climbed down and walked into the forest, glancing back to keep an eye on them.

'We need to tell her,' Jonas whispered to Vernak.

'Yes, eventually. Not until it's absolutely necessary, though. Her love for coin could outweigh her love for safety. But she is trusting us with her problems. That's a start.'

'I don't know. I think she's scared. She wouldn't jeopardise our partnership for a few extra nights in a comfortable room. With us, she has a chance of survival.'

25. Fight or Flight

The tall trees swayed overhead, branches dancing in the wind, leaves cheering happily, rustling loudly. Bird calls she had never heard before drifted from tree to tree, a harsh grating sound, a scream more than anything else. Orana was astounded that the horrible sound came from a big, beautiful bird with white feathers and a very curved beak. Their big eyes followed her where she walked through the forest, heads tilted, inquisitive and curious, skipping along behind her on the ground. For all their beauty and gentle-looking nature, their calls sounded hateful and angry, yet the longer she listened, the more appealing they became. Green parrots flew from branch to branch, chirping a little more lovingly to one another, the males fanning out their tails in a show of magnificence, trying their best to attract the females.

The betrayal on Jorin's face had stayed with her, stuck in her head since the day he found out she had set up the event in the alley with the thugs, sold them out to gain their trust. Betrayal was very often an unintended consequence in her line of business, especially if you wanted to be the one on top. She wandered a little further and heard a sharp snap, the crack of a twig, and spun to her right.

'You are running out of time, Orana Rille. Yelefant is getting impatient, and it doesn't seem like you're making up lots of ground, or that you are in any rush.' Lofka stepped out from behind a tree, twirling a ringed knife around his index finger.

'What are you doing here, Lofka? You've been following me, spying on me?'

'More like staying ahead of you. What did you expect? Did you think we would just leave you to come back on your own?'

'A girl can dream, can't she?' Her boot scuffed a rock as she stepped back and stumbled slightly.

'Now, now. You aren't planning on running away, I hope. I would hate to see your pretty face get all cut up.' She turned and made to run, when another man stepped out from behind a tree on her left. It wasn't a big man, but he had a vile look on his face, one of those that said he despised women. That he was better than them. Thick dark brows rode his forehead, his skin marred with blotches, similar to Jonas's. *The sun has some nasty consequences, eh?*

'You brought company? For little old me?'

Lofka shook his head and held up his hand, showing her the missing digit on his right hand. The ring finger had been torn off at the lowest knuckle. 'You have a knack for injuring me. And I'm not stupid.'

Orana glanced between the two and felt the wetness growing on her palms. 'I still have time left, Lofka, and you are wasting it right now. What do you want?'

'I don't want to keep an eye on you throughout the entire continent of Mayanore just to give you your agreed time. I'd much rather get rid of you and report back that you got killed trying to steal back the items or pissing off the wrong person. It wouldn't be a stretch to see that as the truth.'

She stepped back, heart pounding, eyes scanning for anything to defend herself with. Filthy fingers lunged at her, digits spread out like an eagle's talons, readying to tear her apart. Fear gripped her, knowing how far she had wandered from the wagon, realising that her compatriots might not hear her screams. That didn't stop her, though. 'Help! Jonas!' *Why did I leave my knife on the wagon?*

She sprinted away, running for her life.

Wind howled over her ears, trees swishing past as she ran across the forest floor, jumping from one rock to the next with agility and speed. She had the advantage on a rough terrain, but they weren't far behind. A knife thudded into the tree on her right just as she sprinted past it, the blade wobbling from the impact. *Lofka seems a little bitter about his finger.*

Usually, though, when she was using her agility to gain access to high-reaching balconies or roofs, she did so on her time, planning the route out properly. There was no plan here, and things were coming at her thick and fast. Trees, rocks, shrubs, logs, branches, and even birds swooped down on them angrily for invading their space. A patch of unknown, dark-barked trees stood to her right, closely knitted together with a few shrubs in between. They would need to follow her through, and the space would be limited. She dashed into the patch, placing her feet well, until her momentum was snatched out from under her, and she struck the root of a tree with her chin, blinding lights exploding in her sight, teeth clattering together. Her vision came and went, threatening to leave her as she moaned and stretched her arms out to crawl forward, hearing them close on her heels.

One of them grabbed her boot and started dragging her back, when she grabbed hold of something . . . Something that wasn't a root, or a tree, or a shrub, or a rock. It was leather, round at the front, getting longer on the sides. *How did Lofka get in front of me?* The foot stepped over her, and she wheeled around to see a man pick up Lofka's companion from the ground, carry him in a run toward the tree behind her, and crash into it, exploding the air from the man's lungs.

Orana shook her head and saw it was Jonas, using his elbows to beat the man's face against the tree. Lofka ran in from the side with a cutlass, and she shouted, 'Watch out!'

Jonas spun around and jumped back to avoid the slash, nearly tripping over a tree root, and jumped back again, using his forearms as shields for his face and throat. A wild swing from Lofka opened a cut on his arm, and Orana grabbed up a rock from next to her and hurled it at their attacker, cracking him on the side of the head. The curved cutlass dropped with a grunt. It amazed her how fast Jonas was on top of the man, gripping his arms and head-butting him in the face, shattering Lofka's nose in a gush of blood.

Groans sounded from Lofka's accomplice, who stumbled over to Jonas and started beating him against the ear to drop the man, shoving his filthy fingers up Jonas's nose and dragging him back.

Pain shot through Orana's ankle when she tried to stand, and she dropped back to the ground. She dragged herself closer, grabbing rocks in passing and hurling them, but the man was behind the tree now, difficult to hit.

Jonas dropped Lofka and jammed his fist into the accomplice's throat. A spark of fear gripped the man, the scowl on his face turning slack, brows raised to plead for his life. Jonas had wrapped his fingers around the man's oesophagus and squeezed hard, crushing the windpipe.

The man stumbled away, groaning and heaving, wheezing air through a collapsed throat. His eyes widened and his mouth kept moving, yet no sound came out. He crashed into a tree and sagged to the ground, clutching his neck, legs kicking, heels scraping the ground.

Lofka had got to his feet in the meantime and was now running away, glancing over his shoulder at them. It did not seem to bother Jonas too much, letting him get away. The fight was over, and they were still alive.

'You're bleeding,' she said, pointing to his arm, and dragged herself up from the ground by a low-hanging branch, wincing at her ankle.

'I'll live. Who was that?' he asked with a voice as hard as tempered steel.

She could lie to him. She could say it was a thug, a mere desperate soul that saw an opportunity to steal from her. But they had just spoken about trust . . . 'That was Lofka. He works for the man I owe. It seems Lofka doesn't share his employer's sentiment of waiting for me to return with the goods.'

'Truth . . . I didn't expect that.' Jonas stepped over the dead man and bent down to rummage through his pockets, feeling for things to scavenge.

'His body isn't even cold yet.'

'And? That makes a difference? Would you feel better if I stripped him naked and buried him first?' Jonas muttered while going through the pockets. He undid a sheath and inspected the knife it held, then wrenched some gold and silver rings from his fingers.

'Yes!'

He turned on her with his stony stare and said, 'I'm done with him.

You can dig him a grave or I can carry you back to the wagon. I ain't wasting my energy. You choose.'

It was a simple choice.

Orana sighed. 'There's another blade in the tree, and don't forget that sword. It's a good blade.'

'Wise choice. I reckon it's not the last time we will see this Lofka.'

She had to admit, without Jonas there, she would have been done for. And although it annoyed her terribly, she leaned on him for support, hobbling out of the forest like a wounded creature.

'Thank you,' she whispered, shying away to glance at anything that wasn't him, and saw him nod in the corner of her eye.

* * *

'What happened to you two?' Vernak asked, rising from the front seat of the wagon and calling attention to Jorin, who came running back up from the water's edge, looking much cleaner than before.

'Father?'

'How are you still cleaning yourself, boy? We've been gone for some time!'

Vernak rummaged through a pack, seeing the sheepish look on the boy's face, and said, 'I sent him back after he returned the first time, still covered in muck. Told him to do it properly. It seems you two will also need a cleaning.'

'We are fine. Get the suture kit from your pack again. Got another cut on my arm. Burns like fire. Vernak, can you have a look at her ankle? See what you can do for her. I think she twisted it.'

'Of course, yes. We are friends, after all.'

Orana gritted her teeth from the pain and frustration. 'You are not worth my anger right now, Vernak.'

'What happened?' prodded Jorin again as he brought the little box closer.

Orana shook her head and said, 'I wandered a bit too far and—'

'And some thugs attacked her. Opportunists. But we scared them off.' She looked at Jonas sidelong.

This made her even more curious. *Why would Jonas lie to them?* 'Why were you in the forest, Jonas?'

'You were taking too long, so I went looking. Is that okay, or did I need your permission for that?' His firm hands slipped around her waist, and he picked her up, placing her on the wagon's bed, feet dangling to the ground.

'Oi! You can't just move me around like I'm nothing!'

'Huh. Then at Pikeridge, you can get down on your own.' Trapped in between the supplies on the wagon, she sat on the bed while Vernak removed her boot, feeling her ankle and working his hands up to her calf and back down. Jonas climbed up front and pulled a full bottle of liquor out from under the seat, spilling some of its contents over the needle, and set to work on himself to close the cut on his arm.

'You need help with that!' Orana called. 'It will leave a big scar.'

'Just get yourself sorted. I'll be fine.'

Vernak glanced around and said, 'Jorin, break that crate apart and give me two straight pieces. Her ankle is just bruised, but she needs to take it easy for a while. The splints will help when she has to walk. And make her a cane.'

'Just give me yours.' Orana grinned, hoping to hold the beautiful cane for a while. It was a futile attempt, half-hearted and not even meant, but she could see he considered it for a moment, furtively glancing at his cane. She chuckled. 'Oh, my. That's adorable. It's okay, you keep it. Just get me a stick. Hey, kid, that one over there.' She pointed to a thick, forked branch. 'Cut it at the bole and a bit beyond the split, eh?'

'There are axes in that crate,' added Jonas, groaning as he pushed the needle through his skin, finishing up with his stitches.

The crate cracked open with a last kick, splintering the planks apart, the look of victory and triumph plain on Jorin's boyish face. He quickly gathered the best pieces, long enough to extend from her foot to her calf, and handed them to Vernak. 'Will these do?'

'Ah. They look mighty fine to me. Thanks.' Vernak took the offered pieces and tore strips from a piece of clothing he had pulled from the trunk and began strapping it tight around her ankle and tying it off.

Orana pulled a face, biting on her lip to keep quiet. The planks pushed up hard against the swollen ankle, paining her. This was not the first time she'd had to wear an uncomfortable splint, and unfortunately, it probably wouldn't be her last. These things tended to happen when running and jumping on precarious ledges and terrains.

* * *

Pikeridge came into view as they rounded the border of the forest, the road following the mighty River Parth on its left, houses built on stilts spreading far on its banks. It seemed like everyone wanted a river view. Yet, not all could afford the luxury of living on the banks, it seemed. Some had to settle on the back side, leaving a long winding road through the town.

'A small town should be easily defensible. How would they defend this with so few guards?' Orana observed, shaking her head. 'It would take them forever to run from one end to the other to bring in support. The fight would be over before it began.'

Their wagon rolled onwards, furtive glances were cast their way from men and women going about their business, children shooed from the roads by their worried mothers.

Jonas chewed on his lip and said, 'What does it matter? If they were close to each other, a large army would surround them. They are dead either way.'

'How did you get so cynical?'

'I've seen what happens to places like this if they are attacked.'

'Oh, yeah? And were you doing the attacking or the defending?'

'Bit of both, I suppose.'

'They attacked our village a while back, killed my mother, and kidnapped me,' added Jorin, speaking out of turn where he sat next to Jonas on the front seat, and he quickly got cut off by his father.

'Hey! Shut it. No need to go spilling all our history. She has no interest in that.'

Oh, but I do. I want to know exactly who and what I have got myself into, Orana thought. 'I'm sorry to hear about your wife. And your mother.' *So this must be what started it all.* 'Why did they kidnap you?'

'They wanted to get to my father—'

'Enough. Let's get some supplies and get out of here. We have a way to go still.'

'My father is special,' Jorin said with a smile, quickly finding that not listening to Jonas reaped him some unfortunate consequences. A hard palm slapped him on the head, nearly sending him over the side, his feet quickly searching for the solid planks beneath him.

'Damn it, boy! Don't you listen? It's things like this that get you into trouble.'

'Sorry, Father.' Jorin lowered his head to stare at the wood grains of the planks under his feet, biting his lip.

Orana watched the moment, searching for signs that she could use to probe more, while Vernak lay next to her, snoring loudly. There was a quick glance from Jonas to Jorin, and he cleared his throat before he said, 'Jorin here did his best to defend our home. He stopped four men before they overwhelmed him. I couldn't be prouder of my boy.'

She could tell there was something else to this story by Jorin's silence, his face turned away from his father's praise. And she would find out.

'Over there. Looks like a tavern. They might have some stock. Horse food and such.' She pointed to the left to an old timber building, wood turned grey with years of rain, sun, and wind battering it every which way in relentless pursuit of wearing it down.

'Mornin, fellas, ma'am,' called a cheery man crossing the road, fancy black cane in hand and dusty top hat plastered on his shaggy head. Jonas lifted his fingers to return the greeting. Another man followed closely behind and greeted them with a toothless grin before running to catch up with Top-hat.

Men and women buzzed all around, laughing and talking, going about their business. Orana had never understood small places like this.

Where are they making their coin from? Why would you live in such an isolated little place? The world rushes by you, growing and learning, while you sit here, slowly dying away. She knew she would certainly not make a living here.

She stared at Jonas on the front seat, a big smile glued to his face. He looked like he couldn't get enough of seeing the simple life of these folks, and she had to admit, most of the people seemed happy here. Poor, but happy.

They made their way to the tavern, pulling the wagon up at the front, and Jonas jumped off, Jorin and Vernak following him. 'Hey! Some help here?' she called after them, but Jonas ignored her wholly and strode through the door without a glance back. Vernak paused and gestured to Jorin to help her down. *I guess I deserved that.*

26. Finding Purpose

Far below in the valley, Calmantis could see the river winding through the forest, a green snake slithering across the land. He couldn't believe where he was, and with whom. Never in his wildest dreams did he think he would ever be in this position. To be needed by a god . . . His aspirations were to become a Shadow Guard. To serve Aztar with blind faith, but now, he wasn't sure what his aspirations should be. How could he top this? How did one continue a trivial life after having seen all this? How did one go on living in the same old boring mortal realm if you'd been here, in Tenthis, the land of the gods?

Behind him, a huge tower constructed from larimar stone rose from the mountain's side, its blue-white exterior meticulously polished by Ostarra's servants every day. It was a magnificent construction. Calmantis had been told not to wander far from the tower, in fear of being spotted by another god not so understanding towards Voidwalkers, and he was in no hurry to die.

During the last few nights, he had spent his time listening to Ostarra talk about the abilities he had received and how to use them, then during the day, he tried to put it to use, willing his body to shift between the realms, but so far, he had yet to accomplish the desired effect. Calmantis suspected that Ostarra's patience with him was wearing thin. With every passing day, the god became more blunt and abrupt in their conversations, his scowling face set deep with creases, red eyes glaring through to his very soul.

Men, women, and children in raggedy clothes walked around him, maintaining the gardens, polishing the tower, moving rocks and sand, doing work where needed, their heads bowed low never to make eye contact with Ostarra or any who visited him. He could not help but feel like they were being used like slaves. Then again, what did he know? He was a cesspit cleaner for the Order of Eternal Sacrament. How was that any better? 'Excuse me,' he called to one servant, and the man stopped next to him, turning his face away. 'You may look at me.' The man shook his head nervously, fingers rubbing his palms. 'Who are you?' Calmantis asked.

Strange sounds drawled from the man, a language Calmantis did not know, yet he was sure the man had understood his every word.

Feeling that this was going nowhere, he waved the man on, who eagerly tramped away to continue his work. Calmantis bent down and picked up one of the thousands of blue-white pebbles scattered in the beds around the flowers and trees and walked back to the edge of the gardens where he sat down, closing his eyes.

'You have to become part of the world,' Ostarra had told him one night. *'Make your body ethereal, as though you are spirit walking. Focus your mind on not having a physical body. That is how you move between realms. Once your mind sees the doorway, your body will follow. Focus on the realm you need to get to and open the door.'*

Spirit walking . . . If only I knew what that was, he thought. *Relax your muscles, relax your mind. Drift away.* He rubbed the polished stone in his hands, working it between his fingers, then decided to put it in his mouth, sucking on it, tasting the bit of dirt and some iron and— 'Argh ghr!' The stone slipped down his throat, getting lodged halfway and stopping the flow of air to his lungs. Eyes jumping open, he scratched at his throat and beat his chest, making awful sounds to dislodge the stone, yet it did not want to budge. His face and hands were turning numb, tingling all over and not wanting to react to his commands.

This is a silly way to die.

Calmantis saw between the dark spots in his vision two servants running towards him, and then darkness. It felt like his mind was still working, beyond the fact that his body was on the ground, kicking dirt and stone. There wasn't a way to become more part of the world in his mind. He thought of home, of Baldor, the cesspits, and the Order. He thought of the Shadow Guard. Of Clairvoy Yeron and his shocked expression when he saw Ostarra.

The ground gave way under him, and he fell.

Through his breathless delusion and dark vision, he dropped through the air, albeit briefly, before hitting the ground with a thud, dislodging the stone from his throat to go flying from his mouth, skimming his teeth and nearly shattering them. Calmantis sucked in air with wide, red eyes and clutched his chest, lips still tingling and numb. He coughed and rolled on the ground as his senses reeled, his ribs hurting. The mountains were still there, but the tower had disappeared, and so did the levelled gardens overlooking the valley. *I made it!*

He had done it.

Now if I can only do it again, and this time, without nearly dying. He spat to his right and a large ball of phlegm splattered against an innocent rock. A cacophony of grunting and gasping filled the air as he gathered more sticky goo from the deepest cracks in his body and spewed them with another spray and splash. The choking had caused an unbearable amount of phlegm to assault him.

'Dear me, Cal, how did you manage this?' he asked himself, surprised and proud of himself. If there was ever a time that Calmantis liked himself, it was now. To his own account, he had climbed in social standing from the bottom of the barrel to absurd new heights. 'I don't think there are steps to climb above this, I dare say. Reached the pinnacle, I have. Well, my good man,' he mocked in his father's rich, pompous, patronising demeanour, clinking an imagined glass of wine to himself. 'It seems you have nowhere left to climb now.'

The sun was going down, a bright ball in the sky being pulled behind the mountains. Here he was back in this place he hated, the world of man. Where nobody had ever respected him. Where it was normal to sleep on lice-infested beds, filthy sheets that stank of excrement, or not on a bed at all. Back in Tenthis in the god's abode, soft pillows, smelling fresh and clean on a bed that didn't make him sneeze or itch, had been his for the last few days, reminding him of home when he was a young boy.

Ostarra would be home soon, requesting an update on his progress, and Calmantis didn't want to stare into those eyes, only to disappoint him again. He had to get back to Tenthis soon. Besides, he had no idea where he was, other than on a mountain somewhere, a stiff wind howling over him.

More than a week ago now, Ostarra had slaughtered the beast on the field and taken Calmantis away. Everything had moved so fast that most of it was a blur to him. They had come out on the empty field, having a relative idea where they were compared to the mortal realm, but then everything got sped up by a machine; he had not the faintest idea of what it was. There had been a large, slightly raised metal platform on the ground, and in the middle stood a dark metal arch. Once Ostarra set foot on the platform, it came alive from within, humming with a certain power, making Calmantis feel light on his feet, like he would float up into the air and never come back down. The air within the arch turned dark and swirled slowly, bending the world around it.

'Are we really going through that?' Calmantis had asked, fearing his body would be pulled apart.

'You will be fine, young Cal. The Flow will get us to where we need to go.' They had stepped through the arch, and the world raced by in a blur. His body pulled at his gut, wrenching it back and forth. What he witnessed seemed impossible; to move at these speeds could simply not be. It felt like he had been running the entire day, his legs weak and wobbling, trembling from exhaustion, and the world suddenly stopped, came back into frighteningly sharp focus all too abruptly. He was sure that was what an arrow must feel like, getting shot and hitting a target far away. The arrow, though, he knew, had nothing in its stomach to hurl out. But Calmantis did.

Yellow slime and the red of an earlier tomato burst from his mouth, peeled, and sprayed from between his fingers to cover the dark metal platform with chunks of stink. Ostarra had jumped away from him like he had the plague, scowling at him in disgust. His top lip curled up in anger, and Calmantis was sure the god was about to strike him down.

He hurled again.

Ostarra grabbed him by the scruff of his neck and headed for the next arch, only a few hundred feet away. To his left, through the sprays of puke, Calmantis saw a large city, golden and white, the sun reflecting brilliantly from high-towered buildings, rich arches, and delicately designed gardens. And then it was gone again.

His head felt like it was in his arse, and it stank like it, too. Three more times, the world stopped briefly, giving him glorious glimpses of Tenthis, the world of the gods, and three more times it had sped by, yanking his head back to tear it from his body, until finally reaching Ostarra's home, or that was what Calmantis thought it was, at least. He didn't really care, as long as he didn't have to do another one of those travel jumps for a while.

Ostarra had dragged him from the platform, feet scraping over the metal, legs folding under him feebly as he tried to stand. Then the hard ground and rocks dragged at his shoes, trying to pull them from his feet, so much so that he had to curl his toes to keep them on. It was not a matter of saving his old worn shoes because they helped keep sharp stones or thorns at bay, or that they cost him anything, but because he was afraid that the stench of his feet might be the last straw for the god Ostarra. In the back of his mind, he had seen how the god would keel over and die from the fumes, and he chuckled to himself.

'Dear me. How far is it still to go? My feet are killing me.'

'Your feet are killing you? I've been dragging you the entire way.'

'I hear you, I do. I really do, but you are a god, and I'm a mere mortal.'

'Keep this up and your mortality might run out.'

Calmantis kept quiet for a while, trying to keep up, running and falling, being dragged along. 'Please stop, your holy godliness.'

'That is a terrible title. Do not use it again.' Ostarra dropped Calmantis on the ground and dusted his hands, his breathing slightly increased.

'What then?'

'Why would you call me anything other than my name? You didn't pray to me, you didn't serve me. Why would you now?'

There was truth to his words, and Calmantis couldn't help but admire it. 'Very well, Ostarra. Why have you brought me here after you told me that the other gods would like to see me dead?'

'They won't look for you here. You will be safe.'

A narrow path took them up the side of the mountain, where he first saw the servants toiling to neaten the path, planting flowers in rows and watering perfect red roses. *The god of storms lives in a palace of beauty,* he thought as he first laid eyes on the larimar tower, his mouth hanging open. 'By the way, what were those things we travelled through? Horrible bloody things.'

'Like I said, we call it the Flow. They might be horrible, but there are no quicker ways to travel. You'll get used to them, eventually.'

* * *

One night, Ostarra sat before his great hearth, swirling a dark red liquid in a large glass, delicately crafted and thin as paper. Calmantis could see clearly through the glass with no distortion or blur, and instantly wondered how many of those glasses he would have broken were they in his hands. He could not help but admit that he had been a tad clumsy since his birth some thirty-five years ago.

It was a strange feeling living in the house of Ostarra. No matter how cold or how hot it got outside, the inside of his tower was always the perfect temperature. Calmantis crept closer from the side, eyeing the great red chair and the god within, his white hair bathed in a glorious red from the flames. 'Apologies, Ostarra. I have been here for a few days and still you have not told me what you need my help with.'

Ostarra turned his head, with a flash of the golden prongs sprouting from his head that formed a divine crown. 'You should practise, not skulk around.'

'I have been thinking that it might be the lack of urgency that is causing my momentary lapse in progress. Perhaps if I knew what we stand to gain or lose, then maybe it will motivate me.'

'Huh, you have a point,' rumbled the god's deep voice. The glass drifted up, and he pointed to a chair opposite him. 'Sit. And listen.' The room was lit only by four lanterns on the wall and the fire blazing in the hearth, casting ominous shadows into the gloomy room, stretching and jumping with the dance of the flames. 'Our world is under threat, Calmantis. And the gods – Aztar included – are not doing anything to fix the problem, which will not just affect our world, I might add. It is already interfering with yours as well. You have seen the devastation caused by the event you call the World Storm?'

'Yes, I have been meaning to ask, as you are the god of storms. Why do you allow—'

Ostarra cut him off with a glaring look, then reached for a dark bottle and a glass on the table to his right and poured some of the dark wine, handing it to Calmantis. 'Those storms are not of my doing . . . And they have been growing worse gradually over a long time, getting more frequent. Soon that will be all that's left of your world. A chaotic, constantly raging storm. Uncontrolled and unstoppable.'

'Dear me. That is not good.'

'No, it is not.'

Calmantis took a sip of the wine, smelling the rich fruity flavours, and swirled it around in his mouth. It tasted soft and dry, melting away down his throat and warming his stomach. 'Oh, dear god.' His eyes snapped open at his words and saw the smirk on Ostarra's powerful face. 'I mean, it is just so good. I have never, ever tasted wine so well made.'

'Yes, we took it from you humans, actually, and made some slight adjustments. It is rather good. One truly great thing you have given us.'

'We inspired the gods?' Calmantis couldn't believe it and took another sip, folding into the chair as the taste ran through him. 'Oh, my.'

'Yes, you did.' Ostarra laughed, beginning as a chuckle to end as a rumbling growl, and Calmantis joined in. 'Thank you, Calmantis. I haven't laughed in a long time.'

'Please, call me Cal. All my friends call me Cal.'

Ostarra nodded and said, 'While your world feels the wrath of the

World Storm, Tenthis bears the same pain, although not in the form of the storm. I believe the Light of the Eyavare is growing dim, causing all of this destruction, and soon, it will vanish altogether, taking Tenthis with it.'

'What is this Light of the Eyavare?' Calmantis drank a mouthful, savouring the taste, rolling it around in his mouth.

'A long time ago, when the Eyavare created the realms, they also created the Lights for our realm and the underworld. It keeps our worlds apart, stops the bleed-through effect, but it has long been theorised that our Light was damaged during the war between us and them. We have no means of fixing it. It is beyond our skills.'

Calmantis swallowed hard on the next gulp of wine, getting an air bubble lodged in his throat. It hurt him as it crawled down his oesophagus. He groaned and shifted, trying to force the bubble out in a burp, but he could not persuade it. 'Ooh . . .' He struggled to get any words out, speaking in a whisper until the bubble cleared his chest. 'Ow! This is insane! Why would Aztar not help?'

'We are not allowed to interfere with your world.'

'I would call this interfering if you don't do something. Apologies.' He realised he was near shouting and sat back in the chair, biting his nails.

'I agree with your sentiments, Cal. And that is why I have started my own plan. But in order to do something about the problem, I first need a piece of the Light of the Eyavare, and you're going to steal it for me.'

'I am?' Calmantis asked, his face turning slack.

'Yes. You are.'

'Steal from the gods?'

'For a good cause, yes.'

'Oh, my. Why me?'

'You can enter and leave Tenthis the same as us, but they will not detect you when you enter the Light's Sanctuary. Then there's the barrier that cannot be crossed from this side, unless you can transverse between realms. Not to mention that if anyone from this realm steps foot in the Sanctuary, other than Aztar, they will instantly die.'

That night was a conversation Calmantis had never dreamed of having, nor wanting to have. Now there was no taking it back. He lay on the rock, caught in the world of man, and closed his eyes, then thought, *One night won't do any harm. See you tomorrow, Ostarra.*

* * *

'Where have you been?' rumbled a voice, and Calmantis's back arched with a solid kick. He nearly soiled himself. There was no warning of anyone creeping up on him, none that he could hear. Still, the red eyes of Ostarra forced him back on the dark rock at the darkest hour of the night. No moon shone up high, and thin clouds covered the glittering stars, few finding their way to be seen from the ground. Calmantis crawled back on his hands, chafing his arse over the rough rock, and quickly found the edge of his temporary bed. 'Argh!' Head over arse, he tumbled backwards, hitting the ground and rolling down the mountainside, scrambling to grasp anything with outstretched fingers.

'We had a deal! Are you trying to run away?'

Calmantis coughed and clawed his way back up the steep mountain. 'Nice to see you too, Ostarra. No, I wasn't running. I managed to get to this side, but not back. Thought if I rested, I could try in the morning again. But now that you're here, how about a hand?' He reached up to the god on the rock and found no reciprocating hand.

'Come, you are wasting time.'

27. To Carry a Burden

The gardens seemed peaceful in the waking hours of the morning. Bright orange and pink clouds streaked across a blue sky, while flocks of birds flew in V formations over the horizon. Bellard had risen early to pack, excited to be returning to Forgeholde for a well-deserved break after a long and heartbreaking semester at Kunia, Academy of the Arcane. Despite the eagerness coursing through his veins, his stomach still twisted at the prospect of returning to his home, a place where he had suffered at the hands of his peers for not fitting in. At least now he would have Mila for company.

Bellard waited for her on a bench in the forecourt, watching students drift by to the hall for the last speech of the year, taking this time to reflect on his return home and what awaited him. *I wonder how Mother's doing?* he thought, rubbing at his scalp through his thick head of hair. For seven long years after Opa Anglard had given his last warning to his parents, Bellard had made sure not to be there when his father got home, taking extra care when there was liquor on their breath. He wasn't even sure if they would welcome him back into their home. If not, he was sure that Gallus would organise a place for him and Mila. The more he thought about it, the better it seemed to just stay away from his parents altogether.

'Hey, you waiting for me?' Mila called, skipping down the steps of the girls' dormitory with a rather large grin.

'For you? Pft. No.' Bellard pulled a face and cleared his throat.

'Yes, you were.'

'No, I wasn't.'

'Oh yeah? Then why are you rising from your seat?'

'Because I was getting ready to go. It is pure coincidence that you are here at this time.'

'You are such a terrible liar. If we ever get into trouble, you are not allowed to talk. Got it?' Mila glided by him, white hair swinging wildly at the back of her hooded black robe. 'Stop staring and fall in. We're going to miss the opening.'

The past events had not seemed to dull her wits in the least. Bellard jogged to catch up with her, avoiding a group of students who got in his way, needing to sprint around them like a desperate fool. 'How do you walk so fast, yet your legs seem not to move at all?'

She just smiled at him and walked even faster. His long limbs stretched out, having to sprint every few steps to keep up with her relentless pace across the grass quad, making their way to a building in the centre, heralded by two enormous sleeping golems of stone hearkening for their master's call for protection. Tall and gaunt, they stood carrying large spears in their three-fingered hands, and old swords sheathed and belted round their waist. Rumour had it that the head grandàre of long since past had created them to safeguard Kunia, should they ever be attacked. Bellard glimpsed up at the rock-faced protector, a sense of foreboding overwhelming him when he strayed too close. He had seen more of them scattered around Kunia's grounds, on the edges of the perimeter, hiding in shadowy corners.

'Why didn't you come to witness the claiming of the others?' Mila asked, spinning around briefly to look at him. For the last three days, students had been going back into the Sacred Hall to complete their claiming, some entering in groups, others opting to go solo.

'I wanted to, Mila. But I just couldn't. I'm sorry.' She accepted the apology with a slight pull of her mouth and spun back to continue forward.

They scurried past the statues and under a vine-grown roof, with large white columns spreading in a half-circle to meet the building. A clamour of laughter and conversation echoed as they drew nearer to the hall's doors. Great and polished, their dark wood flowed with golden waves through the grain. Bellard pushed on them, allowing Mila to enter under his arm, and followed her in.

'Why thank you, my good sir,' she said and curtsied with a grin. Bellard rolled his eyes at her, glancing around at those nearby like a wounded puppy.

'Silence! Silence in the hall,' Grandàre Shevira called from behind a podium at the front, a flicker of sunlight bursting through the red drapes, blinding her every few heartbeats. She cupped her hand over her eyes, and a commotion near the wall started up as a student lifted a long pole with a hook at the end, trying to pull the drapes closed properly. 'Thank you, Kelliron. It has been a tough few months for all here at Kunia, but we are proud of what you all accomplished this year. You have grown beyond what any of us could have imagined, and it only goes to show that with hard work, anything is possible.' Shevira glanced around the room with her enormous eyes, always looking like she was one breath away from crying, her wrinkled face showing her age.

Bellard's eyelids were heavy, and Shevira's continuous droning helped him none. No matter what he tried to do, his lids wanted to close, drag him down into the abyss with them. A sudden murmur of students close-by brought him out of his daze enough to wonder what Shevira had said. Not enough for him to find out. He closed his eyes, squeezing them shut, and rolled them about, feeling them scratch against the lids. It was a brief indulgence, and one wrought with a naivety that soon found him tumbling through the air, the ground racing towards him.

Everyone had vanished, replaced by howling wind screaming in his ears. Heart pounding in his chest, right before impact, his eyes flared open with a loud snort and fluttering hand movements. All around him, students laughed into their hands and sleeves, eyes rolling at him.

'What are you doing?' Mila whispered. 'Didn't you sleep last night? Pay attention.' He kept glancing around at the other students, feeling ashamed. He was just so tired. *Maybe some fresh air would do me good. How long is this going to take still?* Bored faces stared back at Shevira, none listening to what she had to say, all thinking of their holiday that was about to start and all the mischief they would get up to.

Behind Shevira, the other teachers and grandàres sat in their chairs, hands on their laps, faces stern and watchful. 'We have seen losses to our school, and endured hardship that should never have been. For the part we played, I sincerely apologise, as head grandàre of Kunia. This will not happen again. Not under my watch. Next semester will be here sooner than you think, so be ready! Until then, congratulations on another year completed! Enjoy the break! You all deserve it!' Shevira shouted, and a sudden roar of voices went up, everyone filing out of the hall to be graced by the warming sun.

The push of the throng guided Bellard towards the door. Tall enough to see over most, he watched them from above while Mila was stuck in a close-quartered cell of bodies, her head tilted up, eyes wide and searching to see. The bottle-necked door approached with short, hurried footsteps, and they were pushed through, quickly gaining freedom from the mass of students around them as they filed away.

'Are you ready to head out?' he asked Mila, re-adjusting his pack after so many had pushed it around.

'Am I ready? Asks the one at the back . . .' Mila spun around with a bounce of her legs. 'Are we taking a horse?'

'No, I don't have the coin.'

'Ooh, do we have to steal one?'

'No. The mountains will be too treacherous for a horse. We will have to walk. There're coaches for hire from Khort-amali. Until then, we are on foot.'

'On foot?' She pursed her lips and scrunched up her face. 'So undignified.'

'Come on, princess. You'll be all right.'

* * *

'You haven't said why we are going to the mountains. Why can't we go directly to Forgeholde?' Mila drawled from behind, dragging her feet up the hill. 'I'm already tired.'

'You really need to exercise more, Mila. We haven't even travelled a mile from the city.'

'Yes, but the city itself was a few miles to get through! And all the people walking around made it no less difficult to get to the other side.'

'Ha! I haven't heard you complain so much since I met you.'

'Oh, shut up! Since you met me, I have been nothing but a proper lady.'

'So what happened then?' he asked with a smile, feeling her glare at his back.

'What do you mean, what happened?'

'Why did you stop being a proper lady?' A rock sailed by his head with a swoosh, making him jump to his left. She dropped her pack and got ready to hurl another rock at him. 'I'm just joking!' he shouted, letting his pack fall as well.

'I'll show you joking!'

He ducked in behind a boulder, hearing the small pebble bounce off its surface. 'You might have to work on your aim as well.'

'Ooh, ya bastard! Get out of there!' Her extreme tiredness had all but evaporated now as she ran up to the boulder and jumped around it with an evil little grin.

'Oi,' he called from above her, startling her. She jerked her head left and right, jumping back when she saw him hanging over the boulder's top. 'It pays to be tall.' Unable to reach the ledge, Mila stood with arms crossed, waiting for him to come down, a hard scowl on her soft face.

'You might have the high ground, Bellard. But you have to come down, eventually.' There was something in her voice that made Bellard regret starting this game, something menacing and dirty. *Wasn't it her words not to mess up our friendship?* She sounded hungry, like a caged tigress ready for her first meal in the wild.

He turned to see the way down from the boulder, marking out the path in his mind, and turned back to where Mila was, or used to be. There was nothing now, just the last indentation of her footprints in the sand. She had vanished. A weight settled on him from above with a giggle and a shake. 'How did you get up here so fast?'

She was not interested in his questions. There were other things on her mind, it seemed, and talking was not one of them. Out in the open in the cold north, on a rock that drew every bit of warmth it could from the sun, Bellard had his shirt stripped from him, and his mouth sealed with wet kisses while he dug his heels against the sloped surface, fighting not to slip down its side. It was not easy, with Mila on top of him, working her pelvis back and forth, her face not so innocent and childish anymore.

Things were getting uncomfortable in his pants again. And she noticed. Sounds of pleasure left her mouth, arousing him even more. He wasn't sure how this had got to where it was, but he was not complaining. She tugged her robe up and undid his pants, the click of his belt a grim reminder of his old life with his parents. It seemed a world away right now. There was only one thing bothering him at the moment.

They were slipping . . .

Could we not have done this on the ground? Or anywhere that had a flat surface? His pants were around his knees now, and Bellard cleared his throat. '*Ahem*, I uhm . . . Just remember it's cold, okay? I mean, freezing.'

She pressed her index finger over his mouth to silence him. 'Shh.' Mila breathed in his ear, slipping over him with a gasp, soft squeals and whimpering escaping her. He held on to her back, felt her warmth as he pulled her near. The damn robe was in the way. He considered struggling with it to take it off, but it would possibly just end the mood completely. Their motion increased, the speed rapidly bringing the conclusion closer, their rhythmic grunts and squeals growing fiercer, their nails digging deeper, fingers squeezing harder.

'Yes! Oh, yes!' Mila shouted and leaned over him.

Bellard kicked his legs up with finality, muscles tense and jumping, spasming from the excitement of finishing the race. With no feet on the boulder to keep them pinned down, his arse slid down, taking Mila with, and they tumbled over each other all wide-eyed and weak.

Everything went limp with the hit on the ground, and Bellard groaned from under the laughing Mila, who worked her way up from the embarrassing position they had found themselves in, flicking his manhood off her chest. Sand and snow were lodged in his arse. He could feel the assortment of gravel and dirt chafe against his buttocks with every move, but picking them out one by one didn't seem like the proper thing to do in front of Mila, so he ignored them as best he could.

'Oh, my.' Mila chortled, placing her hand over her mouth, and Bellard joined in, pulling up his trousers and donning his shirt and jacket. 'I told you you'd come down eventually.'

'Yes, you did. I just didn't think it would be that quick.' He let his head fall back against the boulder and said, 'There is an enchanter by the name of Yosphore Blackstain that lives where the mountain meets the shore. Grandàre Larison told me about him. She said that I could request his services as a favour to her. Apparently, he can imbue my Pillar into something else that is a little easier to carry.'

'That is amazing! I have been meaning to ask what you were going to do with it. So I made you something in the meantime.' She rolled herself up from the ground and dusted some of the grime from her robe on her way to fetch their packs a distance back. Bellard didn't wait at all. As soon as she turned to leave, he went mining down his crack, fishing out sharp little stones and dirt where he really didn't want any of them.

Mila dropped the packs and tossed him a small leather pouch on a leather string and said, 'I think it'll fit. Let's see.'

It was rudimentary, with no frills. Hard leather, stitched with hard sinewy threads, and it fit perfectly. 'Thank you, Mila. I don't know what to say. It's such a pain carrying this thing in my pocket.'

She smiled and set off past him, walking with renewed energy up the hill. 'Then don't say anything.'

* * *

The flames licked and danced under a hanging kettle, light bounding off the wall of the overhang, giving what little warmth it could to them. Mila pulled a blanket around her shoulders, then flicked it over her head as well and pulled it tight, shivering, a cloud of vapour puffing from her mouth in steady streams. She watched Bellard fritter away with a gleaming silver press, constantly rummaging through his pack for something else. He poured something, that sounded like small pebbles hitting terracotta tiles, into a mortar and ground it up. As he worked the pestle, a pungent aroma drifted over the fire.

'What are you doing?' she asked, holding her hand over her freezing nose.

'Making a pot of clastra. It will warm us up.' He poured the warmed water from the kettle into the press and slowly pushed down on a long silver stem sticking from its top, and the smell burst out with pride.

'Is it any good?' she asked, scrunching up her face.

'Have you never had it before? They drink it all the time in Forgeholde. The people there live by this stuff. Can't drink too much, though, or you will get the shakes. Makes your head go crazy.' He picked up the two metal cups from next to the fire, tapping them with his gloved hand to see if they weren't too hot, and poured the black contents from the press. 'Here. It's boiling, so don't burn yourself.'

'How old do I look, two? Of course I've had clastra,' Mila said, pulling her face into a scowl. 'I just didn't know that's how you make it.' She took the cup and brought it to her face, smelling the rising steam. The heat rushed through her nose, livening her airways to new things. Droplets formed on her top lip from the condensation caused as she gently blew into the cup. She took her first sip, the strong acrid taste pulling her lips back, her left eye fluttering closed involuntarily, and she shuddered from her head to her toes, nearly spilling the hot liquid over her hands.

'Ooh, be careful!' Bellard said and laughed, seeing her shocked expression, her brows knitted and creased, eyes begging to understand what just happened.

'Dear me!' she stated, working her tongue over her teeth. 'Feels like I've got hair growing everywhere.' Mila shook her head, racked by shivers, and went in for another sip, unwilling to let this drink defeat her. She was Mila Vashgarde. There was not a drink in the world she was afraid of. *Be strong, Mila, you can't let Bellard see you suffering from this. Look at him sipping on the clastra, as if it were nothing more than hot water.* The strong flavours swirled in her mouth, and she swallowed it, her jaw involuntarily stretching her mouth open, face pulled back, head shaking. 'Whoa!'

'You've never had clastra, have you?' he laughed.

'No . . . Don't go thinking you're all that for drinking this dreck.' She sneered at him.

'Give it here. I'll finish it.' He reached out to take the cup from her, but Mila yanked it back.

'No! It might be dreck, but it's still warm dreck.'

'You are so strange.'

'What? You are strange!'

'I meant in a good way.' Bellard laughed and sat down next to her.

'What are you going to ask from the enchanter?'

'I haven't really thought—'

Mila gasped loudly, and Bellard jerked his head around, searching for any sign of trouble. 'What? Do you see someone? Where?'

She slapped his arm and spoke with excitement ringing in her voice, eyes stretched wide. 'Maybe you can ask for a dagger! Or a shield?' She scanned his confused face, and continued, 'What about a bow? I've always wanted to learn how to use one.'

'I, er . . . Uh . . .'

'I swear, if you get something like a cane, or a staff, I will never be seen with you again.'

'But all grand wizards have staffs.'

'Yes, because they're all ancient!'

'Okay, okay. I'll think about it.' Bellard rubbed his shaved chin, glancing sidelong at her. 'You want another apple?'

'Only half, please. I'm quite full after the broth and bread. Where did you learn to cook?' Mila drew her legs up to cover them with the blanket and felt ashamed of the things she had packed. He had thought of everything: food, water, clastra, pans, and bedding. She was sure there were more things lurking inside his pack but couldn't see there being much clothing. Where her pack contained mostly clothes, only for her, a few combs, a canteen, and The Book of Unmitigated Beauty: A Wizard's Way to a Glorious Life. She had thought of leaving it behind, but there was still so much to learn from it. And even though it weighed an absolute ton, she was sure it would be handy. Bellard rummaged through his pack again and pulled out a small knife and an apple, then cut it in half.

'I had a . . . difficult childhood, growing up. I had to learn to look after myself from a young age. Cook, clean, all that.' He sighed, and Mila saw his shoulders sag.

'Sorry, Bellard, I didn't mean to intrude.'

'No, it's not you. I'm just concerned with how they will react when they see me, or us.'

'Isn't that cute?' a gruff voice said right before a man stepped out from the shadows of the bush. 'Nearly wept from his sad story meself, I did.'

Bellard jumped up in front of Mila, arms stretched wide to protect her, knife flashing in the light of the flames. 'What do you want? Who are you?'

Mila stumbled back and pushed up against the overhang, feeling the cold of the stone siphon through the blanket. The man had a jagged scar on the right side of his face, the pink flashing angrily back in the fire, his eyes sunken, with an eerie blue glaring at them.

Another man stepped forward from the darkness, face hidden behind a dark hood, arms covered in a slew of tattoos, his clothes torn and ragged. On some level Mila felt sorry for the man, wondering how cold he must be with so little to protect him, but he seemed none bothered by the temperature. And she found out why soon enough. He stepped closer to the fire, calm as though they'd been invited, and pulled a burning twig from it, lighting the pipe in his mouth, and sucked at it to stoke the weed. She knew the smell well. Her uncle used to smoke the foul weed constantly back home. He would start the day out sober, eyes clear and white, until he lit his pipe, and that sweet smell would drift and follow him wherever he would go, his eyes becoming bloodshot and dull, his mind slow, his senses numb.

'Stay back!' Bellard shouted again, brandishing the knife, but they paid him little heed.

'You better watch out, little brother,' said another voice in mocking alarm as the third man came into view. 'This fella seems to mean business, eh?' If it was any indication at all, it seemed Little Brother was the one smoking the pipe. Mila saw his drugged eyes scan the third with a vicious smile, lips curled up to one side. The third man removed his broad-brimmed hat and sat on his haunches, eyeing Bellard and Mila for a time.

'You want to make a woman out of him?' Scarface asked Little Brother, who didn't take his eyes off Bellard.

'We have nothing you'd want! We have no coin, no gold, no silver.'

'But you have her . . .' stated the one with the hat. A chill rushed through her at his words, and her hands began to tremble. 'We saw you two humpin' like rats, and we wanted in. Don't you worry, lad. Little Brother here won't forget about you. Get 'em!' Scarface and Little Brother rushed forward, scattering their gear and jumping over the fire.

No, this will not happen. Not today. Mila shoved the startled Bellard out of the way and drove her hands into the flames, blasting fanned fire over the men. It roared from her hands to devour them in a whirlwind ablaze, and both men jumped back, falling over each other to retreat from the heat.

'Let's go!' Mila grabbed Bellard and yanked at his arm, pulling him away from staring at the burning man while the two others beat him with their clothes.

'Put him out! Little brother! Roll, damn it!'

* * *

Bellard couldn't believe what had just happened. Grandàre Larison had told him to be careful out here. He had taken the words of warning as those from an overprotective mother, with little evidence to its validity, and now wished he had been more cautious.

The dark skies would hide them for a while, but daylight would come, and he knew the thugs would not let this stand. Mila was still dragging him by the arm, her fierceness returned, nails digging into his flesh with the power of her grip. He did not know she could be so strong. *How is she even seeing so well in this darkness?*

So much had happened that he was struggling to think. Thoughts raced through his mind, yet every time an idea was close to birth, his body snatched it away with the need to focus. Where to place his feet, not to fall, to watch for branches flashing by, to search for their hunters . . . He nearly tripped over a rock he couldn't see and grabbed hold of Mila's arm. 'Wait, Mila. They are not behind us.'

'What? We can't wait! They'll catch up to us.'

He slowed her to a stop and gripped her arms. 'We have to, Mila. They have all our gear. We won't survive without it. They know it.' He remembered seeing Mila use her magic to see in the dark during Valdor's funeral. It only dawned on him then to do the same. He had forgotten in the heat of the crisis that he was a sorcerer. That he could protect himself and Mila. *I am probably the worst sorcerer to have lived, cursed to be annoyed by the biggest Pillar. Look at me now, everyone, the biggest Pillar for the biggest fraud.* The world opened up to him, changing to a faded daylight, like that of early morning, as his magic altered his sight. 'I think I have a plan.'

They ran to hide behind a humongous dark bole, scanning the scattered trees and shrubs for movement, then focused on the fire still burning in the distance, where screams of pain blended with the streaming curses from the burnt man. 'We have to do it now.'

'What are you thinking, Bellard?' Mila kept tugging on his shirt, wanting answers.

'You distract them. I'll get the gear.'

'They will see us!'

'No, they won't. Trust me. All you have to do is bounce your voice around. Don't let them get close.' He ran back up the slope towards the glow, trudging through cold mud. A good distance away now, Bellard summoned his power, focusing on his objective. His Pillar channelled his thoughts into reality, oozing thick, rolling mist from him in great waves, filling the hill and obscuring all sight.

'What is going on? Where'd all this fog come from?' he heard one thug shout. Bellard moved steadily closer. *Come on, Mila.* He didn't enjoy leaving her alone back there to be bait, but there was a bigger risk in getting the gear, he thought. He pushed through the thick fog, adjusting his vision and waving the mist gently in front of him.

'Let's head this way!' he heard Mila's call, coming from the opposite direction. Then heard it come from the left. 'Move, quickly. Before they catch us.'

'Did ya hear that?' asked one thug. It sounded like Scarface.

'I did,' said the other. 'You go down. I'll go this way.'

'What 'bout your brother?'

There was a bit of a pause. 'He ain't going nowhere.'

As careful as he could, Bellard made his way closer, stepping on rocks and earth, careful to avoid dried twigs. He had his knife in one hand, just in case. Magic tended to be a longer process than a swing of the blade. Although he would never forget the day that he ran late into Grandàre Shevira's classroom. That was a wild ride.

He was getting close to the fire now. Its orange flames created a beacon through the white mist, its heat warming his front. He edged closer and picked up his pack, carefully lifting it not to make a noise. There was a time to be picky and a time to be grateful for what you had, and this was a time he needed to be grateful. They needed the bedding, the kettle, and the press. All else could stay.

The groans of Little Brother filtered through the fog to his ears, and Bellard froze on the spot, too afraid to move a muscle. *Don't freeze up now, Bellard! Move!* The gurgling cries rose and fell, not getting any more threatening, and Bellard picked up the kettle to stuff it in his pack, folding a piece of clothing around it to stem the clinks and scrapes.

'Follow me!' came Mila's voice from somewhere between the first calls, and he heard the other two dash in that direction, breaking through the brush.

Snow drifted down in soft flakes to settle on his head and shoulders. It was only going to get colder. There was no way he could leave without his clastra press. The thought alone was grounds for banishment. Some of their gear lay scattered around, thrown about during the confrontation. A can of opened beans lay spilled on the ground next to the fire and Mila's pack. A fork and a spoon lay in the dust, but he could only see one pair. *At least Mila will eat civilised. I can use my fingers,* he thought, annoyed that this had to be a choice as he scooped up her pack and the cutlery.

A flash of silver caught his eye from under a small bush, and he quickly snatched up the clastra press from the ground, seeing a mighty dent in it, and Bellard's anger flared. *Uncivilised bastards!* It had taken him many months of working all kinds of odd jobs to pay for the press. He had cared for it dearly, and now it was all scratched and dented.

All he needed now was the bedding. But it was not where they had left it. He slung his pack over his shoulder and got low to the ground, searching with eyes squinted, waving the mist away.

A roar sounded, and he glanced up to see the burnt Little Brother charging at him, his face melted on one side, clothes scorched black and in tatters, his arms and chest covered in thick pockets of blisters, pus and blood oozing from them. Bellard jumped up and took the man's weight, getting driven back to crash against the overhang. His ears rang, and his vision was shoddy, eyes blurring, before Little Brother punched him in the ribs, then the face. The pain drove deep into his stomach, his lungs unwilling to suck in air. Bellard dropped Mila's pack and nearly collapsed, when the cold reminder of steel in his hands brought him back, and he stabbed out, pushing the blade through the man's hand with a scream of defiance.

Another fist slammed into his ribs. Bellard yanked out the blade to stab it down into Little Brother's neck, slicing deep into the soft flesh, not hitting any bone. Blood rushed from the man's throat, thick, bright, and fast. A shock of horror spread over Little Brother's burnt face, his lone eye searching for an escape from this terror. The man stumbled away, pulling the knife from his throat, opening the wound more to a waterfall of warm, red liquid, steam rising in the cold air. Bellard stared with eyes wide, breath hissing, as Little Brother's blackened fingers aimlessly pressed at the wound, causing sprays of red to shower over him. The man dropped to the ground, gurgling his last groans, sucking air through the massive hole in his neck. It sounded awful. Frozen, hands trembling, Bellard could not pull away from the dying man.

'Bellard, run!' Mila shouted, her voice sounding far away to his ears, like something from a distant past.

I just killed a man . . . I just murdered someone . . . 'Run, Bellard!' he heard again, then the thrashing of grass and brush being trampled in a hurry. The other two were coming for him. His vision turned red, and he blinked, quickly wiping his face with his sleeve to get rid of Little Brother's blood, his eye stinging profusely. Bellard grabbed up the packs and saw the bedding on the ground, covered in blood and grime. They had used it to kill the flames on the man and covered him with it. There was no time to be picky. Yes, it was disgusting, but it was what it was: this, or an icy death. He grabbed up the bedding and stuffed it under his arm, then ran from the area through the fog.

His magic was fading, the adrenaline wearing off and his vision turning dark once more, the sky glittering up above in flashing brilliance. 'Mila!' he called in a whisper. 'Mila, where are you?'

She came from the darkness, glancing around the forest, and took her pack. 'Bellard! Are you okay? What happened?'

'I'll tell you later. Let's get out of here.'

28. Pressures and Morality

Jonas caught sight of Orana, and he had to look twice. She was an exotic creature with an exquisite body, her sharp green eyes piercing. Most of her injuries had healed by now, and the dark bruises around her face had faded away to nothing but a memory. The only thing bothering her still was that bruised ankle. She walked with a limp, leaning on the forked branch Jorin had cut for her. In the humid air of the rainforest, sweat dripped from her face, leaving a sheen on her skin that made her look like an unnatural creature, the light bouncing softly from her in radiant reflection. He had to admire her tenacity, watching her hobbling along without complaint, pushing through her pain.

'You need some help with that?' Jonas asked, gesturing to the crate she dragged on the forest floor with her one arm, other arm cupped in the branch for balance.

'I can do it myself,' she answered, spraying the last word with a hint of bitterness.

'Huh.' He turned around with a groan and cracked his neck, annoyed at her stubbornness, yet equally impressed.

Everything was sticky. His clothes hugged him too tightly, everything chafed everywhere, and his inner thighs felt like a colony of fire ants had made a nest in his pants. They needed to head out, make what they could of the day, and start as early as possible. Jorin had loaded most of their equipment on the wagon, while Vernak stared off into the forest with his dull eyes, working the *"I'm too old to carry all of that"* excuse, leaning on his cane to look even more ancient. 'Jorin! Help Orana with the last crate,' he called to his son, and watched the boy nod from the wagon bed.

'I told you, I can do it myself!' she stated, brows knitted.

'And I don't care that you can. It's getting late. We need to get going.' He swung away from her glare and climbed over a smoke-trailing clump of hot ashes to join Vernak at the edge of their camp. 'We still not telling her everything?'

'Do you trust her enough with all the information? Humans have a hard time understanding the magnitude at which we work. The mere mention of a god, and they go all crazy-eyed. They want to live in their perfect little bubbles, blissfully unaware. Be shielded from the truth. She might just think us a bunch of lunatics, maybe even turn us over to the authorities for heresy.' A short stint of soft laughter rolled from Vernak's stomach, and he continued, 'Can you imagine that? Me, a heretic . . .'

A chill-inducing screech called for their attention when the crate dragged on the timbers of the wagon, knocking against the other equipment, and Jorin called out in a huff of heavy breathing, 'We're set to go.'

They had made it to Yuronia the day before, and Jonas had been in a foul mood ever since. He climbed to the front of the wagon and waited for Vernak to join him before urging the horses into action, chewing on his bottom lip as he stared at the two in the back. They had been talking way too much for Jonas's liking, getting too close to each other. *She's old enough to be his mother, not his lover,* he thought, watching Jorin chuckle at something she said to him. 'What are you two giggling about?' The wagon rolled through the winding road of the forest, bouncing over roots from enormous trees where the ground had eroded away.

Orana rolled her eyes up at him, head tilted to one side, and Jorin said, 'Nothing.'

'Boy, I will not ask you again,' Jonas rumbled over his shoulder.

'I asked him if you have always been such an arse,' Orana answered, her piercing gaze locked on to his.

He guessed she had a point. That didn't mean he would concede to it. 'Stay out of my business.' There was no reason to be mad, but Jonas had woken with a burning heat in his chest, and everything just piled onto it, making it hard to breathe. His skin burned and itched, muscles spasming and twitching. It felt like spiders were crawling all over him.

Every second heartbeat he found himself rubbing his face, his eyes, the corners of his mouth, his scalp. He had got so frustrated by checking if something was crawling up his leg that he eventually turned to slapping, whether there was something or not.

'When my mother was giving birth to me—'

'Enough!' Jonas swung around, backhanding Jorin with a teeth-rattling hit. 'Do not bring your mother into this.'

'Hey! What the hell is wrong with you?' Orana jumped back, startled at his aggression. 'Let the boy speak about his mother if he wants!'

'You don't understand, Orana!' Vernak began, while Jonas wiped his face and scratched his scalp, eye twitching like a thing gone mad.

'Argh! All of you leave my Ayla out of this. Or I swear I will break every bone in your bodies. Is that clear?' Jorin sat with brows raised, staring at him out of fear, a streak of blood seeping from his lips. The twitching didn't want to stop, and it was driving him mad.

Vernak leaned over to him and whispered, 'I think it's time for you to drink some of that medicine Erechol gave you, eh?' Jonas swung to him, face pulled into a snarl. He wanted to bash the old man's head in real bad, make him stop talking permanently. 'You know I'm right.'

He was sure he could tip this entire wagon with the frustration he felt coursing through him; the adrenaline making his fingers twitch. 'Take the reins.'

Smells of a bitter, poignant fragrance left the brown satchel while he undid the strings to roll it open, and he gagged, shaking his head in shuddering trembles. The sachets needed to be boiled, drunk with tea, and that was not happening now. Just having left, they couldn't stop already. He turned his gaze to the foul-looking orange vials, lip trembling. *A black stag's piss . . .*

Jonas really didn't want to drink it. He removed a coin from his pocket and flicked it into the air, catching it quickly and slapping it on his thigh. 'Tails!' A silver crown lay in wait for him when he removed his hand. 'Bastard heads, every time.' He stowed the coin and took out the vial, pulling the stopper to break the black wax seal. If the sachets smelled bad, these were a torture method. The back of his throat closed up, becoming an unwilling participant in the struggle for survival.

'Oh, my! What is that stench?' Orana called, her face pinned back next to Jorin, who leaned over the side of the wagon to get away from it. Even Vernak had glanced away, his eyes becoming wet, his nose runny.

'Bottoms up.' Jonas quaffed it in one swoop. The thick sludge crawled down his throat, taking its time to move down his oesophagus. He bent forward and jumped up from the wagon, hand before his mouth. 'Blargh!' Jonas caught the rising liquid in his throat, forced it back down with tears streaming from his eyes, face turned red, a long string of snot flowing from his nose. His spine curved again, almost launching him from the wagon, and the horses whinnied, becoming infuriated with him shifting his weight around, causing the wagon to become unsteady. A few moments of uncomfortable gurgling, huffing, puffing, and sniffing noises went by before anyone spoke.

'Jonas?' Vernak asked, glancing up from the road to pat the man's back where he half lay on the front seat over to the side, a pitiful mess.

He waved his hand back at them and groaned, 'I'm fine. I'm fine. Just let me rest.'

* * *

He ran through the village, seeing body after body. These were people he knew well. Good people that wanted nothing more than to live in peace. There was nothing he could do for them. His only concern was with his son, and Ayla. Many sat on the dusty roads, crying in the blood of their loved ones as he ran by, heart pounding furiously in his chest . . .

Jonas groaned and blinked his eyes open, squinting against the sharp rays blinding him from above. He was exhausted, feeling old and stiff, his eyelids heavy and unwilling to open fully. The heaviness on his chest had disappeared, replaced by a feeling of shame for slapping Jorin. 'Where are we?'

'We've left the Elderforest behind. The scrublands of the Southlands are up ahead,' came Vernak's voice from next to him.

Jonas sat up and turned back to see Orana and Jorin also asleep. 'Any trouble?' Mountains with patchworks of grey stone lined both sides of the valley, tall grasses swaying in the winds like an animal's fur coat.

'None, yet. Had a couple of travellers on the road, but mostly good people.'

'Good people? That so? Coming from you, that's saying something. Not sure what, but something.'

'I'm not incapable of seeing people as good or bad, you know. But I am sensing a change in me—'

A groan and yawn sounded, and Orana stretched her arms out wide, tapping Jorin on the head to stop his snoring in her ear. 'You still ready to take a bite out of us all?' she asked Jonas and rubbed her eyes.

There was a time when men had bowed before Jonas. A time when his word was law, and sometimes, he still wanted those days back. To command respect with a quick gaze. Men would fall silent before him, not interrupt while he was busy, but those days were long gone, and so was the man, he suspected. 'How's your leg?'

'Better. The swelling has gone down, and I can move it more. Don't think it was a bad sprain. I think I will walk soon. Maybe in two days.'

'Good. Cause I think we're being followed. Don't make any sudden moves! Just keep doing what you've been doing.' Jonas saw her face go slack, her lips parting with the revelation, and knew how dry her mouth must be. It had happened a lot to him, the shock of knowing something bad was about to happen. But she kept her wits about her and grabbed Jorin's head as he wanted to swivel back and search for their hunters.

'Stop that, Jorin!' Jonas snapped. 'Don't let them know we know. Have you learnt nothing from your sword master?'

'Uh. Yes, of course. Sorry, Father. It won't happen again.'

'Sword master? This kid doesn't know how to wield a butter knife,' blurted Orana with a chuckle. Jorin sat up straight, staring back and forth from Jonas to Orana, and she continued, 'I'm sorry, kid, but you have to tell him.'

'I agree with Orana's assessment. Jorin has no particular skill with a blade,' Vernak chimed in. 'I have seen him sneak away with the cutlass when he thinks we are not watching, swinging it around with little skill. It was rather pitiful.'

'What?' Jorin mumbled. 'Father. They lie! Why would you do this, Orana? Just when I started forgiving you.'

'What are you two talking about?' asked Jonas. 'We have paid for him to go to classes for over three years.'

Orana sighed and said, 'Tell him the truth, Jorin. We all need to know if we can rely on you in a fight.'

Jonas lifted his eyes away from Jorin to the speck behind. No doubt a man on a horse. Another speck drifted apart from the first, and another. *At least three men,* he thought. 'Jorin, what are they talking about?'

His boy's eyes drifted to each of them, searching for support but finding none. 'Fine, I can't do this anymore. Father, I have been lying to you. I have never attended the sword master. Heck, I don't even know what his name is.'

That heavy feeling on Jonas's chest suddenly returned. 'What do you mean? I saw the bodies at our house! Four of them! Who else—' The redness in his face was returning. He could feel himself grow hot all over.

'It was Mother!' Jorin blurted and jumped up to stare down at his father, who steadily rose to meet his gaze. 'It was Mother who took my sword and laid into them. She had been taking the classes instead of me. She knew you wouldn't understand!'

'Ayla?' Jonas muttered her name. He dropped back on the seat, rocking the entire wagon and causing the horses to grunt and snort, neighing their discontent. 'What have you been doing then, Jorin?' he asked, heart thundering in his chest. He finally knew why they killed her. She had defended their home, defended their son, and paid for it with her life.

'I . . . I have been working as an apprentice to master clocksmith Taronbhore Rimples.'

Jonas couldn't believe what he was hearing. He shook his head in confusion, fingers stretched out and working back and forth. 'What do you mean, you've been apprenticed to a clocksmith? To Taronbhore Rimples? That mad old kook? And what for? Do you think that will bring in any coin? You want to marry Tunisia and have a little one on the way. How will clocksmithing support you? How will it provide food for your table, my boy? No, you'll need to join the army, or work with your hands, become a feller or a builder. Not this nonsense. Never in my life have I needed this device or sought council from it.'

'The world is changing, Father. More and more people are requesting clocks to keep track of their daily schedule. And Master Rimples believes he may be able to make them even smaller. So much to be carried in your pocket. And they are being sold everywhere. In the crown's chamber, the council houses, the Order of Eternal Sacrament, everywhere.'

'Are we really having life discussions while someone is following us?' interrupted Orana, nervously glancing over her shoulder.

'Yes! We are! Since you brought this up . . .' Jonas glared at her. 'But you are right. We need to know who we can trust in a fight. Jorin, if there's fighting, you'll stay with Vernak.'

'How do you know I can fight?' Orana grinned at him.

'I don't, but you can shoot a bow.' Jonas turned back in the seat and took the reins from Vernak with a sigh. 'Keep an eye on them. Let me know if they try to flank us.'

* * *

'Who is following us, Father? And why?'

Jonas glanced at Orana and saw the worry in her eyes. 'There are a lot of bad people on these roads, Jorin. They don't need a reason. Are they gaining on us?' he asked calmly, voice even.

Vernak twisted around and handed the two at the back a piece of dried meat, scanning the blurry white specks on the dark brown road, green fields of grass and brush spreading to the left and right, rolling over hills and down into ravines. 'No. It does not appear so.' The sun beetles sang fiercely in the heat of the day, a deafening cry in the waving stalks.

Up ahead, Jonas kept his eyes on a range of gigantic stone formations jutting from the earth, their dark facade clumped with patches of green shrubbery. 'Huh,' he groaned, pulling their attention, and Orana shifted closer from the back, keeping her ankle raised on a crate of fruit.

'What are you thinking?' she asked, following his gaze to the hundreds of rock formations, sharp edges that tapered to a pointy climax. 'Those look like gigantic arrows. What are they?'

'They are called the Penwe Peaks. I'm thinking we can use their cover to set up an ambush for our followers. Are you any good with a sword?'

'I'm not bad, but I'm better with an axe or a knife.' Orana pulled a hatchet from a crate and left it on her lap, the old wood handle polished dark, the blade dulled with fine decorative etching all around.

Jonas chuckled at that and said, 'You know I'm a feller, right? Know my way around an axe pretty well myself. The axe will be a last resort. I want you on high ground with your bow.'

'And me, Father? I can help!' called Jorin, his eyes pleading for a chance to prove himself, brows raised high.

'No. You stay with Vernak. He will look after you.'

'Two more broke off from behind the front rider, making five,' added Vernak.

Five on two, don't like them odds. Can't keep running from these bastards hunting Orana. Jonas surveyed the grounds, searching for a suitable position to strike from. 'Can you get up there?' he asked, pointing to a rock formation on the fourth row in, with a flat top, standing roughly fifty feet high. It was the lowest one around, but he knew with her ankle it would be a torturous climb.

Orana rubbed her ankle and said, 'Yes, I think I'll manage.'

'There's seven now. It seems they are gathering speed. Where do you want Jorin and me?'

Seven, eh? Great. 'You two keep heading through and get out of sight. Stow the wagon if you need to and hide. I will jump off and lead them around to be in range of Orana's bow.'

'Father, there are seven of them!'

'Huh. Thanks for reminding me.'

'I'm serious!'

'So am I. Catch this. Tails, we continue on the road and hope for the best. Heads, we stay and fight.' Jonas retrieved his coin and tossed it in the air.

His son had not expected the coin toss and fumbled it in the air, snatching out both hands, hoping to grab it in one. He opened his hand to the crown facing up.

'The coin has spoken. We have no choice but to do this, my boy.' Jonas glimpsed Orana's thoughtful gaze, and took his coin back from his stunned son, who still sat with mouth agape.

29. The Deep End

Like Mother always used to say, *'There's no better time to learn to swim than being thrown to the sharks.' I do miss you, Mother. You had such a . . . knack with words.* Calmantis lay on the ground, dripping blood from a cut across his lips, heaving ragged breaths, arms shaking from fatigue. He lifted his left hand, finger pointing to the sky. 'One . . . moment . . . please.'

Powerful hands grabbed him by his pants and the scruff of his neck, thick fingers pulling at the folds of his skin, and the tiled courtyard sped by a few feet under him, his arms swinging, legs kicking. He hit the floor with a clatter of bones, skimming his knees, elbows, arms, and legs.

'We do not have a moment! Time is running out! Now focus and make the jump!'

He was pulled up from the ground and beaten with the flat of Ostarra's hand, barely having time to open his eyes before the next blow fell. Bright lights burst in his vision, and his right ear rang out loud. This was not the way he ever thought a meeting with a god would go.

Since Ostarra had brought him back to Tenthis for the second time, the days had been a blur of being yelled at and beaten. The god of storms had laid into him every waking hour of the day. He wasn't sure what this method would achieve other than his inevitable death. Hungry to the nth degree, he had no strength left. Ostarra had ordered the servants to keep food away from him for the last day and a half, only giving small rations of wine and water to drink. His insides hurt, and his head pounded angrily, teeth stained with his blood.

'Do you think this is a game? Do you think I have time to waste?' Ostarra walked up and down before him, loose blue chlamys flapping in the winds, the dying sun blinding Calmantis.

'No, this is not a game. I understand that, sir. I . . . am trying my best.'

'Well, it's not good enough!' roared Ostarra, taking a step towards him, with fists bunched. 'Can't you see what is happening in your world? It will be doomed if we don't do something fast!'

Calmantis dropped his head low and rolled to sit up, groaning as he climbed to his feet. 'Both times I made the leap I had this utter dread flowing through me. A realisation that what was about to happen could be the death of me. I felt myself giving up inside. Accepted the outcome. Maybe if I can find that same feeling—' Ostarra's enormous fist rocked his head back, and tears streamed from his eyes. 'Ahy!' he whelped and crashed on the ground again, sniffing and spitting blood.

Calmantis felt like crying. His nose was sore to the touch, and his teeth were loose. His right eye stung from the blood flowing from a cut on his brow. 'What is wrong with you, mmm?' He wiped the blood from his eye, rolled his tongue in his mouth, and felt the wobbling tooth. It had torn from his gums and flapped around on a thread of flesh. He spat the blood that was accumulating in his mouth on the ground and watched the brown tooth skittering away to the garden bed. 'What was that?'

'Hm. Maybe you need more than that . . . Come with me.'

All servants gave them a wide berth as they sauntered up the grand stairs leading to the larimar tower. It was quite an impressive sight to see the building during daylight. The stone seemed to absorb the sun's rays and use it to light the way inside, making the hallways appear bright and fresh. Calmantis followed the god through the passages of his home to a thick wooden door standing three men tall, four enormous bolt locks keeping it sealed from whatever was inside.

'Er . . . Nope. No. I have learned a long time ago that doors locked like that are done so for a reason.' Calmantis whirled around to walk away, when Ostarra gripped him by the wrist and held him tight, squeezing his arm. 'Argh!' he cried in pain, feeling his bones shift and complain from the pressure applied.

'Do not make me regret saving your friends. I can always reclaim what I've given, mortal. You'd do well to remember this. It is not a request. Now get in here.'

Hardly comforting words, if Calmantis ever heard any, but the icy glare from the god slapped his defiance away. Ostarra reached up and slid the first bolt open with a loud gong, then the next, and the next. 'Beyond this point lies the realm of Darg'ule. These doors are the only way to get there from Tenthis.'

'Darg'ule?'

'Yes, of course. The underworld, as you know it. I've heard you humans refer to it as such many times before.'

The underworld? This is amazing! Calmantis couldn't believe all he had seen since coming to Tenthis. The fear he felt before changed to wonder and excitement. It felt good being the person things were finally happening to. 'Will I be the first mortal to set foot in the underworld?'

'No. Wait, you are excited about this?' Ostarra shook his head, scowling at him over his shoulder.

'Shouldn't I be?'

'Human, you are intolerable.' He unlocked the last bolt, sliding it back to click against the metal clips, and swung the door open. They entered a small room with a long, dark corridor dripping water from its ceiling, a stench of rotten meat burning Calmantis's eyes and nose.

Their footsteps sounded hollow, bouncing from the long corridor's walls as if they were alone, but there was a distant rumble in the air, something throaty, something monstrous, something close. Bones of all sizes lay scattered against the edges of the wall, strings of muscle still attached, yet Calmantis could not make out what it came from. Human, animal, something he had never seen. It was all a guess. The air irritated his throat, making it hard to breathe, and he started coughing. *Okay, it's not feeling so amazing anymore.* 'I get your point, Ostarra. We can go now.'

'I don't think you do,' the god muttered and stepped over a ragged pile of bones held together by a thick bloody pelt with mangled black fur, a string of intestines pulled to spread far from the unfortunate creature. There was no head, but Calmantis saw an enormous paw that looked like a dog's or a wolf's. A loud clatter sounded, like that of pots falling, and Calmantis felt the hairs on his arms and neck stand upright, a cold shiver running down his spine.

'What was that?' he whispered frantically, grabbing Ostarra's arm from behind, and received a menacing look for it before the god yanked his arm away from him. The sound came from a room at the end of the narrow corridor, barred by a large, round steel door.

'The underworld was created to house those of us who caused chaos in the eyes of the Eyavare. And now it serves the same purpose for you mortals, when we gods deem you unworthy of Tenthis. Over time, our kind changed, after being banished from the light for so long, and now they are fit for little else but violence.'

'So why are we here?' There was a sinking feeling in Calmantis's gut. His stomach churned and growled, unhappy and hungry. He'd had his fair share of sleeping hungry. It was not something new to him, but the pain would always be stronger than him, an unbearable torment. It took everything he had not to dive into the pile of bones and start licking them.

Ostarra stopped at the door and turned back to Calmantis, his hand drifting inches away from the twisted wrought-iron handle. There was no amusement in Ostarra's face. His glowing eyes were hard, the deep lines on his forehead creased even thicker as he said, 'If you can't make the jump, I hope you can run fast.' He grabbed the handle, and symbols all over the door burst into life, burning bright red, followed by a gust of foul air released from within like a mighty belch, rolling over Calmantis in a powerful wave.

That was not all that escaped.

Through tear-filled eyes, Calmantis glimpsed a hooded figure in filthy black rags, dark liquid like black ink running down her face from her eyes and mouth, burst through the doorway, her legs and arms inconceivable between the folds of her cloak. Time slowed, he was sure of it, for the figure's long strands of black hair floated from her hood and drifted around her face as she stopped before Ostarra, scanning the god up and down with twitches and jerks, her throat releasing a strange clicking noise similar to what Calmantis had heard bats make. She twisted away with the slightest of bows and charged towards him at a menacing speed.

'Shit, shit, shitshitshitshitshit! What is wrong with you?' Calmantis spun around and ran, his feet barely touching the floor, and slipping when they did on the accumulated water dripping from the ceiling.

'Why are you running?' came a voice he knew well, and Calmantis glanced over his shoulder to see his mother, arms stretched out, crying for him to come to her. 'I'm sorry, Cal. Come back to us.'

'Mother?' Calmantis slowed his retreat as his mother approached, realising that he was in their old home on the second floor, near his bedroom. The smell of onions and potatoes cooking drifted from the kitchen downstairs, and he knew Algo was busy preparing the food.

'Yes, dear. It's me. Who else would it be? Now stop this foolishness and come sit with me.'

He pressed his palm against the timber wall and felt the warmth of the bright sunbeams cast between the thick red drapes fall on his hand. In that flickering light, dust swirled and drifted calmly, waiting for him to decide. 'It can't be . . . My mother never had time to sit and talk, especially not during the day!' He spun around and ran again, hearing a screech and a high-pitched wail. His old home vanished as fast as it had appeared. He did not wait around to see what was happening behind him.

Arms swinging, legs spinning, he ran, hoping to stay ahead of the creature. *I must make the jump!* The cold of steel sliced into his arm, burning fiercely, and he recoiled to his right, the sense of urgency doubling, the need to get away growing serious. *Shit, shit, shit, this is not what I was thinking.* He burst through the bolted door and felt something grab his foot, tripping him. 'Oof!' Calmantis groaned as he hit the floor, sprawled on his stomach, chest heaving.

Something took hold of his leg, the sharp ends of jagged nails digging into his skin, scratching him, and his eyes went wide with horror. 'Help! Help me!' he shouted, hoping that someone might be brave enough, but no one appeared. He tried to push away, kicking violently to crawl to safety, but he was going nowhere.

Long nails dug into his side and flipped him over, and she pinned him to the ground, a rumbling, coarse voice flowing from her in a language he did not understand. *'Qup, mortal, quun qijjan naat a qaap naq qaat qijjan kutiinik quunsaak nguk qaa nuu.'*

The disgusting black goo sprayed over his face, the reek terrible. To his ashamedness, he could not help but stare at the breasts bouncing through the torn rags she wore, even with the existential threat looming over him. Her eyes had no life in them. They were like a broken beast's, caged to remain hopeless. The bitter blackness seeped into his mouth, and he spluttered the acidic bile back to the woman. At least, he thought she was a woman, or was once, a long time ago. She bared her jagged, rotten teeth and licked his lips with a long slippery tongue, wiping the black goo over his face.

He had been screaming for a long time now. Calmantis felt his throat getting sore. He swung his right arm, hoping to crack her on the jaw, maybe stun her to get away, but she moved in unnatural ways, bending her neck far more than should be possible. She leered at him with a devilish look and lunged, her head down, fangs ready to sink into his skin. He fended her off with everything he had, pushing her head away and beating her with his fists, but he was gaining no ground. Sweat ran down his face in his frantic search for freedom, pleading groans leaving him, soft whimpers filling the beautiful blue-white hallway, now splattered with filth flung by the woman-creature. 'Please . . . stop.'

Her head came up and so did her arms, dragging a long dagger to the sky. With both hands, she brought the blade down, roaring a hiss.

* * *

Did she do it? Did she drive the dagger through my heart? Is she already peeling the flesh from my bones and stuffing it down her throat? Calmantis shuddered, air coming sparingly, not wanting to fill his lungs. There were no sounds around him except for the rustling of leaves. He opened his eyes one at a time and, through his fingers as he protected himself, saw a bird of prey soaring up high in the sky. *Where am I? Where is she?* he thought and sat up, feeling rocks and gravel push into his side. Blood seeped from a bite mark on his stomach, but if that was the worst of it, it suited him.

He was back on the mountain overlooking the valley in the mortal realm; the tower had vanished. 'I'm alive?' He chuckled and burst out laughing, jumping up and down, shouting his victory over death. The sheep far down in the valley cocked their heads up to him and continued their grazing, ignoring the crazed fool. Calmantis was happy to be alive, and he spun around on his heel. 'Eek!' he shouted as Ostarra gripped his arms, nearly soiling himself at the sight of the god.

'Good. Now take us back, or I will throw you off this mountain.'

I guess the time for pleasantries is over. Death should not always be the thing that drove us forward. In this case, it was the only thing. Calmantis laid his hand on the god's chest, glancing away nervously with lips pursed, adjusting his hand gradually to Ostarra's shoulder, and focused on how he got here. In his mind, it was the utter fear he felt, and the acceptance of death that brought him through the Fold. To attain it was hard, if there was nothing threatening you. With eyes closed, he visualised himself fading away, dying in one realm and being born in another, feeling the fibres of his body separating from each other, his mind becoming numb, separating himself from the world around him. He felt the Fold surround him and he shed his skin, dropping it away in his mind to walk through.

It was different this time around.

For the first time, there was none of the dread. Not until he opened his eyes, that is. He had forgotten that the woman-creature was where they would come out, and her hissing swipe of the claw reminded him quickly to stay alert. Four servants were fighting with the woman, struggling to keep her in a cage of thick steel.

'I said get this cleaned up! And get her back to Darg'ule!' roared Ostarra, wiping a splatter of black ooze from his face with a handkerchief. 'We should eat. Come.' At the mention of food, Calmantis's stomach rumbled, and his thoughts raced to various cuisines he could think of.

Who would have thought a cesspit cleaner would ever be in this position? Just wait until I tell these stories . . .

* * *

Hands trembling from hunger, he waited at the exquisite table, peering across the long white tablecloth at Ostarra, who sat at the other end. The flowing black-and-blue patterns of a dark marble plate melded together seamlessly where it rested on the splendid white sheet before him, an empty bowl on top. Calmantis slid his finger over the ridge of the silver knife, finding its touch strangely warm.

'You have done well today, Cal. A celebration of food and wine is in order before you do what is needed of you.'

After witnessing that creature, he was reluctant to trespass in Tenthis. 'Is there no one else who can do this? Maybe someone more suited?' He shied away, knowing his question would be received with hostility.

'You know that is not possible, Cal. I have searched long and far for someone like you to help us in the quest. We have to do this today.' Servants with lowered heads, dressed in their finest rags, filed out from two doors with sizeable platters of food, making Calmantis's mouth water. A tantalising, delicious aroma of salty meats tugged at the strings of his stomach. 'You must be hungry. Eat.' Calmantis had not expected the god to be understanding.

He needed no more convincing. Thinly sliced meat covered in rich brown gravy lay in a mountainous pile on the platter, and he grabbed a forkful, dripping sauce all over the elegant white sheet, splattering it with brown stains. Salty and tender, the meat fell apart in his mouth, juices running down his throat. They placed a platter of garnished potatoes next to him, and he stuffed his cheeks with them, eyes rolling to the back of his head with enjoyment.

'Pace yourself. There's plenty more,' Ostarra said calmly, using a knife and fork to cut the meat with a gentleman's touch.

All around him, Calmantis glimpsed the fleeting looks he was receiving from the servants, and guilt washed over him. 'Where do I need to go?'

'I will take you close to the city, but you cannot be seen. Get to where you need to in your world and make the jump to Tenthis. Once you have a piece of the Light of Eyavare, get out of there. Do not linger. I will wait for you in the realm of man.'

* * *

The world raced by him in streaks of black-purple smears, twisting his gut into several knots. Calmantis had nearly hurled twice already, but unlike the last time, the food he had stuffed down his mouth did not splatter on the dark metal platforms this time. The next leg of the journey began as abruptly as the last had ended, yanking him off his feet to fly headfirst onto the next platform, scraping his forehead raw. *Can it never be a safe, relaxing journey to a serene beach, far from danger? Why does it always have to be uncomfortable? Perilous? And to somewhere far from an exquisite meal?*

It seemed their platform stood on the edge of the world, overlooking a grand city with sparkling buildings of silver, white, and gold. A wide river entered from where they stood, snaking through with quick turns, bridges spanning them to the heart of the city, where stood a plethora of buildings, and one in particular.

The wind buffeted them on the cliff, and a thought popped into Calmantis's head. 'So, you all maintain our realm, with the god of the sun, god of storms, god of life,' he gestured to Ostarra, 'and all that. Do you do the same in your world, then?'

'Actually, we do not maintain your world.' Confused, Calmantis swung to Ostarra, watching him gaze at the city down below, his tempestuous nature something to be careful of.

'What do you mean? We pray to all of you for help, and sometimes, you answer.'

Ostarra pulled his eyes from the city with a sigh, and said, 'We look after our world, and yours follows what happens here. A physical act from us affects both realms. Enough of this. Do you see the tower in the centre?'

'Yes.' A thin beam of blue light rose from its top, disappearing through grey clouds forming around them. 'What is that?'

'This is Melloria, the heart of Tenthis. And that is the Tower of Divinity. It is where you must go. You will head up to the top of the building and retrieve a piece of the stone. Just a piece. Without the Light where it is, our worlds will come undone, so be careful.' Calmantis looked around at the fading light, then at his hands, and Ostarra continued, 'What is it now?'

'I have no weapons. Can I get a sword?'

'No.' Ostarra looked away.

'What if I get cornered by guards?'

'Then you jump across the Fold.'

'Are you mad?' Calmantis cried, and cleared his throat with a cough as Ostarra jerked his head to him with an angry glare. 'I mean, what if I am up there,' he pointed to the tower's top, 'and I jump across the Fold? I would plummet to my death on the other side. No. Not a good idea. I'm sorry. And how will I break a piece off some rock with my bare hands? I need something—'

'Argh, fine! Here, take this.'

A strange sensation, like butterflies fluttering in his stomach, took hold of him, the same as when he was only ten years old and lay eyes on Teralee for the first time. She was the best house-sitter he could ever dream of. Beautiful, but in a plain sort of way, no fancy makeup to darken her eyes or make her cheeks red. No fake brows painted on or lashes that seemed to sweep the room every time she blinked. No, she had plain brown hair, with broad brows tapering to a sharp end, eyes so gentle he could stare into them for days. Her voice was a tad rough, but you couldn't have everything perfect, now could you? And that was what the blade looked like that Ostarra pulled from a second sheath: plain, single-edged, broad on one end, tapering to its tip, beautiful, yet rough around the edges. *He knew I'd ask for one . . .* Calmantis nearly ran to hug the god but forced himself to stay back and accept the blade, waiting for the sheath while it was being removed.

Spots of rust accumulated around the cross guard, but the blade was perfectly straight. The black grip was made of a polished stone he had never seen, with a silver pommel at its end. Plain, yet beautiful . . .

'Now go. Time is running out.'

30. The Light

*T*hey couldn't have placed those bloody platforms any closer *to the city, could they? Why have them at all if you are still left miles from where you need to be?* Darkness had settled in already, and with no city lights to guide his way, it was getting difficult to keep track of which direction he was supposed to walk. Calmantis stopped for a moment, turning around on the spot, with the sword gripped in one hand, resting on his shoulder. 'Where the hell am I?'

It was getting easier to jump across the Fold the more he used it. Ravens squawked on his right and took off from a large tree, swaying the branch and rustling the leaves. Calmantis swung the sword in an arch, left and right, switching hands, in awe of his awesomeness, and dropped it, grabbing at the handle and catching it before impaling his foot, dancing away clumsily with a sigh of relief. He decided to sheathe the blade just in case.

Eyes closed, he spiritually stepped over the threshold of the Fold, pulling his body along with him to Tenthis. He snapped them open with a start at the sound of an animal lowing, staring into the eyes of a large beast with horns and a wet snout. It jumped away from him, swinging its neck to skewer him, narrowly missing as Calmantis leapt back with a scream. An entire herd of them started bellowing all around and came running up to investigate. 'Bloody cows!' Calmantis quickly looked around and found the lights of the city, then stepped through the Fold. *This is going to be a long night.*

* * *

It all sounded so simple. *'When in trouble, just jump across the Fold . . .'* Nobody accounted for the mental toll it took on him. And he was not yet close to the tower. Three times he had to make the jump to get his bearings while walking towards the city, until he reached the banks of the river and followed it. Now he was sure he was already in the thick of it. People, gods, servants, large buildings, and all the strangeness of this realm should surround him. But here in the mortal realm there were grey outlines of trees, hills, animals, and the river flowing to his left, its noisy rush pleasantly calming.

I wonder what would happen if I jumped across the Fold and ended up in a wall, or an animal, or a person . . . maybe a god? Who would die? Surely we can't occupy the same space. I can just see it now, Aztar standing with his hands on his hips, thinking he is invincible, and then here I enter, his limbs flying, gut stretching, intestines peeling out. Do they even have intestines? Or is it just hollow in there? There must be something there. I've seen Ostarra eat. Never seen him poop, though.

Calmantis stopped to look around and edged closer to the river, thinking if they built something, it would not be on the edge of the water. It was eerily quiet around him. No cows bellowed, no sheep bleated, no deer grunted. Hoots from a lone owl sounded far away in the rustling trees, the night air feeling wet and uneasy.

The crack of a small twig breaking pulled his attention, and he jerked his head in that direction, squinting to see beyond the dark treeline. Everything seemed quiet, and then the shift of a body, darker than the rest, moved from one tree to the next, hunched over and low to the ground. His breath caught in his throat, and he bolted. Someone or something was stalking him. *I have to jump across.*

Calmantis blinked, and ran into a great white pillar, getting knocked on his arse. *I hate this, I really do.* It was a good thing that it was night out. He searched the area and saw no one around, so he got to his feet swiftly.

Everything seemed quiet. Tables and chairs stood around him, vacant and dark, the river lapping rocks a few feet away. A road wound through the lower section of the city where the buildings were only a few storeys high, gradually growing taller deeper to the centre. Everywhere around him, things were bathed in the strange blue light. He stared up and thought, *The beam didn't look as big from the cliff.* The bright light touched the distant corners of the city, tendrils arching off the main pillar like lightning strikes, turning his skin blue every time he crept from the shadows. It didn't seem so different from Baldor, other than it being extremely neat. Not an ounce of rubbish lay strewn in the streets, the gardens seemed to be maintained to supreme order, and the buildings, although a bit of a disappointment to Calmantis, were cared for. He could not see a brick, or a stone, or roof tile out of place. Everything was where it was supposed to be, lined up perfectly, not a drop of chaos anywhere.

What he had envisioned were flying horses and talking dogs, the black pegasus of Aztar, with its golden chariot sweeping across the night skies. This just seemed subpar.

'Oi! Get off the streets and get back to your master!' called an old woman from across the street, her door cracked open for her to peer out, a faint bit of light streaming from within.

He headed up the road to get out of her sight, keeping to the side of the buildings as he walked, sprinting from shadow to shadow. *Who are all these people? Were they born here? And why are they all slaves?* Sobs came from the low window he made to pass, and he stopped to peer in through the shutters, seeing a man and a woman holding hands where they sat around a table, a lone candle fluttering in the wind while their whispered cries filtered to him. He'd thought this would be a happy place, a place where gods and mortals could live in unity. Yet the more he saw of it, the less he believed it to be true.

Bells sounded in the distance, loud gongs that rumbled through his feet so far from its origin, the Tower of Divinity at the centre of the city, followed by a powerful pulse of the blue light, waves rolling outwards, dispersing and fading as it reached the city's edge. Sounds of laughter and music echoed from far away, growing louder the further he crept. A group of six guards with long spears and curved blades sauntered towards him, calmly walking and scanning the streets, and he took cover behind a large barrel. Above, to his right, a door creaked open on the second floor of a building and an old man appeared, shuffling out slowly, staring up to the stars, a sense of longing in his deep-sunken eyes.

'Get back!' shouted one guard, pointing his spear at him. 'Back in your home, right now!'

Calmantis crossed the Fold, and the dark forest surrounded him again. He'd have to walk a few hundred feet and jump back to Tenthis. Exhausted, his feet hurt. It had been a long day that had seen him beaten, kicked, humiliated, and almost served as dinner for that woman-creature Ostarra had called a Vargul. He had been dragged across the world to sneak about a city and a forest, and being stalked in both worlds had him at the thread's end.

'Aaaiiyu, aaaiiyu!' called a female voice from the darkness, and a flurry of vague shapes darted through the trees towards him. *Shit! Why me? Just leave me alone, why don't you?* He sprinted again with renewed energy as a spear thudded into a tree on his right, splintering the bark to scatter broken shards against his face and chest.

'Ugh,' he whimpered, tripping over unseen rocks, feet scrambling for ground as his arms searched for balance. If there was ever a time that Calmantis didn't want to fall, it was now. Moonlight flashed off a steel tip hurtling towards him, missing him by a few inches, and another sailed through between his legs, tripping him again with the long shaft of the spear. He careened headfirst into the ground, doing a magnificent tumble to land on his feet again, impressing even himself. 'How the hell did I do that?' A menacing collection of wet leaves and branches whipped him in the face, and he burst through the brush to roll down a hill, going head over heels before crashing into a tree, knocking the breath out of him.

Ribs bruised, he gasped for air as a figure sprinted towards him. Long hair whipped around its blurry features while it ran on all fours to get under the tree's branches and down the steep hill without falling, spear clutched in one hand. 'Stay away!' Calmantis called, spittle flying from his mouth, and the figure came in close, invading his space. 'Eek!'

'*Juup voot kun hi are ke. Neen ke uu.*'

Another woman sent to kill me . . . At least this one looks much better.

'What? I don't understand! Please don't kill me!' he flinched as she brought the spear closer to his eyes, holding the blade only an inch away.

'I asked, what manner of man are you? Why are you here?' Her voice was calm and soft, alluring even, yet he preferred her to speak in her tongue again. It flowed gracefully from her mouth, where the common tongue stuck in her throat, coming out in bitter rasps. She was better-looking than he thought at first, her features sharp and feminine, yet she had an edge to her. Not that it would matter how attractive she was if she killed him. It did, however, feel better than being ripped to shreds by that ghastly Vargul. Light green eyes glared at him, and when she turned to the approaching others of her kind, Calmantis saw the pointy, double-tipped ears, and gasped.

'Edelbore?' he whispered, and she whipped back to him with an angry sneer, sharp canines flashing.

'*Ly's:ien!*'

'What's that? Lyssien?'

'*Ly's:ien! Noot!*' Confusion reigned in his head, and she must have seen him struggling, for she shouted at him in the common tongue. 'Fool!'

Yes, I am a fool. He closed his eyes and felt her hand grip his wrist, his bowels becoming loose, fear driving his new abilities forward. There was no stopping it. *Shit . . .* Suddenly, a loud congregation of people shouted and danced, singing loudly, as fireworks celebrated the night sky in red, blue, yellow, and so many more colours of explosions, where darkness had reigned a mere heartbeat ago. The streets were lit with hundreds of lamps, lighting the area to near daylight. They had come out right next to the square where the celebration was happening. The woman's eyes had gone wide at the sight of so many foreigners and buildings around them, letting out a brief scream of shock and stumbling away, spear in her grasp.

'No! Come back,' Calmantis called, wanting to take her back to the mortal realm, but she wasn't listening. Two guards had heard her scream and started running in their direction, pointing to the shadows where she ducked into. *Shit! Sorry, whatever your name is.*

Calmantis sprinted from shadow to shadow, heart thumping in his chest. The tower was ahead to his right. He had not realised with all the things going on how different it looked to where he'd begun. The Tower of Divinity was gigantic. By far the biggest building he had ever seen, reaching for the heavens, with the blue light above. Its sides were perfectly aligned and smooth as silk, a polished sheen to its dark facade. *This is why it had to be tonight, I guess. Most are occupied with these festivities, which means fewer guards for me to worry about.*

He ran across the immaculate gardens in front of the tower, leaping over perfect paths of white stone, and slowed when he reached a humming, barely visible barrier. The entire thing stood over three men tall, flashing patches of red constantly. Calmantis plucked a leaf from a flower on his right and rolled it into a ball. *Let's see what Ostarra was talking about, eh?* He tossed the ball against the barrier, and instantly, it erupted into a small flame, singing and curling up into ash. *I'm in way over my head . . .* He vanished and reappeared on the other side, the thought of touching the barrier crawling up his backside.

Even with all the confidence in the world, he never thought he would be in this position, nor have made it so far. He lay his palm on the building's strange metal and felt it vibrate, cool to the touch. *How did they build this?* Four sides of perfectly aligned stone, packed so close not even a hair could slip between them, dwarfed all the other buildings.

Here he was, in the lands of the gods, and his first act would be to steal from them. Calmantis stretched his neck up for the last time and sighed. He did not look forward to climbing these stairs. Great glass doors greeted him as he drew near, sliding open of their own volition, startling Calmantis, who jumped to the side, scanning for any movement inside. *I've always wanted to be special, but not like this. Couldn't I be special in an important sort of way?* He slipped through the doors and entered a hall large enough to house thousands upon thousands of people with room to spare, magnificent podiums of dark wood in each corner and one in the centre. At the front of the hall, a large throne stood, with smaller ones on each side, the gold reflecting red from the lanterns that shone down on the walls. More elaborate chairs spread out on an angled base, hundreds of them in the surrounds, but none as glorious as the main throne. *The Tower of Divinity . . . This must be where the supreme gods all assemble.*

His footsteps echoed through the large chamber, making him feel small compared to what was out here. On the right of the hall, through some old oak doors, he found the stairs leading up. *Here we go then.*

He started climbing.

* * *

Dry huffs left him with rasping breaths, chest heaving and heart pounding. Calmantis was dead tired. He threw himself halfway over the stone railing and cursed, dragging a long string of spit from his mouth that did not want to break. It clung to his lips like a fly to a turd, unwilling to give way, its strength immeasurable. His legs burned fiercely, and so did his arms, having crawled the last few steps on all fours. With all other options marked in failure, he dragged his lips over the rough stone railing, tearing the spit from his face, and watched it swerve left and right as it fell, disappearing from his sight long before it hit the floor far below.

There was no door at the top, and no guards that he could see. It was a lone archway that opened to an empty rooftop, devoid of any furnishings. *Terrible security, Aztar. Very shameful indeed. Then again, who would be stupid enough to . . . Never mind.* Heavy winds buffeted him this high up, pushing and pulling him left and right, threatening to cast him to his death. Forceful blue light enveloped Calmantis, shoving him with the pulses of the beam.

Great stone arches criss-crossed from one corner of the building to the other, joined by a gigantic pillar in the centre. The pulsing blue light radiated through the stones' joints from the four corners of the building, funnelling up to its centre above, where it culminated into the powerful beam. And at that centre, set in the stones, was the source, the Light of the Eyavare. Blinded by its fierce brightness, he could not tell what it looked like, but he knew it was there. He curled forward, getting lower to the ground, making himself a smaller target for the wind, and moved his legs inch by inch to the Light of the Eyavare. From all the way down below in the streets of Melloria, the beam had seemed big, but up close, here, standing next to it, its breadth was unbelievable.

Step by agonising step, so terribly slow, Calmantis slid back, feet slipping across the roof, the dreaded edge approaching. *Shit, shit, shit.* He felt like a rag in a whirlwind being whipped around and flung to the skies. There was nothing to grab onto, nothing to latch his fingers into and keep himself from going over the edge. He unsheathed the sword and stabbed the metal-like floor he stood on and felt the tip bite into the material, a brief flash of sparks appearing. Dragged for a short while, muscles aching, hands hurting from the grip on the sword, he came to a stop and lowered even further, crawling forward by stabbing the roof, dragging himself closer to the large pillar.

Why am I the one doing this? No. Stop complaining, Calmantis. You've always wanted to be important. Here's your chance! Do not let Ostarra down. We can't let this world and ours fall into oblivion because we are a little scared. A lot scared, actually. The wind changed direction and kicked him in the back, flinging him into the pillar with his arms flailing, sword clattering against stone, chest heaving from the impact. He scrambled for grip and felt the grooves between the stones, pulled himself up one rock at a time. *If I don't die here today, I will be a changed man. I promise. If Mother could see me now . . .*

His ears hurt from the constantly grinding hum created by the beam, feeling the pressure it exuded from above, flattening him against the stone. Hair whipped about crazily, cheeks rippling, tears running from his eyes, he held on for dear life, worming his way up.

Arms stretched out, he grabbed onto the top stones of the arch, legs working him up, sword dangling in the sheath. It was right above him now, a thick beam coursing like a gigantic bolt of lightning with crackling bursts only a few feet away, and the thought of him turning to ash as he touched it came to him. *Hopefully, it will be a quick death, and not an agonising affair.*

He pulled himself up and kept near to the stones, staring up at the wildly chaotic and violent swirls of thunderous lights clashing and circling above him. It spread from the source, starting as a thin beam filled with potential, blooming like a mushroom, showing its power. Whimpers of fear and panic escaped him continuously, ravaging his mind with thoughts of death, of a life unfinished.

Calmantis spun over to lie on his stomach and crawled closer to the source, feeling heat bake him from above. Night had turned to day, a blue sun burning him from above. He could not get much closer for fear of touching the beam, and he dragged the sword from its sheath, taking care not to bend his elbows too high. Wrists aching and fatigued from the worming climb, he gripped the hilt, feeling the weight of the blade bend his hand down, weakening his grip. He quickly pulled it up not to let it drop, and the beam ripped the blade away instantly, shearing it off at an angle halfway, the cut steel glowing red. *Shit! A quick death indeed.*

'Cal, you will never amount to anything if you keep turning your back on things,' his mother had said when he was twelve, grabbing the wooden sword from his little hand. *Well, here I am, Mother, and I still have a sword . . .* He worked the shortened blade closer to the source of the light, shielding his eyes as much as possible, and chopped at it from the side, hitting the stone clamps used to hold it. Again he swung the blade, and again, each time spraying large chunks of metal in bright hot flashes. *Come on!* Over and over, he beat the stone, the world sounding distant, the clanging far away.

The chipped blade came down with all his strength and struck the source, shattering into a million pieces over him, its sharp edges cutting into him everywhere. For the briefest of moments, the gigantic beam flickered, like a deer breathing its last shuddering breaths, a tremor running down the tower and into the world. 'Argh!' he shouted, and nearly rose, quickly lowering beneath the malevolent light. *Swine shagger!* Hands trembling and bleeding all over from shallow cuts, he was about to give up.

Angry at himself and the situation, he all but threw the broken blade into the light, when something caught his eye. A dark lump melted to the remaining steel. 'Ha! Yes!' He carefully sheathed the blade with the lump stuck to it, and shimmied down the pillar, scraping his stomach and thighs against the stones. *Time to get out of here!*

31. A Promise Kept

Dusk was approaching fast, with the sun hanging low over the fields, waning, being cut to shreds by the jagged pillars rising above them. 'Yah!' Jonas whipped the horses, pushing them hard to stay ahead of the chasing dust cloud, and saw Jorin over his shoulder, clambering over Orana for a better view. 'Stay low!' he crowed, pushing Jorin down on his arse, and both of them cursed, with him falling on her.

'Jonas, over there!' called Vernak, pointing to the right where a road split away to higher ground. The crates in the back shifted and bounced as the wagon swung right, nearly crushing Orana and Jorin. 'Hold on to the supplies! We will need them still.' Vernak bounced on the front seat, clutching the rails with his old, wrinkled fingers.

'No shit! You hold on, and I'll sit at the front.' Orana pushed the crate back with her leg, keeping the bruised foot out of the way.

'Father, what can I do?'

Eyes darting over the darkening fields, Jonas searched for cover, glancing over his shoulder to see their hunters drawing closer. The wagon was slow, and they had nothing else to work with. 'Keep out of sight! Do not let them get to you and use you as bait. We will take care of them.'

A terrifyingly loud crack sounded from up high, a flicker of light flashing. Vernak mumbled something on his left, staring up at the clouds gathering above, his dull eyes worried, brows knitted. 'What was that?' called Jonas, jerking his head towards the old man. 'What did you say?'

'Something is not right . . .'

It was a whisper barely reaching Jonas's ears, quickly amplified by a booming crack of lightning from above. A tree exploded a few hundred feet away, blazing an angry fire, smoke rising from its top. The crack echoed over the world, as more lightning rolled in waves through the clouds. 'Balls of the abyss! What the hell was that?'

'That is trouble! That's what it is.'

Jonas didn't need more information. Trouble had seemed to follow him his entire life. This wouldn't be any different. He nodded and whipped the reins, felt the wind shift on his skin, the air becoming tense and cold.

'This isn't right! Another World Storm? We had one a few weeks back. How can it be back already?' Orana shouted from behind.

Jonas glimpsed Vernak side-eyeing him and returned to the problem at hand. These events were nothing new to him, but he had to agree. This was strange. 'Huh. Never one thing at a time, eh?'

The mountainous peaks grew large. Some standing hundreds of feet tall, others reaching maybe fifty feet in height. Spread over the vast distance of the entire Penwe Peaks, different coloured igneous rock lay scattered. Jonas had never been a man to care for the way of things. He never wondered why steel was so hard or how an axe was made, simply that it was and what the most efficient way to swing it was; be that for a log or a head, both would tumble soon. That didn't mean he found nothing interesting or beautiful. It meant he could focus on the important things.

Rain pattered down. First as a solitary drop here and there, to be joined by a flood of thick drops pouring down in bucketloads. They rode through the first group of peaks, scanning left and right for a good vantage point for Orana, wind howling and screaming in their ears. It was asking a lot from her to climb one of these monstrosities with her injured leg, but what choice did Jonas have? He could not trust his son with a bow and arrow, and Vernak was an uncertainty. It was hard to judge how far the old man's willingness to help or intervene would stretch. That only left her. At least he knew with her neck on the line, she would do anything to be rid of these hunters.

'Jonas, turn left! Now!' Vernak shouted just before a kink in the road.

'What do you see?' Jonas called over the wind and thundering rain, jerking the reins left, causing the wagon to slide all over the slippery road, wheels gliding across the surface.

'It's not what I can see! It's what I know.'

A thin slit between the peaks was visible now, looking too narrow for a wagon. 'Damn you, Vernak! We won't fit!'

'We will! Trust me. Just beyond these peaks is a good perch for Orana.'

Jonas glared at the old man, jaw clenched. He'd had to rely on advice from many men in his life, and he was still alive. The key to that was making sure those who were giving the advice were trustworthy friends or allies. Vernak was neither. He was a temporary acquaintance with similar goals. *Trust? You can't trust what you don't know. It's more like indulge and be ready for anything.* They followed the winding road, slipping and sliding, bouncing off roots and small trees down the narrow length, drawing closer to the crevice.

The horses were skittish, snorting and neighing, while their hoofs pounded onward, and they entered the dark slit. Jonas twisted around for a heartbeat to see if they were being followed, and the wagon careened into the side of the cliff, wheels scraping and digging grooves into the softer sections, horses bounding into each other, their meaty bodies clashing violently, wagon shaking and nearly tipping. He quickly pulled them back, slowing them some to adjust their course slightly.

'There! Pull over to the right just beyond these peaks when we exit this tear.'

'Yah!' Jonas whipped the reins, driving the horses further, and saw the peak Vernak had pointed to. It stood probably forty feet high, with a slight slope at the back, where if you didn't know about it, would make for hard climbing. 'Can you make that jump?' he asked Orana over his shoulder, pointing to a large crack between the two peaks.

'Yeah, I think so. Where will you go?'

'I'll draw them in from the south. That way!' he gestured, then reined in for her to get off the wagon, watching her limp away. 'Hey, I might not be the cleverest man alive, but I do know it is unwise to make yourself tall in a storm. Keep low.' She nodded and hooked the bow over her back, limping up the slope.

'You better come back for me!' she shouted as they set off again, and Jonas flicked his thumb up.

He'd have to keep his wits about him in this place. It was already a maze, and with the falling of day, it would be treacherous. 'When I get off, you two get to higher ground, sheltered and hidden away. We will find you afterwards. Got it?'

'Father, I don't like this. Let me come with you.'

'No! Stay with Vernak! Maybe if you had listened to me and trained as we agreed, then none of this would have happened. My Ayla would still be alive, and you would not have been kidnapped! Do as you're told!' Jonas swung back in his seat, too worried about the hunters to be concerned about his son's feelings.

* * *

Sinister flashes of lightning struck the peaks up high, their rumbling and quaking sending shivers through the earth at his feet. Jonas pulled the hood over his head and gripped the cutlass tight. He'd always preferred axes, but this had a good weight to it. And why not use the tools given to you? How much more special could he make it for this Lofka than to greet him with his own blade? Scanning his surroundings, he stopped and knelt, digging his fingers into the mud, smearing it all over the shiny blade. *It won't last long, but it will dull the shine for a while. And any advantage counts.*

Ahead, in the darkness and the pouring rain, men on horseback rode in at a trot, the angry effulgence of lightning casting their shadows in streaks of ominous warnings. Faces hidden, the front rider gestured to two men over his shoulder and pointed left, then to two others he pointed right to a path leading away through more peaks. *Lofka . . .* Jonas saw the man's sharp eyes and his missing finger in the flash of lightning while he twirled the ring knife round and round. He heard him whistle softly to another man, gesturing with his head to follow, and said to the remaining man, 'You keep watch here. Call out if you see anyone.' Water poured down Jonas's hood, and wind tore at his frame, whipping his wet robe about, but he remained focused.

There was bloody work to be done tonight.

He would need to move quickly and hope that the lightning worked in his favour, not giving away his position as he snuck up to the man on his horse. Jonas gripped the sword tight and kept low, creeping through the plants being whipped around by the terrible wind, following the man on his right, keeping out of sight. It was always difficult to fight a man on his horse, especially when they had a spear at their disposal, like this one. *Fuckin' hate spears. Getting skewered from a distance feels like being cheated.*

He knocked a rock loose from the soil and picked it up. *You might do.* The size of a lemon and a good solid feel to it. He bounced it in his palm, eyeing the man on the horse a few feet away, and sent it flying. A flash from above struck just as the rock crashed into the man's head, knocking him off the horse in a grunting cry of pain and a splash, leather helm flopping to the ground, and Jonas charged in, brandishing the cutlass.

The man stumbled back on his arms, eyes wide, slipping in the mud, spear lying off to his right, and Jonas roared his anger, momentarily losing himself and bellowing his outrage with a swing of the blade. Half a hand went flying as the man cowered behind his arms. The cutlass took no favourites, had no mercy. It had a job to do, and its master was overbearing. Jonas returned the swing and got his legs kicked out from under him, nearly falling into his own sword. The damn flashes made it hard to see the man's movements.

Jonas got back up to see the man running, his back illuminated by the lightning, clutching his severed hand, his shouts barely heard over the pouring rain. Jonas ran for the horse and jumped up, whipping the reins to charge the man from behind, sending him flying to the ground with the weight of the animal, and trampled his body, breaking many bones. *One down, six to go.* He spurred the horse on to the two that went right.

Breathing hard, the mount and its rider pushed through the

darkness, searching for the two men that came this way. They were heading in the direction Vernak and Jorin had gone. *I hope those two have hidden well.* Deep gulleys formed, streaming down the Penwe Peaks, water gushing down the jagged cliffs to soak the ground, glittering in the flashes from above.

A mighty clap of thunder sounded as a thick purple bolt arched to the jagged tops above, an explosion of rock following the bright flash, and debris came crashing down the side, hurtling towards the ground. In that flash, he had seen the two men milling about an entrance to a small cave, turning their horses round and round. Gigantic rocks crashed to the ground around them, the horses dodging left and right, narrowly avoiding being crushed. They were not reacting hostile towards him, and one called out to him. 'Ehfilga, is that you? We found something here!'

Jonas did not slow his horse, and instead put his heels to its flank, letting the cutlass fly. It spun in the air, haft over blade, and sank through the chest of the one man, skewering him with a drawl of pain. The other, who had called to him, yanked on the horse's reins, making it rear up, and he drew his sword from its sheath. Jonas leapt from his mount in the sprint, tackling the man off the horse. Stones, bush, grass, soil, and water all tumbled with them, fists swinging, boots kicking.

A vicious left hook cracked Jonas on the chin, making his eyes roll back, stunning him, his teeth clattering together. His head was in a daze of misty confusion, muscles feeling heavy and unwilling. A punch to Jonas's gut doubled him over, sucking the air from his lungs. He dropped to the ground, reaching in his haze of dizziness for a handful of mud, and threw it in the man's face, rubbing it in hard with his rough fingers. The man pushed him away, wiping at his face, screaming and staggering back to get to his feet, unable to see. Jonas ran at him and slammed his fist into the man's throat, feeling the fragile bones shatter, crushing his windpipe. Gurgling cries sounded as the man dropped to his knees on the ground, fingers grasping his throat, searching, trying to find a way in, hoping to fix what was broken, whimpers and soft squeals leaving his mouth. Jonas pushed him over and stood there watching him take his last breath, catching his own in the meantime.

Four left. Wait . . . Yes, four. My head hurts.

* * *

Foreigners . . . I have to trust my life in the hands of foreigners. Orana climbed to the next rock, leaning on her walking stick for support on the slippery scree. *How do you keep finding yourself in these messes, Orana?* She had made it up the slope and to the crack in the rocks, and realised it was larger than it appeared from down below. Cold and defeated, she sighed loudly and moved her bruised foot up and down, seeing if it would hold for the jump across. *This is dumb.*

A harsh stinging pain lanced through her leg when she put her weight on it, and she bit her lip, cringing and pulling her shoulders up. A small, flat, wet surface waited to greet her on the other side, running up to a vertical wall steeped in moss and lichen, a thick root from a determined tree wrapping around its side.

She tossed the crutch over and took a step back, gauging how many steps she'd get in to push off with her left foot, seeing that the gap was around seven feet wide. Arms swinging for aided momentum, Orana readied herself and steeled herself for the coming pain. With a huff, she set off at a run as fast as she dared, and pushed off.

It was all running through her head, how much skin she was about to lose, how many broken bones she would have. Being a thief had the advantage of having strong legs, though she felt the weakness of her left leg doing its best to get her across. It felt dumb and wrong, not jumping with her dominant leg, and she was sure it would feel even dumber landing on the injured one.

The moment of truth arrived faster than she had hoped, the ground rushing closer. She landed on her foot and yelped, legs buckling beneath her, the scree quickly slipping away. Her palms thrashed against the wet stone, skinning and cutting herself, but luckily, she avoided banging her head. With a groan and sigh of relief, she turned over, hands trembling, small sharp rocks pressed into her bleeding hands. She had made it, and her foot still moved. *A good jump then.* Tearing into her shirt, she cleaned her hands in the pouring rain and bound the rags over the wounds.

Behind her, she heard the moving of rocks and sharp claws scraping, and quickly got to her feet to search the ledge, holding a knife at the ready. A flicking tongue and beady eyes stared back at her, a large dewlap flapping in the wind. *Bloody lizards!* She sheathed her knife and waved her arms at it. 'Shoo, shoo. Get out of here.' It did not appear to find her threatening, and slowly scraped its long-clawed feet across the stone surface, making its way to a hole in the rocks.

Nearly there. She gripped the thick root of the tree and dragged herself up, avoiding the slippery rock at all costs. It wasn't a hard climb, but the wind tearing at the small tree, making the roots pull free from the stones, was not her idea of having fun. A last push to the top and she collapsed on the ground, sticking her hand into the quiver to ensure she had lost none of the arrows.

She let the rain wash over her face and opened her mouth, waiting for it to fill before swallowing. 'Those bastards are probably already here.' Orana waited for another mouthful and savoured the cool water, then got to her feet, using the crutch to get closer to the edge. Crouched down, she scanned the darkness below, searching for signs of movement, and realised she had no way of telling Jonas apart from the hunters if they were to come on foot.

How am I supposed to shoot my bow in this bloody wind and be expected to hit anything? Where is Jonas? What is taking him so long? She was sure that if she didn't give away her location, they would not find her here this night. The problem was with the next night, and the one after that. To the right, a few peaks from her, a thick bolt of lightning arched to the top, and an explosion rocked the world, scattering debris in the flash that followed. *Shit! Better stay low, like Jonas said.*

Movement in the darkness below. Two men were on horseback, walking steadily closer, and she waited for them to get in range. 'Easy day . . .' She drew the string back with the arrow nocked, calmly breathing. *Deep breaths, in and out. Forget about the pouring rain, the gusting wind, the flashing lightning.* If only it were that easy. Accounting for the wind was a difficult thing, and these gusts came from everywhere all at once, but she had to take the chance. She sent the shaft flying, hearing the string thrum in her ears, watching the arrow buck and weave through the air.

A gust tore at her from the north, sliding her forward to the edge, and she had to grip the flailing tree, branches getting torn off by the force. 'Oh no!' She turned back to see the two figures jump from their horses, running to find cover. Fingers numb from the cold, she fumbled the arrows in her quiver, adrenaline making it hard to take action calmly. The shafts dropped and slipped through her wet fingers.

Finally grabbing hold of one, Orana aimed ahead of one man sprinting for new cover, and skewered his leg, dropping him to the ground. His screams filtered through the howling wind, and another one shouted something at her, shaking his fists and ducking down quickly as an arrow flew at him, striking the boulder he cowered behind.

'Over there!' shouted the one she had skewered, while he dragged his leg through the mud, pointing up at her location. An arrow shattered against the stone just below her from another direction, and she swivelled to see a dark figure running closer, the outline of a bow in his hands. She was getting boxed in, and there could be more than the three she knew about. A call of surprise sounded, and she glanced around to see two men rolling in the mud, fighting, throwing punches. *Jonas!* He had sneaked up to the one she had pinned down behind the boulder.

They wrestled and cursed at each other, unidentifiable in the darkness. She nocked another arrow and watched the one man throw the other to the ground and lock his arm around the man's neck, squeezing hard, choking him. *Shit, who's who?* She pulled the string back and took aim, moving between the two targets, then saw a third limping up to the man doing the choking, and she let loose. The third man dropped with the bolt through his throat, and the whizz of an arrow sang in her ear, nicking her arm. 'Argh!'

Heart racing, she nocked another arrow, searching for the archer, seeing nothing on the ground, and then, in the corner of her eyes, a sharp glint flickered. She spun around to see Lofka raise his knife above her, ready to stab, and loosed the arrow she had nocked, throwing him off balance. It zinged by his face, disappearing into the darkness, but his lunge missed as she rolled away, the blade sparking with the hit on the stones.

'Your time is up, Orana! Yelefant wants payback!'

'We all knew I would never make the deadline!' Orana dragged her hatchet free just as he stabbed at her, parrying it away, blades sliding over each other in a shrill scream of metal crying. 'Don't do this!'

'I have no choice! It's you or me. And if I don't succeed, he will just send someone else, so spare us the trouble.' He swiped the blade at her again, and she jumped back with a grimace, scowling at him when she put her weight on her sore foot, buckling from the pain. She swiped back at him, keeping him at bay, making sure he stayed a little nervous, buying time to figure out what to do.

The sounds of other men fighting came and went with the change of the wind, their screaming and cursing, gurgles and coughs a reminder that she was not alone, but she had her own worries to deal with. A terrible clap deafened her, and a blinding bolt of lightning turned the brave tree into a fiery inferno. They leapt away from the frightening event, eyes wide, slipping and sliding across the slick rock. Lofka lashed out at her while they hastened to the brink, and her palm flared with pain, burning with an intense heat. 'Argh!' Her little axe bounced away from her with dull clinks against the stone.

She kicked his hand that was holding the knife and saw it fly away, skittering over the edge just as they did. Orana scrambled for grip on the slimy rock, palm getting sliced from the rough edges. Fingers digging in, she scrambled for grip. Everything came at her so fast, it was hard to judge when to reach for passing handholds. A jutting rock rushed at her, and she grabbed at it, nearly rending her arm from her shoulder. She screamed in pain, feet dangling over the edge. Suddenly, a mammoth amount of weight was added when Lofka grabbed her legs, straining her shoulder even more.

'If I'm going down, you are coming with me!' Lofka shouted, and he punched her in the side, air exploding from her mouth. She felt the grains of sand on the slick rock roll beneath her fingers, the edge pulling away from them. Both hands reaching and grabbing, she gathered only air and water.

32. Blizzards and Bastards

Terrible winds howled through the jagged peaks of the mountain range, whipping snowflakes into a blinding frenzy. Apple-sized hailstones thundered into the mountainside, bouncing off trees and breaking branches, vanishing into the deep layer of snow that blanketed the ground, sending up puffs of white. In the midst of this chaos, Bellard and Mila lumbered through the drifts, their cloaks flapping behind them. Exhausted, they still used their magic to keep the projectiles away from them.

Since their encounter with the thugs, they had been on the move, constantly looking over their shoulders for their stalkers. Rest was little and far between, and their bodies were paying for it, mentally and physically. Mila stumbled and dropped into the snow, an action that seemed so slow and easy to overcome, yet her legs just would not move fast enough to catch her.

'Mila! Are you okay?' Bellard asked, turning back to help her up, and saw the defeat on her face. Everything, the relentless pace, the constant watchfulness, never resting, had sapped the will from her. She was at a breaking point.

Tears streamed down her face, quickly becoming streaks of ice while she sniffed her whimpers away. 'I'm fine.' He reached out to her and dragged her up, dusting the white flakes off her dark cloak, hands covered in thick gloves.

They knew that somewhere behind them, the two thugs were still pursuing relentlessly and, without a doubt, gaining ground. Bellard could see in his mind their eyes glinting with malice as they drew closer with each passing moment. He had killed Little Brother, and there was zero chance of them letting it go. They would want revenge.

Bellard drew his scarf up over his nose, breathing in the icy air, lungs, throat, and nose burning from the cold. Beside him, Mila clutched his arm as they trudged through the snow, their clothes wet, their mood sombre. Her usually dark brows turned white with a layer of frost, her green eyes looking even colder, like a partially frozen river flowing over a frosted riverbed.

'Stay out of blizzards,' he remembered his Opa say. *'They are a sure way to a quick death up in the North.' Opa Anglard, where's your wisdom today when we can't wait out the storm?* With chattering teeth, they pressed on, struggling against the numbing cold, aware that if they wanted to survive, they must keep going.

As they climbed higher and higher up the mountain, the blizzard grew fiercer, severely limiting visibility to only a few feet ahead. Snowdrifts formed as immense waves, sculpting the mountainside to look like a roving, frozen ocean, the debris of large trees stuck in the ice, laden heavily with the white powder. Bellard's nerves were destroyed. His face muscles twitched while his eyes jumped and jerked, jaw clenched and barely able to talk. Still, they pushed forward, their hearts pounding with fear and adrenaline.

We must be getting close to the sea now. It can't be far off. Mila sagged in his arms, and he caught her fragile form, felt her go limp while he struggled to hold her up, getting pulled into the snow with her. 'Mila!' he called, seeing her tired eyes.

'I can't . . . I just can't,' she breathed heavily, 'I need . . . to rest.'

Wind ripped at their cloaks, rain, sleet, and snow peppering their faces, hail crashing into trees, bouncing off with dull dings. They could not stay where they were, so out in the open. If it wasn't so dangerous out and about during the blizzard, it might have been beautiful, with the green and brown of the trees sticking out in patches, dark stones protruding through the cover of snow. Now it all looked quite bleak to Bellard. To the right, he spotted a large drift and dragged Mila up. 'Just a little further, we have to get out of here,' he called over the howls.

Hands trembling inside his gloves from the cold, he dropped to his knees against the snowdrift and dug into it, scooping out large mounds with his arms, while she groaned next to him. Their energy was getting sapped, and using their magic would only sap it faster, but he had no choice. He removed the gloves and pressed his blistered palms into the cold snow, felt a wave of energy seep from him, his hands becoming warm. Water started flowing away as he burrowed deeper, melting the snow to create a snow cave, scooping the water out with numb fingers.

He dragged her groaning form into the cave and blocked the entrance with a piece of fallen timber. Sitting her up, he shook her and rubbed her shoulders as he said, 'Come on, Mila. You have to stand. You have to get to the warmer section up there.' He had made a ledge for them to climb up, with a small platform to rest. With her remaining energy, she managed the climb and collapsed on the hard surface, and Bellard wrapped himself around her, dragging a blanket over them. A gentle warmth spread from him in pulsing waves, heating the chamber and thawing their frozen bodies.

Mila began to breathe more naturally, the air not being restricted by jerky shudders, her shoulders growing calm in his arms, the heat placating her and bringing some colour back to her face. The young mage, Bellard, struggled to keep his eyes open after the use of his power. His heavy lids closed, and his mind slipped away from the harsh reality. Sleep took them both.

* * *

'Bellard, my boy. What are you doing out here?'

'Opa!' Bellard called, skipping over the stones of the babbling brook, arms out at his sides for balance. 'It's a great day to have an adventure! Don't you think?'

'You know your father will get upset with you again, and that man has a bad temper. Why do you give him the chance, boy?' Opa Anglard stood with his fishing rod, clasping the line between his fingers, and turned in his stride up the hill, following the brook to where it got much deeper and broader. Bellard had ventured out with his Opa to the secluded spot between the trees on many occasions, watching him fish.

'I'm a boy, Opa. I need to learn how to look after myself.' He glanced away and muttered, 'Besides, what else am I going to eat?'

Opa Anglard sighed and rested the butt of the rod on the ground, shoulders sagging. 'I know they are not ideal parents, and I wish I could take you away from them. But I am getting old, my boy, and soon, I might not be around anymore.' Those words rocked Bellard, shattered his world.

'What do you mean? You can't go anywhere! You're too old.'

'Bellard, don't play dumb with me. You know what I meant. No one lives forever, child. Now, how about we leave all this talk of leaving and dying, and catch some fish, eh? Bellard? Are you listening?' His old, coarse voice morphed into a high-pitched, frantic one, and the world jerked back and forth as someone shook him.

'What's going on?' he asked, rubbing his eyes to see Mila hovering above him, a mask of worry stretched over her face, and he quickly got up. She already had her pack slung over her shoulder.

'Voices . . . I hear voices.'

Voices? Oh, no! They've found our trail. 'We've got to leave right now!' His words hadn't trailed away when someone kicked aside the piece of wood they had used for a door, spraying snow all over as he pushed through the hole. Nearly of equal height, it still felt to Bellard as if Scarface towered over them.

'Got you now, ya shits!' he growled and unsheathed a large knife, his bulky form blocking their exit. Mila didn't let them wait on her. A sparkling stream of hard ice ripped away from the shelter's wall and collided with the thug, lifting him with a groan from the ground to smash against the doorway, breaking it apart with his back and hurling him a distance away to flop against the bole of a tree.

'Don't just stand there!' Mila shouted, and they dashed from the snow cave. With most of the roof ripped away, they saw Scarface slowly climb to his feet, shaking his head dizzily, stumbling around with a smear of red on his face. *It won't keep him off for long,* thought Bellard.

However brief it might have been, the sleep had done them good, replenishing their strength. 'Over there!' he heard the thug shout and assumed Big Brother was nearby. The cruel chill of the tempestuous winds, laden with sleet and rain, crashed upon them, their cosy haven fading into a distant dream.

Bellard glanced around, trudging through the snow, dragging Mila along with her shorter legs while she struggled to make her way. He glimpsed Big Brother coming from the left up the mountain, a long blade in his hands. *Too short for a sword.* The storm was not yet done with them. It raged on all sides, groaning angrily with flashes from up high, shaking trees and shuddering the earth. Daylight had turned to darkness by the seething clouds, hurling down what they could at the four on the mountain.

A crazed scream came from Big Brother only a few feet away, gaining on them fast. Trees whipped by as they found a shallow stretch of snow, their feet crunching into the sleet, their grip slipping. Bellard slammed his palm against the bole of a tree as he passed it, a ripple of power rushing from him, and the tree groaned bitterly before erupting into a spray of gigantic splinters, speeding outwards, pinning into other trees, ground, snow, and Big Brother's arms, rocking him to the side momentarily. The tree toppled, and Big Brother jumped out of the way, vanishing into a puff of snow.

What should I do? I can't get her killed. Air exploded from his mouth, and it felt like his ribs had shattered as something heavy crashed into him from behind. The world spun and tumbled around him in swirling colours of white, dark purple, and green. Once, twice, three times he saw the pattern repeat, and then another hit, his spine cracking from the blow. He struggled for breath, watching through a haze of coming darkness, searching for Mila. Salty blood seeped down his throat, his head pounding furiously. Bellard drew in a ragged breath. She was to his right, faltering in the snow, trying to rise, a dark stain seeping through her cloak from her leg. *Where did that come from?*

Scarface had appeared out of nowhere and tackled them both, and all of them rolled down the mountain a way. Struggling for air, Bellard numbly grabbed at Mila's hand and rose, staggering further. Their grim-faced hunter rose from down the slope and shook his head, started towards them again.

'I didn't mean to kill your brother!' Bellard called, but Scarface just spat at them. 'Run, Mila!' He crashed into her from behind while he kept his eyes on the man at the back, nearly sending her to the ground, and jerked his head back to see Big Brother waiting with his blade on the crest of the rise.

Mila turned and glanced at him, her eyes filled with worry, but also something else. There was hope there. She whispered from the corner of her mouth, 'On the edge of the cliff.' His eyes followed her words and saw the faint glow through the whipping snow. *It must be the enchanter's home. We made it . . . almost.*

Bellard and Mila turned to face their attackers, their hands raised to prepare for battle. They were mages-in-training, young, naïve, and outmatched. A physical fight they would not win, and they were exhausted. Magic was their only way out. 'Are you ready for this?' Mila asked, drawing deep breaths to calm her raging heart, and glanced up at him. She had to look twice and grabbed him by his cloak, searching over his chest.

'What are you doing, Mila?' Bellard asked, watching Scarface approach from the rear while Big Brother cautiously came at them head-on.

'Your Pillar! It's gone!'

Those words ripped his feet from under him, his entire body growing colder than the blizzard could ever make it. 'What? No! No, no, no, no, no, no!' He worked his hands over his chest, rummaging inside the cloak to feel if it had slipped down, if the pouch's string had broken. But there was nothing. He had lost his Pillar. She was their only hope now.

'We'll come back for it, Bellard. First, let's survive!' She was right. He couldn't argue with her logic. He went to draw his knife and nearly yanked his entire belt over his head. The blade was stuck in its sheath, frozen solid. *Argh! I'm useless! No wonder everyone always picked on me!* Bellard lowered himself to the ground and picked up a fallen branch. Scarface came from the back, rushing in like a madman, and Bellard swung the branch as hard as he could, clobbering Scarface across the arm and chest.

Shrugged off like faint annoyance, Scarface tossed the branch away and sank his big fist into Bellard's stomach, doubling him over. Mila's screams and pleas sounded dull in his ears. The fist came again, slashing open his brow, blood spurting into the snow; another, more red spraying to the ground. Bells went off in his head, flashes in his eyes, and suddenly Scarface was not above him anymore. Mila had replaced him, standing with a piece of timber in hand, her Pillar glowing bright.

'Run, Bellard!' He felt a frail hand grab onto his where he lay face up in the snow, and a mighty crack sounded, the earth below them quaking loudly. They were hurled from their feet by a great eruption of snow and earth and were flung a distance away. The mountain was unsettled, prone to landslides and avalanches. They had to be careful not to wake the *beast*.

'Run, Bellard!' she shouted again, dragging him up, limping away from a snowy crater formed around them. Most of the snow had slid a fair way down the mountainside.

For an instant, he thought they'd made it, but then Scarface climbed out from the snow, and Big Brother walked from behind a boulder. *Come on!* The blizzard was growing more intense, and the snow was piling up around them, making it even harder to run.

They were getting closer to the cabin, seeing smoke drift from its chimney up high. He glanced over his shoulder to see the two catching up to them. *Maybe this is it. Maybe I should give myself to them as a sacrifice so they might leave Mila.*

A brilliant burst of magic exploded from the enchanter's house in waves of glorious beauty to Bellard's eyes. 'Grab on, Mila!' he shouted, holding out his arm to her. They clasped their arms around a tree, holding tight to it and each other. It was as if the very mountain had come alive, shaking the snow and ice off its slopes, causing the thugs to tumble down the mountainside, their screams echoing softly, fading fast.

The magic dissipated, and the mountain settled, rocks still tumbling down the side fierce and fast, trails of dust and snow drifting down. One boulder rammed the tree ahead of them, tearing its roots from the ground, snatching it away and over the edge, down the hill to join the rest of the tumbling debris. 'Run!'

With the blizzard still raging, Bellard and Mila hurried towards the enchanter's home, their bodies aching, dodging rocks and other debris. As they approached the wood cabin, the door swung open to reveal the enchanter himself, a tall and imposing figure with eyes that radiated annoyance like burning embers.

'What are you doing here?' he grumbled, his voice deep and commanding, blocking the doorway, leaving them out in the cold of the blizzard, his long black hair getting whipped around.

Bellard stepped forward and nearly sank to his knees, wanting to beg to be let in, but he was sure it would have got him nowhere fast. 'Grandàre Larison sent us. She said you owe her. This is payment.' For far longer than he'd hoped, the enchanter said nothing, did nothing but stare at them. Bellard leaned on Mila for support, his ribs hurting, face burning.

'Huh. Did she now? Come inside, the mountains are not a safe place . . .' He stepped aside to let them pass, eyeing them with a great frown. Bellard and Mila stepped into the warmth of the house, relieved and exhausted, not sure who was carrying whom. The enchanter closed the door behind them, shutting out the howling wind and snow. 'You've come a long way,' he said, his eyes fixed on them. 'Let's hope it was not all for nothing.'

* * *

'So let's hear it, then. Who are you and why have you come? And what does Larison want from me now?' Yosphore Blackstain fell back into his chair, a puff of dust erupting from the pillow covers, the wood creaking from the sudden weight. It was a humble little home, with wooden floors and walls, plain furnishings scattered about. Dull chairs and a plain dark table stood in the centre of the main room, and three doorways led to other rooms at the back. The wooden roof groaned from the force of the gusting wind while the snow, sleet, and hail tried their best to break it down.

'Are you not worried about the storm or those thugs coming back?' asked Mila, having a similar worry in her head as Bellard.

'I'm an enchanter. My cabin is . . .' He gestured with his hands, as if wanting them to fill in the blanks. When they kept staring at him in silence, he sighed, dropped his hands, and continued, '. . . enchanted. They can't come in if I don't want them to. You two are as thick as the snow in this blizzard. Now, why are you here?'

'I'm Bellard. This is Mila. Grandàre Larison sent me so you could enchant my Pillar, imbue it into something of my choosing.'

'That so? Let me see it then.' Yosphore leaned forward, waiting for Bellard with hand stretched out, snapping his fingers open and closed impatiently.

'I'm afraid I don't have it . . .'

Yosphore dropped his hand and chuckled. 'So for nothing, then. You know how long I've been waiting to say that?'

Bellard glanced at Mila, his feet throbbing, and shifted nervously, hoping they'd be given permission to sit down, but none came. 'No.'

'Honestly, I have lost count. And you want to know why?' He continued before Bellard could say anything. 'Because the people that do make the trek all the way out here have the good sense to remember all the things that are needed, like payment, their Pillars, rings, what have you.'

'I did bring it!' Bellard's exhaustion was getting the better of him, the pain shortening his fuse. Mila grabbed his arm, holding him back. He calmed himself and said, 'In the fight with those bastards, it came off my neck. We will wait for the storm to pass and search for it then.'

Yosphore had his arms up in mocking surrender. 'Okay. Okay. What do you want me to make then?'

'I don't know.' Bellard stepped back and planted his arse in the chair opposite Yosphore, not caring if they were given permission or not, and Mila followed suit, lowering herself into the chair next to him.

'Ha! Of course you don't. That would be too easy. You do know how this works, right?' The enchanter slapped his palm on the table between them, startling Bellard and Mila, making them jump.

'We've been a little busy trying to stay alive! There was no time to think about what I want.'

'Oh, hush. Where are my manners? I haven't had company for a while. I'll make us some tea. It seems you two will be here for a few days. You can share the room over there,' he said and pointed to the right. Yosphore rose slowly, made his way to the other room separating the two bedrooms, and rummaged through the cabinets, the sound of porcelain cups scraping and clinking filling the house. 'You two do drink tea, right?' He poked his head back out into the living room and found both of them fast asleep, heads resting on their arms on the table. 'Maybe tomorrow, then. Huh. This means I have to make more food . . .'

33. Unwanted Memories

The image of that ledge pulling away from her was seared into her brain. Orana shook her head, trying to rid herself of the memory, and looked at Jonas, who sat on the front seat as if nothing happened, the entire fight forgotten or suppressed. The act of killing all those men nothing more than an insult, easily shrugged off. No matter how hard she tried to forget that image, it kept crawling back to her, kept digging its nails into her.

Sharp, slick pieces of scree had cut into her fingers, and time had slowed, the ledge stretching away. Flashes of lightning ruled from above with great anger, while thick drops of rain wet her face, her hair whipping over her eyes. She had screamed, not wanting to die horribly disfigured and in pain, having no control of the outcome. Orana could already see herself lying on the ground, limbs bent and broken in all the wrong ways, blood seeping from grievous wounds on her head and body, lungs crushed and unable to breathe. She knew it wouldn't be long before her eyes closed permanently.

Yet, it never happened.

Here she sat, slightly the worse for wear, her ankle still hurting, the cut on her arm burning, but she was alive. Unlike poor Lofka, who had broken both his legs. Blood frothed from his mouth in ragged breaths where he lay with eyes staring to the sky, until Jonas stepped on his neck, pushing his weight down on the gurgling man, waiting for him to die.

Halfway to the ground, Orana had closed her eyes, accepting her coming death, when Jonas stampeded into her, tackling her in mid-air and hitting the mud, rolling in an embrace down the slope. It hurt like hell. Her left shoulder took the brunt of the impact, snapping out of place with a loud click, getting dislocated.

She had rolled around in the mud clutching her elbow, unbearable pain running up her arm, through her shoulder, and into her chest. 'Are you okay?' Jonas had asked.

'My arm . . . I can't move it. It hurts.' There was little more than a sympathetic look from him before he grabbed her wrist and yanked as he pushed back on her shoulder. A deafening pop sounded, and her shoulder throbbed terribly. Orana nearly fainted. She was a thief, not a soldier, and certainly no warrior. It didn't seem right that she had to endure these treatments. In the pouring rain, pummelled by the winds, they had sought Vernak and Jonas's son and found them in a cave a distance away, where she saw two more lying dead on the ground. Orana was starting to understand that Jonas was not a man to be trifled with. *The sooner I can get away from them, the better, I think.* They had waited for the storm to pass over, then continued on their way.

Orana slitted her eyes against the sun's rays at the slight angle over the horizon and rubbed at her arms. The world still waited to be warmed by it. And so did Orana. Beneath her, the wagon bounced, the bed hitting her bottom again and again. 'Thank you,' she said, speaking to Jonas, 'for saving my life.'

'Huh. There's nothing to thank me for. I couldn't just leave you to die if there was something I could do about it.'

'But how'd you know it would work?' asked Jorin, brooding in the corner. It was the first time he had spoken since they were all brought together again.

'I didn't.' Jonas turned to him, eyeing him from the corner of his eye, and turned back to the road, greeting a passing traveller with a wave of the hand. 'But I hoped. I actually wanted to catch her, but I was too slow.'

Jorin shook his head in disbelief and jumped up as he said, 'So if you'd timed it wrong, either she'd be dead, or you'd be dead if she landed on top of you. Timing . . . See? It is very important!'

'Oh, not this nonsense again! Sit down. Winterbourne lies ahead.'

Orana joined Jorin and stood up behind him, arm in a sling, staring at the approaching city in the distance. Farms and small settlements spread out before it, buildings painted a variety of colours. Yellow, black, blue, red, and so many more. *This looks like a city confused to whom its allegiance lies,* thought Orana. Queues of wagons travelled to and from the city, loaded with supplies all bound for delivery elsewhere. This was a thief's mecca.

A grand coach with dark polished wood and elegant trimmings of carved flowers rolled by them, followed by a train of five wagons filled with supplies, and an armed escort of thirty men at their flanks, swords dangling, arbalests hanging on their side. Hard stares followed them from all the guards, their hands drifting ever closer to their swords. Horses neighed and groaned, tossing their heads about. Her fingers itched, and her heart drummed in her chest. A thief needed to keep practising. 'How long are we going to be here?'

'We are heading straight to port,' said Vernak, stretching his legs out to the side of the wagon, then rubbed his thighs to get the blood flowing. 'There will be no time for . . . sightseeing.' He glanced at her, as if reading her mind, and Orana slumped down on a crate, annoyed. The buzz around them grew more urgent the deeper they ventured into the expanding city of Winterbourne, the streets becoming difficult to navigate with the wagon. Men, women, and children kept cutting across the road in front of them to get to other sections of the city, causing them to move at a snail's pace.

Steam rose from grates in the ground, leaving a foul smell that stung their noses. There seemed to be a strange tension in the air, a feeling of unease with every passer-by. Rubble lay strewn on the sidewalk, scattered to the walls and doors of buildings. To their right they passed a row of abandoned buildings, windows all shattered, with signs of char on the bricks covering a stretch of murals of men in brown uniforms, brightly coloured bands of red, blue, and yellow strapped around their chests, stern faces following Orana as they crawled by. 'What happened here?'

'Huh. I don't know. Best keep a lookout,' Jonas mumbled.

'Damn, it's cold here,' she muttered and drew her cloak around herself, teeth chattering.

'This? This isn't cold yet. You are just used to the heat. It will get colder the further we go south.'

She shot Jonas a look and said, 'For me it is cold, then.'

* * *

It didn't get any better the closer they got to the docks. If anything, it stank a lot worse. An overturned garbage bin lay off to the side of the road, its foul contents spilt from its gaping mouth, with a pair of filthy legs sticking out, snores rumbling inside. People climbed over the homeless man, ignoring his corpse-like body. Orana tapped her finger on the frame of the wagon. 'And just who will fund this next stretch of our little adventure?' *I am a thief! Not an investor! Coin and all things valuable are supposed to flow towards me, not the other way round.* She knew what the answer would be, but damn it if she was just going to hand it over to them.

'Er . . . We were hoping you'd have some coin to spare,' mumbled Vernak, his dull eyes straying for a heartbeat to hers before shying away.

'Just what I thought. And just what exactly do you bring to this wonderful gathering of misfits?' She planted her legs sideways up on the railing and leaned back, resting her eyes, and continued, 'I mean, so far, it seems like it is only me and Jonas that've been doing all the work. No offence, kid. We keep you two safe. I pay for everything, and Jonas drives us everywhere. Seems like we really don't need you, Vernak.'

'I provide information!'

'Oh, yeah? And when last did you do that? I, for one, have heard no information.'

'Vernak is not from here,' interrupted Jonas. 'He's—'

'A god,' blurted Jorin.

'What?' Orana shook her head and spun back to them. 'Oh, ha! Joke's on me.'

'Jorin! I said keep quiet!' Jonas called, and Orana caught something in his eyes that told her Jorin wasn't lying.

'She has a right to know what's going on!'

'Oh, bullshit!' Orana said. 'Why would a god be slumming it with us?'

Vernak glared at Jorin, then turned to her and said, 'Because there are things at play here that transcend your world, Orana.'

Their wagon rolled forward, the clip-clop of the horses' hoofs a rhythm she could hold on to. 'And what? You are our saviour?'

He grabbed her hand, and Orana was about to yank it from him, when a feeling of calm flooded over her. Deep-seated emotions of guilt, anger, and sorrow came rushing forward, with flashes of her father and her brother vividly in frame, replaced by a peace she hadn't felt in a very long time. Her breath was caught in her throat, wanting to become a sob, and she jerked away. The peace she felt vanished quickly, leaving her staring at the far corner of the wagon. 'What was that?' she asked, not turning to them.

'I am the god of balance. That was me bringing you back from all the self-loathing you believe you deserve.'

'Pff. Never heard of no god called Vernak. So glad I'm not one of those religious folks.' She wanted to sound tough and angry, condescending, but it felt rather pathetic. 'What a disappointment it must be for your followers when they meet you.' Orana laughed, unable to believe what she was hearing. 'So. How does it work then? Where do people go when they die?'

'They go to the realm of Tenthis, where they will serve their master,' said Vernak, clearing his throat while he looked around the docks. Few boats bobbed around, skiffs and small fishing vessels anchored against the chop, people rowing from the shore to where the big ships sat anchored.

'Please don't oversell it . . . Now I can't wait to see it.'

'Don't hold your breath. You won't see it.'

'Ah, no. Really?' she said mockingly, swinging her fist in disappointment. 'So close. Where will I go then?'

Vernak swung on her, his eyes suddenly fierce, angry, his brows knitted with deep lines. 'Tenthis might not be perfect. And yes, some gods treat their servants atrociously, but at least they know relative freedom for eternity. You will not have that, I'm afraid. Where you go, darkness breeds suffering. Terrible beasts roam the realm of Darg'ule.

You will know fear forever.'

'Ooh, gloomy.' She waved her hands about, poking fun at him, but those words scared her some. Religious factions had long since used stories of the underworld to scare people towards their doctrine, towards their god. She had thought it a fairy tale, like most other mythical superstition. But to hear it from the source directly had a little more effect. *Tenthis doesn't sound so bad after all.*

'There.' She pointed to the right of the docks, where a tall ship was moored, men running around offloading its cargo, stacking great boxes onto pallets for storage until they got hauled away, large nets being cast over all the stacked boxes to secure them for a time. *I wonder what goodies they have tucked away in there? Maybe some fine wine? Or perfume? Ooh, some hair soap. They are worth a pretty penny now.*

Jonas swung the wagon right to a causeway leading over a section of the harbour, where the dying sun shimmered on the water, an icy breeze coming from the sea. Orana ducked down and shivered, feeling the cold tighten and dry her skin more than it had ever been. She stretched her hand open, and closed it, feeling the skin crack. Every move burned her. 'I hate this place already!' she spat.

'Huh.' Jonas said nothing else, nor showed that he would elaborate. She was starting to hate his stoic silence.

'So how did you get tangled up with a god? And why does he care about you and your soul?' She tried again, hoping for an answer. Soft sprays of the thrashing water against the causeway's boulders drifted over them, making the air that much colder, and Orana drew her scarf over her mouth.

Vernak sighed thoughtfully and said, 'If she hasn't run away yet, then I think we can tell her the rest.' He turned to her. 'I am admittedly a low-ranking figure in the world of Tenthis. Normally, we are not allowed to interfere with the mortal world, but I have felt a shift of balance. I investigated the matter and found that Jonas here was being used as a pawn in a greater game by godly figures. Therefore, I intervened. As his punishment for not doing their bidding . . . Well, you saw what they did to him. But I fear they are not yet done with what they plan. All I know is the goddess of the wind is in on it. She has his soul, and we're going to get it back. Whatever Danu is planning needs to be stopped before a terrible disaster befalls the mortal realm.'

'Oh, okay. That sounds fun and all, but I have places to be. So if you could just drop me off anywhere here, then I'll find my own way to Baldor,' she stated, inching closer to the back of the wagon.

'We need your skills, Orana, please.'

'Nope! No. I am no warrior or adventurer. I'm a . . .' She glanced around at the people they passed, hearing her voice drift in the quietening dusk. Here and there a shout echoed from a labouring shipmate to another, working fast to get the job done so they could take to the streets, enjoy the brothels, or drink themselves into a drunken stupor. The gravel track beneath them crunched under the wheels, silence filling the void. 'You know what I am.'

'What do you want, Orana?' asked Jorin, wanting to be helpful but getting a glare from his father, and he sat back.

'It's not what she wants, it's what she needs.' Vernak followed her gaze carefully, judging her, reading her.

'What I want is to find the damn merchant and the things I . . . *borrowed* and survive.'

'No. That is not it. No, you seek absolution.'

'What? Stop it with your crazy eyes and ideas.'

'You seek forgiveness for the death of—'

'Oi!' She had her knife out, pressing it against Vernak's wrinkled throat in the blink of an eye. 'Don't you dare! I've spent my entire life trying to forget. Don't you dare bring this back up to the surface!'

'Whoa! Orana, put that down!' Jonas demanded, nearly running the wagon off the causeway with the startle she caused. Pedestrians jumped out of the way, swinging their fists, their curses drifting far. Jorin had fallen back, waited for her to calm down.

Vernak slowly pushed the blade away from his neck, and she noticed a line of blood where the blade had pressed. 'A god that bleeds?' she asked, slowly sheathing the knife.

The old man wiped the red from his throat, working the slimy liquid between his fingers. 'Yes. We all pay a price for our role in this adventure, as you call it. The mortal realm does not discriminate. It is happening faster than I would have hoped.' He sat for a while, staring at the drying blood on his fingers, rubbing them together slowly. 'I can give you what you want, Orana. All I ask is that you help us in return. I can let you speak with him.'

Her breath caught in her throat, and she struggled to get the words out. 'You . . . Uhm. You can? Really.' Vernak reached for her face, a frown appearing on his, and she quickly pulled away. 'I'm messing with you. I don't want it! Now let me down. Keep the wagon, I don't care.' She wiggled to the back of the bouncing cart and grabbed her crutch, dangling her feet off.

'They will not stop looking for you, Orana!' Jonas called from the front. 'More will be sent, and we will not be there to protect you.' Their wagon came to a grinding halt as Jonas pulled on the reins near to the ship. The horses neighed and tossed their heads, happy to stop moving for a bit. 'But if you want to go, then go. I don't have time for this shit.' He jumped off the wagon and sauntered over to a lean man sitting on a crate before the ship, ticking off boxes as men carried them out and stacked them.

'They won't stop looking for you.' She knew that to be the cold, hard truth. Jonas turned back to them, pointing in their direction, their voices not reaching them, but she could see their lips moving. She reached for the ground with her left leg, inching closer with the right, and settled her weight slowly to the ground, pushing on the crutch to help her balance.

'Orana, please!' called Jorin, staring at her with desperation.

'I'm sorry, kid. I'm not getting myself killed for this . . .' She waved a careless arm, pressing down with her good shoulder on the crutch. '. . . whatever this is.'

'Let her go, she ain't worth it,' Jonas said as he returned to the wagon. Orana paused for a moment, feeling the sting of those words, and heard him call to her, 'The ship is leaving tomorrow morning at first light. If you want to join, meet us here.'

* * *

Orana had wandered a distance from the others, discovering the maze of the city slums, and winced at the pack pulling on her shoulders. She hobbled along on her crutch and felt she fit in perfectly with her ailments.

A man and woman sat on a bench outside their little home, the roof sagging, floorboards rotting, see-sawing back and forth in their rocking chairs with a cloud of smoke hanging above them. A strained cough left the man, hoarse and dry. She felt it in her throat, listening to him suffer through it. *Damage from the floods of the World Storm.* They had covered the roads with layers of gravel, but the World Storm had churned them all into dredges of mud. Still, she was impressed the waters had receded by so much already, thinking it had to have something to do with those steam-spewing grates in the streets.

Why can't anything good just happen? Why do you always need to risk your life for anything good? God of balance, my arse! You don't have to lift a finger for the bad to come your way. Why not the good as well? Orana brooded and limped forward, her thoughts dark. People kept falling in her path, pushing and shoving her with grimy hands. Not that it mattered, she supposed. She was one of them now.

She walked and walked, evading rushing men and women, seeing dark faces in the dark suburb, the sharp outlines of jagged structures set against the full moon, feeling vulnerable with her limited mobility.

'What? Wait, how did I get back here?' Back at the causeway, near to the beginning, she hobbled up to the shore and sat down on the beach, cursing the spray from the salty water crashing over the rocks ahead of her. A warm bed would have been ideal right about now, defrosting her tired bones in the comfort of soft sheets, but her leg throbbed terribly. She was going nowhere.

Her heart was heavy. It had taken everything she had not to sob before those three, listening to Vernak's words. Taken everything to play it off as a mocking joke. She let her head hang between her pulled-up legs, breathing deep. Her heart was running its own race, beating furiously in her chest. *Who gave him the right to drag up old and forgotten memories? Bastard!* Long-winded breaths left her slowly as she calmed herself, and tickling tears rolled down her cheeks. *Bastard.*

A mighty crash of water thundered over the boulders, spraying their mist up high. Orana shuddered for an instant, seeing her father disappear behind the wall of water, seeing it rush towards her, feeling her helpless baby brother's tiny fingers clasping hers. She shuddered again and sobbed, her chest heaving as breaths came rapidly, shaking her where she sat. Her fingers slipped into the sand, the cold, coarse grains wet and clumpy, sticking to her hands, and she hurled handfuls at the darkness before her, screaming out loud. The quavers returned, heart aching. *Bastard.*

34. Cheating Death

The dispirited mob of the dead went about doing their masters' bidding, crowding the streets in their slow walks to nowhere. They had nothing to live for. Death'd brought them only servitude. Calmantis had found a bleak, woven, beige blanket, a rag of a thing, dirty and dusty, and wrapped it around himself and over his head like a hood, concealing his face as best he could.

His deeds had caused a great fuss. Throughout the night, guards searched the grounds and the tower for trespassers. But Calmantis had already made his way down to the ground floor and hurried to hide at the foot of the dais, watching them run past. He felt invincible. Doors were getting kicked down from nearby buildings, and the dead were being dragged from their homes, questioned with their faces in the dirt. It was an unfortunate consequence he wished they did not have to endure, but he was finally doing something important with his life. Something that mattered. Something that would change the world, for him especially. He leaned against the sun-baked brick, panting, and set off again.

Now if he could only remember where Ostarra said to meet him . . . This had happened not just once with Calmantis. His inability to keep listening when he got excited was near legendary in his house as a child. And he had received more cuffs on his head than he would have liked because of it. It had taken considerable patience to get away from the tower, silently slipping between worlds until he was far from the premises. Calmantis was not yet done with Melloria, though. There was much to see still.

The sun was high, its rays warm. Unlike Baldor, the buzz of the crowd was barely perceptible, even in the throng milling about. People whispered to themselves in hushed voices, avoiding eye contact, continuing with their business. He had made it away from the taller structures in the city, following the neat streets, the perfect gardens, the sombre crowds, blending in with his slow walk, avoiding faces. On his right stood a magnificent golden statue of a god wearing a silver circlet on his head, a winged sceptre with a large jewel set in the centre planted firmly on the ground. The god's face was youthful, elegant, clean-shaven, but his eyes were older, much wiser, with long hair flowing down past his shoulders. Those that walked ahead of Calmantis all reached out their trembling hands to rub the foot of the deity, whispers of *'Aztar'* in prayer filling the area.

So this is his domain? The king of the gods, their Primarch. He looks so young. Calmantis reached out and rubbed the worn foot in passing, mumbling nonsensical words, and knocked into someone. The man stopped in his stride, hood drawn over the deathlike pallor of his face, and slowly turned to him, mumbling something. At first it began as a whisper, 'Voidwalker. Voidwalker,' pointing at him accusingly, and grew to a humming chant echoed by those around him, more fingers being shoved in his face.

'No! I'm not,' he tried. They didn't listen, and the chanting only grew.

He backed away from them, getting caged in, feeling the walls close in on him. The grey-skinned man jumped forward, fingers reaching to grab hold of his tunic, and Calmantis closed his eyes, feeling his body being pulled across the Fold. But this time, there was something else, a strange sensation emanating from his broken sword. He opened his eyes to the glimmer of the Fold, and the pale man with deep-sunken eyes clutching his tunic in both hands. Fear radiated from the man while he stood with mouth agape, staring all around them at the flickering lights of the Fold. Calmantis's sword grew hot, a wave of heat flowing up his body, through his chest, into his arms, and out to where he held on to the man's arms, a faint glow spreading outwards.

It all should have taken a mere heartbeat to cross the Fold, yet this felt so much longer, so much stranger. The world blurred and faded, the cityscape disappearing to be replaced by the shadows of gigantic trees, a forest filled with many colours, and now a man that should've been dead was back into the world of the living. They stood there in each other's arms, unsure of what just happened. *This should not be possible. The dead should not be able to cross the Fold. They have no bodies, yet here he stands.*

The man stared around at the trees. His once-dead, haunted eyes turned radiant blue, his grey visage getting colour to his cheeks. He left Calmantis's arms and wobbled to the closest tree, placed his hand on it, and began to chuckle, then he hugged it fiercely, laughing out loud. *This should not be possible.* A hail of sobs echoed through the forest as the man sagged to the ground, tears streaming from his eyes.

'What is your name?' asked Calmantis, shocked at what had just happened, realising that he'd just raised someone from the dead. He crept a little closer to the man, who suddenly pushed away in fear and hid behind the tree. 'It's okay. I won't hurt you.' *But I will have to take you back to Tenthis. Ostarra will kill me if he finds out what I've done.*

'I'm not going back there!' His voice sounded hoarse, dry.

'Of course not.' *Yes, you are.* 'Why would I take you back?' Calmantis carefully stepped closer, placing his feet between the twisted roots sticking out above the ground close to the tree, and lunged at the man, trying to grab him by the arm. The man jumped away, rolling over small bushes, before getting to his feet and running as fast as he could, glancing over his shoulder at Calmantis still lying against the tree, a new scrape mark on his forehead. *Shit . . .*

That's twice this happened on one quest. Ostarra will be fuming. Calmantis climbed to his feet and looked around, trying to figure out which direction to walk in order to get out of the city, then sauntered what he thought was east. He stumbled over another root, nearly going down again. The running speck of a man caught his attention where he made his way across the grass and wildflower field, arms swinging, before he disappeared over the rise, and Calmantis thought, *Someone is going to be really surprised to see you.*

* * *

Calmantis stood in the open field where he remembered the Flow platform to be in Tenthis, staring down at the valley below, imagining the lights of Melloria as he saw it last night, the bright beam racing to the skies. The world blurred around him, a shimmer folding over him, landscapes blending together, and before he blinked, the familiar beam was there, ever prevalent in the sky.

'What is this?' called a coarse voice behind him. Calmantis nearly jumped off the cliff, and grabbed at his chest with brows raised, a girlish yelp escaping him before he found himself on the metal platform, knees weak.

It was a man standing on the other side of the platform with a spear in hand, weapon held ready for use. There were three of them, two of which seemed to be an armed escort. The other was a tall, lithe woman, adorned with wooden accoutrements around her ears, fingers, wrists, ankles, and neck, her arms and feet clinking with dull rings as she stepped closer. She stopped halfway, bending down to look at him curiously, head tilted to the side.

'Tell your Lichens to lower their weapons or I will burn their hearts with the flash of thunder.' Ostarra stood off to the left of the platform. He seemed ill at ease, his hand straying close to his sword at his side.

'What have you got here, Ostarra?' asked the woman, gesturing to her men to lower their weapons. This was a bit of inconvenience he'd hoped to have avoided. Calmantis pushed up from the platform and quickly joined Ostarra's side, keeping his head low and avoiding her gaze, hoping to be seen as a servant of the god. He certainly looked like one, but his unfortunate entrance to their world was a dead giveaway to something more.

'Maloriffe. This does not concern you,' said Ostarra, keeping his eyes on the two guards. 'Go, be on your way.'

Maloriffe? The goddess of trees? Calmantis grinned, then remembered what Ostarra had said, *'Most want you dead,'* and his smile quickly vanished.

Regal and elegant, she approached them carefully, dressed in a long blue gown adorned with leaves and thin vines. She was exceptionally beautiful. Her slender, tan face shimmered like it was made of gold leaf, supple lips glistening in the dying light. Soft, slanted eyes focused on him, melting his heart. Her dark hair flowed down to the small of her back. Calmantis had never been one to shy away from a good-looking woman. How could he do so now with this magnificent goddess before him?

'Are you mad, Ostarra? He is a Voidwalker! Seize him!' Her guards rushed at them, spears swinging, the crescent-moon blades singing with each slice.

'Argh!' Calmantis screamed, leaping out of the way, and Ostarra caught a spear, yanking it back to fling the guard across the platform, close to Calmantis. 'Egh!' he screamed again, seeing the man's face twist in anger while he scrambled to get up. He ran from the platform, legs scything through the air, and the ground exploded under him in a convoluted jumble of branches and roots, lifting him to the air while it closed around him, sharp pieces of rapidly growing timber closing in to crush him to death.

The sky vanished above him, and the fighting sounds grew muffled, the space around him getting frighteningly small. He pushed with his legs against the thick bole on one side, his back to the other, grunting and sweating. He could already imagine his body's juices flowing into the new tree, giving life to its murderous rampage in dark streams. It was getting hard to breathe, and his feeble attempts at saving his own life were doing little to aid him.

He fumbled the broken sword, letting it drop twice, fingers reaching down to grab the hilt, and stabbed into the wood, chipping small splinters from it. Air rasped through his teeth, but nothing filled his lungs. His sight became fuzzy and his head light, the world drifting, his limbs weak.

A tremendous clap sounded, reverberating through the surrounding structure, a bright flash its companion. The trunk split apart as if sliced by a flaming sword, and he was sure if his ears worked at all, he would hear the wood groaning its death cries while it collapsed piece by piece, but all he heard was a sharp ringing in his ears. Calmantis rode the falling tree to the ground, dodging flames and other sharp objects by merely falling in the right direction, sucking in great gasps of air. He had no balance. His legs wobbled and sent him to the ground more than once.

Another bright flash appeared, coming from a sky now filled with rumbling clouds. *There were no clouds that could do this earlier.* The clap was horrifying, engulfing the one guard in a blaze of blue fire. The man didn't even have time to dodge it. He dropped to the ground instantly, his screams short-lived. Calmantis stumbled closer, in time to see Maloriffe doubled over Ostarra's sword, the blade through her back reflecting a dull light cast from the city.

'No!' he mumbled, the words sounding strange to his ears, muffled and hollow, dragged out from his mouth as if he couldn't speak. He knew she'd been about to kill him, but he couldn't bear to see the goddess murdered like that. She spluttered up blood over Ostarra's chest, holding on to his shoulders as she stared into his eyes, and he twisted the blade, jerking her body up, a squeal of pain leaving her contorted face. 'What have you done?' Calmantis gasped.

Ostarra ignored the wobbling Calmantis and yanked out the blade, dropping the goddess to the platform in a pool of her blood, her eyes left open to stare at the sky. There was no doubt in his mind that this thunder show would attract attention. The other guard lay to the left, his throat opened wide. Chest heaving, the god of storms licked his lips, then wiped the blood from his face with the back of his thick arm. 'Did you get it?'

The sound was returning to his ears, the ringing slowly growing dim. Calmantis knelt by her side, stroking her hair, and closed her eyes.

'Did you get it?' Ostarra roared, stepping closer with that dreadful sword.

'Yes!' Calmantis called out, falling back, tripping over Maloriffe's limp arm. Ostarra reached out to him, gesturing for him to hand it over.

'Give it here, now!' With a start, Calmantis quickly pulled out the blade and handed it to the god. 'It melded with the sword. There was no other way.'

'Huh. This will have to do. You have done well.' His eyes came up from the broken blade, and he calmly stared into Calmantis's very being, and said, 'I regret having done what I did here. You were not supposed to come back to Tenthis.' He looked around at the carnage at his feet. 'There is one thing she was right about, I'm afraid. You cannot leave here alive . . .'

* * *

His spine grew ice-cold, and a flash of adrenaline pumped through his body. All his senses jumped to alertness, his mind working overtime. He was a dead man walking. *Calmantis, you buffoon! Of course he would want to kill me now. Someone will have to take the blame for killing these three. And what better for Ostarra than if he apprehended Maloriffe's killer, the Voidwalker? He would be heralded as a hero, never suspected of anything.*

Ostarra took a step towards him, and Calmantis squealed with panic. He spun around and ran for his life, then jumped through the Fold to the mortal realm, hoping to lose the god in the forest. If this was indeed Edelbore like he thought, he needed to head southeast. Feet sloshing into soft mud, he slipped and slid across the forest floor, grabbing hold of passing trees for balance, using them to turn at sharp corners. *How am I going to escape from a god?*

'Don't make this harder than it has to be, Cal. You are doing this for a noble reason. They will revere you as the human who saved Tenthis. And besides, once you are dead, I can make a case for you to be transferred to us, not the underworld. You will sit by my side, drinking that fine wine you so like.' Ostarra's voice sounded sinister, a hollow promise to the tone.

Dark shapes rushed by him, and soon he was not running alone. Animals bounded next to him: deer, rabbits, wolves, all running the same direction he was, monkeys swinging in the trees above, their screeches loud enough to be heard miles away.

'You can't hide from me!' shouted Ostarra, and the world groaned as clouds formed above. The wind picked up around him, shaking the trees and bushes terribly, howling like hungry wolves past each bole. He was getting pushed back by the gale, slowed in his run, and rain poured from above. A bright burst of light exploded on his right, and a tree trunk stood in flames. 'Shit!' he called and dived to the ground, worried something would take his head off. He quickly gathered his wits and ran once more, when another groan sounded. Calmantis grabbed hold of a tree and turned to see a gigantic tornado forming above. *Oh no.*

The urgent bugle of an elk sounded, and stampeding animals ran for their lives, all knowing what was about to happen. He had never seen a thing like it before. Predator and prey all running together, uncaring of what was next to them, only thinking of their self-preservation. He joined the crazy run, skipping over bushes and logs, jumping over small ravines, skirting low cliffs. The tornado touched the ground with a tremor-inducing force, instantly ripping trees from the soil, sending them crashing into the others.

Something solid rammed him from behind, knocking him to the ground, and sent him tumbling down a small slope. There was no time to worry about injuries. He had to keep going. His balance was still lacking, and he quickly found the ground rushing at him again, knocking the wind from his lungs. It was chaos all around. Animals were fleeing the vicinity, lightning flashed all around and fires raged, winds tearing at everything. The tornado had no mercy. He jumped up from the ground, seeing the deer that ran him over bound away into the darkness.

Terrible sounds of roots snapping filled the air, timber cracking and animals bellowing. *You have got into many bad situations before, Calmantis, but you have outdone yourself here.* He knew he could not outrun this. And seeing all these animals getting slaughtered because of him made him sick. It had always been easier for Calmantis to care for animals than humans. There was just something in their innocence he could relate to, never getting that gnawing feeling of imminent betrayal he always got when he spoke to other humans. With all the courage he could muster, he turned to face the tornado, readying to call out to

Ostarra to finish this, when a faint whistle sounded to his left in the forest's gloom. The flashes of lightning strobed through the trees, revealing a tall woman next to a tree, holding on with one arm while gesturing for him to follow her.

Do I go with the definite death sentence and call out to Ostarra? Or do I follow this very ominous-looking woman found in the middle of nowhere? Neither seems very safe to me, but if she can get me out of this, I'm sure Ostarra will tire of searching for me eventually. He ran after her, following closely, hoping that he had not just exchanged killers. From what he saw in the flash of lightning, it was not a stretch. Her eyes were painted dark, with white jagged lines crossing her face, a small bone stuck through her nose. And he couldn't help but wonder if it was the bone from some poor fellow's finger.

She led him to a small crevice in the cliff and squeezed through, pushing against the wall to help her forward. Skin tearing from the rough edges scraping his back, he winced in discontent. All around, the smell of wood burning made it hard to breathe, and then he saw ahead of them a flickering light a little further away. The storm raged above them, yet here, in the cave, no water poured on them, no winds tore at them, no thunder reached them. Finally, the crevice opened up, revealing the fire in the middle of the small cave, a few crude huts built around it with animal skin.

Most worryingly, there were four others waiting around the fire, licking their lips while they chewed on the bones of something he could not make out. *Maybe I'll take my chances with Ostarra . . .* He turned to re-enter the crevice through which they had come, and found two more men blocking his path, and he noticed their double-tipped pointed ears. The Sidhe.

'Where is Tirveeä?' one asked from the fire, slowly approaching him.

'Who?' Calmantis asked, glancing at them. He turned to look at the two behind him again but saw too late the butt of the spear racing for his head.

35. Finding Solace

Bellard drew in a deep breath, his eyelids fluttering, yawning and stretching his back, arms, and legs. A tangled and dishevelled mess of white hair blocked his view out the frosted window, and he poked at the body beneath it, hearing a groan of unhappiness. Mila turned around on her stomach slowly, a lone green eye staring at him through the white fur. 'Ew! Wipe those eye boogers from your face.'

Peepers flared wide, he wiped the gunk from them, and brought the fingers he had used closer to her face, threatening to smear it on her. 'No! Don't you dare!' she chided, slithering away from him under the covers, pulling them over her head and drawing the blankets away from him.

'Hey! It's cold! Give that back,' he said, rubbing his naked arms and chest, feeling the goosebumps come alive on his skin, while she giggled with glee, the covers shaking with her laughter. He shoved his icy hand under the blanket, grabbing hold of any warm skin he could find, and Mila squirmed underneath, kicking her legs to keep him away.

'No! You're so cold!' Mila giggled, feigning the anger in her voice. She poked her face out of the covers and blew her hair out of her face, but the unwilling strands settled back over her eyes, concealing their evil little plots. She jumped like a frog, covers in tow, wrapping herself around Bellard, instantly bringing heat back to his body.

'*Ahem!*' came a clearing of the throat near their doorway, and both of them froze on the spot. Bellard poked his head out from under the blanket. The old enchanter stood uncomfortably a few feet from the doorway, glancing around the living room as if everything was very new to him, then he met Bellard's eyes briefly. Snow fell from his thick blue robes to the wooden floor while he rubbed his hands against each other for warmth. 'Yes, well. When you're ready, food is being prepared.'

'Yes, of course. Thank you, Yosphore. We will be out shortly.'

'You two have been sleeping for nearly an entire day. You must be starving.' The old man glanced away again, searching for new things to look at. 'Huh. Okay then.' His footsteps drummed away from the door, his face set in a scowl of annoyance, mumbling sounds drifting through the little home.

Bellard pulled his head back under the covers and saw the innocent look on Mila's face, knowing it not to be the case. He laughed and said, 'Let's get ready. I am starving.'

* * *

They sat round the table in the main area, laughing, making jokes with one another in hushed tones, while meat sizzled over a hot fire in the kitchen, the smell drifting to them. Yosphore sauntered from the kitchen with two plates in hand, steam rising above. He placed it on the table before them and turned back to fetch his own. It was a rudimentary meal, one that served to fill their bellies, not to whet the appetites of the crown with garnishes and silly decorations.

A thick cut of fresh bread lay off to the side of the plate, covered in a dark gravy, with a slab of meat next to it, a big bone in its centre. Stomachs rumbling, they grabbed a knife and fork from the centre of the table and began cutting into the meat, dipping the bread into the salty gravy and taking large bites from it. Meaty juices ran down their mouths, making their chins glisten with fat, their stomachs rejoicing at the taste of food.

A chair screeched across the floor as another plate was placed down harder on the table than was necessary, and only then did they realise they had not even waited for their host to join them. 'I see they do not teach manners or etiquette at Kunia anymore. In my day, you'd get whipped for this behaviour.'

Bellard swallowed a large chunk of meat he had half chewed, feeling it stick in his throat, painfully going down at a snail's pace. 'Apologies, Yosphore.' The words that crawled from his mouth sounded like it came from an ancient figure, old and hoarse. He cleared his throat, eyes twitching as he waited for the pain to subside. 'I think the hunger brought out the worst in us.' It was only when he really looked at the enchanter that Bellard saw the fine red splotches of blood across the man's robe. 'What happened?' he asked and pointed to his chest.

'What?' Yosphore looked down, stretching his robe so he could see. 'Agh! And this was a clean one as well. Must have happened when I slit the throat of . . .' His eyes drifted back up to them. 'It seems it is my turn to apologise. No need to be so crude at the table, especially when there is a lady present.' He smiled awkwardly at Mila, before his face went slack, eyes stretching wide, mouth suddenly agape, and he snapped his fingers with a loud clap. 'Oh, yes. That reminds me. Here you go.' He stabbed his hand into a pocket and pulled it out to slide the Pillar satchel Mila had made for Bellard across the table. 'Found it in the snow when I went hunting this morning. I see now why Larison sent you to me. I'd hate to lug that around everywhere.'

Bellard's eyes lit up, and he grabbed it from the table, quickly flipping open the front flap to see the amethyst crystal within. 'Thank you! Isn't it great, Mila?' He turned to her, and her face morphed from a thoughtful haze to a smile as she grabbed his hand, her eyes straying towards Yosphore.

'What about those thugs that were after us?' asked Mila, nervously holding Bellard's hand. 'Were they still out there?'

'Oh, I have a feeling those two won't be bothering you again.'

Mila shook her head, narrowed her eyes at him. 'What does that mean?'

'It means, girl, that you don't have to worry about them anymore.' His stare was cold, stern, eyes pulled into a scowl. The air had turned a little sour. Bellard could feel the tension rising around him, seeing Mila and Yosphore not averting their gazes from each other.

'Argh, that's disappointing,' Bellard said, trying to tie the broken strings around his neck, finding them too short. They had snapped during their tussle with Big Brother and Scarface.

'Don't worry about that. You have no need for it any longer,' Yosphore held out his hand, waiting for Bellard to hand his Pillar over.

'Have you decided what you want? I would like to start on it today.'

'I have. For far too long have I been the victim, unable to defend myself, always cowering behind someone else to fight my battles for me. No longer will that be so. I will not be a victim again.'

'What will you have me forge then?'

Bellard gestured with his finger for them to wait and ran to their room, footsteps pounding. He quickly reappeared, holding his old, rusted knife in hand. 'Here it is.'

'Wait. No! I will not waste my talents on that garbage. Just look at it.' Yosphore grabbed the hilt and pulled at the bits. 'The blade is loose, and the handle is skewed and worn. There's rust all over the edges, nicks and scratches throughout! The cross guard is split. Oh, dear. This is just terrible. No! I will not do it.' The enchanter sent the knife flying past his two guests, pinning it into the wood wall with a thud.

'What do you mean, you won't do it?' Bellard asked frantically, arms waving about angrily. 'You have to do it!'

'No! I will not let my good name be sullied by making second-hand junk! I have worked far too hard for it.'

'Does it mean nothing to you that you gave your word to Larison? Is this really how you would repay her?' Bellard had his hands in the air, shouting at Yosphore, who was halfway out the door.

The enchanter froze on the spot, ready to slam the door shut behind him, and stared at the two ponderously. He grumbled something under his breath, whining incoherently, legs bending, back stretching, fist swinging like a child about to throw a tantrum, then he said, 'Follow me.'

* * *

A thick blanket of snow covered the mountain, reflecting the bright sun, blinding them when they ventured outside. Patches of green pine trees poked out all over, laden with the white fluff. They walked around to the back of the house, feet crunching, disappearing below the cold snow. They had not realised how beautiful it was up here during their fight for survival.

A soft mist drifted over the sea below, the sparkling blue water coming in from afar, fading into a glistening green as it got shallower, crashing onto the boulders to the right, a loud roar applauding with every slap. White foam formed in the surf on their left, lapping the strand, soft and gentle, dissipating on the sand before more water rushed over it. A stiff breeze came from the east, and Bellard shivered through the frosty gust, rubbing his arms through the coat. It didn't seem to bother Mila as much, though, and for a moment, he felt embarrassed, quickly stopping the rubbing to act like nothing was wrong.

The back of the home stood on wooden stilts, the mountain having fallen several feet to make its way down to the strand below. Mila ran her hands along the planks nailed from post to post to keep the wind out, staring at the sizeable gaps between some of them, and followed Yosphore through a narrow door ahead of him.

Having been embarrassed by Mila's unwavering strength already once this morning, he really didn't want to admit how good it felt to be out of the wind. Long tables stood against the wall, raggedy sheets covering items on them, the sharp edges forming shapes not unlike the mountain range they were on, with hidden valleys and long sweeping bends, where Bellard could imagine beautiful fields of wildflowers blooming in the springtime. A clay forge stood in the centre of the room, with a long piece of old iron wedged in, just waiting to be heated and shaped into something new. Next to it stood an anvil on a block of wood, raised above a strange collection of unknown symbols depicted in the ground, all linked with crisscrossing lines.

Yosphore scowled and mumbled something under his breath. Dust fluttered and swirled, lit up by the rays of the sun beaming through the gaps in the wood as he yanked the sheet from one table, then the next, and the next. Bellard took a step back and knocked into the long table behind him, and a conglomerate of tools and equipment shifted and bounced from their neatly stowed locations. 'Sorry, sorry. I didn't see it behind me.' Yosphore ignored his woeful pleas and waved him over to the shiny pieces on the table.

Many items lay in wait. Daggers, short swords, axes, rings, belt buckles, earrings, necklaces, cutlery, and so much more, made from various metals. 'These are great!' said Bellard, turning back to Mila who only smiled.

'Pick an item and it will be yours.'

'Any item?' Bellard asked.

Yosphore nodded. 'I was just going to sell them. Make some coin. But giving them away seems close enough to my goal.' Bellard didn't find his sarcasm funny at all. He wished he could repay the enchanter, but he barely had enough for them to make it to Forgeholde as it was.

'One day, Yosphore, I will repay you, my friend. This I promise.'

'I won't be holding my breath, but thank you for the sentiment. Go on then. Which one?'

Daggers with short blades, thick and wide, long blades, curved and edged, straight and narrow, double-edged blades, throwing knives, and other triangular throwing weapons with sharp edges greeted him with their lustre. He moved on, gawking at the rings, seeing strange symbols inscribed on them.

'What about this one?' said Mila from the corner of the room, face turned away as she studied the item in her hands.

'What did you find?' Bellard asked, feeling like a kid about to receive a toy for the first time. How many times growing up had he wished that things could be different in their home? That his parents could be loving and caring. How many times did he dream as a young boy that his father would come home with a new toy instead of more lashings? A horse like all the rest got, or a sword, or some books, anything really. He crowded behind her, glancing over her shoulder. 'Let me see.' She turned around and handed it to him.

'Ah, an interesting choice,' stated Yosphore, drawing closer to them. 'The hilt is old deer antler, hence why it's so curved. And the blade is folded steel. Thousands upon thousands of layers rolled over each other to form that pattern, you see.'

'I'll take it.'

'Of course you will. It's the one that took me the longest to make.'

Bellard flashed a great big grin and pushed his luck. 'And a belt, please. A decent one with a sheath that will never let it fall to the wayside.'

Yosphore took in a deep steady breath, releasing it slowly while he glared at him. 'Might as well. Looks like you need all the help you can get.'

A glint reflected from a piece of metal from another table, blinding him with a flash, and Bellard stepped closer to it, lifting the sheet half covering it. 'What is this?' he asked, astonished at what he saw.

'That? Oh, it's something I've been working on for a while. It's not yet done.'

'Forget the belt. I want this.'

'Let me see,' Mila said, walking closer.

Yosphore shook his head, spreading his hands wide, the folds of his neck swinging in dismay. 'I'm afraid I have to object. It will be a terrible burden to carry for the rest of your life.'

'I would listen to Yosphore. I don't—' Mila began, quickly cut off by Bellard.

'Is my Pillar big enough?' the young mage asked, eyes wide with wonder.

The old enchanter looked around and stammered over his words. 'Er . . . Yes, in theory, it should be sufficient. But—'

'Then it's settled.'

Yosphore grunted a long sigh, and said, 'It will take a while to complete.'

'Are you sure about this, Bellard?' Mila asked, concern ringing in her voice.

'It's not a staff . . .' Bellard said with a chuckle, 'but it will do.'

* * *

'Something isn't right with that man,' Mila said, pulling Bellard aside when they walked outside, taking a good look around to confirm that

Yosphore wasn't in earshot.

'What's wrong, Mila? I know he's a little strange, but what did you expect from a man that lives out here all alone, away from civilisation? I'd be worried if he wasn't strange.'

'Don't be daft!' She whacked him on the head with the flat of her palm. '"I was just wandering around, hunting,"' she said mockingly, rubbing the bridge of her nose, '"and just stumbled upon your Pillar?"'

'What does that mean?' he asked, also rubbing the bridge of his nose.

Mila crossed her arms defiantly, chin pointed to the sky. 'You are so out of the loop . . . It means that I'm being ironic.' Bellard chuckled at her haughty nature. 'Do you really think Crabface and Littlefinger would just let him waltz around and not attack him?'

'Who?'

'The two idiots chasing us! I swear, sometimes you make me so angry.'

'Scarface and Big Brother?'

'I know who I'm talking about!'

'You're overreacting, Mila. He was probably just very careful.' Bellard held her by her arms, smiling at her.

'Oh yeah? Tell me this. Did you see any deer up here in the cold mountaintops the entire way we came?'

He had to think for a while. *There must have been one, somewhere.* He was sure of it. Though he could not recall the encounter. *But if there were no deer . . . then what were we eating?* Just the thought alone made the contents of his stomach want to rise. *No, it's not possible that so many bad things can happen to two people all at once.* He suddenly felt queasy but saved face before Mila, not wanting to show her she had him concerned.

'He killed something, right?' she continued.

'I believe so.'

'Ask him to show it to us.'

'Shh, Mila. He's going to hear you. Look, let's just be careful, and as soon as he's done, we leave, okay? He has my Pillar. I can't leave without it. Let's take a walk, clear our heads, eh? Think of something.' He took her by the hand and led her away from the cabin, following what looked to be a recent trail made in the snow, and he thought, *Must be Yosphore's trail from this morning. Maybe we can see what he was up to.*

Feet crunching, birds squawking, snow melting, they trekked through the mountain, keeping an eye out for the two that had chased them, hoping they had not made a third enemy in Yosphore. Bellard couldn't think that Grandàre Larison would lead him into a trap like this. Or knowingly send him into the clutches of a possible cannibal.

The trail they followed changed, grew more chaotic, with fallen trees ruining the perfectly sculpted snowdrifts, pine-needled twigs and branches spreading the chaos further. Deep tracks cleaved through the snow where something or someone had tried to run. Then something caught his eye. Red droplets stood out from the white, screaming for them to be seen, a splattered mess. Mila gasped, and Bellard turned her away. She angrily shook him off and turned back around, finger pointing at his face. 'I told you! And don't treat me like some little girl!'

Hands held up in surrender, he backed away and trudged closer to the scene. There were no bodies, just lots of blood, some clumps of hair stuck in the now-frozen viscous liquid, bits of skin and meat scattered about, the white of the bones merging with the snow. *Whoever's blood this is must be dead,* he thought. Drag marks led away from the scene around a few trees to pool at a patch where little snow had fallen under a large tree, the bole as thick as three men. They searched around the tree but found little else.

Bellard looked up and took a step back with a start, trying to conceal his shock with a faint gasp, but Mila had already followed his gaze, and a shrill scream was born from her lips. He wanted to cover her mouth quickly, make her stop screaming, when the high-pitched wail died instantly, replaced by the muffled whining of a person being gagged. Yosphore stood behind her, his eyes dark, one hand cupped over her mouth, the other holding her firmly in place.

'Let her go!' Bellard shouted, ready to run at the enchanter.

'For all the boring days I have endured, I'd love to find out what the rest of that threat would entail. But alas, you have us at a rather unfortunate moment. If you care to listen, I will be glad to answer your questions. Just stop screaming. And don't try to burst my head or whatever. It won't work. You are far too young and inexperienced to take me on. Got it?'

Mila nodded, and Bellard backed away a step. Yosphore slowly released his hand from her mouth and let her go. She jumped away towards Bellard, her fists up. 'I might not know how to fight properly, but I will make you hurt one way or another. Now speak!'

'Your friend up there,' the enchanter pointed to the headless body hanging upside down by his legs from a rope, 'had been stupid enough to get close to a bear's cave. She mauled him real good too, left his carcass for me to find. So I hauled him into the tree so it didn't attract more animals.'

'Liar! What did you hunt this morning? Did we eat the other one?' Mila shouted, stepping forward and getting dragged back by Bellard.

A harsh, discordant laughter burst from the enchanter, holding his belly as he arched his back, his body shuddering. 'Oh dear. That's precious. And completely crazy. I caught a fawn in a trap a few hundred feet from here. Not proud of it, but you two needed the food. There's a small container I made from the snow outside on the right of the house. Keeps the meat nice and fresh for a while. You are welcome to go look.'

Bellard and Mila glanced at each other, and Yosphore turned, starting to walk away, when Bellard asked, 'You said they wouldn't bother us again? Why was that? What happened to the other one?' He stared at the body above, trying to figure out which one it was, thinking it had to be Scarface. Big Brother seemed to be the leader of the little group. He would have stayed where it was safe. Sent in his underlings to do his dirty work.

Yosphore didn't even look back. In between his rolling laughter, he asked, 'Would you stay here after seeing one of your men like that?' Bellard had to admit, no, he wouldn't. They followed the old man back to his cabin, feeling a little safer, and a little more embarrassed.

36. An Honourable Thief?

Water sprayed over the hull, raining down a soft mist on Orana's face. Hidden in those sprays lurked a rainbow, faint but alive, giving voice to the colours of the world. She stood on the bow and stared out over the grey water, wondering what prowled beneath the surface in the dark depths. Men briskly walked around, pulling on ropes, making knots, tightening them, releasing others, letting them run through the pulleys up high, the friction singing songs of seaward tales. Seagulls squawked above, following their trail across the Forgotten Strait.

'I'm glad you joined us in the end.'

Orana didn't turn to the old voice. 'As long as you stick to your promise, Vernak.'

'I'm a man of my word,' he said, drawing near to stand beside her, hands cupped together behind his back.

'Interesting saying that, eh? Strange how they didn't make the expression "a god of his word", seeing that you're so trustworthy.' She scoffed with a chuckle, shaking her head. In the distance, she could already make out the raised land of the island, the white-capped mountains, looking cold and unwelcoming. Gusting cold spray racked her with shivers, and she wished she were back in Skalg sweating the day away, having a refreshing drink to cool her down. Here, she couldn't see anything warming her up.

It sounded as if Vernak was about to say something, then swallowed his words with an audible sigh and peered at his feet. He tried again. 'We are not so different, you know. Humans and gods. We both have ambitions and failings. We both get embarrassed or are proud of what we have accomplished. It is just the scale that differs. You work on a mortal scale, we on the eternal. What we do affects the lives of millions to come after you have long since been forgotten.'

'And I'm sure you will keep reminding us of that.' The ship rolled over a large swell, its bow dipping at a steep angle, and Orana had to brace with her feet, grabbing onto the foremast as she slid forward, wincing with the pain running up her leg and arm. Vernak clutched onto the other side, his beard flapping in the wind. All around her, there were groans and creaks coming from within the ship, the wood planks bending and grinding against each other, sounding most ominous. One crew member slipped on the deck and slammed his head against the boards with a loud crunch, instantly knocked unconscious with the hit. He slid around, knocking against the crates, and headed for Orana.

'Grab him!' one crew member shouted. Other men tried getting to the rolling man, but they were too far away. *Argh! Why did you have to pick me? I can barely hold on to the mast myself. Now I have to grab your unconscious arse!* For a moment, she considered leaving him to his own fate, and realised it would be a little too obvious, especially with Vernak right beside her.

This was going to hurt.

She bent down, arm ready to grab up the sliding man by his clothes, and to her surprise Vernak stood ready as well, his thick, hairy fingers stretched out, eyes focused. 'Grab his leg if you can. I'll grab his collar.'

There was no time to think about positioning. The man rushed at them like a rag doll. Vernak snatched out his hand, grabbing anything he could get his fingers around, and Orana did the same, closing her fingers around his wrists, but the momentum nearly tore the man free from her grasp. His arm slipped through until she latched on to his triceps and dug her nails into his skin. She pinched the meat in her hands and wrestled him closer to grab a wrist. Bent in a very awkward position with one leg and arm around the mast, the other around the man, she could do scant little as gravity left them. They slipped into the air, the deck pulling away, arms drifting up, hair waving in flux.

Crewmen shouted to brace from somewhere to her right, and the bow tilted up, the floor rushing back. Head shaking from the impact, she nearly let go of the man, crying out in pain, with her buttocks taking the hit. Her rump was numb. Gradually, the ship levelled out, and the strain on her arm lessened.

Hand trembling, Orana forced her fingers open, the spasming muscles struggling to let go from their strained position. Other crewmen ran up to her and hauled the man away, their incoherent calls for space and grabbing positions dwindling as they made it down the stairs inside the hull.

It was the little things in life, like surviving an unfortunate encounter with a gigantic wave, that made life interesting. Orana lay panting on the deck, watching the tall mast and sail above her and felt the solid wood beneath her, the boat careening and bobbing in the winds and waves. Vernak's hairy fingers were suddenly in her face, palm waiting to be grasped, and she did not let it wait long. The old god pulled her up effortlessly, not even a groan escaping him. 'Thank you.' The words felt like razor blades cutting into her tongue, and she quickly shifted the focus somewhere else. 'Where's Jonas and Jorin?'

'Ha. It turns out our friend has a strong disinclination to be on the sea. Seems his feet want solid ground beneath them. Jorin is trying to cheer him up, though it looks to be only elevating his annoyance. They are downstairs.'

* * *

'Hard to port! And drop the anchor! Don't let the current take her afore we settle!' shouted the captain. 'Put your backs into it, lads, we have no sails to guide us further! You there! Drop that rigging and go help the lads haul in the foresail.' He was a big fellow, clean-shaven, with long, black, bushy sideburns and an imposing stare to threaten any naysayers. Orana watched him call out to his men, giving orders from the quarterdeck. She wondered how much of his shouts were just for show. *A commanding presence, or a man that likes the sound of his own voice?*

Jonas and Jorin emerged from the stairs, and the captain turned to them. He cupped his hands over his mouth and called, 'My men will take you ashore. We leave on the morning of the third day. Be here, or we leave without you. Got it?' Orana had paid handsomely for the transport to the island, a route they rarely ran. And she was not at all happy at the prospects of being left here with no way back to the mainland.

She glared at the captain and called to him, drawing the attention of his crew. 'You better wait for us! We didn't pay you for a one-way trip.'

'We'll be here. Just make sure you are. Any more 'n three days, though, I can't promise.' The big captain turned around when one of the crew slipped and dropped a crate behind him, and he started shouting at the man while Orana descended the ladder to the awaiting skiff.

Her finances were dwindling faster than she would have liked. They had to pay extra for the storage of their wagon, the horses, and all the gear they couldn't take with them. And while they had to slog through the wild snow-covered terrain of the island, their horses would be lavishing in luxury aboard the vessel, filling their bellies and sleeping, resting after the long journey to get them here.

The skiff pushed through the water, forming a small wave at the bow, where Jorin and Vernak sat staring at the island's shore. Jonas sat across from her, glancing at her, then to the island, saying nothing, letting his eyes do the talking. Four men paddled them closer, a sweet ripe smell drifting from them that made Orana's eyes water and nose burn, forcing her to hunt for fresh air.

She dipped her hand into the icy sea, feeling ice crystals hit her palm as the water rushed by, her skin turning blue and numb from the cold. The fact that creatures had to live in this cold astounded her and made her miss the scorching Skalg even more. Dark spots of brown and black pockmarked the white sheets of snow on the island, burned grass swaying in the winds, dying in the consistent anger of the freezing weather. Shards of timber lay scattered on the water and strand, the remnants of ships getting too close to the rocks that lurked below the surface.

The bow pressed into the strand, grinding over pebbles, sand, shells, and ice, wobbling to a standstill, and two men jumped out, heaving as they pulled the small craft from the calm lapping waters to higher on the beach. A shudder rolled through her at the thought of stepping into that cold with her boots, then having to slog her way up further, freezing from the inside out. It was an act of kindness she had not expected.

Their boots crunched through the thin layers of ice and into the sand, their packs weighing on them, dragging their energy away with each step. Her ankle felt much better now, with the bit of rest it had, but she was sure the workout would take its toll. 'Which way do we go?' she asked, eyeing Vernak as she adjusted her pack.

'During the retrieval we embarked on with Erechol, I saw the cave below a tower, more like a dungeon of a sort.' Vernak turned slightly in his stride, glancing at them past the hood covering his head and face. 'Have you ever wondered why towns, villages, cities were built where they are?'

'Resources,' grumbled Jonas and walked by them, trudging up the slope to where an animal trail awaited, dead grass flattened under the heels of a herd not long since passing through. Orana wondered what animal it was.

'True enough, for some of them, I suppose. Have you ever walked or stood somewhere, and suddenly, inexplicably, you feel this presence with you? Around you?' No one answered. They didn't need to. All knew the feeling. 'Well, that is because the Fold is not as thick as you might think. More than not, they built directly over the dwelling of a god because there was a strong connection, a feeling of not being alone, because in truth, they weren't. The god is there, living just on the other side of the Fold.'

'That doesn't mean shit. God or no god, we mortals are still alone,' Jonas said, and squeezed sideways between two trees on the trail, his pack scraping against the sheet of snow on the bark.

'Not my point, Jonas. If you take away your anger towards the gods and listened to what I say, you might learn a thing or two.'

'I can be angry and learn at the same time. We are heading to Harkenfell. It's not very hard to decipher your babble.'

Roads were not a common thing on Keltorison. There was one main road going in and out of Harkenfell from the small port town of Bayor to the west, but not needing to transport many goods, the group cut through the woods and joined up with the main road, closer to Harkenfell.

A terrifying growl sounded a few feet away on their right, and Orana nearly jumped out of her skin and shouted, 'Argh!' Jorin leapt in behind his father, who stood ready with the cutlass, steam rising from their mouths and noses.

Vernak lowered Jonas's blade with a gentle hand as the powder blanket moved, the snow falling away to reveal a large white walrus with gigantic tusks curving down its meaty body while it bellowed and roared. 'It's harmless. Leave it be. Not everything needs to die. Let's keep moving.' Orana watched it drag itself towards the beach, its moustache bristling with frozen water.

'Father?'

'What?' Jonas had become increasingly distant over the last few days, blunt with his answers and retorts, as if the care had seeped from his pores, taking any kindness with it.

'Do you think that creature will be there? The one that stole you away.'

'Huh.'

'*Huh*, as in it will be there, or *huh*, it won't be there?'

It made Orana laugh just listening to Jorin. The way he pushed his father's level of frustration to new heights amused her. And even with the horrible remarks Jonas had made, Jorin kept at his side.

'Do you know how long till nightfall?' Jorin asked, looking up at the dark skies, the grey clouds making it impossible to tell the time of day.

'Huh, as in keep quiet. And the time does not matter.'

'If only we had a clock . . .' Jorin scoffed with a mocking sigh, shoulders shrugging. Jonas spun around, eye twitching, and for a moment, it looked like he might smack his son, who jumped back at the glare he received, apologising profusely. 'Sorry, sorry!'

'Boy, why do you test me so?' Jonas turned back, and they kept walking, lifting legs higher than normal to clear the snow, quickly draining their energy. 'Vernak, you will look after Jorin at Harkenfell. Wait for our return,' he said, pushing Jorin back a step with one arm, not even glancing at him while doing so.

'Is that wise, Jonas? I could be a tremendous help over there.' Vernak inclined his head, brows curled to a frown.

'The more feet we have there, the easier to get caught.'

'Talking about getting caught,' Orana said, glancing up from the slippery snow track, 'If they capture me, you will come get me, right?' The moment of silence that followed instilled little confidence in her. 'Jonas!'

'Yes! Of course I will come get you. I've saved your life twice already. Why not a third time?'

'Hey! Just remember who we're doing this for!' she snapped. 'How are we getting to this realm of the gods anyway?'

'Yeah, yeah, yeah,' he grumbled, waving her comments aside. 'I'm a Voidwalker. I will get us there and back.' They stepped onto the main road, or what they considered was the main road. If they had not been paying attention, they would have missed it. A road no wider than a wagon snaked through the forest, covered by the snow, with tufts of brown grass stalks springing up all over, rocks scattered around. It would have made for a bumpy ride on the wagon. 'We go left.'

Behind them people walked the road, hugging themselves in their thick cloaks and jackets, trying to keep warm, smoke billowing from their mouths with every breath. Orana couldn't feel her fingers anymore. She knew they must be there still, but damn it if she knew where. And the same went for her toes. There was just no telling anymore.

Strange screeches from strange birds and strange critters followed them, as if the critters themselves were wondering what strange humans these were. And who could blame them? They did not belong here. Orana had never felt further from home in her entire life, even after she had run away.

'A Voidwalker?' *Why not? We already have a supposed god in the mix.* 'I've never met a Voidwalker. I thought it was a myth.'

'And why would you meet one? It's not like there are thousands of us running around. I have never met another either. And until recently, I thought I might be the only one.'

'There have been a few. Most are dead. Killed by . . . unfortunate accidents,' added Vernak, averting his gaze from the staring Jorin.

Jonas snorted a chuckle and said, 'Yeah, those unfortunate accidents are called worthless gods, running scared of the beings we've become. I'm surprised you aren't more afraid of sorcerers, mages, and all the wizards and druids of the world. They seem to have grasped the power of the gods.'

'Oh, we are. But they do not have the ability to cross the Fold. Not yet, anyway. Therefore, they pose little threat to us.'

'And what if they find an ally in a Voidwalker? What shit would you cast to the mortal realm then?'

'It is not I who makes these decisions, Jonas. And here I am helping you, working against these other gods, putting my life on the line to save not just Tenthis, but the mortal realm as well. So stop your complaining! Not all gods are the same, just as no human is the same. You, Jorin, Orana, Ayla—'

Jonas spun around, hand on his cutlass, eyes cold as steel locked to Vernak's. Just like a row of ducklings following their mother, they nearly walked into him, keeping their eyes peeled on the ground. Startled by the sudden stop, Vernak, Jorin, then Orana lifted their hands before ramming into each other from behind.

'This is your first and final warning, God of Neutrality. Continue with your remarks, and it will be the last remark you make.' His hand slipped away from the sword, trembling, and he followed the road again, picking up the pace substantially. If the threat scared Vernak, he hid it well. Those dull eyes of his didn't blink, and he said nothing, merely fell back in line to keep moving.

The drumming of hooves sounded, their heels pressing through the snow, tapping on the ground. 'Whoa! Whoa!' called a man from a wagon drawing near to their backs, bringing the horses to a standstill.

'Where you folks headin'?' he asked, all serious. Jonas glared at him, then at Orana and Vernak. 'Ha! Just winding your knob. Need a ride? Got some room to spare. And the horses ain't so tired yet.'

She wondered how many times the man had tried that joke on travellers. As if there were destinations other than Harkenfell. If she hadn't been so focused on worrying about getting murdered, or waiting for Jonas to murder someone, she would have chuckled or rolled her eyes at him.

How many times had her father done the same thing, making the same old stupid joke day after day? Every night he'd get back home after a long day of fishing, all filthy, smelly, and tired. He'd settle down at the table, waiting for Orana and Besmitz to join his side. Mother would bring out the food, and as everyone dished up, he would strike out fast, grabbing either Orana's or Besmitz's little hand, shoving their fingers into his mouth and gently biting down with his lips, growling and shaking his head like a crazed dog. It was stupid, yet they had laughed every time.

Jonas nodded to the man, and Vernak said, 'Thank you, stranger. It has been a long and weary journey.'

It would not be a long journey to Harkenfell on foot, but why walk when you could be driven there? Only a fool would not conserve his energy and decline a generous offer like this. At the very back, she climbed in last, felt the wagon teeter with the added weight, and pulled her legs up, watching the wheels slowly dig new grooves into the snow and mud.

37. Lies and Deceit

'We should rest for tonight. Get our energy up and go in tomorrow night,' said Jonas, unstrapping his pack to drop it on the floor.

'Tomorrow? We should go in tonight, stupid bakghor. We only have three days to get back to the ship, and we've already wasted the first getting to Harkenfell!' Orana shrieked, dropping her pack as well.

Jorin and Vernak fumbled with cut timber near the hearth, stacking them and pressing tufts of dried grass and twigs into the mix. Sparks flew with every hit of the flint rock, setting the tinder alight, and soon the fire crackled in the room's corner, quickly spreading its warmth.

Fire bathed the side of her face, lending a red glow to her features in the gloomy cabin. Jaw clenching and unclenching, Jonas kept staring at her. 'Huh. You look weary. Some rest might do you good. Might be in for a few scraps once we are there.'

'You do the fighting. I'll get your soul, that's the deal.'

'What about the darcöle?' asked Jorin, rising from the hearth, still warming his hands.

'That concerns me as well,' added Vernak, eyeing Jorin and Jonas.

Calm on the outside, a storm-filled rage swarmed Jonas's mind. He turned to each and said, 'That's why we have the thief! To avoid the darcöle.'

'What is this bloody darcöle?' Again, Orana had been left in the dark, and it irked her terribly. Her face pulled into a sneer. Much of her grace seemed to evaporate with her temper. 'You promised not to keep anything from me!'

'We kept nothing from you! It just never came up.' Jonas sat down on one bed and wiped his face, feeling the tension behind his eyes, pain blossoming around his fingers as he dug deeper. It was strange how causing pain also lessened it somehow. 'It is the creature that is guarding my soul.'

'Is it dangerous?'

'I would say so, yes . . .' Vernak chuckled with a snort. 'That is why I think I should come with.'

'Might not be a bad idea for him to come along,' added Orana, gulping water from her canteen. She wiped her mouth with the back of her arm and took a deep breath. 'Damn, that's cold! Can you make something warm for us to eat and drink, Jorin?'

The poor, useless Jonas needing someone to hold his hand . . . I've needed no one to fight my battles for me, woman. I'm sure as hell not about to start now. 'No, he stays. He will slow us down. We'll need to move fast. If we don't return, then only do you come for us. Got it?' Blank stares looked back at him, all wanting to say something, their lips unmoving. 'Got it!' They nodded reluctantly and drifted away. Orana collapsed on the bed, and Vernak rejoined Jorin, helping him set up a stand to cook some meat over the fire. 'We will rest, eat, regain our strength, then go in later tonight.'

'Don't you reckon you should drink some more of that . . .' Orana waved her hands about, struggling to find a good word, '. . . filth Erechol gave you? Seemed to calm you down some before.'

Jonas turned on his side and closed his eyes. 'No, I will need all the anger I have to spare tonight. Wake me in a short while.'

* * *

'Do you have what you need?' Jonas stood by the window overlooking the pale town of Harkenfell, watching the snow drift down before the lantern lights.

'I don't know what we are breaking into. How could I possibly be prepared?'

His eye twitched, the frustration causing it to flutter wildly. *Going back into that lair. We must be mad.* 'Just make sure you will be able to pick a lock. I doubt it will be anything fancy.' The cold coin pressed against his palm, and for a moment, he couldn't help but wonder if this was actually worth it. To risk their lives for his benefit. Dull and rubbed smooth, he tossed it to the air, watched it spin there, and called on its way down, 'Tails, we leave here and don't return.' He already knew the outcome before he opened his hand but grinned down at it just the same. *Heads.*

Soft snores came from the bed on his right, where Jorin lay fast asleep, tucked away under the thick blanket to keep himself warm. For all the boy's bravado and macho nature, he was still a boy, seeking warmth in the arms of his father. Warmth that Jonas wasn't able to provide, not now. His eyes lingered on the blanket's consistent rise and fall from Jorin's breathing. It had been the happiest moment in his life when the child was born, yet here, now, Jorin might as well have been a stranger to him, the memory itself so far removed, he could barely recall it, and he hated the feeling. Hated himself for it. 'Look after him, Vernak.'

'I will. Danu's palace should be only a few hundred feet west, at the centre of town, near the temple.'

'And the lair?'

'Presumably below the structure, like a dungeon.'

Jonas nodded at the old god and turned to leave the room, when Orana grabbed his arm.

'Are you not going to say farewell to your son? If this ends badly . . .'

'And what would you have me tell him? That everything is going to be okay? I'm not in the habit of lying, never was. He's a man now. And men need to grow up with hard truths. He will be fine.' Jonas wasn't sure he believed what he was selling, but he was there now, no point in turning back. Like his father used to say when he got hurt, *'Soldier on.'* He pulled his arm from her grip. Her green eyes called to him, soothing his temper slightly. 'You need to do something for me.' Jonas's voice was suddenly unsure.

'What?' Orana asked, stepping closer.

'I need you to strangle me.'

'Are you mad?' she began, speaking louder than she wanted, quickly lowering her voice and staring at the sleeping mound past Vernak, who rose from his bed, yawning wide and stretching his arms.

'Just get me close to death. It is the only way for me to get to Tenthis.'

'This is absurd!' Vernak shouted as he walked closer. 'It is not sustainable.'

'I used to control it, although that was years ago. The skill might be lost, but the instincts remain. Once I'm close to death, I will get us—'

Orana didn't wait. She jumped in behind him and slid her arm around his neck, clasping it with the other, squeezing hard. His body wanted to fight it. He grabbed at her arms wound so tightly around his neck, wanting to pry them loose, searching for air, gurgles of spit spraying from his mouth. Jonas had not expected her to agree so easily. A little too eagerly, for his taste. He fought with himself not to crack her in the ribs with his elbows, but his hands wanted out. Handfuls of hair clasped in his grip, he pulled her closer, and she kicked his knee out from under him, sent him to the floor in a thrashing heap.

'Father, what's going on? Get off him!' Jonas heard the panic in his son's voice coming from the bed but could not see his face. He strained his neck up to see, eyes bulging, lips turning numb. Fist beating against the floorboards, he forced himself not to fight her, scratching grooves out of the timbers with his nails when the world started slipping into darkness, wafts of cold air rushing over him, mixing with the heat of the fire in their room. Red glow, long shadows dancing, silent night, large snow-decked trees, their comfortable room, the hoot of an owl, the shouts of his boy . . .

* * *

A sudden rush of air filled his lungs, and with it, the freezing cold of the outdoors. The pressure on his back disappeared, and he rolled over, sucking more air, coughing it out in hoarse bursts, rubbing his sore neck where she had done her business. His eyes floated around, searching, hunting, scanning his surroundings, and found Orana huffing and puffing above him, wiping away at a bleeding nose. He brought his hand up and felt a slight bump at the back of his head. 'Sorry,' he muttered, gesturing to his face. 'Instincts for survival are hard to force away. Is it broken?'

'Shit on your instincts! I won't be so gentle for our return home.' Orana sniffed, then blew out a spray of red through her nose, covering the snow with dark spots. She stalked off through the trees to where lights flickered in the distance, and he climbed to his feet to follow, coughing all the way.

'So this is the world of the gods?' he heard her ask ahead of him. 'It doesn't seem like much.'

'Huh.' He coughed again and growled in his throat, spitting phlegm into the snow. 'I hate this place.'

'You've been here many times, then?'

'Too many. And each encounter has been . . . disappointing.'

Orana spun around, guiding her hand over the bark of a tree, and said, 'You are too hard on Jorin. He only seeks to make you proud. So what if he can't fight with a sword?'

'He's a man! He needs to defend his family if and when it's needed. And we all know they will need it in today's world. I will not be here forever to protect them. I'm hard on him because I must be.'

'Cut him some slack—'

'Are you a mother?' he interrupted, frowning down at her, feet crunching in the snow, hot steam rising from his mouth.

'No.'

'Then you wouldn't understand. As a parent—'

'Oh, don't give me that as-a-parent nonsense. We all have people we care for, be it a friend, a lover, a husband, wife, child, dog! And none of us want to see them hurt.'

'Yes, but you can walk away from those. You can't walk away from your child.'

'Apparently you can. You just did.'

He froze on the spot and watched her continue walking through the gloomy forest. She had punched him in the gut with her words, left him searching for air. 'It's not like that!' he called from the rear, but she didn't stop. Jonas quickly made his way closer, keeping an eye on their surroundings, scanning for guards patrolling outside. A twig broke under his heel, snapping with a loud crack. *Nice going, Jonas. Why don't you just call out to Danu? Tell her you're here.*

'Shh! What the hell is wrong with you? I thought you'd be better at this!'

'I am!' he whispered and shoved her aside. Orana stumbled back, hitting the tree behind her, when an arrow zipped between them, shattering against a boulder they had just passed. Jonas was already at full sprint, bearing down on a guard fumbling with his bow. The guard decided it was too late and dropped the weapon, unsheathing a sword just in time to parry a blow from the Voidwalker, steel ringing out.

Jonas pushed the guard back, feet sliding on the slippery surface, steel flashing in the moonlight, grunting and punching with his free hand. A fist bounced off his biceps, numbing his arm to drop his sword, and a flash of steel headed for his throat. He stepped in close to the man, the blade zinging by his ear as he spun around and grabbed the exposed wrist, bringing his shoulder up below the man's triceps, and yanked the arm down, snapping it at the elbow.

The man uttered a quick scream, swiftly silenced by the broken arrow shoved into his neck by Orana, dark steaming liquid pouring from the wound instantly. She clenched his mouth closed and kept staring into his eyes, waiting for him to grow still. Unlike Jonas, taking another's life had never been an easy thing for Orana. Guilt rode her mind, seeing the guard's life leave him while she held his head. Jonas dropped the man, waited for the right moment to meet her eyes, and whispered, 'I thought you'd be better at this . . .'

Orana pursed her lips and shook her head. 'What is he?' she asked, hands trembling and covered in blood. 'Why are there people here?'

'What did you expect? Angels and fairies flapping their wings from cloud to cloud, spouting love songs to each other? They are called Lichens, the errand boys for the gods, born here in Tenthis. There are many of them.' Orana grabbed up the guard's bow. 'Beware of their weapons. The steel here disagrees with our flesh. It burns us.' Jonas stepped over the corpse and dragged it behind a tree, hoping it would go unnoticed.

Ahead of them, the palace loomed with its gigantic walls, a neat and tidy garden with many beds shaped in patterns of flowing wind spread through the grounds, the darker moonlit curls and furls sticking out from the snow-covered surroundings. Lantern posts lit long walkways beneath arched coverings, crept over by a rush of green with spots of small white flowers visible in the light. A great many windows faced them from the wall on this side, and Jonas could only imagine how many rooms there were in this place. At least three storeys high, it ran close to four times the length of Barren Hollows.

'I don't know what I expected, but it wasn't this. How can it be like this? It snows here, but not there,' Orana said, nocking an arrow to the string. 'And this bow . . . I have never felt one so light. It barely weighs anything.'

'Huh. Let's go find out.' They stepped from the frostbitten forest to a strange rippling sphere of power covering the entire compound, its barrier holding back the cold snow. Cloaks flapping in the icy winds, Jonas stuck out his arm, glancing at Orana, seeing her back away from him, and cursed the coin. His fingers touched the near-invisible barrier, felt them tingle, the hairs on his arm standing upright, yet it was not solid. It felt strange as the current flowed through his body, and he shuddered, pressing on to stick his hand through. 'It's warm inside,' he said and stepped through. There was no point in waiting any longer.

It was just another day for Jonas, and all he needed to do was not die. Getting his soul back would be a great bonus, but truly, he cared very little for it right now, the same as for anything else. A soothing warmth engulfed him, dispelling the cold from his bones.

He saw no slaves toiling in the gardens, no inhospitable environment for them to live in, finding it strange and counter to what he expected. Jonas thought back to the days when he led the charge against the western territories of the Northlands. How many times did he sneak through the world of Tenthis to get into cities unnoticed, to steal away when he was being hunted?

What he had witnessed in the gods' realm had shocked him, turned him against them so much so that he would never pray to Hobohr – the god of war – again. The doomed, wretched souls who had passed in the mortal realm received the gift of unending servitude to their masters, getting no rest after a lifetime of subjugation. The stories he'd been told as a boy were a lie. The Hall of Elyantra – supposed final gift to the brave warriors of Hobohr, where they would feast and celebrate their victories, where they would watch from above and spit on the crowns of those that opposed them – was an utter lie.

They kept low and ran over the soft lush lawns of the garden towards an arched gateway, keeping away from the lantern posts, searching for guards on patrol. Leaning against the wall of the building, Jonas peered around the corner and saw it stretch even further to the left and right, closing off a large garden in the middle. Another building stood encased in the squared-off gardens, a cut above the rest. Silver-and-gold artwork glistened against its facade of alabaster stone, curved stairs leading to the front door. Four towers stood at the corners of the building, with intricate patterns of swirling winds.

A humble goddess? Is that it, Danu? Don't make me laugh. He had expected her to be egotistical, selfish, and uncaring to her followers, but here he walked past windows, glimpsing the dead in their gifted apartments, laughing and enjoying each other's company.

They stood at the main gate of the squared palace that worked as curtain walls for the goddess's home. 'You ready for this?'

'Have to be,' Orana whispered, returning her focus to the open grounds. 'Don't have any other choice.'

Do any of us really have a choice? 'There's a guard to the right, behind those pillars. He might see us.'

'Yeah, I see him. We'll have to get into the building quickly. Follow the path on the left and keep to the shadows. He might not see us moving between the flowers.'

Jonas nodded and set off, running low to the ground. If there was ever a time to keep their eyes peeled, it was now. His feet gnawed at the pebbles beneath, eyes scanning left and right, stretched wide to see in the dark, when his foot hooked onto a row of neatly packed stones sticking up to act as boundary for the pathway. He hauled in a gasp of air right before slamming down on the ground, head bent back, his chin scraping the ground with a thud. He had been so busy scanning for guards he had not expected his attacker to come from the ground. Air exploded from him, and he heard a shout of alarm on their right.

'Hey! Who goes there? Hey, you! Stop!'

Balls! What have I done? Orana was no longer at his side. She had kept running for the building, disappearing into the darkness and leaving Jonas alone with the guards rushing at him. *Treacherous bloody woman! Knew I shouldn't trust her.* He scrambled up in time to meet the guard, flicking his cutlass out right and dangerously exposing his chest to parry the stab. The deadly edge of the blade slipped by his stomach, cutting the leather straps of his cloak, and he felt his cutlass reverberate in his hands. On the back foot, he retreated quickly, jumping away from a wild slash to sprawl on the ground. Wet grass scraped his left ear and face.

The guard kept shouting for help, swinging the sword and chopping into the ground as Jonas rolled away, tufts of grass and soil flying into the air. A momentary slip on a wet patch caused the guard to lose his balance, and Jonas jumped at the opportunity, leaping like a frog with steel in hand and stabbing down through the guard's boot into the earth, severing half the foot. The guard screamed in pain, flopping to the ground with no way to stand, clutching what was left of his foot.

Jonas yanked his head left and right and saw more guards converging from doors in the square of buildings, all rushing towards their prize. It seemed like a contest, and usually it was. *Promotion for the man who stopped the intruder. Three cheers for the man who saved our goddess from the heretic . . .* And the winner was the guard coming from the same direction they'd been headed, being closest to him, with another at his back. But the eager worm would taste the soil faster than anyone else, in this case.

An arrow whistled by Jonas's head, pinning into the leading guard's chest, sinking to the fletching to come out on the other end. *Maybe she hasn't abandoned me completely after all.*

There was no time to think about it. The next guard was upon him. An angry scowl charged at him, and a spear swung down, a large metal blade at the end ripping through the air with a swoosh, biting into Jonas's back as he spun away to run, stumbling instead. He smelled the burning of flesh, felt the heat on his skin, and nearly flung the blade from his hands, his fingers wanting to jerk open. But the cutlass's leather hilt clawed at his hand still, lodged securely enough to be swung as he twisted around, crashing the blade into the thick shaft of the spear. It felt like he had hit a wall with the sword. The shock ran up his arm and into his shoulder, rattling his brain, yet the guard seemed unfazed and kept coming, stabbing the spear out to skewer him.

'Run, you fool!' he heard Orana shout and saw a guard drop to the ground no more than five feet from him, a shaft lodged sideways through his neck, hands tearing at the feathers. 'Watch out!' he heard again and dived right, sliding over the grass and into a rock garden, tumbling the stones and scraping his skin on the sharp edges.

Jonas spun around and hurled the cutlass, flicking the heavy blade away to tumble in the air, tip over hilt. A dull thud sounded, like it had hit a piece of timber. At first, the guard did not understand what had happened, but instantly knew something was wrong. Groans and moans escaped the guard – pleas to be helped – while he sagged to his knees, clutching the hilt sticking from his chest.

Jonas jumped up and ran at him, knocked his hands away and grabbed the hilt, kicking him full in the chest to draw out the sword. *We are in it now. No point in crying about it. They must have been off duty.* Some wore no armour, while others only had a helm, but from the far corner, he saw guards now running in with armour flapping and glinting on their chest, arms, and legs. He needed to get out of here.

The ground rushed beneath him, and an arrow skimmed past, cutting into the grass next to him. It was coming from the roofs. More zinged by, missing him as he spun and danced, stepping left and right to make it difficult. There was little he could do, except run for the goddess's home and hope there were no guards inside. Their element of surprise, well . . . was no surprise any longer.

'Up here! I'll hold them off!' Orana shouted from a window on the third floor. 'Use the creeper wall. Their roots are strong!'

Huffing, Jonas fumbled to sheathe his blade in the run, struggling to find the slit with all the shaking and bouncing, and it slid into its mark unwillingly, thirsty for more blood. An arrow thudded into the wall, shattering against the stone only a few feet from him now, and he jumped, fingers stretched to claws, ready to grip the vine's roots. He hit the wall, boots slipping on the wet leaves. Orana was above him where he climbed, loosing arrow after arrow, downing as many as she could. The thin stems of the creepers had intertwined and grown strong, holding firm while he climbed up.

'Argh!' A cursed arrow of the immortal realm sliced into his calf, burned like fire where it dangled, wobbling with every move he made. 'Shit-balls!'

Orana stuck out her arm, reaching towards him. 'Take my hand!'

The fire spread from his calf into his heel and knee, cramping the leg up. He had to get the arrow out of him quickly. He snatched her hand with his right and climbed with his left, pulling himself higher as she groaned from above. Sticking halfway out through the windowsill, he wormed deeper inside, feeling the wood grind into his pelvis. His crotch dragged over, the sill catching on his pants, knees and shins scraping, skin tearing away. He dropped to the floor in a miserable heap, rolling on his side with the arrow pinned in his leg. 'Get it out! Get it out, now!'

Flustered, Orana dropped to the floor as an arrow raced through the window, hands frantically doing nothing. 'Uhm . . . Er, what should I do?'

'Balls in a vice! Cut it out! I don't care! But get it out!' It was like it was a molten arrowhead that didn't want to cool.

She dragged her knife free, hands trembling, eyes wide, and handed him an arrow. 'Bite down on it.'

Eyes watering, he bit down on the thick shaft, rasping breaths leaving him, and turned over. She stuck the blade into him next to the arrow in his leg, and he felt her digging around. 'Argh! Argh!' He heard her gagging, then more pain assaulted him as she dug deeper, cut wider. He was about to pass out from the pain, when the extreme burning suddenly vanished, replaced by a sort of pain he understood and was old friends with. The arrow dropped on the floor next to him, streaked with blood and bits of flesh. Small pieces of him left behind. Orana gagged again.

If he could only close his eyes now. Sleep a little. Rest and recover. Then life would be grand. But when had life ever been grand? He still had a job to do. *Get up, you lazy bastard!* He rocked himself on his back and rolled to sit up, staring at the woman hunched over, a string of drool running from her salivating mouth to the floor. A stream of curses left him as he took hold of the bloody arrow, cursing the thing, and bent awkwardly to reach the back of his leg, pressing it against his skin with the flat head, singing the wound closed. Always more pain. He tore a sleeve off his cloak and wrapped it tight around the wound.

'My knife's pretty clean, but you might want to keep an eye on that wound, eh? When you said their metal does not agree with our flesh, I didn't expect this. I thought you were exaggerating.' Orana leaned out the window with her bow, loosing an arrow, then stepped back behind cover. The thuds and cracks of the arrows slamming into the building next to the window kept droning on for a while.

'Thank you,' said Jonas, rising from the floor. 'We are not yet done.' He hobbled over to the door and grabbed the cool handle. Loud shouting and fast-running footsteps echoed up towards him, and he cursed under his breath, knowing more guards were coming from below. 'Danu! You ugly sow!'

'Where are you going?' Orana demanded, yanking him around by the arms. She was in his face, glaring into his eyes, her angry, heaving breaths wafting over him.

'Did you really think I came all this way for my soul?'

'That was the plan!' she shouted, stepping back.

'That bitch destroyed my life! She killed my wife, kidnapped my son, and tortured him to get to me. I am not here for my soul. I'm here for vengeance.'

'Well, I'm not! If you want revenge, get it yourself, and leave me out of it!' Orana spun away as if to stalk from the room in anger, but there was only one way out, and that way had guards coming towards it.

'Fine,' grumbled Jonas. 'You go look for my soul. Free it if you can. I will look for Danu.' Enraged, heart pounding, he stepped through the door and saw in the gloomy darkness the shape of a mallet, or a mace, heading for him. He turned his head just in time to avoid a deathblow, but not enough to come away unscathed. Stars exploded in his sight, and he spat out a tooth from the back of his mouth, tasting iron.

* * *

Orana screamed, covering her mouth with her hands instinctively, as she saw the blow glance off Jonas's jaw. For a moment, she thought he was done for, and was already plotting her escape from this situation. No soul was needed if he was dead, after all. Only thing was, then she would be stuck here in Tenthis forever. The berserk Northerner shrugged off the blow, spitting out blood and teeth, and stormed from the room, tackling the guard and laying into him with his fists, dripping dark drool over the guard's face. She tiptoed around the fighting pair, avoiding their kicking legs, their scything arms, and made her way down the hall. She glanced back to them and saw Jonas headbutt the guard multiple times, a dark stain growing on his forehead with each hit.

Quick-running footsteps came from the stairs ahead of her, urgent shouts drifting through the home. Even with all the bloodshed and danger lurking around every corner, Orana couldn't help but wonder how big an opportunity she was missing out on. Here she was, in a goddess's home, where who knew what riches awaited her, and she had no time to waste searching through drawers to fill her pockets. That was according to Jonas, though. Her heart lay elsewhere. There was always some time to spare for her glittering beauties. *Maybe just a little peek . . .* She slipped into the room on her left, hearing the guards draw closer. Orana swiftly closed the door behind her, gently leaving the handle and hearing it click into place.

She fingered the wooden walls, amazed at the perfectly polished surface, not feeling a grain out of place. Moonlight shone through the window, giving everything a shade of grey, a colour her eyes had grown fond of over the years. A sheet covered a device in the centre of the room, with a stubborn metal arm protruding from its base, not wanting to be concealed. A tray lay waiting in its talons. Fascination drove her closer, ignoring the shouts, and beatings, and cusses being spewed outside her door.

Orana gasped as she reached into the tray, feeling the warmth of the jewels, a sense of enormous joy radiating through her. She scooped them out into her pockets, rings, earrings, bracelets, thin delicate chains, and pure nuggets that glimmered yellow and silver, the shimmer of diamonds reflecting light into her eyes. What had she stumbled upon? She yanked the sheet from the device, sending a plume of dust to the air, and she jerked away, filling her nostrils with it. It tickled her eyes and nose, not wanting to give up its relentless pursuit to make her sneeze.

Orana stifled it as best she could, glimpsing through her watering eyes an amulet stuck in a metal monolith she presumed to be made of gold. She drew in some air, feeling the tickle increase, and again, and again, and, 'Ha-choo! Ha-choo!' *There was no way they didn't hear that,* she thought, and grabbed the amulet, prying it loose with her fingers, when Jonas and a guard crashed through the wall, wood splinters flying all over. Time was indeed running out . . . She jammed her dagger beneath the amulet and broke it free from its protector, wanting to laugh out loud with it in her hands.

Another guard burst through the door, screaming bloody murder, a weapon resembling a shortened scythe raised to be swung at her, its deadly, sharp tip coming down fast. She dive-rolled across a dresser, avoiding the weapon, seeing it spark as it hit the wall.

Gurgled cries sounded behind her, a plea for help. She twisted around and saw Jonas on his back, being choked from the rear, a difficult position to get out of. She scowled and tossed him one of her knives. Her eyes lingered on him for a brief moment as she jumped away from the other guard, seeing Jonas grab the weapon from the air and immediately stab the guard repeatedly in his side.

She did not wait to check on him. This was his stupid revenge, not hers. *Stupid bakghor! Lying piece of filth!* Orana leaped over the two men on the floor and out into the hallway, dashing through into a chamber on her right, and heard footsteps running by a heartbeat later. *This is not how I do business!*

The amulet was still in her hands, a reason for her to make it out of here alive. *Better put you away, my pretty.* Orana tucked the amulet in her pocket. She slipped from the room, back into the hallway, hearing an awful hubbub from the adjacent room, and again, the poor magnificent wall was punished as three men crashed through it, Jonas having tackled both of them, laying into them with his fists, screaming like an enraged beast. The sight of the man's eyes scared her. There was nothing there but death, and she didn't want to stand in his way.

Down the staircase she ran, skipping two or three steps at a time, her knees so used to the effects of dropping from heights. *If I had a lair, it would be in the basement. No use in searching these floors.* She reached the main floor in the gaping mouth of the luxurious foyer, where gigantic crystal chandeliers hung from the roof, jingling and glittering, then another guard burst through the front door. His eyes locked with hers, and he unsheathed the sword at his side. Feigning left, she then ran off to the right through multiple rooms with furniture neatly placed all over, now being tossed around by the guard on her heels, trying to get to her.

He leapt at her and grabbed her foot, tripping her, and she hit her head against the floor. Blood gushed from her nose, and she spat it into the guard's face, who dragged her near, clawing at her legs, thighs, hips, and received a thunderous kick to his nose. They were in a desperate situation, but all she could do now was run.

She overturned a cupboard filled with glass ornaments and heard them shatter on the floor. The guard tripped over the mess, colliding with wood and glass, sharp edges piercing and cutting flesh between the unarmoured sections of his body, his hands, and face. His shouts of anger and pain echoed through the chamber, and he scrambled up to come at her again. 'You will die here today!' he growled, wiping the blood from his face. 'You should not be in our realm! How did you get here?'

'Really? I shouldn't? Maybe I took a wrong turn somewhere . . .' She brought up the bow and let loose an arrow, watching it skim by the man as he arched his back.

He jumped over the couch standing between them and swung his sword. 'Worthless mortal!'

She had waited for just this moment. Orana kicked what looked to be a tea table into his knees, and the guard doubled forward. An egregious sound followed as Orana thrust the spiked end of a three-pronged candelabra in under his chin, and it slid all the way to the top and out. Disgusting matter exploded from his head, and she wanted to throw up. 'Argh! I did not expect that.'

'Danu! You maggot! Come out and face me!' she heard Jonas roar from somewhere on the floor above.

'Now to find this lair.' A few candles flickered their light from sconces on the walls, giving some guidance through the gloom. She searched for the lowest part of the house, seeking a door that would lead further down into the depths below. It seemed an endless construction, with more rooms appearing the further she walked. Down the hall she went, striding past hangings of other authoritative figures. Men with great beards and strange armour, strange clothing, all brightly coloured and commanding, crowns on their heads and arrogance in their eyes. Women with stern faces, elegant features, tough demeanours, graceful yet focused, forces to be reckoned with. Then there was one man with a youthful face, clean-shaven, seeming not much older than Jorin. 'Strange fellow. Don't seem like you belong in that crowd.'

A stairway led down on her left, to a low door left ajar, a glow emanating from within. *That doesn't look good. Keep clear of the darcöle, whatever that is.* She descended the stairs, one at a time, bow ready with an arrow nocked. For all the anger she had towards Jonas, she could not deny that this was very intriguing.

The heat bathed her fully as she entered and took her breath away. Blinded by its brilliance, she lowered the bow and covered her eyes. It was a vast chamber, with fires raging all over. Air rippled with the heat, making it hard to see while shadows jumped all around her, the walls radiating the torridity. She could not get near them to stay in their shadows, following the trail leading through the cavernous lair.

There was no movement anywhere that she could see, and she made her way deeper. Sweat poured down her face, stinging her eyes. Gigantic pillars that looked like dripping wax stood everywhere, some running from the roof down, some from the floor up, some already reaching both ends, getting only thicker. Soft sand was underfoot. That alone was strange to her. Most caves she'd seen were rocky. This felt like the dunes near Skalg.

The roar of the flames sounded in her ears, the combination of everything making her lose her balance. Dizzy, she leaned against one of those pillars, instantly regretting it, and yanked her hand away. A searing heat had scalded her, the smell of burned flesh drifting from her fist. 'Argh!' she screamed and saw a small blister forming on her palm. 'Bastard!'

Steadily, she backed away and realised she was staring at an enormous stone chair, and turned to scan the room. 'What is this place?' A big, mangled cage lay destroyed not far away, and she wondered if this was where they held his soul. Through the heat haze, she could not see clearly, and she stepped closer. There was someone there, sitting on their haunches, and Orana quickly brought up her bow.

'What is it you seek here, daughter?' came a female voice, stern and direct.

Orana's heart jumped into her throat, her breath coming fast. 'Are you a darcöle?'

The woman laughed and rose, stepping a few feet closer. 'That is an insult I will only let slide once. I am Danu, and although I might not be the feared beast, I would caution you not to try me.'

Orana wasn't sure if she should be more afraid or less, having seen

Vernak's face when speaking about the creature. Then again, Danu was a goddess. 'Where is Jonas's soul? I am here to claim it and it alone.'

'Oh, really? He sent a girl to come get it? Rather cowardly of him, wouldn't you say?' Piercing blue eyes looked at her, an uncomfortable feeling pulsing through her. She pulled the string back on the bow, aiming between those radiant eyes, and Danu paused in her stride towards her. 'It is not here anymore. You are too late, I'm afraid.'

'What do you mean, we're too late? Where is it?'

'Everything you need to find it is right there. Now answer me. Is Jonas here?' Danu asked, head tilted to the side. 'Of course he is. Upstairs? Searching for me?'

Orana felt compelled to answer. 'Yes. And he will kill you.'

'He can try.' Danu stepped closer again, and Orana quickly drew back on the string again, having relaxed it a little.

'Don't!' The string wanted to be let loose. It wanted to sing songs of its heroic cries as the arrow bucked from the bow. Her hands trembled. She could not hold the bow for long.

'Are you really going to murder a goddess? Make all my followers orphans? You've seen what they have with me. Do you think all gods will be as merciful to their followers? Jonas was an unfortunate casualty, one that he could have avoided if he had worked with me, and not against me. You must see this, my child. That man is a monster, more than I could ever be. Do the right thing and let me go. You do not want to end up in the underworld because of him.'

She had never wanted to be part of this. And the killing. And even worse, killing gods . . . *It would not end well for me if Jonas found out I let her go.* 'I can't let you go.'

* * *

'How many of you bastards are there?' Jonas shouted and swung his blade at the evading guard, steel grinding over steel, parrying for his life not to be decapitated.

'More than you will ever defeat!'

Their swords cleaved into the walls, splinters flying, and Jonas's shin burned from a kick that made his leg buckle backwards, nearly snapping it at the knee. He grabbed at the stairs' railing, fingers slipping over cold steel, and gripped the guard's tunic, pulling him down with him. The world spun, dark and gloomy, and the sharp edges of the treads crashed into his back, then his head, lights exploding in his sight. Entangled with the guard, arms flailing, legs swinging, more bumps and bruises assailed him while they rolled down, groaning and moaning from every hit. His arm burned, then his side, and the weight of the guard crashed into him at the bottom of the stairs with a yelp.

Jonas pushed with his left arm against the guard's chest, keeping him at bay. A trembling dagger was in the hands of the guard, being pushed down towards Jonas's throat. The guard lay on top of him, beard dripping red, face pulled into a snarl, groans escaping him as he leaned on the blade, and Jonas was slowly losing the battle. He shifted left on the ground, and searing pain lanced through him as the blade slipped in beneath his right clavicle.

'Argh!' Blood seeped from the man's mouth onto him, followed by a gasp of air, slowly drawn in with eyes wide. The pain was worth it. He had needed the extra room to get his knife out, plunging it into the man's stomach. Warm blood leaked over his right hand and the bitter steel of his knife, and he twisted his hand. The guard jerked from the pain, his mouth pulled into a snarl, and Jonas pushed him away to roll off to the side.

Everything hurt, everything burned, and he was no closer to finding Danu. She was nowhere to be seen on the two floors above, and he was sure she wouldn't have stayed around after all the fighting started. At least for the moment, he could catch his breath in peace.

'Orana!' he called, still lying on his back, breath misting in the dark. No answer came, and he rolled over to climb to his feet, muscles trembling from exertion. *Shit on me. Where did that thief go?* He bled from myriad cuts and bruises, where the guards had got through his defences. It didn't feel life-threatening, though, except for maybe the last stab he received. It would need to be stitched soon.

He limped away to the next room, seeing the turned-over furniture, the broken glass, and called again, 'Orana!' In the next room he entered, lay a guard in an awkward position, with his arse pointed to the sky, and his head on a table, the tip of a metal prong stuck through his skull from below. *She must still be alive then.*

'Down here,' came a faint call to him.

He made his way through the door where light poured forth, the heat of the fires making him sweat in his fur cloak. *Back into this damned cave we go.* Step by step, he crept deeper, cutlass in hand, eyeing the darker corners for the beast that had held him prisoner, but he saw no movement, except for the jumping shadows. 'Are you alone?'

Orana sat on the ground, head lowered, dabbing at a red streak on her brow. It took a while for her to answer. 'Yes, there's no one here,' she said and looked up at him. The cut on her forehead ran down to her left eye, splitting her brow.

He reached out his hand for her to grip and pulled her up, inspecting the wound. 'What happened?'

'That Danu is tougher than she looks.'

His muscles tensed up, teeth grinding over each other. 'So she was here, and you let her get away.' His anger flared, and he felt like beating her with the pommel of his sword. Were it not for the kind-hearted nature of his mother and how she had raised him, he might have spilt more blood right now. *Oh, Ma, please hold me back. Stave off my rage.*

'Excuse me?' she demanded, folding her arms and cocking her head, scowling at him. 'You put us in this damn mess! Needing your revenge and all those stupid things! You put my life in danger, and I still saved your arse out there! I fought a bloody goddess for you and nearly lost my eye in the process, and you have the balls to get angry at me?'

They glared at each other, each waiting for the other's move. Jonas sighed and asked, 'Which way did she go?'

'Forget about her. She's gone. If you didn't catch her on the way in, then she could be anywhere by now. We have to get out of here, back to the mortal realm.'

'*Ahem.* And my . . . soul?' Jonas cleared his throat, glancing towards the mangled cage a few feet from them.

Her eyes flashed to him, then to the cage. She drew in a deep breath. 'You will not like what you see.'

He stepped closer to the cage, sheathing his sword, and grabbed hold of the iron bars. Their heat burned his hands, but he did not release them, and he shouted as he lifted a section to get inside.

A grisly scene of human remains – his remains – lay scattered on the floor before the cage, framed by the rusted iron surface and the broken bar he had pried loose. There wasn't much to tell it was his, merely a bit of hair, skin, flesh, and bone. But he knew nonetheless. 'Huh. This does not look good.' In the midst of all the gore lay a broken sword, only the hilt with a small section of the blade left attached to it. The rest was not there.

'Well, don't get too emotional about it,' Orana sneered and squeezed past to pick up the blade, revealing a leather parchment underneath with strange symbols and squiggly lines on it.

It was like nothing he had ever seen before. She was right. It should have bothered him more, but it just didn't. 'Maybe Vernak will know what this means.' He shot her a look and asked, 'You ready to strangle me again?'

'More than ever.'

* * *

They burst through the door, startling Vernak and Jorin awake, making them jump upright on their beds in the darkness, letting in the stiff cold from the outside. 'Close the door!' Vernak called, throwing the covers from himself as he strode over to the hearth to stoke the fire, adding another log to the pile of ash. Jonas limped into the room, held up by Orana, and slumped down next to the old man and the hearth. 'What in the blazing fires of Darg'ule happened to you two?' Orana turned to close the door, shivering as the latch fell into place.

'Father? You're back already?' Jorin rubbed his eyes, yawning and stretching his face, waking himself.

Daylight was not far off. Even with the drapes closed, Jonas could see the darkness slowly subside, hoping for a magnificent display of colours over the frost-covered island. He climbed to his feet with some difficulty and limped to the window, drawing the curtain open.

A rather dull grey sky greeted him. 'Hmm. Yes, I'm back, Jorin.'

Vernak stomped up to the feller and grabbed his wrist in a deathlike vice. Jonas wanted to shrug him off at first, then felt it was too much effort and just let him do what he wanted. The old god stood staring at his chest, dull eyes scanning him, the creases on his face deepening. 'You didn't get it, did you?'

Orana and Jonas shared a glance.

'Your father nearly got us killed,' she said to Jorin, sitting down near the hearth, warming her hands in the growing fire. 'We wasted our time coming all the way here. All we found was this.' She pulled the broken sword from her pocket and lay it down before the fire, watching the glow reflect on the polished steel, and heard a gasp behind her.

Vernak hurried over and knocked her back, then kicked the blade to skid away. 'Did you cut yourself with it?' he asked urgently, grabbing tufts of his silvery hair, sprouts sticking out between his fingers, causing tensions to rise in the room. Orana looked confused, her eyes darting between them, evidently taking too long to answer for his liking, and he shouted again, 'Did you get cut?'

'No! At least, I don't think so. Not by that, anyway.'

'Very good,' Vernak said, breathing deep.

'What did you get cut with?' Jonas interjected, ''Cause it sure was nothing from Tenthis's side, otherwise it would have been a burned scar, like the one on my leg.' He turned and lifted his tattered trousers, revealing a jagged scar with boils around it, his skin an angry red. 'Not like the clean cut on your head.'

Orana's fingers went up to touch the dried blood on her forehead, and she said, 'Danu punched me in the face, and I dropped my knife. She must've grabbed it up and cut me with it before running from the cave.' Jonas stretched his neck and saw her sheath was empty.

The old god walked over to the broken blade and dropped a rag over it, picking it up with care. 'The Darsfiëre is a sinister weapon used by cowards and thugs! It has no business being in the hands of the goddess Danu. It's a foul piece of sorcery created by a vile sorcerer eons past. We had locked it away in Tenthis for good measure. I have no idea how she got hold of it.' All eyes were on him now. Jorin sat on the bed, Orana waited, arms crossed, and Jonas sagged to the bed beside him. *Just more bad news.* 'Once this blade kisses your skin, it sucks your soul into it.'

'What?' squealed Jorin, beating Orana to the outburst, and got up from his warm bed. 'What do you mean by that?'

Jonas hung his head to the floor, his shaggy hair filthy and streaked with blood. 'So that's it then . . . It means Orana is right. This has been a waste of time.' Jorin sagged back to the bed, clutching the sheets tight.

Orana drew the parchment from her pocket and handed it to Vernak. 'We also found this with it. Do you know what it means?'

He glanced over the scribbles and stumbled back as if hit in the chest, sweat propagating on his forehead. 'Did you find anything else with it?'

'Some blood, skin, hair, and such,' Jonas said offhandedly. 'Look, let's just forget about my soul and continue on without it. I'm fine as I am.'

'You might be now, but for how long can you live off elk piss, eh? How long before you lose yourself? How long before you kill one of us for staring at you wrong? Danu is messing with us. She has pulled your soul into this blade and shattered it. She sent her pet, the darcöle, to scatter the pieces far and wide. A sort of treasure hunt for us, to keep us busy, I guess. Without all the pieces, you will never be whole. Things will only get worse now.'

'What's next for us, then?' Orana asked, glancing at Vernak, then Jonas.

Vernak was about to speak, when Jonas said, 'We get to the ship and set sail to get as close to Barren Hollows as we can to drop off Jorin. Then we will continue on to Baldor as promised for you to get back what you stole. But first, let's get stitched up and get some rest, Orana.

It's been a long and unpleasant night.'

'I thought you didn't like the sea, or ships?' Orana prodded with a smirk.

An angry stab of irritation washed over him, and he glared at her. 'I'll get over it.'

To be continued . . .

AFTERWORD

Thank you for reading The Way of the Walker. I really hope you enjoyed this novel. If you have a moment, please leave a review on your preferred store as this will allow me the opportunity to write more books such as this. I would really appreciate it. Reviews are especially critical in today's world. Help other fantasy readers and tell them why you enjoyed this book. Thank you!

* Leave a Review: Here
Or scan this:

Want to stay updated with news about my books?
* Join my mailing list at:
https://www.mariushvisser.com/contact
* Like me on Facebook:
https://www.facebook.com/mariushvisserbooks
* Follow me on Instagram:
https://www.instagram.com/mariushvisser
Thank you again, reader. I hope we meet again soon amidst the battles to come in a new adventure.

* There's a sneak peek of Echoes of the Darsfiëre, Book Two of the Stormfall Cycle, on the next page.

Echoes of the Darsfiëre

A big bruise spread across his left rib-cage, grey-purple and sore to the touch. Calmantis was sure they had cracked or broken at least one of them. Then again, he had never been able to withstand pain as well as he would have liked. He dropped his shirt and softly caressed the wound, wincing at the touch.

Cold floor brushed his bare feet where he walked towards the narrow window in the wall, a ray of dying light warming his numb fingers as he wrapped them around the bars. *I should be proud!* he thought, clenching his jaw. *What I did could possibly save the entire world, and that of the gods.* He was sure he should have felt great about what he had done, yet there was something that just didn't feel like he had won in the end. *Oh, wake up, Calmantis! You were used, like always! You were expendable . . .* He dropped his head against the cool iron between his hands, the momentary pain of the hit – a little too hard for his liking – a grim reminder of what Ostarra wanted to do with him.

It had been nearly ten days since the night Ostarra had hunted him. Ten days of nothing but deliberation on both parties' side. His circumspect behaviour, and his unwillingness to be manipulated again, resulted in a stalemate that granted neither any benefit. He knew he was being a stumbling block.

Fear was not his concern, and neither was dying – although the thought of his last breath escaping him was a very disconcerting one. No, it was the thought of failure that haunted him. A deep-seated fear that he would never be good enough as a person on his own. That he should have listened to his mother and father, and joined them in the business *they* created. The legacy *they* carved.

He opened his eyes to a shuddering breath released from his lips and took in the beautiful surroundings he could see of Yelavantia. Elaborate bridges of intertwined vines and delicate crystal tracery spanned great chasms, connecting terraced gardens where vibrant flora cascaded in riotous blooms next to the crystalline waters. Here and there, towering spires of quartz stood as a monument of their capable engineering. Calmantis had marvelled at those buildings at night time, when an iridescent glow from the moon and stars reflected from the surfaces, bathing the entire city in its glory.

Looking at the wondrous place he found himself jailed in, he could not help but think that this was what he hoped the gods' realm would be. *What would the Shadow Guard do?* Calmantis burst out laughing, a pained shudder leaving him where he clutched his ribs. *They would have no idea what to do . . . This is new territory, for daresay anyone. In all honesty, they would probably leave her there to her fate. They would not risk the wrath of the gods. Especially not that of Aztar. They would be stripped of their rank from the Order, branded as heretics, and imprisoned for even suggesting such a thing as they want me to do. I can see it now, heads rolling from the guillotine, citizens shouting and laughing.*

He shuddered at the thought, and stepped away from the window, chains rustling around his ankles. A short shuffled walk back to his pallet then, trying to keep his mind numb to all that was happening. He thought back to the very first time Tay'la had walked through the door, cringing at the memory . . .

Calmantis had awakened with a throbbing head, mind foggy and slow, eyes unwilling to focus, a sharp, spicy smell burning his nostrils. Blurry faces had surrounded him, crowded in close, only to jump back when his eyes fluttered open, groans of pain and indignation leaving him. 'You will pay for this,' he drawled, a long string of drool reaching for the ground from his mouth, where he stood propped up by a device of ornate steel, a flurry of symbols emblazoned on its shiny surface. His head and hands were locked in the device, same as he'd seen criminals in Baldor secured in the pillories, people hurling rotten fruit and insults at them. 'Do you know who I am?' he mumbled, and for a moment, he wished they could tell him. His memories were a mess. He wasn't sure where he was, who he was, or why he was there to begin with.

Faces blended and merged, their clothing a dizzying array of colours and patterns coming into sharp focus. A silver-haired female Sidhe stood before him, face set in a scowl, brows stern. She handed a small sachet over to a younger female on her right and gestured her to leave. Gradually the air became more tolerable, the pungent smell slowly drifting away from the area. Calmantis's head reeled. Groups congregated all around, some in silence, some whispering to others, their voices filling the chamber with a low buzz.

'What are you?' The silver-haired woman asked, arms crossed, tapping her middle finger on her arm impatiently.

'Wha . . .' Calmantis mumbled confusedly, turning his head to look around. A vast hall with towering archways carved from gleaming quartz reflected glints of the sun piercing through the high windows, intricate vine motifs chiselled into the stonework. High above a vaulted dome ceiling that seemed to stretch to infinity, lending a sense of boundless space to the chamber. Tapestries adorned the wall that seemed to come alive when an observer approached. It was a unique chamber. Something he had never seen before, but the most impressive, was the enormous tree in the middle, where crystalline pools reflected the sparkling sun, arranged in a circular pattern around the tree.

'Your mind is muddled. It seems you are weaker than we thought. They assured me they did not hit you very hard.' She turned to another Sidhe, a male standing some distance away, glaring at him for some time. Calmantis sensed how the man squirmed beneath her stare. When she turned back to him, she continued, 'I am Thasalla Maelis, the Sylvan Sovereign. Adjudicator, arbiter, mother, matriarch. These are all titles I am known as.'

Thasalla stepped closer, her soft footfalls a drum beat in Calmantis's ears. Nothing else stirred. 'I ask again. What are you?'

What am I? Memories of his recent adventure with the god Ostarra came rushing back to him. 'I am a Voidwalker . . . and I shall take my leave.' He had no want to be kept caged any longer than was necessary. Calmantis reached out to touch the curtains of the world, and draw them, hoping to step through and disappear from this realm and make good his escape. A fierce jolt ran through his spine, a charge like a lightning bolt coursing through his bones, twisting his limbs and body. Spasmodically, he thrust out his pelvis, slamming his hip bone against the device, and nearly lost all control of his bladder. All around him, the Sidhe leapt back in fear, angry scowls on their faces.

'You shall do no such thing,' Thasalla said, a smirk on her elegant, old face. 'You have been bound to this world until I say otherwise.' Anxious, a bead of sweat formed on Calmantis's brow. 'Bring in the girl,' the Sylvan Sovereign called to a guard stationed near a gigantic door that glimmered in the light. For its magnanimous size, it opened at a touch, latches falling away with loud, echoed voices, scraping the inside of Calmantis's skull.

It was an odd method of interrogation, bringing a child in to talk to him. *She must be a sorceress or something even more powerful. Maybe it's a calling card, or a nickname they gave her*, he thought, lifting his head as far as he could, stretching his eyes wide to see what would appear. To his somewhat disappointment, a regular little Sidhe girl strolled into the chamber, frail, thin arms, as pale as the moon pendant held near to her chest, freckles lining her nose. Eyes wide in fear, she approached with caution towards Thasalla, who held out her hand with a loving smile. 'It's okay, dear. He can't hurt you.'

'I would never hurt a child!' Calmantis shouted. 'I've never hurt anyone! Well, physically, that is. But they could always recover from a bit of lost coin. Let me go! This is a mistake.' Thasalla gestured to the two men at her side, and they marched closer, determined, angry. They took up positions on either side of Calmantis, their presence stirring a sense of foreboding through his veins.

The crowds were hushed as the girl slowly approached him, their eyes locked on each other. 'We will talk, you and I. See what you have done,' the girl said in barely a whisper. Rough hands grabbed him with the device and hauled him up, dragging his feet across the pristine floor towards the pools. Kicking and screaming, Calmantis's nerves were frayed. Were they about to drown him in these magnificent pools?

A beating of drums started, joined by others hitting the butts of travel canes on the floor in rhythmic unison. A group of ten Sidhe, men and women, formed a circle before one pool on their knees, the girl waiting in the centre, trembling, lip quivering. Thasalla initiated a melodic chant, which the ten in the circle took up, their humming voices beating against Calmantis's sanity.

The chant grew in pace; the ten Sidhe's upper bodies were in constant movement, chests swelling, shoulders shaking. On and on they droned, until a shimmering thread came into being in the palm of their hands, little Tay'la included where she still sat in the centre. Another chant started up from Thasalla, different from the ones of the ten, making it hard for Calmantis to focus on anything. He had never been good at listening, not to mention when there were too many noises, his mind very adapt at blocking out what he could not follow.

The Sylvan Sovereign walked around the group, chanting, sweeping her hands back and forth over their shimmering threads, each time taking a little more, weaving together an ethereal tapestry of energies, with Tay'la at the centre of it all. It was taking a long time, and

Calmantis's legs were growing tired, the muscles spasming, not being able to stand up fully. The splendorous moon and stars replaced the glimmering rays of the sun, yet their voices never seemed to grow tired, or lose track of the chant. Threads dwindled from their hands into the magic tapestry, and finally Thasalla guided Tay'la towards the pool.

Eager to see what was happening, Calmantis craned his head until the sharp edge of the device dug into the back of his neck. The chanting softened, and Tay'la's voice echoed over the water, merging with the magic in the air. 'Liin röyt touo, maas pei na ke, tortiirva. Hy köi mä nä pat nuis ral.' Even though he did not know Sielish, he heard the words spoken in his head. *Across the Fold, I call to you, sister. Let me be your guide back home.*

Thasalla worked her hands on the invisible threads, binding them together, and leaned over the pool, whispering under her breath. The moon's light danced on the surface of the water, sparkling with Tay'la's reflection within. Calm and docile, the surface quickly changed to one of contempt, bubbling and boiling, steam rising to waft over Tay'la's young face, waving her silver hair back. Tay'la's visage turned ethereal, her features changing, the surrounding quartz walls behind her shifting to that of darkness. In that gloom Tirveeä emerged, slamming her fist against the surface of the water to break through to the mortal realm, yet the water did not allow her.

Thasalla jumped back, and with the help of the other ten, they weaved the threads together, intertwining them to resonate like a symphony of magic and nature. Tay'la placed her hand upon the water's surface, and so did Tirveeä, their minds melding, their thoughts merging. 'Thank you, sister, for doing this.' Tirveeä's words echoed through the minds of the participants.

Tay'la started screaming, her hand drifting away from the boiling water until Thasalla gripped her shoulders re-affirmingly, rubbing her arms while guiding her through the pain. The threads of energy converged, funnelling through the young girl Tay'la, coursing through her small body and into the pool, enveloping Tirveeä on the other side while the chanting continued, sealing the connection between the two.

Once-calm water now danced as waves in a storm, as if the girl's screams were the driving force. Calmantis's ears rung and ached, yet he could not look away. One by one, the pools exploded up in a steaming spray, causing havoc to those closest, who leapt away in fear of getting burnt.

The violent display settled, shocked faces all around, staring at each other, wiping the water from their clothes and faces. Near the edge of the pool, Thasalla stood hunched over the girl, frantically trying to get her to breathe. 'Come on, child! Not like this! I beg the Eldertrees. Give her breath!' A short, sluggish gurgle sounded, and Tay'la drew a ragged breath of air.

Expressionless, she lay there, and said, in a new voice, Tirveeä's voice, 'Being hunted . . . Need to get home soon. This is not our world.' Tay'la's body spasmed, her neck twitching, and suddenly her fearful eyes returned. Instantly tears flowed from them.

'I want to go home.'

Thasalla helped her up, and said, 'And so you shall, child. Take her to her room and tend to her wounds.' One guard stepped forth and scooped the girl from the ground with ease, striding past Calmantis with not so much as a look.

Here, now, back in the gaol, Calmantis cleared his mind of the memory and took a shuddering breath. He lay down on his pallet and closed his eyes.

Bound by fate, forged in adversity, heroes carve their own path.

With Jonas on the brink of losing his humanity, Jorin, accompanied by Vernak and Tunisia, undertakes a perilous mission to retrieve the shattered pieces of the Darsfiëre – a blade holding the essence of his father's soul. Their journey takes them into the heart of darkness, where ancient secrets lie dormant and dangers lurk in every shadow.

As they navigate treacherous landscapes and confront formidable adversaries, Jorin grapples with his own identity and the weight of his family legacy. With each step, they inch closer to unlocking the mysteries that bind their fate to the fate of Tenthis itself.

Amidst the chaos of battle and the machinations of gods, Jorin's journey becomes a crucible of courage and determination. With the fate of worlds hanging in the balance, he must confront the demons of his past and embrace the true nature of his destiny.

The echoes of Jorin's choices resonate through the tapestry of time, shaping the course of events in ways he could never have imagined. As heroes rise and alliances are tested, Jorin's quest becomes a beacon of hope in a world consumed by darkness.

A professionally trained Information Technology Specialist Marius H. Visser spent the better part of a decade honing his writing skills and pushing the bounds of imagination after his début fantasy novel Mercury Dagger - A Tale From Kraydenia. When Marius H. Visser is not off exploring the wilds of Australia, he is dreaming up new adventures and monsters to cause chaos in a fantastical world filled with twists, loyalty, honour and great and terrible battles.